MAIL-ORDER MAN

MAIL-ORDER MAN

Martha Hix

KENSINGTON BOOKS

ZEBRA BOOKS are published by

Kensington Publishing Corp.
850 Third Avenue
New York, NY 10022

ISBN 1-57566-072-5

First Zebra Paperback Printing: July, 1994
First Kensington Hardcover Printing: March, 1996

Printed in the United States of America

Jack and Leslie Bird,
for making Mother happy and proud,
this one's for you.

Special thanks to
Gary L. Willmann, D.V.M, & his wife Ann
for a decade of giving so much
to the four-legged & two-legged Hixes
and . . . special thanks to Sharon & Chris
for helping out while Mama played in Corsica
and . . . more special thanks to
René & Eileen Boulogne
because you are good times and all the fun.

Chapter One

U.S. Army stockade, Vicksburg
July 4, 1865

"We're in luck."

That would be a switch. Braxton Hale, prone in his hammock, scowled between bars at the swaggering, footloose youth who shared the Hale surname. Brax centered on an issue more important than that vague announcement of good fortune. "Where the hell have you been? It's been three days since I've seen the whites of your eyes. Dammit, boy, I figured you got knocked in the head. Or thrown in the Mississippi."

Geoff tucked a periodical beneath his armpit, the frays of his sleeve fanning the newsprint. "That guard you cheated in three-card monte wouldn't let me in."

"Why am I not surprised?"

For a swig of lunch Brax picked up a bottle of whiskey that he'd swindled from the captain of the guards. Something brown and ugly skittered over the lip. Brax muttered a curse, then flicked a roach to the wall of the dank humid cell. The war had reduced better men than Brax Hale, late of the defeated Army of Northern Virginia, to worse acts than drinking after an insect, but he wasn't that desperate for lunch.

"Don't you want to know the luck?" Geoff Hale asked.

"Not particularly." Too long, luck had been nothing but snake eyes for the Mississippi cavalryman drafted into the medical corps and the clever half-caste boy, now seventeen, who'd followed him to war. "Did you get that sack of flour to your mother?"

"Bella got the flour." Hurt in his light brown eyes, his voice elevating, Geoff said, "Doggone it, Bubba, I've been getting us help, and you aren't even interested."

Brax glanced at the door separating this cellblock from the antechamber where Blue Bellies stood guard. "Keep it down, or they'll hear you." Beginning to get infected with Geoff's enthusiasm, though, he whispered, "What's the luck?"

"You were wrong. Your friend Petry isn't dead."

"That's what you call *luck*? Who gives a damn?" The sissy lawyer was never more than an acquaintance. Until March of 1861.

"Massa Petry's got a lively law practice." Geoff leaned into the iron bars. "Yankees like him. Especially the brass."

"That lard-assed weasel is the sort to cozy up to the enemy." His mind working, Brax ran his tongue over his pearly whites. "But I *could* use a lawyer to get me free. And to look into the debt Titus St. Clair died owing me."

"Sure wish I'd been with you in Texas when you were cowboying for the major." Geoff snickered. "I wish I'd seen how he let the Indians ride onto his ranch, then let them steal a whole casket of topaz from under his big ole red nose."

"The bastard did let the Comanches get to him. But you're wrong. I wasn't around for his comeuppance. Dammit."

Brax hated Titus St. Clair. Hated him with a vengeance, even though the major was three years in his grave. Some types of hatred never die, and Brax held such an animosity for the supposed friend who'd employed him awhile in Texas, then coerced him into Confederate service . . . only to let him down. Hard.

"I am going to call in that marker," he promised.

"But the major changed his gold to Confederate money."

"I know there's no cash recourse. Petry could write the courts in Mason County, see about restitution, say an exchange of my marker for the deed to the Nickel Dime Ranch."

"Speaking of the Nickel Dime—"

"Hell's bells, though, Geoffie! It could take years for a deal like that to go through. Even one year is the same as a life sentence to a man itching for California." Brax sat up in the hammock, planting his worn-out Wellingtons on the floor and his elbows on the knees of his threadbare britches. "What we need is an easy way to get paid."

"That's what I was coming to. Bub—"

"Hey, youse guys." Clearly, the speaker addressed his fellow guards. "Want I should bring you some blackberry cobbler?"

Hunger twisting his gut, Brax called out, "Why, yes, kind sir, my man and I would be mighty pleased to enjoy a couple of bowls of it." Despite Geoff's warning extension of his hand, he added, "If y'all can see your way clear for a pot of coffee, we—"

"I ain't talking to no dirty Reb gyp-master that cheated my buddy, so shut up!"

"My apologies." Brax shot the bird toward the doorway. "You being a city boy, I doubt you know what chiggers do on blackberry bushes. Say, how are those chigger bites of yours?"

The Blue Belly slammed the solid door, unwittingly giving the black and white Hales the favor of privacy.

"I wonder what he'll have for lunch," Geoff said, wistful.

It seemed like forever since Brax had sat down to a real meal along the lines of ham and hominy, turnip greens, pecan pie, and gallons of cool, cool tea laced with sprigs of just-picked mint. "Wouldn't a nice big bowl of strawberry short-cake taste good right now?"

"Strawberry shortcake?" Gone was the wistfulness. Geoff's voice flowed mellifluously, contrary to his age. "Before long the two of us, and Bella, too, will eat the richest and sweetest of pound cakes fresh from the oven, topped with the biggest and juiciest strawberries west of the Mississippi.''

"Couldn't happen too soon for me." Brax stared at the condensation dripping through the patterned mildew on the wall. "Tell me you've talked to Petry and he's parlaying with the provost marshal."

"Let me read you something." Geoff fished for the periodical, anchored it between thumb and forefinger, then set to the unfurling. " 'Husband needed. Strong back and good sense of humor required, as ranch work in Texas is expected. Talent with firearms a must. If you are not of excellent morals and attitude, or if you are over thirty, do not apply. Comeliness not a requisite but helpful. Ref—' ''

"Oh, I see," Brax cut in. "You're wanting a bride."

"Not me. You."

"I was right all along. You did get knocked in the head."

"I've never been more sane, I assure you. You've got three of the requirements. Strong back. Talent with firearms. Comeliness." Geoff scrunched up an eye to peer into the cell. "Leastwise the ladies used to think you were nice looking."

"Used to?"

"Ain't no mo'," Geoff replied in a voice that had served the two of them in a few schemes. "Massa, you best stay away from da looking glass. You so skinny you's only gots one side."

"That's not funny. Besides, I'm a year over thirty. And I'm of ignoble character. I don't qualify."

"Stuff like that never stopped you before."

True. Brax considered the advertisement, painting a grim picture of the writing between the lines. Giving Texas its due, though, it had primitive beauty and prospects for riches untold, the latter appealing to the hardworking set. Of which Brax would no longer count himself.

He imparted a stern glare. "Do you have any idea what that 'strong back and good sense of humor required' malarkey means? Some woman is wanting a slave in husbandly chaps. Count me out. I've done all the hard work I intend to do."

"Let me finish reading the—"

"No. Not no—hell no!" *Patience. He's just a kid, and he means well.* "Fetch Virgil."

"Soon as I finish this." Geoff snapped the newspaper open again. " 'References demanded. Travel expenses paid. Con—' "

"I like the travel-expenses-paid angle."

" 'Contact Virgil Petry, Esquire, for interview.' "

"Petry, eh?" The glint in the younger man's eyes told Brax he really did have something figured out. "Go on."

Geoff didn't. He reached between the bars for sour mash, tilting the bottle up before Brax could warn him off, then wiped the back of his hand across his mouth. "Mammy, Pappy, and Jeff Davis's hound dawg Sammy—lawdy, dat stuff shore am good."

"Cut the field-hand patter. I don't like you swilling liquor, either. It's bad on an empty stomach."

Beyond his knowledge of medicine, Brax had bossing rights, even though Geoff had been free since the age of two. It was a matter of family, the youth and his mother being the same as kin. *Don't be hard on him. He's known enough hell. And he and good-hearted Bella are all you've got left.*

Brax Hale, at his pappy's knee, had learned to live by the credo, Do unto others before they do unto to you, but those two were exceptions to the rule.

"Did Petry suggest you read me that piece?" Brax asked.

"No. But he is anxious to get his client married off. He said so himself."

Undoubtedly. "What about the woman wanting a man? Do you reckon she's like Petry's new chums, from up North?"

"Nope. I hear she's from as far south as you can get in Mississippi. She's a Biloxi belle. You know the kind. All salt air and boiled crabs and 'Rastus, faster with that fan.' "

"I guarantee she's miserable in Texas." Brax snickered. "But why isn't she advertising for hired help?"

"The frontier's out of cowboys. The war, you know."

"That'll change."

"True. But that rancher-lady is green enough to hand you

her place. She's our golden opportunity. You can make a marriage, and we can get us a home and a fresh start in Texas."

Brax smashed a mosquito that buzzed his leg. "It's California or bust for us."

"Count on 'bust.' " Geoff drew himself up, tatters and all. "You're looking to do hard time, we don't have two bits. And me and Bella, well, we're just two more darkies."

Geoff's frustration and resentment gave Brax pause. How true those words. The coloreds were suffering as much as, if not more than, the defeated whites in the ruins of Dixie. Being on the western edge of the Confederacy, and having hosted few battles, Texas had the best shot at recovery.

Then again . . . "I'd do anything for you, Geoffie. But I won't chain myself to a marriage just because you think life'll get easier. Besides, once we get where the money has value for more than outhouse duty, you and I can run a few grifts."

"Who said anything about forever after? Once you marry her, the ranch becomes yours. Sell out. Then take off with the proceeds. Cal-i-for-ni-a, here we come. Bye-bye, Miss—"

"And who'd buy it?"

"Carpetbaggers."

Squinting, Brax smoothed his upper lip with a thumb and a forefinger. "Not a bad idea."

Regardless, he had doubts about the mail-order-man deal, and knew how to make Geoff think twice. "Let's go for it. Once we get there, when the Rastus-and-the-fan lady wants the cows rounded up and the Injuns gunned down, you can pack the pistols."

The youth froze. Recovered, he replied, "I doan know 'bout dat, massa. You know dis boy too dumb fo work."

"I doubt the lady would let you nap while her man's riding the range." Brax chewed down on a grin. "You know, I think the honeyed aroma of fresh cow patties will round out your education nicely. Did I tell you they have rattlesnakes ten feet long out there?"

"S-snakes?"

"By the thousands. Scorpions by the millions." Brax nodded. "Yes, I do think my marriage is our ticket to the good life." He pointed at Geoff. "You do the work and the gunning." He jabbed that fingertip against his own chest. "I'll keep the lady's bed warm. Why, I may never want to traipse off to the poker dens of San Francisco—if she's good-looking, and her biscuits aren't as hard as the boot heel of Missouri."

In just one of war's cruelties, it had been since Richmond, early '64, that Brax had known the pleasure of a woman, so he couldn't help wondering about the advertiser. He imagined shiny dark hair and big brown eyes lighting a porcelain doll's face. "How did Petry describe her?"

Having changed his mind about the prospect of frontier life, Geoff replied, "Said she's hard up, that's what he said. Sounds pretty bad. Bad as bad can be. She's desperate for a man. No telling what kind of mess you'd be getting us in to. Why, she might be one of those black widows ready to kill her mate."

"Stop exaggerating. And don't judge things you don't know anything about. Southern men are dead, by and large, and the women need anything they can come up with to get men." A pause. "Is she a widow?"

"Uh-uh. She izzzz . . . Isn't."

"Is she young or old? And what's her given name?"

The lesson unlearned, Geoff kept the ball of exaggeration rolling. "Young. Very young. Probably not a day older than fourteen. And it's Skylla."

"Sky-lah. Different. Not bad." Brax smiled. "Sure would be nice to see a woman with meat on her bones. You reckon she's fat or skinny?"

"Skinny. She's gotta be. Probably ugly, too. Teeth all rotted in her head, big old moles with hairs growing out of them. Probably dips snuff and dribbles it in the biscuit dough."

"Typical for fourteen."

Geoff cleared his throat. "There's something else. The lawyer's pretty little washerwoman said the heiress and her pappy and stepmammy were in cahoots with the occupiers of Biloxi. Vigilantes hanged Ambrose St. Clair on the lawn of his ocean-front property and ransacked the mansion itself, but they let the women go. Provided they got out of town and stayed out. So Miss and Mrs. St. Clair took refuge inland, but beat for Texas at the first opportunity. On a U.S. Navy ironclad. I know you hate Blue Belly lovers . . ."

Brax abandoned the hammock, taking a giant step over to the bars. "What is—? What did you call them?"

"Blue Belly lovers."

"Not that. What's their name?"

"St. Clair. Like I told you a while ago, it's St. Clair."

Brax threw back his head of golden hair. *Hot damn—my luck's just changed!* "You didn't say anything about any St. Clair except for Titus. But everything's tying up, all neat and sweet. I've heard of Ambrose. He's the major's brother."

Geoff shrugged, unconvincing in his nonchalance.

"You're afraid I'll take the deal, and make you work."

As weary as Brax from the long walk from Appomattox Courthouse in Virginia to the ruins of Vicksburg, Geoff exhaled. "You're right. I'm not wanting to face hard work. But you got me wrong, Bubba. I did mean to say Skylla St. Clair is the major's niece and heir. His only heir."

"Titus did mention a niece." After the first rambling report, dispensed in the early days of his stay at the ranch, Brax had shut his ears. Now he wished he'd paid more attention. Being a head taller than his partner, he bent to eyeball Geoff. "Did you ask Petry if those women have cash on the barrelhead to pay off the marker?"

"I did. They don't. Massa Petry says he put up the traveling money. Mrs. St. Clair fell on hard times after Biloxi, and Miss St. Clair doesn't have two nickels to rub together."

"She's got the ranch."

"It's probably all run down and grown over."

Brax shook his head. "You know better than that. You heard Titus say he left his foreman to take care of the place. Oren Singleterry will have it in fine fettle."

"Bubba, forget it."

"No way." Arms akimbo, he boomed, "My brilliant pal,

thank you for pointing out how I can get the law on my side. Thank you very much. I aim to get us the Nickel Dime."

If some oily swain beat him to the tinhorn bride, Brax might never get that ranch—much less a grubstake for California or his revenge upon the ghost of Major Titus St. Clair.

"Geoff, find out how much it'll cost to send Bella by ship to San Francisco. Then fetch Virgil. Tell that fop of a mouthpiece to sashay on over here."

Mr. Reluctance did not hop to attention.

"So this is the way it is, eh?" Brax dug a gold piece from his pocket. "Let's flip for it."

"Nawsir. Not on your life. I know about that trick coin. The only luck it'll bring is yours."

"My luck is yours." Brax returned the coin to its place. "Be warned, Geoffrey Hale. I *will* get my money. You're either with me or you're not. What's it going to be?"

"You won't work me too hard, will you?"

Chapter Two

An hour after sending Geoff on his unmerry way, Brax found himself face to face with the roly-poly Virgil Petry.

The attorney shifted his weight from one new shoe to the other. "I'm not comfortable recommending you to Miss St. Clair."

"Does this have anything to do with your failure to pay me a call in the hoosegow—of your own volition?" Brax watched Petry's Adam's apple go north, then south. "Whatcha got against me, Virg? I seem to recall a day in March of 1861. I'd been back from Texas a few months. I tried to save my mother's life . . . but I saved yours instead."

Petry removed his silk top hat to run a nervous hand on thinning hair thoroughly glazed with pomade. "You pulled me from the path of a runaway team."

"I did. And you did what?"

"Said thank you."

"Now, Virg, I recall a more enthusiastic response. Like, typical Virgil behavior. Crying, blubbering, slobbering gratitude. I believe I recall the words 'hero nonpareil' and a promise to be forever beholden. I'm collecting on the forever-beholden part. Do whatever you must to recommend me to Skylla St. Clair."

"I-I . . . I just can't do that."

Brax reached through the bars to grab a fistful of Petry's collar. Twisting it, he ground out, "By God, you can. I mean to marry the woman, and you will help me."

His face grown purple from lack of oxygen, the lawyer managed to nod in agreement. Brax let go of the silk cravat and starched linen. Petry fell back against the corridor wall, gasping. Enjoying the space now between him and the cell's bars, the little man quibbled, "But I'm not at liberty to help you. I'm grateful for my life, but I'm not Miss St. Clair's solicitor. I represent Mrs. Claudine St. Clair, her stepmother."

Brax itched to finish choking him. "Don't play games with me, Virgil. Your name is in the advertisement. Tell me what the heiress looks like."

"I've never even met the young lady. Mrs. St. Clair and I have communicated by correspondence."

"What's the matter? Is the heiress illiterate?" Suspicious, Brax steadied his eyes on the lawyer. "Does Skylla St. Clair know her relative is trying to find her a workhorse?"

"She knows. Claudine wrote to save her stepdaughter the indelicacy of appearing overeager."

That made sense. Southern belles did have their standards. What sort of Biloxi belle did she resemble? Brax decided the looks of the deed took precedence over her physical appearance, though he did hope she didn't resemble a warthog. After all, celibacy stank.

"I want her. Get busy, Virg."

"But you're a Lothario, not to mention that nasty business of two weeks ago."

"The latter being when I beat the shit out of two Blue Bellies after they laughed about Hale womenfolk dying 'with their noses to the ground' in the Siege of 1863."

"I suppose you were upset over Larkin, too."

"I've had three years to mourn my brother." His death still hurt. There was little in Brax's life to celebrate.

"And then there's the matter of your father."

Brax went cold. His muscles locked. Willing himself not to appear too disturbed, he said, "Ah, dear dad. Dr. John Hale, who sold the Hale holdings downriver, then abandoned his family to their own devices."

In 1850, Elizabeth Hale and her children, along with Bella and her son, migrated up the Mississippi from Natchez, settling here. From the start, they were shunned by Vicksburgers, even the relatives they had counted on. Once Brax reached puberty, though, a goodly number of ladies sought him out. But those were bygone days. "I'm not responsible for my father's actions."

"Claudine is from here. Likely, she'll know about you."

"I'm not marrying Claudine. Get busy, Virgil. I want out of jail, quick like, so I can be on my way to Texas."

"Well, I, well, I . . . I mean Claudine—"

"What's the matter with you? What kind of lawyer can't string two words together? Why are you scared of the woman?"

Petry licked his bulbous lips. "Claudine doesn't scare me. She's a friend of long standing. She used to be Claudine Twill. You know, the Twills of River Bend. She's their daughter. You remember her, I'm sure."

Brax knew some highfalutin Twills, but he didn't recall any Claudine. One thing cleared up, though. Virgil Petry had been, or was, close with a particular Twill, closer than two dogs huddled together in the Klondike.

A wicked chuckle accompanied this thought. Brax now knew how to blackmail the weasel. "Speaking of human frailties . . ."

A quarter-hour later the lawyer was all too willing to recommend Braxton Hale to the post of prospective husband. Two days later Brax and the black Hales boarded the steamship *Jackie Jo*. Onward to the good life.

* * *

Gunfire banged from the cookhouse, aimed at a quartet of thieving, and now retreating, Comanches. It masked their savage whoops and the roar of Indian ponies' hooves striking the hard dry earth. The rifle butt bruising her thin shoulder, Skylla St. Clair fired yet another futile bullet.

Suddenly the stick that held the flap-window aloft flew away from its mooring. The heavy wooden closure slammed down. It caught the rifle barrel. The butt kicked up to catch Skylla's chin. She screeched in pain and fell hard on the earthen floor.

The events of this sweltering morning in July were enough to reduce a woman to a bucket of tears. One of the other two females in the enormous cookhouse was already so reduced, but Skylla wouldn't let herself cry.

"It's over." She got to unsteady feet, brushed the skirt of her widow's weeds, and forced a smile at her fearless adopted sister, who blew on the pistol barrel she'd leveled at the marauders. Skylla walked to the whiskey still, then lent a hand to her cowering stepmother. "You can quit crying. Stalking Wolf is gone." *For now.* "We'll be okay."

"Will we?" Claudine lifted trembling fingers to her thick red hair. "That evil Indian and his awful band are stealing us blind. I told you, you should've let me at the Spencer."

Skylla wouldn't point out that her stepmother could barely hit a grazing longhorn, not to mention Claudine's debilitating fear at the first sign of Indian attack. While Skylla, too, had been tempted to hide, and while her aim was nothing to brag about, she'd never entertained the idea of handing the rifle to Claudine.

Kathy Ann lowered the pistol. "I nicked an Injun."

"Better you had killed him," Claudine said.

"Better he didn't kill me." The fifteen-year-old's gaze cruised over the cupboards. "What's for breakfast?"

Claudine's face went as red as her hair. "Is that all you can think of! You're already big as a moose. God, what was I doing when I allowed my late husband Mr. Lewis to adopt his misbegotten! You are too dreadful for words."

"Claudi—don't." Skylla turned to her stepsister. Tears welled in the girl's eyes. "Lovey, she doesn't mean it."

Kathy Ann rushed from the cookhouse.

"Claudi, try to be more prudent with your words." Skylla had learned to be cautious with hers.

The redhead chewed the bottom lip of her Cupid's bow mouth. "Every mother wants her child to behave. *She* would try the patience of a saint."

"All she asked for is something to eat. We all get hungry." Forcing the accusation from her tone, Skylla said, "Kathy Ann was your third husband's daughter, and you did agree to adopt her."

"She's had half her life to recover from the upbringing of that prostitute mother of hers. You'd think she would've straightened up by now."

"If you wouldn't be harsh with her, she might respond."

"You've never been harsh, and what good has it done?"

This was no time to extend the debate over childrearing. Skylla stared at the door Kathy Ann had exited, and thought about what else awaited outside. "I'll cook her a special treat for lunch. That should make her feel better. For now, though, we'd best survey Stalking Wolf's damages."

Leaving the cookhouse and glimpsing her late uncle's two-story granite home, Skylla felt older than her twenty-three years. A rope dangled from a rung of the porch railing. The Comanches had stolen the piglet that had been tied there. A quick look at the henhouse yard gave evidence that the chickens were also gone.

Skylla feared Stalking Wolf was on the verge of stealing her dream—making something of her legacy.

As had the foreman who'd made off with the ranch's string of horses not long before the three St. Clair women arrived in late January, Stalking Wolf undermined Skylla's efforts to get the ranch on its feet.

The Nickel Dime had once been a prosperous spread. Uncle Titus had made a fortune herding cattle to the market in New Orleans. As well, he'd gotten a king's ransom in gemstones from the creek, only to lose them to thieving Comanches. That was before he'd left for the war, taking the cream of his cowboys with him and impressing friends and acquaintances along the route to Virginia into Confederate service.

Her eccentric uncle had then perished at Second Manassas, a battle Northerners called Second Bull Run.

His fortune gone, he left a ranch stocked with unbranded longhorn cattle. Skylla knew nothing about prospecting for topaz, nor did she have the reference books necessary to learn the skill, and she was ignorant about longhorns. Not that there was any local market for them, anyway. Even seeking to hire help had been a lesson in frustration and aggravation.

She took note of the positives. "The Comanches didn't trample my garden this time," she said to Claudine, who lagged behind. "And we've still got a horse."

"Monroe is on his last legs."

"He's better than nothing."

"Always the optimist, that's my daughter and best friend."

They were best friends, and had been for a decade before Ambrose St. Clair had married the widowed Claudine in 1860. Best friends, mother and daughter, business partners, inept frontierswomen—their bonds were strong.

Claudine caught up, took Skylla's hand. "Daisy," she said, using the pet name she'd bestowed on her at their first meeting, "let's sit for a spell. There's something I need to tell you."

The two women made their way to a picnic table under a spreading oak near the house, Skylla's gait the slower of the two. Seated, Skylla took off her bonnet to brush a wayward lock of dark hair out of her face. "What's wrong, Claudi?"

"I've done something," the alluring redhead admitted, her eyes on the flask she kept on the table. "You may not approve."

Skylla picked up the cold cup of coffee. She'd abandoned it upon hearing the arrival of marauding Comanches. "Go on."

"We need help with this awful ranch."

"Please don't say 'awful.' The Nickel Dime is our only

hope." Skylla had inherited the place upon her uncle's death. Having been stranded by war, only recently had she been able to claim it. Never again would she, or her kin, be homeless. "This ranch is our promise for the future."

"It could be. With the proper help."

"Uncle's cowboys will return to help us," Skylla said, ever hopeful.

"A pipe dream." Claudine poured a snifter of whiskey—part of the small stash she'd found in the cookhouse last January. But she set the glass down with deliberate purpose. "I've come to the conclusion that a woman in Texas, even if she scrapes the bottom of a barrel, can't come up with a fine and decent man."

"Unless she can tame an Indian brave," Skylla joked, hoping to scare the redhead off her favorite subject. The lack of suitable men hereabouts.

"Tame an Indian? We're lucky they haven't scalped us."

"If they were after our scalps, they'd have taken them by now," Skylla replied with bravado. "You know, some people even say the Comanches can be good people."

"Forget Indians." The widow fiddled with the neckline of her faded gingham dress. "I have a plan to solve our dilemma. I've sent for a mail-order husband."

Mail-order husband?

Claudine desperate enough to seek out a husband? Insanity. Pure insanity. Claudine was the loveliest blossom in the Magnolia State not so long ago. She'd had her choice of suitors each time she'd wed, and when she'd married Ambrose St. Clair, he'd been hailed by Jeff Davis himself as the luckiest man in Mississippi. Claudine had a knack with men.

But gentility and appreciative beaux were no more. On the Texas frontier, no admirers came courting, not to the most divine widow, never to a spinsterly and scarred brunette.

Yet Skylla didn't seek a husband. Her heart still beat for a dashing young ensign who'd given his life in service to the Confederate Navy.

"Go on," Skylla urged, swallowing her sorrow. "What have you done to get a husband?"

"I've written to the Twill family attorney. I asked Virgil Petry to advertise for decent men."

Skylla took a sip of coffee. "Men?"

"Dearest, Virgil is procuring husbands for us both."

The cup slipped from Skylla's fingers.

All day, all night, Skylla scrambled for an alternative to the mail-order husbands. At first light she rode into Ecru. Her best shot? Selling her mother's string of pearls, the proceeds of which would be earmarked for another go at finding and hiring decent cowboys. No one had money to buy pearls.

Charlie Main did offer his dubious services in exchange for all the whiskey he could guzzle. (A talented jewel-cutter, Titus had also possessed skill at the distiller's art, and false rumor had it he'd left a bountiful legacy.) Skylla declined the filthy sot's offer.

The grocer, Emil Kreitz, agreed to take the pearls in trade for a sack of flour, a bushel of potatoes, and a box of bullets. He even threw in a dozen sticks of horehound candy—a true delicacy in these times—for Kathy Ann.

It took two more days of soul-searching before Skylla gave up. She went to Claudine. Bent over the writing desk in her second-floor bedroom, the redhead set her pen down.

"You win, Claudi. I won't fight you over the husbands."

"Thank heavens." Claudine quit the chair. "I'll post a letter to Virgil Petry, and remind him to be exacting and discriminating. I insist on the best of men for the two of us."

"One should hope."

Reaching to open a desk drawer, Claudine extracted a long envelope, then pulled papers from it. "From Virgil. It has to do with legalities. We must discuss them before we tie ourselves legally to anyone."

Skylla read six pages of flowery script, one a dummy deed of trust. Marrying could have its repercussions, if the St. Clairs weren't careful. Thankfully, Solicitor Petry was a master at his craft.

"Where's my cat?"

The ladies swiveled around to face the insolent Kathy Ann.

Claudine gritted her teeth. "You're supposed to be confined to your room, young lady."

Earlier, the girl had charged from the house when Claudine had insisted she couldn't have all the horehound candy at once. Kathy Ann had stayed away for hours, scaring Skylla half to death, for she'd feared the Indians had gotten her sister.

"Where's my cat?"

"Lovey." Skylla spoke gently, moving across the room to put her arm around corpulent hunched shoulders. "I thought you were going to hem the hand towels. We do need them so, and your handwork is the most delicate I've ever seen."

Kathy Ann jerked free. "Where's my cat?"

"I put Electra outside, where she will stay," Claudine snapped, her fingers twitching, as if they tingled to cane the girl. "And you know why."

"I wish you'd left me in New Orleans." Kathy Ann whirled around, stomping away and rushing down the stairs.

Skylla wilted onto the edge of the bed, closed her eyes, and dropped her chin. "Oh, Claudi, let's pray our husbands will guide Kathy Ann with more sense and sensibility than we've used."

"Let us pray."

Three weeks after collaring Virgil Petry, Brax and company sailed into the Texas port of Indianola. He arrived filled with vim, vigor, enthusiasm. Get to the Nickel Dime, get it sold, get gone. Piece of cake. In between? Three hot meals, a feather bed, and a dutiful wife to tumble in that feather bed.

How simple the future seemed as he and Geoff disembarked the *Jackie Jo,* then waved goodbye to Bella, watching as she sailed away, bound for San Francisco around the Horn. Then . . .

It was just one thing after another, the deflating of Brax's great expectations. Nothing was as he remembered. He'd assumed Texas would remain basically unscathed. Wrong. The whole 'state had gone to pot, and July's blistering heat helped neither matters nor tempers. While the rumor mills had it that a provisional governor had been named and Federal troops were landed at Galveston to the east, the streets of Indianola were rife with the anarchy caused by rowdies and their shoot-'em-ups. Price gouging had reached ridiculous proportions.

Posthaste, Brax and Geoff headed their newly purchased elderly geldings—embarrassments to ride, little better than traveling by foot, but all they could afford after paying Bella's passage—in a northwesterly direction toward Mason County.

Arriving at the eastern edge of the Nickel Dime, Brax got a gander at the valleys between hills of limestone and outcroppings of granite. "Look at all those cattle," he told Geoff. There wasn't just a profusion of the longhorns that had made Titus rich; the herd had increased tenfold during the war. Who needed the bother of cows? Cattle meant work. Culling, branding, castrating, herding to market.

"We've got to get rid of this place as soon as possible," he said to Geoff. "Thank God we've got a plan."

Lately the partnership of Hale and Hale had discussed the easiest way to offload the ranch. They'd decided to seed Topaz Creek, which would give the impression topaz could be had by the ton, for the mere scooping up rather than from the elbow grease required for prospecting. Their saddlebags held a collection of blue glass fakeries.

Brax clicked his tongue to keep the bay gelding Impossible on the trail. Molasses started to step into a hole. "Careful!" Brax yelled. "A snake."

Yelping, Geoff got Molasses out of the line of trouble. " 'Bout scared the heck out of me, Bubba. I thought I was gone for sure."

"Watch the trail, Geoffie. You can never be too careful in Texas." The youth nodded; Brax changed the subject. "I've got a powerful hunger." He eyed a choice cow with rust and black spots. "That mean-eyed heifer sure would make good steaks for a couple of hungry Mississippi boys."

"Pappy, Mammy, an' dat ole Sammy. Dat right fine, suh." Geoff reverted to his natural speech pattern. "Do you reckon Miss St. Clair will cook us a big supper?"

"I imagine. If you show up willing to work. Let's see," Brax goaded. "You could anchor your foot in a snake hole and get yourself bit. That ought to impress the heiress."

Geoff clammed up.

Growing pensive, Brax saw too much work ahead for any one man. Or for a full battalion. *Now what? Let the Blue Belly buyer worry about it.* He sallied forth, Geoff in his wake. They rode past a copse of oaks—the gaits of their mounts uneven. A rise speckled with trees, outbuildings, and a house came into view. Nickel Dime headquarters. Brax's spirits plummeted.

Any fool could see Oren Singleterry hadn't ridden out the war at his post. Desertion had done nothing to preserve the value of Titus's legacy. "Damn, Geoff, it'll take more than seeding the creek to fool a carpetbagger into forking over cash."

"Don't get down at the mouth. Look at the major's magnolia trees. He spoke of them often. They look right nice, don't they, Bubba?" Geoff pointed to the grove by the well. "Reminds me of Mississippi, seeing those pretty blooming trees."

"They're the only thing that looks nice." Brax eyed the homestead. A wide porch ran across its front. The widower had built the house in anticipation of remarrying and raising a family, which never came to pass. "Correction. The house weathered the war."

Conflicting sentiments curled through Brax. When last he'd laid eyes on the residence, he'd still considered Titus a straight shooter. *What's going to greet you on this go-around?*

He kneed Impossible. "Let's go meet the women."

Brax and his partner were tying up to the hitching post within five minutes. By the time he knocked the second time on the oaken front door, a young blonde, plump as a piglet, responded and offered a pouty yet toothsome smile.

In no way did she resemble any of the russet-haired Twills. Nor did she favor Titus. But this had to be the heiress, though she was way too young to be the former Miss Twill.

Skylla St. Clair stood in the shadowed doorway. Her hair curled in ringlets, her eyes too beady for classical beauty. Wearing a hooped frock with a crocheted bertha that extended to the waist, she was not dressed for chores.

Rastus, faster with the fan.

Chapter Three

Facing his bride-to-be, Brax removed his Johnny Reb kepi. He ought to call in proper clothes, not the tatters of his gray uniform, he told himself. He used to take pride in looking presentable.

She took a half-step forward. "What do you want?"

"Are you Miss St. Clair? Miss Skylla St. Clair?"

"Could be. Are you peddling something?"

"In a manner of speaking."

Assessing the female he would take for his second wife, Brax saw that her coloring appeared more pasty than alabaster, alabaster being the complexion most prized in the South. And those eyes were not only beady, they had a nasty little cast to them. No matter how low his expectations, he'd truly rolled snake eyes one more time. This St. Clair woman was no prize.

She wasn't even a woman. She was a girl. Probably no more than a well-developed fourteen or fifteen. Geoff's lie had come to pass. No wonder Brax hadn't recalled Titus's description— she'd been but a babe at the time. Damn. Double damn. "Are you sure you're Skylla St. Clair?"

"Are you some sort of pervert, or are you plain deaf and stupid? I said I'm Miss St. Clair."

Great.

Damning the fates, Brax patted his pocket to make certain the envelope containing the St. Clair marker hadn't slipped. "May I present myself?" He sketched a bow. "I am Braxton Hippocrates Hale of Mississippi and Texas. Descendant of Charlemagne and the first families of Virginia. A—"

"Who?"

He repeated the lineage that had brought his mother great pride, but had elicited yawns from Brax. Until now. When he needed to make a good impression. ". . . and I am a combat veteran of Major Titus St. Clair's company, Hood's Texas Brigade, the Army of Northern Virginia. As well, I was a subordinate to your late uncle before his demise at Second Manassas. Later I served the Confederacy as physician to the maimed lion, General John Bell Hood."

I'm straight from the hoosegow, and I'm here for the deed to your ranch. How ya like them apples, cupcake?

He took her hand and feathered a kiss across its chubby, stubby fingers before handing over an ivory chess piece, the queen. The signal of Petry's approval. "Virgil Petry sent me."

The scrutinizing gaze she took was one normally reserved for a persnickety cook picking through a mess of okra to cull the wormy ones. "I kinda wanted a darker haired fellow."

"How 'bout I slap some boot polish on my head?"

"It's worth a try." She dropped the antique chess piece into a pocket of her skirts; it clinked, as if solid had contacted solid. Miss St. Clair turned, her hoops billowing. "You might as well come on in. I guess."

Geoff, who'd stayed out of sight on the porch, but close to Brax's right, handed over a jar of peaches and a pan of chocolate fudge. These luxuries, bought from a farm wife near Fredericksburg, had taken the last traveling money, but Brax had felt it only proper not to arrive empty-handed.

He started to cross the threshold. Sensing Geoff in his trail,

Brax thrust the heel of his Wellington back toward his accomplice's shin. "Tend the horses," he mouthed silently.

Titus St. Clair's niece wheeled around. "Are you just gonna stand there all day, staring off into space like some lunatic?" she demanded. "Are you head-shot or something?"

Her uncle had been many things, but not ungracious. On the other hand, his niece, if she had ever learned anything about Southern hospitality, had forgotten it. When Brax attained the house's cool and shadowed interior, he said, "These are for you. Thought you might enjoy a treat or two."

"Yum!"

Standing in the middle of the front room, she snapped up the gifts as fast as a hound gobbled a pan of scraps. She dug out a piece of the fudge, stuffed it into her mouth, tucked the pan under her arm, unscrewed the jar lid, and was sucking the syrup off a slice of peach. All in the blink of an eye.

A person could be ravenous for sweets, but it was downright greedy not to offer to share. Brax's favorite treat happened to be the sweetness of a woman, but how many months—years— had it been since Geoff tasted a candied repast?

On the forty-mile trip between the candymaker and the nearby community of Ecru, it had taken much guarding to keep Geoff out of the fudge and the melting sun off the pan.

His gaze slid to the Belle of Biloxi, who was chewing with her mouth open. He couldn't imagine getting it up for her, despite his long dry spell since that gal in Richmond. Now what?

Skylla St. Clair slurped the last of the syrup, then looked up. "Oh, you. Sit down." She waved the pan; he remained standing. "What's your age?" she asked. "You look pretty old."

"Thir— Twenty-nine." He recalled the age limitation. "Thanks for the compliment." His lip curled. "How old are you?"

"Old enough. Fifteen."

Girls sometimes got married as young as twelve in Mississippi. Judging from first impressions, this girl would forever be eleven to Brax.

California slipping between his fingers, Brax had a word with himself about judgments. "Miss St. Clair, my batman is outside. It's a hot, hot day. He's mighty thirsty. Do you think he could impose upon your well? He has his own dipper."

"If you're so broke you're here about the advertisement, how come you can afford an attendant?"

"He works cheap."

She wriggled over to a window near the staircase, drawing back the drape. Brax took a look around. The front room and the dining room—connected by an archway—hadn't changed since Titus's days. Racks of horns decorated the walls. Four chairs, with cow horns for arms and legs, were clustered incongruously around a lyre-shaped settee. The house still had a masculine cast to it, with none of the doodads women like to set around. Certainly nothing in the soft-currency line of plate or cut crystal caught his eye.

But the jewel-cutting wheels and polishers remained on a bench by the window, just as Brax remembered them. A strange feeling of familiarity went through him. After a life of upheaval, Braxton Hale took comfort in that small anchor.

"Those sure are nice-looking horses," the girl baited, smothering a laugh and catching his attention.

"They got us here." Offended for Impossible and his sidekick Molasses, Brax glowered.

"By the way, your batman's helped himself to the water." She dropped the curtain, leaving the room in shadows again. "What are you doing with a darkie? We aren't supposed to have them anymore. You'll have those awful Federal people down on us the minute they reach Mason County."

"Would 'awful Federal people' bother you so sorely? They're downright friendly with *some* Southerners."

"If you're referring to that nasty Biloxi business, hold your tongue." She made for the settee to sit down, Brax rushing to help seat her. The springs groaned as her weight hit them. "Sometimes people have to do what people have to do," she explained. "And if you don't like it, tough."

He chewed aggravation. California rearing its beautiful head, he asked, "Miss St. Clair, may I call you Skylla?"

"If you call me Skylla, I won't answer to it."

He read the situation. She was obstinate for the sake of obstinacy. Could it be she played some sort of game? It wouldn't surprise him. She had all the earmarks of deviousness.

"All right, Miss St. Clair, be that way. You do have to do what you do have to do," he mocked. "But we might as well get acquainted as quickly as possible."

"Aren't we doing that?"

"If you'll indulge me in a question or two, I'd be appreciative." She lifted a shoulder in answer; he asked, "Why did you open your door to a stranger? A ragged stranger who might have been out to slash your throat."

"If you'd been all gussied up, I'd've found that peculiar. I haven't seen a man in a nice suit of clothes since before the war." She patted the area near her hip. Her fingers dug into her pocket, extracting a pearl-handled pistol, which she aimed at his face. "I knew there wouldn't be any trouble."

Brax's heart slammed against his chest. He wasn't a coward, but he did have a healthy respect for bullets.

"Your face is white as biscuit dough." She snickered, then lowered the barrel. The last of the fudge stuffed in her mouth, she made a trip with her tongue around the outside of it. "Got any more candy?"

"No, ma'am, I don't."

"Too bad."

Into the lull that followed, Brax said, "I was given to understand you have a stepmother. Where is the good lady?"

"Claudine's out trying to shoot one of those dumb cows. Makes me sick just to look at those ugly old animals."

Plainly the heiress didn't fuss about eating the result. "Who does the rest of the chores?"

She opened her mouth, then shut it quickly. "We hired a few stragglers. Stole everything they could get their hands on, even one of Claudine's many wedding rings. One guy got scared off, once he realized the Injuns are at our back door."

"I can help there. I know the ways of the Comanche." No doubt the ones from past years had moved on, but Brax felt confident of his abilities. "I'm fluent in their language."

"I guess you came by that from your mother." Before he could ask for an explanation, she screwed up one of those pellet eyes. "I don't have any use for Injuns."

If there were any avenue short of committing as much as an hour to this odd girl, Brax needed to find it. "Miss St. Clair, your uncle passed on owing me a large amount of money. Since you aren't disposed to accept me as a bride-groom, I'd like to retire the debt. Do you have five thousand dollars, U.S.?"

"I didn't say I don't want you for a husband."

"You and I aren't meant to be, if for no other reason than the gap in our ages." He took a forward step. "I do have a valid claim against your uncle's estate, though. And I mean to collect. Nevertheless, I *might* be willing to settle for two thousand dollars."

"You're out of luck."

"How about a thousand?"

"Nope."

Searching for honorable escape, he asked, "How 'bout two hundred? Confederate."

"Are you trying to renege on the wedding?"

Patience. Forget exits. Keep your mind on the better life you can get for Geoff and Bella. "I look forward to marriage. But I—"

"You'd better not expect to sleep with me."

A warning sign went through him. If the marriage wasn't consummated, he'd have no legal hold on the Nickel Dime. "I can only assume you're jesting."

"I'll let you know after you tell me whether you stick your tongue in a girl's mouth when you kiss."

She was a rotten child, worrying a bug to death, and Brax thought about turning the tables on her. *Worry her like she's worrying you.* He might be a louse, but he wasn't a child. "A marriage in name only is for the best. You're young, you might find true love someday and want to marry the man. I, of course, wouldn't wish to stand in the way of lovers. And you'd want to give the flower of yourself to him.''

"Flower of myself?'' Her features contorted. *"Flower* of myself? What does that mean?''

God, he would love to choke the girl. He walked to the fireplace and ran his hand across the place where Titus's favorite rifle used to hang. Was there any way to best the porcine beast? "Flower doesn't refer to your manners.''

"Prig.''

Brax couldn't help but laugh. He'd been called many names in his thirty-one years, but prig hadn't been on the list.

She wiggled on the settee. "You said you were a doctor to General Hood, but you're wearing a sergeant's stripes. If you're a sawbones, how come you weren't an officer? All I see is a regular ole soldier.''

He started to ask if she got her training in social graces at the W. T. Sherman Academy of Compassion and Comportment, then he couldn't bring himself to be that awful to the detestable girl. "I got demoted,'' he finally answered. "I got demoted for pounding my fist into Titus St. Clair's nose.''

"I love it!'' She laughed. "How come you punched him?''

"Because he crossed me.''

Right then he heard laughter from outdoors. Geoff's laughter. A woman's laughter, too; probably the stepmother's.

"Oops.'' The blonde left the settee and waddled past him.

Brax twisted the kepi in his hand, yanked it on his head, then wondered what the heck to do next. He couldn't marry this girl. No way. She was a child. A loathsome beast.

Somehow he'd get the money for a Texas lawyer to get the ranch for him. True, he didn't hunger for ranching. He pined for the easy life, but an asset was an asset. Someday the Nickel Dime would become his, without marrying the girl.

When was someday? The courts weren't in session. Hell, no one was even keeping the peace, much less arbitrating civil disputes. All that, of course, would change, once the Reconstruction people got settled in. But what about now? *Are you ready to walk out that door, and forget the debt?* During the sweet stupidity of his youth, he would have traipsed off, depending on serendipity and his looks, along with sleight of hand, to sustain him.

What did he have at present?

No money, and not even a good horse or a sidearm to call his own. The Yankees had shot the black stallion Rapier from under him after he'd parted ways with John Bell Hood. He'd gotten separated from his medical instruments on the last day of fighting at Appomattox. There, he'd been forced to give over his rifle and sword.

The only thing of value now in his possession? A cameo brooch which had belonged to his mother. That, and one gold piece. A double eagle—with a pair of eagles on each side. This, he'd never part with; it was a tool of his trade. Alas, his trade demanded suckers with something to gamble.

Broke, desperate, and out of luck, Brax needed time to regroup. It would be at least six months before Bella docked in San Francisco, so he didn't have to worry about her, not at the moment. In the meantime he and Geoff needed decent horses, decent clothes, and more than a few decent meals before they set out to cross the Indian lands of the great desert to the west.

His choices were marry the girl, marry the girl, or marry the snot-nosed brat.

Use your head, he advised himself. Marry the girl, sleep on the floor. When the courts go into session—lie! Lie about the consummated part. No jury would believe a tactless child who chewed with her mouth open and left no good impression.

His bride-to-be opened the front door, allowing sunlight to spill inside.

"Kathy Ann!" a woman called. "Do come on outside, lovey. And bring our guest. He must be parched from his long trip. Did you offer him something refreshing to drink?"

Kathy Ann?

He took a giant step toward the door. "Why, you little fiend. You tricked me. You're not Skylla St. Clair."

She stuck her tongue out while poking her thumbs into her ears and waving her fingers. "Had ya fooled, had ya fooled."

Brax parked his hands at his waist, throwing his head back, and let a laugh vibrate him from head to toe. It felt good to laugh. He couldn't remember the last time he'd done it. "Piglet, you'll keep me on my toes, I'll wager!"

Now—on to meeting the real Skylla St. Clair.

Chapter Four

The moment Braxton Hale caught sight of the real Skylla St. Clair, he exhaled in relief. He wouldn't be marrying any piglet, he'd be getting himself a pioneer princess who held herself like a queen.

They stood near the well, a semicircle of magnolia trees behind them, she and Geoff. Dressed hoopless and in faded black, she held two things in one hand. An old hoe and the strings of a slat bonnet. The hard scrabble of ranch life softened to whimsy, though, for her free hand lifted toward the boy, a butterfly batting its wings from the perch of her fingers.

Piglet grabbed his hand. "Come on, Sergeant."

The girl dragged him forward. Brax caught up, taking a long look at the true heiress. Her hair, a rich brown with sparkling highlights, was piled atop her head and secured with hairpins, yet a long curl had come loose to drape over her shoulder, fetchingly.

His luck was rolling sevens.

He had itched for a brunette.

"Here he is." The child's voice disturbed the butterfly; it flew away. "He brought the chess piece."

"Yes'm, he be de massa," Geoff said. "A fine, fine one."

Brax, in spite of the hot afternoon, felt the cool tingle of excitement heighten as he turned his attention back where it belonged. He called, "Good afternoon, ma'am."

Doffing his kepi and inhaling the fragrance of magnolia, Brax made up his mind. Some night—and soon—he would make love to her on a bed of magnolia blossoms. Damned right he would.

Cocky as hell, he reached the trees Titus had transplanted from Mississippi, halting a respectable distance from the lady in old black cambric. Halfway between tall and short, she'd be just right for his six-one.

Her cheek had a streak of dirt, her clothes the evidence of manual labor. Thin, almost frail, described her, yet her posture showed straight, ladylike, proud. Brax saw eyes of brown. Dark, dark brown, like the deepest of chocolate. Strength fused with naiveté shone from them, as if she dared the world to defeat her, all the while conceding that it could. Braxton Hale had fought a war for states' rights, not for slavery. But at this moment, he had the damnedest wish to beckon a cadre of slaves to do her bidding.

Where was Rastus when she needed him?

Brax introduced himself.

"Welcome to the Nickel Dime, sir." She answered his bow with a wobbly curtsy. "Thank you for responding to the advertisement. We need you so desperately."

Her voice matched her demeanor. It held a sweet sadness, almost a defeat, he noted as he took her chapped hand to touch his lips to the base of her fingers. Be she sweet or sour, though, he wouldn't get blindsided. He couldn't afford to feel anything for her, not anything above his waist at any rate.

Play his cards and play them right—even though there would be a lot of dealing from the bottom—that was the task. "Whichever way I might help, ma'am, I will serve with pleasure."

"Oh, yuck. Get a bucket, I think I'm gonna be sick. I don't believe *he* said that." Piglet made a show of gagging, which Geoff seemed to enjoy. "You better listen up, Sister Skylla. He's a scalawag. Just a few minutes ago, the sergeant was wanting to head on out. And he's aiming to leave thousands of dollars richer."

Damn the piglet, he didn't want all the cards on the table during the first hand.

A question appeared in Skylla's features. "We were specific on the subject of character, and I would have expected better from . . . Surely Mr. Petry wouldn't have—" The agreeable light in those brown eyes faded. "You aren't here to become a husband. You want money."

Why did she say a husband instead of *my* husband? Did it have anything to do with that "first husband" business? "I am here to be your husband."

"Dat money, it a debt your uncle made dis here massa. Dey wuz in de army together, da major and da massa."

"Geoff, I'll do my own talking. Ma'am, I do hold your uncle's marker. But I suffered under a wrong impression when I offered to settle the matter with your sister. She engaged in a game of deception that drove me to an unseemly suggestion. I won't press my case, now that I've seen the whole situation."

"What about the part where you punched her uncle Titus and got in trouble?" Kathy Ann prompted.

"My later deeds reinstated my worth to the army."

Piglet didn't let up. "I don't believe any old half-breed. He said himself he's the son of Pocahontas and that old drunk from town, Charlie Main."

Brax shook his head. "You misunderstood. While Pocahontas might be from the original first families of Virginia, I am not related to Charlie Main. I said Charlemagne. Charlemagne of the Holy Roman Empire, for heaven's sake, child."

"Don't call me child, soldier. I'm going on sixteen!"

Brax retaliated, but not to Piglet. "Miss St. Clair," he said to Skylla, "the young lady has a way about her, and I doubt it's a new development or needs clarification. I should imagine the proportions of the dear child's pranks are monumental."

"Are not!" Kathy Ann stuck her tongue out.

"I beg that you draw your own conclusions," Brax continued, his eyes on the woman he would, by damn, wed and bed.

Geoff chuckled. "Oooh, wee . . ."

Aggravated at the intrusions, Brax barked to his partner, "Those horses are still saddled. See to them."

Geoff was smart enough to know Brax meant business. He excused himself after Skylla suggested he put their gear in the log cabin that served as bunkhouse. Brax would sure be glad to move into the ranch house. It had feather beds.

Kathy Ann, her arms crossed over her chest, darkened her round face with a pout. "Well, *what about* the part where you punched her uncle Titus? What about the part where you said you're a doctor? I bet you lied. Liar, liar, pants afire."

Skylla sighed. "Lovey, dear, please. We all suffered the past few years, so we shouldn't jump to conclusions."

"Don't you tell me what to do. You're not anything but a gimpy old sister, and not even a blood one at that."

"Now, Lovey." Skylla explained to Brax. "When my late father married Claudine, I finally got my wish for a sister."

"Aren't you fortunate."

"When my father married my former governess's niece"—a spark of pain flashed in her eyes—"he was finally able to put away his awful grief over losing my mother."

Her compassion appealed to Brax. Usually a daughter would have her claws out when her father took up with a new woman.

"Kathy Ann, you see, is her daughter," Skylla went on, "from a previous marriage."

"Am not. My mother is buried in New Orleans. Claudine and two of her husbands adopted me, that's all."

"Let's take a walk," Brax said to the true heiress, having heard enough of Piglet's genealogy. *"Alone."*

"Yes, of course. And you'll want a refreshment."

Skylla shook the rake, then smiled. While Skylla St. Clair might not have been the most beautiful woman in Dixie, she was damned fine looking. And she blinded him with that smile.

"I was on my way to put this rake away and see after supper," she said. "Perhaps you might join me?"

He took the rake into one hand, put the other on her elbow, and they started toward the cookhouse. The lurch of her step caused his gaze to turn. Her eyes and chin were elevated as she limped along.

My God, she's crippled.

Despite his curiosity about the source of her limp, Brax didn't ask Skylla about her affliction. It took less than a couple minutes to reach the cookhouse. By then he'd decided it would be a favor, freeing her from the hell of ranch life.

You ought to set her up in town when you ride out.

No.

That was the sap's way out. When Brax had needed help for defenseless women, Skylla's uncle had laughed.

Brax faced the present. His olfactory senses had kicked in. The scent of pinto beans filled his nose—boy, those beans smelled good. Pinto beans sat well with him. And he speculated about the quality of Skylla's biscuit-making. *Be careful.*

He took a look around. It was a big rectangular kitchen, designed to accommodate a slew of ranch hands. Titus built it of granite walls and wooden shutters, the latter opening from the bottom to lend a view of the cattle-dotted south pasture and to let in the breezes. No breeze blew on this late afternoon.

Gone were the row upon row of canned goods and provisions that Titus's cook had stockpiled. Some items remained, however. A shelf held a collection of ointments and unguents, as well as a cracked leather satchel, a black bag typical to physicians.

Brax continued on. A whiskey barrel sat next to a dusty contraption with coils and tubes that stood in the corner, same as always. One evening in this kitchen, he'd entertained a lady from Ecru. Titus and a candidate for Mrs. St. Clair had retired to the ranch house after a supper of brisket and potato salad, leaving Brax and Jane Clark to sit at the rough-hewn oak table and chairs. They had drunk from a jug of aged corn liquor, making more than small talk.

"Why don't you sit down?" a different woman now suggested.

He looked at Skylla St. Clair. Jane was a pretty little gal, near as he recalled, but he had eyes for the heart-faced brunette stirring a pot atop the iron stove.

"Meow."

An insolent calico cat, perched atop the pie safe, grabbed his attention. She imparted a dirty look and hissed, then jumped to the floor—heavily—to flounce out of the kitchen.

"That's Electra." Skylla chuckled. "She thinks she's our queen. Definitely, she has little use for her subjects."

"Powerful name. It fits her." Thinking about Electra's avoirdupois, Brax commented, "She must be quite a ratter."

"Don't talk about rats. Please." Skylla, shuddering, rushed on. "Supper will be beans and cornpones."

"Sounds plenty fine to me. Plenty fine." Peaches and fudge would have been a nice treat for her.

She eyed him squarely. "Sergeant Hale, what is the true reason you've backed down on my uncle's debt?"

"I need a woman." That was partly true.

"Oh, uh, um." Skylla picked up a potholder and waved it in front of her face. "My goodness, it's hot in here. Heat of late July, added to this cookstove fire, phew!" Her hand shook. "How . . . how about a nice cup of tea, Sergeant? I'll just put on a kettle of water, and—"

"No tea, thank you. I'd prefer a slug of something stronger."

"Help yourself." She gestured toward the still. "There's a jug hidden in a box."

"I know where Titus kept it." If memory served him right, Titus had also hidden barrels of aged whiskey in the barn. Brax selected one of several crockery jugs from a sawdust-packed wooden crate. Pouring corn liquor into a glass, he added, "I used to cowboy for your uncle."

"I know."

Damn, he hoped she didn't know everything. What all had Geoff said?

She lifted a pristine white apron over her black dress, and Brax moved behind her to tie it around her trim waist. Skinny she might be, but she had a nice shape. With no corset to get in the way. *Behave, this is a lady.* It wouldn't do to make her think he was an American Romeo, especially since the stepmother might have a lot to say about his reputation.

He settled on the situation at hand. "Tall order, keeping a ranch going without cowboys."

"It hasn't been 'going.' We expected . . . more than we found." She looked away. "We thought the cowboys would come back, since the fighting's over."

While Brax sympathized with her predicament, what was the use of pussyfooting around the truth? "Forget the cowboys."

He knew what he was talking about. According to Titus, most had quit, then scattered, when he'd volunteered for the army. Of the eight who followed the major, five died in battle. That left Tennessee Frost, Snuffy Johnson, and Luckless Litton. Tennessee lost his sight at Gettysburg, which sent him to a sister in Flat Creek. Brax and Geoff had stopped there on the way from Virginia. Ole Tennessee had taken up preaching.

"After Chickamauga I lost contact with what was left of the Nickel Dime cowboys. That's when I parted from Hood's Texas Brigade, Chickamauga. When John Bell Hood took a shell in his leg. He recuperated in Richmond. I was with him," Brax explained. "If Snuffy and Litton are alive, they may or may not show up. It's a long haul back to Texas." Brax thought about his once brutalized feet. "Especially if they're walking."

"We had so counted on them. Claudine and I have considered mounting a trail drive to the port of Indianola."

"You've named a trail boss?" He suspected not.

She licked her lips. "Would you be willing . . . ?

Yep, strong back required. "It takes thousands of dollars to get a herd to market. Salaries, grub, supplies."

She blew a stream of air toward the ceiling. "What about a tannery? We've heard there's good money in hides and tallow."

"You ever been around a tannery?"

"No."

"The stink would gag a buzzard."

Her cute little nose lifted. "I assure you, I am no shrinking violet. I have smelled many putrid things, Sergeant. A tannery couldn't be worse than the smell of rotted flesh."

Ah, the bliss of ignorance. Tinhorns always came to Texas thinking they were tough enough. Many a man and woman had turned tail and sprinted east in the face of hardships much more demanding than the whiff of rotted flesh. "Maybe you ought to look into tanning supplies."

"We bought a few. Indians stole them."

"Pig—" He brushed his fingers across his mouth. "Your sister. She says the Comanches have given trouble. What about the soldiers from Fort Mason? Why haven't they helped?"

"The fort is deserted. Has been for a couple of years. We must have a guardian angel looking over our shoulder, as far as Stalking Wolf and his people are concerned. They've helped themselves to this and that, but they haven't scalped us."

Titus had mentioned Stalking Wolf. Brax didn't know the Comanche's temperament, since the chief had arrived about the time Brax left. No telling what he had in mind.

Somebody's got to set this ranch to rights.

That somebody won't have the initials BHH. No way would he be that much of a sap. Interesting woman aside, Brax decided to call Geoff, saddle up, and ride out. He started to make the motions of leaving. He stopped.

He needed a place to roost. Damn, be needed something to hold on to. For a while. Besides, he was in too far for backing out, now that he'd seen the woman who reminded him how much joy could be gotten from being a man.

Thus, he had to set this ranch a bit to rights. Like getting a proper herd together. To make it appealing to a carpetbag-toting buyer, he reasoned. It would take effort on his part. Dammit. Why was nothing ever easy?

Brax eyed the jug. "Have you sold Titus's reserve of whis-key?"

"No. There's not much. And Claudine does enjoy a nip now and then."

"Are the hay bales still in the barn?"

At her nod, he said, "There's a chance it's still there. Fire-water could come in handy. For trading to the Comanches."

"I want nothing to do with those demons."

Pity the tinhorn. "How much do you know about ranching?"

"Nothing."

He'd gathered as much. "Are those beans about done?"

"They are."

"Take 'em off the stove. You and I are going for a ride. I'll show you the ranch through the eyes of a cowpoke." He eyed her skirts, naturally wondering what they covered, but he checked his prurient interest. "Have you got a sidesaddle?"

"There's one in the tack room."

Reading something in her face, he asked hesitantly, "You do ride, don't you?"

"I ride."

"Then let's go."

"Surely your horses are winded. Shouldn't we wait until they've rested awhile?"

He offered his hand. "I have no intention of riding either one of those nags. We'll saddle a couple of the Nickel Dime's mounts."

She flushed, and his hand went back to his side. "It seems the foreman even stole Uncle's string of horses," she said.

"Why am I not surprised?" Brax exhaled in frustration. "Petry said you sailed to Galveston. How did you travel over-land to get here?"

"By cart. Our horse died a couple of weeks ago."

Great. Just great. Next she'd tell him someone had stolen her Bible.

He took a look out the window to all those unbranded long-horns grazing in the south pasture. No way could this ranch be worked with Impossible and Molasses. Moving his line of sight to the empty kitchen shelves, he saw that everyone on the place needed sustenance.

"Does Emil Kreitz still own a store in Ecru?" he asked, re-calling the good-hearted Prussian's bent toward credit. "I could send my boy . . ."

Those brown eyes flashed. "What do you mean by 'boy'? He does know he's freed, I trust."

"By boy I referred to his youth. And, yes, he knows he's free. He's been free for as long as he can remember. He's with me because he doesn't have any place else to go." Yet.

She sighed; her bosom rose and fell. Brax noticed that de-spite her lack of weight, she wasn't hurting for bosom.

"As for Emil Kreitz," she said, "don't bother sending Geoff unless you've got gold to pay with. Herr Kreitz isn't in a po-sition to do business like he did before the war. He's a dear and considerate man, but he must have payment upon pur-chase."

Damn. Double damn.

"What exactly do you have in mind?" she asked when Brax didn't reply.

Studying Skylla's exquisite face, and seeing a slight resem-blance to her uncle in the way her eyebrows arched and the determined upward tilt of her chin, he gave thanks she hadn't inherited the St. Clairian potato nose. "I can't recall what Ti-tus said about you."

She jacked up one of those St. Clair eyebrows. "I remember everything he said about you. Uncle Titus mentioned you at length."

Mentioned at length? That Titus would mention his name even once took him aback. Worry worked its way into Brax's surprise. "I'd be interested to know what he had to say."

She set the spoon aside. "In '61, when my uncle was on his way to impress you into the war, he stopped at Beau Rivage.

That was our home in Biloxi, Beau Rivage. Uncle Titus told me what a fine young man you were. He loved you like a son."

Deliver me from a father's love, if it comes from Titus St. Clair or Dr. John Hale. Twice, a father figure had let him down. John deserted his family, damning them to hell as he left. Then Titus did his part to destroy the Hales.

Not wishing to discuss either bastard, Brax reached for the handle of the big shoo-fly fan suspended from the ceiling. He tugged on the handle that moved the wide paddle from side to side; the motion fanned the heiress. "How's that? Cooler?"

"Much." She smiled her appreciation, then opened a canister of meal to begin preparing cornpones. "Thank you, Sergeant Hale."

"My pleasure, ma'am." He stared at the mourning clothes. "Forgive my forwardness, but are you a widow woman?"

"No."

"Whom do you mourn?"

She took a moment to answer, "The death of innocence."

He chuckled dryly. He liked this lady. What a shame, her reduction to searching out a husband. The South might be hurting for eligible men, but a woman this lovely ought to get the pick of the paltry crop. "Do you mind if I call you Skylla?"

She added sprinkles of salt to the cornmeal. "Not if you allow me to call you Braxton."

"Most folks call me Brax."

"All the more reason to call you Braxton." A rosy blush tinted cheeks of alabaster, an intake of breath harmonizing her appeal. "Please don't stare at me."

He gave the fan three more swings before he said, "Couldn't help myself."

"You stared as if you'd never seen a cripple before."

"No, ma'am." The beans boiled over, juice sizzling onto the stove, and Brax got a sizzle in his loins that reminded him of how little her affliction bothered him. "I was looking at you because I was thinking how much I'd like to kiss you."

She studied the floor.

His heart beat a tattoo. His blood started swirling to places

it ought not to swirl in front of a maidenly lady. And his lips—
damn! If he didn't taste her delicious lips, and soon, he'd
starve to death. *Settle down. Ease into this.*

As he continued to fan her, she bolted her gaze to his.
"Braxton, something's troubling me. Why did you hit my uncle?"

"He refused to pay his marker."

"You hit an elder over money?" Censure filtered into the
open features that would never make it at the poker table.
"That doesn't bespeak the Southern gentleman."

"Neither does welshing on a debt."

It had been an eye-opener, the year and a half between the
poker game here at the ranch and Major Titus St. Clair's
death. The night before a Yankee cannonball got him, Titus
let it be known in jeering terms that he'd never pay his debt.

Brax liked to keep the past close to his chest, but he decided
the less intrigue in this relationship, the better it would be for
not rousing suspicions. "I was out of my head that night. My
brother's brains were still wet on my grays." The calmness of
his tone belied the rank hurt and sorrow that still tore Brax's
heart. "I had my brother's widow to think about, be responsible for. My sisters and my niece, too. My sisters were widowed
at Shiloh, you see. But what could I do? I couldn't desert. I
couldn't get Titus to give me the money to send to my womenfolk. So I pounded my fist into his laughing face."

Compassion in her expression, Skylla sat down on a chair
and looked up at Brax. "How cruel of him not to understand
your predicament. Did he give you a reason?"

"Said he didn't have that much money on him, that he'd
have to write to his banker in Galveston. That I was making
a fool of myself by nagging him. Said that I should have made
better provisions for my family before I left Vicksburg. He also
said I was a fool for taking his marker in the first place, that
I should have demanded the money here in Texas." Swallowing the bile that soured his tongue as well as his soul, Brax
closed his eyes for a moment. "And he was right."

"Uncle Titus was a strange man, but I find it hard to believe he'd be so callous. He spoke warmly of you."

"Who's to know his feelings? They died with him."

Sensing his needs, Skylla refilled Brax's glass. He quaffed the shot of mean-eyed moonshine, which whirled like a tornado in his stomach. She started to pour him another, but he put his hand over the glass.

"Your family in Vicksburg," she said, "did they come through the war all right?"

"They did not. And I've said all I'll say about them. Ever. So, I'd appreciate your not broaching the subject."

"If you wish." She closed her small chapped hand over his fingers. "There's one thing I feel compelled to say, so I beg your indulgence. From what you've said, I presume you answered the advertisement for a special reason. Since Titus St. Clair let you down, you feel you deserve a stake in his ranch."

"That about sums it up."

"Then something good has come out of your pain. You will fight for this place."

Lying to a straightforward woman didn't come easy. "All of my efforts will be for this ranch."

The lyrical sound of a woman's contralto floated through the open shutter. "Skylla sweet? Where are you?"

Skylla smiled a smile that gripped Brax smack in the solar plexus. "That's Claudine. You'll love her!"

Chapter Five

Her nerves ajitter from meeting Braxton, Skylla found relief in hearing Claudine beckon from outside the kitchen. Agreeing the Nickel Dime needed husbands, then facing the first one—different propositions altogether. Yet he had her mightily impressed. He was a good man, a family man aggrieved for lost relatives. Just as she knew loss, he had suffered it.

"Shall we go?" he asked, offering his arm.

She took it as well as a certain comfort, despite her discomfiture, in his arrival here. Uncle's indifference would be remedied. While Brax would have to marry to be part of the ranch, he was a man with a stake in its success. He would be good to, and for, the Nickel Dime.

That's not all you feel for him. Her gaze lifted to his face. The intriguing patina of burnished gold in his hair, plus the green of his eyes, reminded her of another man. James. Her fiancé who had been lost at sea.

Braxton opened the door and waved her outdoors, where Claudine stood by the well, calling, "Hello, hello!"

Straightening her spine, Skylla led Braxton to the beauteous redhead. She didn't doubt, he'd be smitten. It was always that way with men.

Somehow Skylla pushed introductions past her tumbleweed-dry throat. As suspected, his attention centered on the cameo-fair Claudine; he took her hand and his lips seemed to linger on her knuckles. And the redhead went into action.

"My dear Sergeant Hale, never in my wildest dreams did I think a man so handsome and gallant would come our way."

"You're too kind, ma'am."

Claudine batted her lashes, then whirled around. Sunlight sparked the brilliance of her hair; she lifted her arms skyward. Her exuberance sliced years off her thirty-three.

"This is truly a day for celebration! Let's do celebrate. After your long journey, a man deserves to be pampered."

Like others of his gender, he puffed his chest. "Name me a man who doesn't enjoy pampering? I, myself, like to give as good as I get." He winked at Claudine, then had the benevolence to gift Skylla with a second one.

They had a tiger by the tail, Skylla decided on the uplift of a brow. Braxton's ragged uniform, too-thin frame beneath wide shoulders, and courtly manners did nothing to mask the sensuality of a passionate man just waiting to brand a woman his own.

Which could be overpowering.

Claudine performed some sort of little dance step, one not uncommon in flirty females. It was the unspoken language of a woman showing her approval to a man. "Did Skylla offer you a nice drink of something strong, hmm?"

"She did." He was beginning to look uncomfortable, but Skylla couldn't imagine why.

"Let's do sit down for a spell and get acquainted." Claudine gestured majestically toward the picnic table.

"Actually, I asked your stepdaughter to take a ride around the pasture. I'd invite you to go along, but I'm afraid my two horses aren't of an age to carry a double load."

"Now, now. A ride can wait a few minutes."

Skylla considered giving up her spot to let Braxton and

Claudine have time together, but decided against it. While the redhead had a vested interest in the ranch, Skylla and the soldier would be the working partners.

"Okay, let's sit down." She longed to get off her aching leg. Besides, why not give them a moment to get acquainted?

When they got to the table, Claudine maneuvered Braxton into seating her first. The redhead reached for the glasses and jug of whiskey she kept at close hand. And Skylla felt the electric charge of his touch as he helped her to the bench.

Dainty hands placed drinks in front of each of the threesome. Claudine lifted her glass. "Here's to the future."

Skylla did no more than touch the lip to her mouth. Straight whiskey never appealed to her anyway, so how would she react if it hit her already knotted stomach?

'She stole a glance at Braxton. His thumb moving along the glass, he gazed at Claudine. No doubt admiring her beauty. For the first time in years, Skylla wished more beauty had come her way, but she gave orders to her heart to stop being silly.

"Were these mint juleps, my, what a toast we could propose!" Claudine refilled glasses. "You do like mint juleps, don't you, Sergeant Hale? Skylla and I find them divine."

"They beat straight whiskey," Braxton replied.

"Heavenly days, don't they?" Claudine sighed.

Skylla agreed, but she was practical enough to know that the good life which that symbolic drink represented had died with The Cause. "Why don't I make a pot of coffee?" she suggested.

"Don't trouble yourself, Daisy. Whiskey will do fine." Claudine turned her smile-of-a-thousand-lights to Braxton. "Let's pretend these are mint juleps. We shall cast aside the sorrows of the war, right here under the blazing sun, with the rustle of oak leaves in our ears and a stiff drink in our veins!"

Such prattle caused Skylla to shudder. As much as she loved Claudine, it was rather embarrassing when the woman acted ridiculous in front of men. Braxton showed nothing but approval, for he chuckled at the remarks, becoming infected by the inanities.

"Y'all are truly something." He grinned. "When I left Vicksburg, I never imagined I'd find such vibrant ladies at the Nickel Dime."

"Vicksburg, you say? Why, of course, you're from Vicksburg. Where else would you have seen the advertisement?" Claudine rose from the table. With her hands reaching skyward, she twirled around. "Oh, how I miss the antebellum days of Vicksburg. Mama and Papa and I, and my dear uncle, Teddy, and Virgil, of course, used to picnic on the bluff overlooking the mighty Mississippi. What lovely memories those are!" Claudine closed her eyes. "I left as a girl of fifteen, but it's as if I can hear the foghorns from the steamboats and the lovely voices of the dock workers as they sing and load cotton on barges."

"Those were the days," Braxton commented dryly.

Those were the days, all right. Skylla grew weary of all this reminiscing. When Claudine stood behind Braxton, laid her hand on his shoulder, and bent to touch her cheek to his, she tingled with jealousy.

Claudine purred, "If you close your eyes and let your imagination flow freely, you can hear them. Can you hear the sounds of Vicksburg, Sergeant Hale?"

"Prettiest sounds on earth, the river and the gospel."

He was hooked.

Happily, he would accept a lesser interest in the ranch, the downside of becoming Claudine's fifth husband. The next candidate would take the leavings, but as Skylla's husband, he'd have control of the Nickel Dime to console him.

So be it.

Claudine patted Braxton's shoulder. "What is your first name? I do declare, I don't believe Skylla mentioned it. Surely I would have remembered."

Jumping in to answer, Skylla said, "As a lad, Sergeant Hale knew Uncle Titus in Natchez. Later, he worked here at the ranch." Before today, he'd been just one more cowboy with an odd twist to his background. Before today. "His name is Braxton."

"Call me Brax."

Claudine blanched. "I—I've heard of you," she said to him. "From friends in Vicksburg. Virgil Petry . . . Surely he wouldn't—I seem to have a headache. You'll excuse me. Skylla, come along. You need to rub my scalp."

"I can't imagine why in the world Virgil Petry would send a libertine to the Nickel Dime," Claudine said as soon as the front door was closed. "I was specific about character."

"Claudi, he's here. He brought the chess piece. Mr. Petry surely sent him, and your solicitor and family friend wouldn't do us ill."

Chewing her lip, the redhead nodded.

Skylla explained about the lost Hales, Uncle Titus's misdeed, and Braxton's natural interest in the ranch. "I feel badly for him. Somehow it seems he needs us more than we need him, needs family and the security of having a home."

"Always the nest-maker, my Skylla."

Skylla recalled the conversation she'd had with her uncle upon his visit to Biloxi en route to the war. Limping over to the staircase and taking hold of the newel cap, she turned back to her confidante of long-standing. "When Braxton was first here in Texas, he searched for his father." Since Claudine didn't like Indians anymore than Skylla did, she decided to omit the part about his captivity with the Comanches, then his marriage to a widow named Song of the Mockingbird. "It was only natural to stop here at the Nickel Dime, to see if Uncle could give him a clue. Titus St. Clair and John Hale were acquaintances of old, you see. In Natchez." It went without saying the St. Clair brothers grew up there. "Uncle once courted Braxton's mother. Braxton sent his salary home to her," she added to show his character further.

Always one to lap gossip up, Claudine said, "No one in Vicksburg had the vaguest idea where the mysterious Dr. John Hale ended up. Did Titus know where to find him?"

"I think so. Uncle acted strange when I asked. He said,

'Some secrets are best left a riddle.' " Hindsight being clear, she concluded, "If Uncle knew where to find John Hale, he should have put Braxton's mind at ease."

"Well, I wouldn't bring up the subject of Brax's missing father if I were you. After all this time, why ask for trouble?"

"Good idea." If she must *wait* to bring up a subject, then Claudine must not want to send him off. "Shall we send him away?"

It took a long moment for Claudine to answer. "He can stay. I can handle a libertine. And we have Virgil Petry's advice to protect us. You won't forget our pact, will you, Daisy?"

"I won't forget."

"I do have a headache." Claudine rubbed her temple. "I need to lie down. Go for your ride, Daisy. But don't get too close to him. He might make an advance."

"He doesn't scare me." It was a lie. She kept thinking about those eyes, those nice lips, and his undeniable sensuality.

Skylla opened the door, then went into the light, where a stony-faced Braxton waited with a pair of pitiful horses. Was he concerned that she might throw him off the place?

"Is she all right?" Brad asked slowly.

Skylla decided to take the light approach. "She said you're a libertine and that I should take heed with you. You won't make a pass at me. Will you?"

He grinned. "Not unless you want me to."

"I do not."

Something akin to disappointment flashed. "Then I'll help you into the saddle, and we'll be off."

"I can get in the saddle under my own steam, thank you."

From her second-story bedroom window, Claudine watched Skylla ride away with the greatest lover Vicksburg had ever known. The redhead champed at the bit for not taking the younger woman's place on the tour. Alas, her monthly flow had started today, so she hadn't chanced the embarrass-

ment of soiled clothes. *It won't last forever.* She'd be back in
the saddle soon.

"He's hers today," she said aloud, "but he'll be mine."

What fun they would have in bed. Claudine needed a man.
All her nights of being in a lonely bed had driven her to acts
that would blind a boy. Soon, a man would fill that bed.

Just as she began to pull the shade down, she caught sight
of Brax's quadroon servant walking toward the cookhouse,
Kathy Ann at his side. "Boy!" Claudine called down. "Boy, get
up here. There's something you must do for me."

Within a couple of minutes, he entered the bedroom, where
she sat in a chair. He was a fine-looking specimen. Light skin,
light eyes, mostly European features. His hair waved rather
than kinked, but there was no mistaking his African heritage.

"Geoff, isn't it?" said Claudine.

"Yes'm."

"I've heard about you."

"What part, ma'am?"

"The part about you being Dr. John Hale's son. You're
Brax's brother."

Geoff paled. "Half. Half brother."

"Why do you let him pass you off as a batman?"

"He doan no nuttin' about we's bein' brothers."

Claudine examined her nails. "Don't you think it's time he
learned the truth?"

"No'm. I doan think it no good idea. Da massa, he gots
enuf troubles. Me, I doan like ta think about him gettin' hard
feelin's 'bout Bella."

"Then I won't say anything. It'll be our little secret, Geoff.
Yours and mine. Just remember who your friend is. Me."

"Yes'm. Dat be awful nice of you."

She drummed her fingers. "You needn't play games with
me, Geoff. I know Elizabeth Hale had a soft heart for you and
that she educated you along with her own children. It wouldn't
do for Miss Skylla to find out you're a fraud, so don't start
speaking with a learned tongue in her presence. But you can
in mine."

"Whatever you think is right, Miss Claudine."

"On the subject of fraudulent behavior, what did Brax Hale do to get Virgil Petry to send him here?"

"Asked him. That's all."

"That's all? What about his reputation as a womanizer?"

"He's taking life more seriously now, Miss Claudine," Geoff answered smoothly. "The war, you know. I asked to go with him, and I saw his transformation. It made him realize how much he wants to be settled with a wife and family."

"That's good to hear." She smiled, convinced. "Let's talk about John Hale. Tell me where he is."

"The family hasn't heard from him since he left in '50."

"Has Brax ever looked for him?" she asked, knowing he had.

"Bubba looked from '56 to '60."

"What took him so long?"

"He helped his mother raise the children."

"How noble." Actually, she knew much of the Hale history from gossip. She waved in dismissal. "You're excused."

He turned to leave.

"Geoff, keep your hands off Kathy Ann. She's a mixed-up young lady, and I won't have her influenced by her hormones."

Again, he turned. "You needn't worry. I know my place."

"You could be her friend, though."

"She's not looking for friendship."

"Then make certain she stays out of trouble."

This time he departed. And Claudine congratulated herself. She had an ally. Furthermore, it wouldn't hurt for Kathy Ann to have a keeper. It was time sweet Skylla had a break from the exhausting chore of trying to be sister and disciplinarian. As she demanded the best for herself, Claudine wished it for her beloved stepdaughter and friend.

Again she went to the window. Where was Skylla? What kept her and Brax on their little tour?

* * *

Braxton, astride the mount he called Impossible, pointed to a horseshoe-shaped limestone bluff capped with juniper and oak. "See that canyon over yonder, Skylla? I call it Safe Haven Canyon. I used to hustle cattle into it, to get ready for cattle drives. Notice the unfinished rock fence between that squat hill and the bluff? I started it in '60. With help from Luckless Litton and Snuffy Johnson. It needs to be finished."

Her fingers trembled around Molasses's reins. Still, Braxton had her jittery as a cat cornered by a litter of puppies. *Stop it, Skylla. You'll never learn to be a rancher if you don't pay solemn attention to the master's lessons.*

"We need to gather a herd," he said, "get them ready for market. That won't cost anything but the sweat of our brows." He rode toward a collection of spotted cows with horns as wide as a man was tall. "We'll worry about money later."

Skylla tapped Molasses's flank. It took a few more taps to get the gelding going. Shame came over her. The least the ranch should have offered its savior was a good string of horses.

"We'll cull the bulls, first off," he said. "Make stew meat out of the troublemakers."

"How do the cows get to water in the canyon?" she asked.

"There's a spring flowing from the rocks on the canyon's floor. It flows back into a pool. We can't see it for the oaks, but it's there. With water and a good crop of grasses—which are there—you've got a fine corral." He patted his mount's neck. "Without fences, a cowboy must ride guard, but a sizable herd can be confined, corralled, branded, and when the need arises"—slightly downturned lips twitched—"castrated."

Skylla blushed, not solely from his mention of castration. Braxton might be speaking of business, but his deep baritone hinted at cockiness and dare.

Seeing her flush, he said, "Pardon my choice in word."

She looked him straight in those splendid eyes. "You needn't tiptoe around my sensibilities."

"Considering all the work to be done here, have you ever thought about selling the place and moving on to civilization?"

"Never. It's my home. And I'll be buried here."

He got very quiet. His mien relayed a strong message. He couldn't understand what a greenhorn woman would want with a piece of property on the frontier.

He might as well hear the whole story. "You think I'm a weakling, too sensitive for the frontier. Know something, sir. I won't run scared, and I will carry my weight."

"Are you sure you're up to it?"

"My leg is impaired, but I'm not crippled."

A moment passed. "From the way you favor the leg, I gather you were injured. Most likely, you weren't born lame."

"It happened two years ago."

"I've seen cripples. Lots of them. I've done my share of treating the afflicted. I always felt it an honor to strap General Hood in the saddle. He'd lost his leg and the use of one arm, you see. Valor on the battlefield hobbled him. It didn't quell his fighting spirit."

She liked the matter-of-fact way Braxton addressed her problem. "There's no valor attached to my gimp. I was cowering in a cave in Vicksburg when a Minie ball got me."

"Vicksburg?" he asked, his shoulders going rigid.

"I was there. During the siege." *Like your family.* She squeezed Molasses's reins. "We—Claudine, Kathy Ann, and I—were there after, after . . . Biloxi."

"That explains your aversion to rodents."

It had taken months of carnagé to starve and bombard the men, women, and children in the city once pegged the Gibraltar of the West into submission. "Everyone ate whatever was available."

"So I've heard." His gaze swiveled away.

Was she bringing up the subject he'd warned her off?

He cut his eyes back to her. His brows furrowed, his mood further darkening. "Why didn't you ladies send up a white flag to Grant and his men? I understand his camp followers had it easy enough. Easy as a Sunday afternoon picnic."

Skylla made a concerted effort not to fall from the saddle.

Did he know about the original sin that it took for the St. Clair women to get aboard a naval ship bound for Texas?

She ordered her back to straighten. "Are you accusing me of treason against the Confederacy?"

"Are you a Blue Belly lover?"

"I judge a man on his merits, not his patriotism."

"Don't toy with me, Skylla. I heard about Biloxi."

With false cool, she replied, "Let's get something settled. The matter of Biloxi isn't your concern. And if you can't accept that, Sergeant Hale, I suggest you gather your knapsack, and your serving boy, then ride on out."

"Braxton." He sucked his teeth in an arrogance that she reckoned he in no way felt. "You wanted to call me Braxton."

"I mean it about the knapsack."

He reached to close his long-fingered hand around the pommel of Molasses's saddle. "By damn, I didn't return to Texas to be turned off the place. You are the same as promised to me, and I have a problem letting promises go by the wayside."

"You're in no position to be choosy. Or bossy."

She stared him down. A full minute passed before Brax admitted, "I've got my own afflictions. Everyone who came through the war—Yankee or rebel—bears the scars of it. You've just gotten a gander at my ugly wounds."

"I have wounds, too. And not simply from my leg."

"Such as?"

"My father reared me to believe no human should be a slave. He died for his beliefs. I take pride in his sacrifice, but I'm a Southerner. All I know is the South. My friends and family fought for the Confederate States because that was the patriotic thing to do. Right or wrong or in between, I ultimately cheered for a Southern victory. Yet I can't forget the sight of my father's lifeless body swinging from a tree. Nor can I forget Grant's relentless attack on the defenseless people of Vicksburg. I am a living contradiction."

Braxton squinted at the setting sun before soldering his gaze to Skylla. "You and I don't have a quarrel about the war. I'm a Southerner who never accepted slavery. We're kindred spirits."

She did nothing to tear her eyes away. And when he said, "I'd appreciate a second chance," she relented.

"Second chances are the stuff of miracles." Confessing more than she ought to, and hoping she didn't ape Claudine's style, she said, "I've always wished for a second chance at the dance." With James.

Braxton leaned over to take her hand. Her bony work-worn hand. He brought it to his chest, where she felt the beating of his heart. When he spoke, his heart went into his words. "I'd consider it an honor if you'd dance with me."

What sweet words. The words of a gallant. Yet she wouldn't be swayed by mere utterances. *He's being nice because he doesn't know he won't have to fight to marry Claudine.* Somehow she couldn't bring herself to set him straight.

Speaking in generalities, Skylla said rhetorically, "What's the fun of dancing with a cripple?"

He lifted her chin with the crook of a finger. "Your limp doesn't take away from you. Not in my eyes. To dance with you would be my honor."

"Just like when you were honored to strap John Bell Hood in the saddle?"

He chuckled. "Believe me, Skylla St. Clair, you're the one I want to settle in a . . . saddle."

"You're a flirt, Braxton Hale." *A nice flirt. And I'm a cripple. A skinny cripple with little to recommend me.* "We'd best head back. Supper won't wait forever."

Chapter Six

"I'm sick to death of beans," Kathy Ann complained to the three other diners at the picnic table. Candles flickered, crickets creaked. Night had fallen. Her voice drowned the creaks. "Beans, beans, beans—that's all we ever eat."

Oh, dear. The ranting and raving again. Skylla saw her sister as a rose in difficulty blooming, and she sympathized with those difficulties, yet she wished Kathy Ann wouldn't misbehave tonight of all nights, Braxton's first night at the Nickel Dime.

She peered over the rim of her coffee cup at the hearty eater. Here in Texas, lots of men didn't dress for supper, but Braxton had changed into another suit of Rebel grays, these not quite as threadbare as his traveling clothes. His hair had been slicked back, his face scrubbed, his uniform brushed. His features, while lean, were handsome in a mannish way, with a strong nose and jaw, and nice teeth sans a rotten one.

The siren, meanwhile, batted her lashes and clucked over him. Skylla was thankful Claudine hadn't put up a big fuss about Braxton. Now that he was here, it would be terrible to lose him. It would be terrible for the ranch.

Kathy Ann turned to face the youth sitting on a stump a few feet away. "Say, Geoff, what do you think about beans?"

"Dey real good, Miss Kathy Ann."

"Traitor." The petulant girl fell silent.

Geoff simply smiled.

Earlier, Skylla had asked the likable lad to sit at table. Why uphold the custom of keeping help in their place? He'd declined the invitation. She pegged him as brighter than he let on. He had his reasons, she supposed.

Kathy Ann spoke again. "I don't know why we can't send into town for the fixings for a nice blancmange."

Ignoring her sister, Skylla continued to eat the tasteless overdone beans—devoid of salt pork—and an even less appealing cornpone. Cornbread without milk and eggs, well, it was something to chew. Land's sake, a blancmange would be nice!

Braxton remarked, "I'm appreciative of this dinner."

"Dat's what I said," Geoff reiterated.

"Then you both must've been head-shot."

Claudine glared. "Kathy Ann, that will be enough."

"You needn't fuss at me," the girl came back. "I was expressing an opinion. Ambrose told me it was all right to express my opinion."

"Father didn't mean insults," Skylla pointed out.

Braxton tried to make peace. "Geoff and I are just out of our heads being in the company of all you lovely Southern belles."

"Oh, pulleeze." Eyes rolled, a tongue lolled, and Kathy Ann fanned her face. "I'm choking to death on cane syrup."

Surprisingly, Braxton laughed. Claudine and Skylla didn't join in, and Geoff merely slipped the calico cat a piece of cornbread, received with contempt. Braxton's gaze welded to Skylla's.

"Are you always this quiet at supper?" he asked her.

"No." She motioned to his plate. "You'd better eat up. You're going to need all the fuel we can feed you."

He chuckled, winked, and started to say something.

Claudine, frowning at his wink, stopped him. "I just can't get over that you, Braxton Hale of Vicksburg, would be the very man to answer our query. Amazing!"

"The world is filled with coincidences." Braxton leaned back on the bench. "Or are you implying it's strange a Hale of Vicksburg would dare to answer the advertisement?"

"I mean I find it amazing that a former ranch hand at the Nickel Dime would see the query." Claudine smiled. "By the by, I knew your uncle in Vicksburg. Harry Braxton. Your mother's brother, I believe. Fine people, the Braxtons of Magnolia Mill."

"That's the story."

"Isn't it a shame you and I never met?"

Braxton poured a shot from the crockery jug, then swirled his glass. "I suppose, Miss Claudine, if you'd been of a mind to hang around Woody's Blacksmith Shop, you'd have found me."

"Blacksmith shop? Her? The high-and-mighty Miss Claudine Twill?" Kathy Ann slapped the table. "That's rich."

"It am, missy. It shore am." Geoff slapped his thigh twice. "Pappy, mammy, and dat ole Sammy, it am rich."

Upstanding ladies didn't frequent such shops. They all knew it. Had Braxton meant to be rude? Probably he was letting everyone know he wouldn't hide from his reputation.

Claudine smoothed over the moment. "I left the city at an early age, before you arrived in Vicksburg, I should imagine. I wed at fifteen, you see, and moved south to Biloxi. I must admit I wasn't severed from Vicksburg chatter. You were the talk of the town, Brax. Everyone said you weren't living up to your potential by working as a blacksmith. What made you decide to choose horseshoeing over continuing your education in medicine?"

"Hunger."

"Harry Braxton had money, at least he did then. He would see after his family."

"My uncle didn't feed his sister and her four kids."

Claudine fiddled with the lace of her shawl. "I never dreamed Harry wouldn't be kindhearted. We assumed Elizabeth Hale lived in her quaint little cottage because pride wouldn't let her intrude upon Harry and Mary Esther."

"I'd rather not discuss my family."

"I second that. I'm sick of hearing about Vicksburg." Kathy Ann leaned toward him. "Hey, Sergeant, why don't you send that darkie of yours into Ecru to buy some sugar and eggs?" She stuck her tongue out at Geoff. "Nice speckled eggs. And butter and milk. We need lots of milk for blancmange."

Skylla spoke gently but sternly. "Mind your manners."

"I don't have any. And I'm not gonna eat these stinking old beans!"

"Don't talk to your sister like that," Braxton boomed as she threw her fork to the table.

"Go to hell!" Kathy Ann jumped up to flounce away.

"Mm-mm, dey gonna be trouble."

Braxton threw his napkin to the table, as if he'd go after the unruly girl, but Skylla stopped him. "It's best you let her deal with this on her own."

"She needs discipline."

Skylla looked into his irate eyes. "We'll work this out. Not tonight. But we *will* work it out. Have patience."

"Ladies, massa, iffen you be excusing me, dis boy be checking da horses. Thank you, ma'ams, fo de hot food."

Claudine nodded, dismissing the batman. She said to Braxton, "Yes, please do be tolerant. Skylla and I are doing our best for Kathy Ann."

"Do you know what's best?"

Braxton glanced from Skylla to Claudine and back again. "If you're looking to spoil her, why haven't you done it right? Why don't you have ingredients for that pudding she's craving?"

Skylla set her fork aside. "There's no money. Except for Confederate notes."

Of course, there were the four gold coins discovered in an empty snuff jar in Titus's dresser drawer. She was saving those for taxes. Talk in town said a tax collector would be appointed first off and any day. She wouldn't chance not having the funds to pay up.

Braxton crossed his arms. "Ladies, you must learn not to count on money. If you want something, find a way to get it. Nothing comes to a seated man. Or woman. Not anymore. You've got cows, thousands of cows. Milk one or two."

Don't let him shame us. "We've heard longhorns aren't good milkers. We can't waste time on unproductive undertakings."

"They give milk. Not like some breeds, but they give milk. You can bet there's enough milk for a simple blancmange."

Claudine fingered her swanlike neck and bit her lower lip. "Brax, we, um—my goodness!—we don't know how to milk cows."

"None of you?"

"None of us," Skylla replied, bravado elevating her chin.

"As I suspected."

Her pride wouldn't let him think the St. Clair women had done nothing but sit on their hands and gobble down the canned goods discovered upon arrival. "Claudine is an excellent shot and butcher. She's provided us with nice cuts of beef." She had gotten lucky with a shot *once.* "Kathy Ann is an excellent seamstress. She's made bonnets and so forth. I put in a garden. Within a couple of weeks, we should have snap peas and summer squash."

Perhaps one meal of each. While it was considered good form for ladies of station to have at least a passing interest in agriculture, Skylla hadn't studied the finer points of farming. Besides, farming hurt. Carrying water from the well always sent her calf into spasms of lightninglike pain. Since she'd bragged on her determination out in the pasture, she boasted further, "I've been watering a hill of berries. Strawberries."

By moonlight Brax's eyes lit up like the brightest star in the galaxies beyond. "I'll be damned—Uh, pardon me. Geoff and I have dreamed about strawberries here lately."

"Aren't we blessed fancies come cheap?" Claudine laughed.

"Shall we have a picnic someday soon? We shall feast and feast on strawberries!"

"Why not? One of you ladies on this arm." He lifted his right hand. "And the other on this arm." He raised the left. "At least until the wedding. Then rest assured"—his gaze returned to Skylla—"there'll be no woman on my arm but my wife."

Guilt went through her, even before Claudine quirked a brow. Naturally, he supposed the ranch owner would have first rights to the husband. She ought to ease his mind. Now wasn't the moment for such frankness.

In her lonely, lonely heart, Skylla knew she made excuses, to buy time . . . to revel in his attentions. Why would he need to mention his past? On the other hand, she shouldn't tarry in telling him the whole truth. Not tonight. Tomorrow. In the morning she'd get an early start explaining things to Braxton. Mornings were always better. Tomorrow she'd tell him the truth.

For legal reasons, Claudine must be his bride.

An hour after dinner and a half-hour after he'd strong-armed Geoff into keeping watch at the ranch, Brax pushed open the swinging doors to Leander's Saloon, Claudine's rifle in his right hand, his trusty double-eagle in a pocket. The latter was useless at the moment. In what seemed like a life-time ago, the coin—a Christmas gift minted by Titus, meant as a joke—had debuted in this very tavern. Debuted and got caught.

Upon a quick inventory of the ranch's valuables, Brax had decided it was the Spencer or his mother's cameo that had to go on the line for blancmange with strawberry sauce.

He scanned the saloon. What a difference four and a half years had made. Gone were the gaggle of customers, the up-right piano, the portrait behind the bar of a painted sporting lady. The bald proprietor, wearing a dirty apron and chewing on a toothpick, pointed to the *NO NIGERS OR CHEETERS* sign, then hid a jar of pickled pig's feet marked *HEP URSEF* under the counter. Some things never changed.

Brax flipped Leander the bird, but got worried. His earlier days in Mason County had been upright enough, save for a particular accusation of fraud connected to the trick coin. It wouldn't do for that story to get back to the heiress.

He thanked his lucky stars for Skylla St. Clair. If either the brat pig or that silly twit Claudine were the bride-to-be, he'd collect Geoff, get on Impossible, and ride.

His line of sight moved on. Hatted head leaning to the side and his gray swollen tongue lolling forward, Charlie Main was propped in the corner. Drunk. Passed out. A wet spot staining the placket area of his denims. A credit to white supremacy and Leander's desire for excellent clientele was the bony, coarse Charlie Main.

Brax made a beeline for the lone table of poker players.

A small pile of chips lay on the surface. Two gray-haired men sat playing. He recognized them both. "How ya doing, Luke, Daggitt?" He cottoned to Luke Burrows, but Homer Daggitt wasn't worth the gunpowder to put him out of his misery, in Brax's opinion. "Long time no see."

The farmer, Daggitt, tipped his chair back, planking a palm on the wooden arm, which emphasized his beer gut and strained shirt buttons. "I'll be dipped in rat shit if it ain't the cowboy from hell. I thought the hogs done et you."

Putting in his two cents' worth, Leander called out, "Ain't no purty boy no more, that's fur durn sure."

Brax lifted his hand to offer the barkeep a second shot at the bird, then sized up one of Ecru's most decent citizens. Luke Burrows was thinner than ever, like older men were wont to be, but he looked healthy enough. Brax was pleased to see him looking no worse for the wear.

Luke stacked red and blue chips on the baize-covered table. "You do look a mite drawed, son. Did you get shot up bad in the war?"

It didn't take bullets to get shot up. Brax felt about as wrung out as he'd ever felt on the battlefield, not that he'd ever admit it. "No Blue Belly's a good enough shot to get me."

"You was prob'ly ducking."

"Yes, Leander, now that you mention it, that's what I was doing," Brax snarled. "Every chance I got."

Luke chuckled, then took a sip of beer. "Have you been out to the Nickel Dime?"

"Could have."

"You ain't looking to put a claim on the place, are you?"

"I just might, Luke."

"You're too late, son. Mississippi gals beat you to it. One of them inherited the place from Titus St. Clair. Deed got all changed and everything afore the war was over."

"I'm working for Miss St. Clair, is all."

"Iffen she hired you, she shore must be hard up—" Daggitt clamped his overstuffed lips when Brax shot him a glare that dared him to finish the insult. "Welcome back, I guess."

Luke eyed the proprietor. "Leander, bring the boy a glass of beer. On me."

"Much obliged." Brax pulled out a straight chair, sat down, then anted the Spencer. "Deal me in."

"Nawsir," Daggitt objected. "I ain't forgit that hunnerd you tried to take off me with yore two-tailed gold piece, Christmas of '60."

"What about that fifty you won from me a week later?" Brax countered. "Deal me in, boys. I haven't had the challenge of playing cards with"—*picking clean*—"a couple of topnotch Texans in much too long."

"Our cards." Luke pointed to the deck on the table.

"Suits me," Brax replied with a smile.

Within an hour he had all the chips in front of him. And it hadn't taken sleight of hand. Brax took the rifle and leaned it against his chair. "Had enough for an evening, gentlemen?"

They had.

Brax was in no hurry to settle up. "What's going on around here? Seen any Yankees toting carpetbags?"

"Not a one," Luke replied, "but I heared there's some over to the east. The scalawags are headed this way, I reckon."

Good. A buyer on the move, with any luck. Since Brax's fortunes were definitely looking up, he had every reason to be tickled over the prospect of a sucker approaching.

What about now, though? His first thought centered on Skylla. The lady was a dervish, even with a lame leg. A grin edged its way around his mouth. A woman that energetic ought to be hell on wheels in bed. First, he had to get her there.

Which meant planning, workwise and otherwise.

What about what she said out at the canyon? Straight out, she said she was glad to have a home and would work for it. Can I turn her off the place? Damn tootin'.

In the meantime, the Nickel Dime would be better off if Titus's horses were back where they belonged. "Say, either of you know what happened to Oren Singleterry?"

"Whud if I do?" was Daggitt's response.

"I heard something." Luke ran a hand down the gullies of his face. "Heard he stolt Titus's horses when he pulled out last November. Also heard Singleterry was over in Menard. Raising horses. Wouldn't surprise me none if them horses've had a running-iron put to their hides."

Brax's sentiments exactly. "Sounds like I need to see about collecting Nickel Dime property."

"Now that ya mentioned Menard . . ." Daggitt took a fat wad of tobacco into his fat wad of a mouth. "Ya know that gal ya used to spark? Jane Clark be her name." He dribbled brown juice onto his stubbled chin. "Didn't wait on ya, naw she didn't. Got herself all married off. Why, you was hardly outta the county."

Relieved he wouldn't have the bother of a lady wanting to take up where they left off, Brax shrugged. "Jane and I didn't make any promises to each other."

"Ain't you lucky?" Daggitt sucked, then spat, missing the spittoon. "Oh, did I tell ya? She's aliving over to Menard. She was left a widder woman. The war, ya know. I heared she was working as a—"

"You yap too much," Luke interrupted.

Choicer words were never spoken. Brax surveyed his chips. "Time to pay up, boys."

Each pulled out bills.

Confederate greenbacks.

"That's not money." Brax leveled a glare at each man in turn. "You owe me. Gold."

"How the heck can you expect anything different than dixies?" Daggitt's face turned the hue of purple cabbage. "Where would we get any gold? I done give near on everything I had to ole Jeff Davis."

"Me, too." Luke nodded. "We just play for fun nowadays."

"I wasn't playing for fun."

Leander came over to collect dirty glasses. He screwed up an eye, smirking. "Luck's run out, ain't it, purty boy? Warms the cockles of m' heart."

"Will you take our markers?" Luke waited with bated breath.

Brax was finished with markers. But he wasn't finished with Daggitt and Luke. The farmer might be friendly, and Brax did cotton to the man, but all men knew poker playing to be serious business. "Tell me something, Luke Burrows. You still raising hogs?"

"I am."

"Then I'll settle for one."

"We only got two breeders. And a half-growed shoat."

If Luke weren't the most decent fellow around, Brax would demand one of those breeders. "I'll take the shoat. Deliver it to the Nickel Dime tomorrow. Before noon." He turned to the corpulent farmer. "I suggest you hightail it over to your place. Bring me a couple of chickens. Caged. Raid your wife's pantry while you're at it. For butter and sugar. A bottle of vanilla would finish off the debt." Kathy Ann would have her dessert, by damn. He didn't give a hoot in hell about her, but he knew the hurt of a craving gone too long unsettled. "I'll wait right here for you."

Neither acted excited about giving over such prizes, but each left.

Brax stood up, stretched a kink out of his shoulder, then strolled over to Charlie Main. "Get up, asshole." He thumped the toe of his boot hard against the drunk's butt, twice. "Get up. It's time to go to work."

Charlie mumbled incoherently. He swatted an arm. His sweat-stained sombrero fell to the floor, exposing greasy hair in a shade which might be kindly described as dung brown.

"Get up."

A bellow of foul-breathed indignation met that demand. Charlie Main did have a temper.

"Sober, you used to be the best damn cowboy in Texas, outside of me. And I'm betting you're still tall in the saddle. Get up, Charlie. I've got all the booze you can guzzle back at the ranch. All you have to do is rope a few cows during the day. Then you can wallow in piss and rotgut all evening long."

"Getthehellouttamysight!" Charlie came alive, and roared to his feet like a mad bull pawing the ground. "You sumbitch!" He drew back his fist to plow it into Brax's face. "Getoutta—"

Brax lunged for the cowpoke's arm and twisted it behind his back. "Make some coffee, Leander."

By midnight Brax was riding Impossible back to the ranch. The Spencer nestled in its holster, the foodstuff in the saddlebag. A cage of upset hens hung from the saddlehorn.

On a complaining mule rode Charlie Main. Brax intended to set the cowpoke on a path—with Geoff's assistance—to repairing the outbuildings, collecting stolen horses, and rounding up a herd to show off to a sucker.

Once Brax taught those women—preferably Skylla alone—how to milk a cow, he'd have done his part to get the Nickel Dime presentable. Here on out, he would do nothing but kick back, wait for a sucker, and eat milk pudding.

Chapter Seven

"Milk that cow? I can't. I simply can't—won't!"

This was not a good morning, certainly no venue for true confessions. The blood drained from Skylla's face as she eyed an expanse of sharp horns and wild beast. Even though the cow's horns were tied between the corral fence and Molasses's saddlehorn, Geoff atop the gelding, Skylla drew no comfort.

Braxton wanted her to learn to milk a cow.

Furthermore, he'd brought that awful Main drunkard to the Nickel Dime. Already, Charlie Main had insulted Claudine and had rendered the outhouse unfit for even Kathy Ann, much less for those of delicate sensibilities. On Braxton's orders, the derelict was hauling water to clean up after himself.

"Come on, honey," Braxton prompted.

"I'm not going near that creature. Or her calf." Skylla cut her eyes to the bullock hogtied nearby, then back to the mother. "Her horns . . . ! Braxton, I don't want to be gored. I'll do anything else. Whatever you deem me fit to do. Why don't I take care of the laundry?"

"Not a chance." He dangled the pail from a forearm, and

took hold of Skylla's elbow with his hand. "We're gonna walk over to that mama cow, and you're gonna talk real sweetlike." His eyes half-lidded, he gave Skylla a meaningful look that sent her heart to pitching from something that had nothing to do with cows or milk. "Talk like you used to talk to the swains of Biloxi, back when the moss swayed in the oak trees and Rastus used to turn the ice-cream crank."

"I gots to tell ya, Miss Skylla, he know milking. He a good hand at it. He real good at eberthing."

Skeptical about herself, she said, "I don't know . . ."

Braxton laced his fingers with hers. "Come on, sweetheart. I promise she won't disturb a hair on your head."

He said it. Skylla decided to believe him. He has lots of fight, she realized. The sun hadn't been up any time, yet she'd already marveled for an hour at the amazing Braxton Hale.

Moreover, wasn't it gallant, Braxton spending his money on supplies and livestock? Imagine—setting hens and the ingredients for dessert. The prospect of a shoat. Lots of milk. *Braxton, you're a wonder.* And he'd called her sweetheart. What would be the shame in basking in that for a spell?

"Are you ready to give milking a try?" He winked one of those impossibly wonderful green eyes.

She took a breath, squared her shoulders, and advanced on a ton of beef on the hoof. "Let's do it."

Electra got wind of opportunity, prancing up with a meow. She really was a tart, going to whoever could do right by her.

No milking stool to sit on, Braxton crouched back on his heels and motioned for Skylla to do the same. Recall flashed across his face as he glanced at her skirts. "Claudine is better suited for this chore," he said, pandering to her affliction.

"I won't let my lame leg get in the way of chores."

He looked up at her with the gaze that turned both her legs lame. "Skylla, would you let me examine your limb? I've had some experience along the healing line, you know."

"I can't be helped. Several doctors have told me so."

Braxton nodded, understanding and carrying on without comment. Thankfully. "Since I've sent Claudine and Kathy

Ann out on a hunt," he said, "why don't you stand here and just watch? I'll milk ole Bossy this time."

"Th-thank you."

Why had she stuttered? Skylla had never been anxious of speech. *It's because you're too chicken to 'fess up.* Or did it have to do with the feelings she'd thought had died with James? Braxton, the model of indomitable spirit, reminded her she was far from dead. With Claudine just as alive, Skylla realized hers was a collision course with disaster.

Rather than dwelling on it, she glanced at the comical calico. Electra posted herself to Braxton's left, then licked her paw and imparted a hurry-up-you-laggard look his way. He began to address the cow. She tried to turn her head in his direction, the ropes restraining her. Yet the look in her round bovine eyes spoke an eloquent language: "Who is this fool, and what the dickens is he up to?" She expelled a moo that thundered across the corral and set Electra's hackles on end.

"There's a good girl, good, good girl." Shoulders hunching, Braxton reached for an udder. Bossy danced from one leg to the other, flipped her tail. With sure, expert motions, he quieted her and guided a stream of white liquid into the pail. "Good girl," he crooned. "Giving us nice milk for blancmange."

"Oooh, wee!" shouted Geoff. "Puddin' wit' berries on da top. Oooh, wee."

Upon getting a smell of and a gander at all that heavenly milk, the usually independent Electra compromised her principles, twining herself around Braxton's ankles, her whiskers upturned as if to say, "Big boy, how about sharing some with li'l ole me?"

He pointed an udder at her. She lapped appreciatively. Skylla laughed, so did Geoff and Braxton when Electra caught a stream in her eye and huffed off with feline indignation. Skylla couldn't recall the last time she'd really, really laughed. She'd thought she'd forgotten how.

On a forward step she bent closer. "This is fun!"

"I aim to please," he said, a sensuous pitch to his voice that sent Skylla's nerve endings to tingling.

He lifted his eyes to her. His lashes were thick, long, and much darker than his gold-shot head of hair ought to allow. Brax's big hand moved up Bossy's tricolored coat, patting and petting as he went. The cow leaned into his hand. And Skylla had the most sinfully luscious desire.

She wished his hand would caress her.

Sitting under a magnolia tree and finishing off the strawberries she'd found picked in the cookhouse, Kathy Ann said to Electra, who was dining on a scorpion, "I want to talk about the soldier. I sure like his looks. Why shouldn't *I* have him? What's so special about Skylla or Claudine? Skylla's an old gimp. And Claudine's just old. She's had enough husbands. It's my turn. I'm old enough."

Finished with her feast, the calico licked her whiskers and crawled onto Kathy Ann's lap.

Pleased at being the person Electra trusted, Kathy Ann stroked an appreciative chin. "Lots of girls in Mississippi marry young. Not from the plantation class, of course. Doesn't that sound just like Claudine, plantation class? Who cares about any old plantations? I want something different."

Maybe she could get the soldier to take her away, somewhere nice. Say, California. She'd read about that faraway land in a storybook, and a hankering like nobody's business had been after her ever since.

"I wonder if he's heard of California, Electra?" She frowned. "If he has, he wouldn't remember it right now. All he does is gaze like a lovestruck puppy at Skylla. She makes me sick. What a goody-goody."

Kathy Ann was jealous that her sister had all the luck, when she had none. " 'Course, Claudine'll tear into sister over the sergeant before it's all said and done. You wait and see. Then we'll see who's lucky."

Her gaze on line with the cat, she caught sight of the soldier's boots as he walked up. She looked up to see him frowning, just as Ambrose had frowned. Like a father.

"Girl, what are you doing lollygagging? You haven't earned the right to sit around. Find Skylla. She'll need your help with supper."

"Quit ordering me around." She gifted him with the sort of face most often seen in a schoolyard. He put his hands at his hips and got all aggravated. "Why are you scowling at me?" she asked. "Are you still mad because I tricked you yesterday?"

His feet spread, he bent forward and rested both hands on his thighs. Glaring, he replied, "I'm not mad at you. But let's get something straight, *little girl*. Don't mess with me."

"Why don't you give me a kiss, and we'll talk about it?"

"Not interested. I don't kiss children."

"Oh? You were ready to marry me yesterday."

"I'm doing the talking. You listen. And you listen closely." He pointed at her. "Mention five thousand dollars one more time in front of Skylla, or your mother, and I will throw you down the well."

"Have you done stuff like that a lot? Are you cruel to girls?"

"I'm willing to start with you."

"Skylla will run you off if you aren't nice to me. So there!"

"Don't press your luck. If I catch—" His expression got tight before he said, "Wait a minute. What's on your mouth? It's red."

"These lips are ripe and ready for kisses."

He got in her face, but not for kisses. "Listen closely. If I catch you talking to your mother and sister like you did last night, bet your britches you'll know worse than the bottom of a well."

"Oh, really? Do you think you can catch me?" She pushed herself to her feet and shoved her palms on his chest. Giggling and picking up her skirts, she spun around to run away. He caught her before she took five running steps, and when he pulled on her arm to spin her around, she yelped in pain and kicked his shin. "Let me go, bad man!"

"Quit acting like a spoiled brat and I will."

She stopped struggling.

"Thank you," he said. "Now go to the kitchen. Skylla needs your help. She's cooking a"—he smiled and his eyes got soft—"blancmange with strawberry sauce."

Strawberry sauce. Oh, no! Kathy Ann felt shame, for she'd eaten every last one of the berries. She bolted, running past the stables and toward the creek. At the edge she kicked pieces of deadwood and small rocks, sending them airborne. Nobody loved her. Nobody had ever loved her. Except Electra. Claudine and Skylla, they were obligated. Kathy Ann needed love.

It was at that moment she saw three Indians atop ponies. She recognized Stalking Wolf, fierce young leader of the Comanches, and his braves, Black Sky and Head Too Big.

Naked as worms, their skin like copper pennies, the chief and his braves were on the other side of the creek. Their black hair having grown to their shoulders, and with feathered spears in their hands, they looked exactly like what they were.

Savages.

Were they? Emil Kreitz, the grocer in Ecru, had told her that during the republic days a young girl had been captured by the Comanches—and she'd turned happy. Cynthia Ann Parker had been torn from her Injun husband, returned to the white world, and she'd died of grief. The Comanches couldn't be all bad.

How would Stalking Wolf treat a wife? Well, he couldn't own a broom closet to lock up a wife when she was bad.

The Injun chief kneed his pony, and horse hooves slashed water as he started across the creek. Kathy Ann didn't scream. She had the urge to stay put. She liked danger. And she wanted to ask him about Cynthia Ann Parker.

The closer Stalking Wolf got, the less adventurous she felt. She whirled around, running as fast as her legs could carry her. Never once did she glance back, for fear of losing ground. It seemed like forever before she gained the ranch.

Goody. She was safe.

As she exhaled, Geoff sashayed from the barn and over to her. "Anythin' da matter, Miss Kathy Ann?"

"Nothing!" She pushed him out her way. "Go 'way, you little black raisin. Go 'way before I box your ears."

Busy making up her mind, she chewed a fingernail. Why mention the Injuns to her elders? Maybe Claudine or Skylla would venture into the woods . . . and get captured. Then Sergeant would be Kathy Ann's.

Her big grin collapsed when her sister stepped in front of her, the soldier at her side.

Suspicion in her brown eyes, Skylla asked, "Did you do something with the strawberries?"

"I ate them."

"You little fiend—"

"No, Braxton, no." Skylla took his hand. "They're only strawberries. We still have the blancmange."

At dinner, Claudine couldn't care less about sweets. She had an awful feeling. She feared Brax found Skylla attractive, even though he was obviously angry that she hadn't scolded Kathy Ann over the strawberries. Would the incorrigible imp provide the link to bond Skylla and Brax together?

If he married Skylla, where would that leave a redhead with too many years and too few prospects?

If you don't watch your p's and q's, you'll end up the pitiable old auntie to their brats. Never! When Brax Hale begat children, Claudine would make certain they were hers.

Eating dinner, Brax ignored the changeable redhead, and stewed over the strawberry incident. He'd be damned if he could understand why Skylla coddled the fiend. Once he was legal head of this family, Kathy Ann would change—or the sun wouldn't set in the west!

"Dis am nice smothered steak," Geoff complimented.

"Mr. Main provided us with a cut of beef," Skylla said. "Thank you, Mr. Main."

Charlie Main belched in reply.

Kathy Ann rolled her eyes and chowed down.

"You never said anything about the roasts I provided." Claudine didn't cotton to having attention centered on anyone else, but who the hell cared what that twit thought?

Charlie Main pushed his plate toward the center of the table and stood up. "I'm going to bed."

No doubt to down the jug of moonshine Brax had promised as a reward for the ranch hand's afternoon of butchering, carrying water, and chopping wood.

Once the main course was through, Brax didn't tarry. Certainly he didn't hang around for blancmange. He made for the bunkhouse, his partner behind him. As the Hale men prepared to bunk down for the night, Main already snored on his cot.

Geoff shook the empty crockery. "He drank the jug dry."

"I watered it down." Brax glanced at the sleeping cowhand. "He hasn't done an honest day's work in who-knows-when. He's out like a light."

Geoff rolled a shoulder. "Won't take much to rock me to sleep, Bubba."

"Tell me about it," Brax concurred.

"I thought we weren't going to do much work."

"What else can we do?" He turned up his palm. "I can't sit around and watch Skylla work like a section hand."

"You're getting sweet on the lady. Next thing, you'll hem and haw about running out on her."

"I won't." Skylla had gotten in over her head with this place, but in an easier setting, she'd do just fine. "She can take care of herself. She's a scrappy woman."

"You shore gots eyes fo dat crippled girl. Pappy, Mammy, and a hound dawg answerin' ta Sammy, you does."

"Cut it out." He eyed Main again, to be certain of confidentiality. "Before we got here I told you not to use that field-hand patter, but it's been thicker than ever. If those ladies find out you're fooling them, we're in deep shit."

"We may be in it already." Geoff sat down on his cot, leaning his back against the log wall. "The redhead knows I'm a fraud."

"What does she know?"

"The usual. Very little."

Brax hooked his shirt on a peg. "Keep it that way."

"I will." A pause. "What if you get so fond of Miss Skylla's, um, *biscuit-making* that you get an idea to stay put?"

"That won't happen."

"I wouldn't bet on it, Bubba, my man. I think you might forget California altogether."

"Wrong."

"You may claim to want your pound of flesh, but—"

"Pound of flesh?" Brax cut in. "I'm not after revenge. I want . . ." His voice trailed off as he came to grips with his intentions. "You're right. I was after vengeance. I wanted a St. Clair to pay for Vicksburg . . ."

"You speak in the past tense."

Brax realized he had spoken as if his feelings had changed. Perhaps they had. That was the frightening part.

"I don't want to hurt Skylla," he admitted and felt better for it. His irritation over the strawberries vanished as he considered that decent and fine woman. "I ought to do right by her."

"Then we're making a home here?"

"Not a chance. But I'll do something to help Skylla get a new start in the town of her choice."

"Watch your back in the meantime, Bubba. That Claudine isn't to be trusted. She's one conniving redhead. Already, she's cornered me. I think she figures to set me against you."

"I don't need to tell you how to handle her."

"That you don't, Bubba. That you don't."

Needing a breath of air, Brax quit the log cabin and wished he could lose himself in a fine cigar. He ambled past the ranch house and outbuildings, and had every intention of soaking his feet in Topaz Creek. Someone had beat him there. A woman strolled along the bank in the moonlight, her head down and her arms crossed under her breasts.

Skylla.

She looked like an angel, decent and pure, what with the silver of moonlight spilling down on her; Brax gazed upon her almost with awe. He cut the gap between them.

Chapter Eight

"Evening," Brax drawled as he approached Skylla in the moonlight, the sounds of night around them.

She said hello, her eyes on his bare chest. He liked her looking at him. She needed to start thinking of him as a *man,* which would be the next step in getting her to the altar.

"Mind if I join you for your walk?" he asked.

"I'd be delighted."

They strolled along the creek bank for five, maybe ten minutes. Then he lent a hand to seat her on a cypress log. She stared at him. He did the same to her. Sitting down beside her, Brax warned himself off putting his arm around her.

When she spoke, she was all business. "I'm amazed you've gotten Charlie Main to work. He has a reputation for laziness. I had grave doubts this morning. Tonight is a different story. You've had no trouble encouraging him. You are"—her heart-shaped face brightened into a moonlit smile—"you're amazing."

Brax took pride in her praise, but . . . "I didn't come out here to talk about Main."

"You're still upset about the strawberries. Please forgive Kathy Ann. She didn't know we had plans for them."

"She knew you didn't pick them for the fun of it."

Skylla sighed, a mixture of weariness and frustration. "She craves attention, any attention, even the wrong kind."

"I've noticed."

"Kathy Ann is, was . . . illegitimate. You see, her mother was once Ben Lewis's kept woman, but they had a falling out. She gave birth in New Orleans. Yvette, Kathy Ann's mother, turned to prostitution." Skylla had no trouble saying the word usually whispered by women. "But she did more than sell her body. Yvette neglected her daughter. Many times Kathy Ann was locked in a closet. For various reasons."

"Sounds rough," Brax murmured, not unaffected.

"I don't know all the particulars, but I do know the police found Kathy Ann in a locked closet. She'd been there for days. Her mother was dead on a bed. Kathy Ann hadn't met her father, but she knew his name. Ben and Claudine took her in.

"My sister is a very troubled girl. And I don't want her to run away again."

"Again?"

"Yes. She's prone to taking flight. I won't chance her running into trouble, especially not here on the wild frontier." Skylla shivered. "I shudder to think what would happen if the Indians got her."

They might try parboiling the brat.

Skylla hugged her arms. "Truth be known, I don't have much experience dealing with a troublesome girl. I don't know what's best. I'm just doing what I sense is right."

Brax took Skylla's hand. "I'll do whatever I can to help," he said, though he'd just as soon volunteer to have a tooth extracted.

Her voice rang with relief. "Thank you."

Enough about Piglet. "Skylla, it's time we talked about me and you. We haven't discussed the wedding."

"You . . . you've only just arrived."

Brax frowned, confused by her withdrawal. "Why did you send off for a husband if you don't want a wedding?"

"It was Claudine's idea. She contacted Mr. Petry."

"But you went along with it." He hoped. He prayed!

"Yes, I went along with it."

"Then what's the problem? Let's set a date."

A moment passed, peppered only with the sounds of moving water and insects calling in the night. Skylla studied the ground. "You're free to marry Claudine."

"I don't want to marry her."

Her line of sight hastening to his, Skylla's eyes got even bigger. "You can't be serious."

"I came here to marry *Miss* St. Clair, not Mrs."

"But you must. She's . . . she's counting on it." There was something suspicious about the way Skylla spoke. "I . . . I'm not ready for marriage."

Brax didn't like the sound of this. Not at all. "What does that mean?"

"It means I still mourn someone very dear to me. A sailor. An ensign. His gunboat went down off Florida." The chill of grief shook her, evident even in the muted light. "He's been gone a good while now, but the concept of marriage is just too fresh for me."

The strangest feeling came over Brax. He understood her loss. Why not let her adjust to the idea of becoming Mrs. Hale? It needn't be a lengthy wait, regardless. Not with his eagerness to take her into his arms and teach her the delights of the bedroom.

Geoff had been right. Brax had big eyes for her.

She deserves better than the likes of you, Braxton Hale. True, but that wasn't the problem. Or was it?

He owed her something. What could he offer? As sweet and kindhearted as Skylla was, she deserved a wedding gift. At least a ring. If worse came to worst, he could give her the cameo. Yes, that's what he'd do. Give her the cameo.

His palm brushed a stray lock of hair from her cheek, his fingers settling against her ear. He feared she'd retreat, and when she didn't, profound relief rushed through him. "I know your mind is troubled, Skylla. There's a lot to be settled. But I have a terrible hankering. Would you allow me a kiss?"

Her eyes widened as she drew in a quick breath. Then a tiny smile tugged at her lips. "I would allow it."

Slanting his lips over the lushness of her mouth, he put his arms around her thin yet womanly body. He tasted the sugar from the blancmange; it mixed with the natural sweetness that was the dark-eyed belle. He yearned to explore the depths of her mouth, then did. Every nerve in his body sparking, he discovered the joys of kissing his bride-to-be.

His fingers combed her hair, disturbing her hairpins, and he loved the feel of that heavy dark wavy mass as it cascaded down his arm. When he pulled her closer, the sensation of her breasts against his chest evoked such a craving that he ached to lay her on the grasses and make love to her until dawn's first rays . . . and then start over again.

Careful. She's skittish already over the wedding. Don't do something to turn her against it forever. He broke the kiss, but his palms framed her face. Gazing into thick-lashed eyes silvered by moonbeams, he let his feelings override his sensibilities. "Marry me, sweetheart. Marry me tomorrow."

Her head turned away. Without a word she left the log, distanced herself from him. He'd pushed her too far, too fast.

This was not going well.

Having deserted Braxton at the creek, Skylla shook and shook and shook as she hurried to the sanctity of her first-floor bedroom. She wilted onto the edge of the bed, lest her legs give out. One hand gripping the brass bedstead, she carried trembling fingers to lips still tingling from his kiss. Had she lost her mind, allowing herself to feel anything for Braxton? She didn't *want* him to matter. To forget James so easily was almost criminal!

To forget her pact with Claudine, worse.

The confusion of her feelings twisted her insides.

Claudine opened the door and ducked her head into Skylla's bedroom. "What happened to your hair?"

Guiltily, Skylla reached for her hairbrush. "I was just beginning to brush it."

The redhead walked over to her. "What did Brax say when you said he's mine?"

"I didn't tell him. All I could bring myself to say was that he's free to marry you."

"And he didn't jump at the chance?"

That remark hurt Skylla, even though Claudine had spoken the bald truth.

"Forgive me, Daisy. I didn't mean to sound cruel."

"You needn't apologize. I'm more upset by Braxton."

"Are you attracted to him?"

"Yes."

"Understandable. He does have his charms." After a gentle kiss on her stepdaughter's cheek, Claudine said, "Let me handle him. Just go about your business, and I'll take care of everything. Including our handsome soldier." She gave her a hug of assurance. "Daisy, it's best we do what we decided weeks ago. I must take the first husband. Braxton Hale would chew you up and spit out the leftovers."

"That is an unkind thing to say."

"I know whereof I speak. I know men. After four husbands, I surely do." Both women chuckled nervously. "Of course you realize I don't degrade your father with that statement. Ambrose was my finest husband. My only love."

Skylla and Claudine laced fingers.

"I want you to have that kind of love." The redhead sighed. "I pray to God a wonderful man will arrive on our doorstep and sweep you off your feet. One who isn't carrying the baggage of a lost family and a tarnished reputation."

"What if God sent Braxton to me?"

"Darling, don't forget that I know of our newly arrived knight-in-tattered-armor. He was quite the lady-killer in his younger days. Many upstanding matrons waited until the dark of night for their carriages to stop near Woody's Blacksmith Shop."

"The libertine business."

"Yes. When a lady wished to be a wanton, she turned to Braxton Hale. I never heard a whisper of disappointment. But he never gave anything but his well-endowed body. He doesn't have a heart to give to a lady."

What about the Indian girl? Uncle Titus claimed Braxton had loved Song of the Mockingbird dearly, and somehow Skylla didn't doubt the depth of the fair-haired soldier's feelings. For ones he held dear, he had a huge and generous heart.

"He's too forceful for your gentle sensibilities."

"If you mean to repulse me, dear Claudi, I'm afraid you've failed. I find it intriguing that so many women desired him . . . when he could be ours forever and evermore."

"Daisy, I wish you wouldn't—"

Unfazed, Skylla nailed her colors to the mast. "We should rethink our pact."

A frown lessened Claudine's beauty. "Shall I remind you of the legal repercussions that could come up? Moreover, we decided not to change the rules, no matter what." She stood, staring down at Skylla. "Daisy, we must abide by the rules, or the Nickel Dime could be jeopardized. He may be a charlatan after no more than the ranch. He could sell it from under our feet, if we don't protect ourselves."

"He could have demanded the ranch in payment for Uncle's debt, but he didn't." Skylla trusted Braxton, but she left the bed to pace and ponder. After a few trips up and down the carpet, she decided caution was the prudent course. "The future of the ranch must remain our first consideration."

"I'll have a chat with him."

"No. The Nickel Dime is my responsibility. So, it's my duty to bear the tidings." A chill went through her. "I'll tell him everything. Later. In the morning. At daybreak, when he milks Bossy. Then I'll tell him the truth."

"Don't put it off, Daisy. The longer you do, the more difficult it'll be."

"I know."

Instead of retiring to her bedroom to wait for Skylla's honesty, Claudine marched outside into the night. She would not sit on her hands and allow her stepdaughter to steal Brax Hale.

She considered forging a note "from Skylla," asking Brax to meet her in the stable. She'd take down her hair, throw off her clothes, and offer him a midnight ride. She remembered her monthly. Drat! It was then that she saw a shadowy figure open the barn door. "To heck with the monthly. That's Brax, and I'm going after him."

She took down her hair as she marched toward the barn, throwing hairpins as she went and shaking her thick red curls into a cloud around her shoulders. Two blouse buttons unfastened, she moseyed on in. It smelled musty inside. Musty, dusty, and too much like cows. Oh, well. "Hello, hello. I know you're in here. Come out, come out, wherever you are."

She scanned the dimly lit barn, her eyes stopping in the corner. Noises from there ceased.

"What are you up to, naughty boy?" She simpered. "Do you need help?"

"No."

"Now, Brax." Actually, he didn't sound as cocky and confident as a golden-haired warrior, but what man would, getting caught doing something that seemed suspicious? "Are you playing with yourself?"

"No."

Knowing the open barn door would limn her body in silver, she swayed her hips while walking toward him. Brax was sitting down now, she imagined . . . watching her. She lifted her hair, let it drop, then fanned her face. "I do declare, it's close in this barn. Shall I take off a few of these clothes?"

"Yeah."

She stopped a good ten feet from Brax. Oh, for a good look at him! He had to be getting hard, what with her stripping off her clothes like this. "Do you like what you see?"

"Yeah."

By now she was down to her chemise. "How about you take care of the rest, hmm?"

"Yeah."

A smile of glee lifting her lips, she rushed forward and threw herself into his waiting arms. Even before she landed on a lapful of something round and hard, she was screeching—the stench had gotten to her. "Good God!" She rolled away. "You're not Brax Hale!"

" 'Course not. I'm Charlie. I found Titus's good whiskey." He lifted the crockery jug from his lap. "How 'bout a drink, missy? Then we'll get on to the sparkin'."

Desperate as she was for a man, Claudine considered his offer. Then she reconsidered. "I would never let a filthy peon touch me!"

She made a quick exit. This is a sign, she warned herself. This is a sign to let matters take care of themselves. Skylla had said she'd talk to Brax, and she would. It was only a matter of time until wedding bells would ring for Claudine.

Over and over, those words echoed in her head. All night she tossed and turned, arguing with her decision. At first light, she'd changed her mind slightly. Yes, she would wait for Brax, but she wouldn't wait too long.

Skylla couldn't spoil the breathtaking sunrise with her announcement, not the next morning or the next. And not for the three days after that. A tennight passed, and still she hadn't been honest. The more she put it off, the harder honesty got.

Cowardice kept her from admitting to Braxton the advertisement had been for two husbands. If only some wonderful candidate would arrive and sweep Claudine off her feet, Skylla's troubles would be over. None did. And she said nothing. Every moment, every day gave her a little more time to live in a dreamworld of what-should-not-be.

What would Papa think if he knew he'd reared a spineless daughter? Always, Papa had taught her that St. Clairs didn't wear their hearts on their sleeves, that it was weak to cry or to raise one's voice in anger or frustration. Yet Papa had died with her irate words in his ears. And her parting words to James had been spoken with annoyance. Never again would she part from someone dear with angry words between them.

She sensed Braxton would be angry.

Then Claudine began threatening to tell him herself.

When the men had been at the ranch two weeks, Skylla promised herself and her stepmother, "Tonight will be the night."

They had settled into a routine by then. Miraculously, Braxton had brought item after item to the ranch, which made the living easier. Everyone was putting on weight. Everyone but Kathy Ann, who had fallen into a black mood that nothing or no one could bring her out of.

Supper tonight was roast beef, boiled potatoes, and snap beans from the garden. Skylla barely touched her food, in spite of all these weeks spent dreaming about harvesting and preparing her measly bounty. *You've got to tell him.*

Once coffee was finished and the diners scattered, Claudine set out to do up the dishes. Skylla started toward the bunkhouse, but met Braxton on his way out of the stable. He carried a saddle and kept walking. She followed along.

"Charlie and I will be gone awhile." He tossed the saddle atop Impossible, then bent to fasten the cinch. "Could be three or four days. Geoff will stay to watch out for the place."

The women had spent months here without male escort, yet Skylla didn't protest Geoff's guard. There were no guarantees Stalking Wolf and his tribe of Comanches wouldn't attack, even though they had been keeping their distance of late.

"Where are you going?" Skylla asked.

"Menard."

"Why Menard? And what for?"

"There's an old Spanish aqueduct over there. I've seen it

before, but I want to study it. An irrigation ditch could water your truck garden. And make farming easier for you."

His ideas and consideration roused her appreciation, yet she read between the lines. She'd heard that Oren Singleterry could be found near Menard; she imagined Braxton had heard the same. It wouldn't surprise her if his plans included an attempt to retrieve Uncle's horses.

That spelled danger. If he wasn't inclined to go looking for trouble, then she didn't wish to give him any ideas. The last thing they needed was trouble.

He stepped toward her, saying, "I think it might be appropriate, a goodbye kiss between us."

If they kissed again she'd never be able to explain herself, for their one and only kiss lingered too much in her thoughts and ignited her selfish passions. She turned. As fast as her maimed leg would carry her, she bolted. Once again.

Dammit.

What was wrong with her?

Tightening his jaw, Brax watched Skylla flit away, if you could call her pace flitting. Every time he brought up the subject of marriage, or even so much as a kiss, she ran like a crippled rabbit.

She'd better not expect him to keep on working like a dog and bringing in the bacon, not without reward. Unfortunately, the bacon was at end. The poker tables of Ecru had closed to Brax, none of the boys wanting to lose more livestock or goods. So much winning bespoke bad gambling, and Brax had known it going in, but he'd been set on bringing home the largesse and hadn't taken any chances.

Now he was just as set on reclaiming Titus's horses, though he'd changed his mind about sending Geoff on the mission— too green. No show herd could be collected without good horseflesh.

Brax's eyes followed the path Skylla had taken during her latest retreat. If she hadn't started the wedding plans by the time he got back from his showdown with Singleterry, he was going to hogtie her and make her tell him why not. There wasn't an excuse in the world that would be good enough in his ears.

His patience had run low. Into the empty zone.

As he started to put his booted foot in the saddle, Claudine appeared in the moonlight. "Isn't it a lovely evening? The stars look like diamonds in the sky. And that·moon—oh, mercy! Could there be anything up there but cheese?"

He told her he was in a hurry, but she kept on jabbering.

He didn't trust this iron magnolia. Her whimsical act was just that, an act. He much preferred Skylla's practicality. In fact, her calm mien offset his hair-trigger temper. Nicely.

"Kind sir, may I beg your indulgence for a few minutes?"

The Spencer settled into its scabbard on Impossible's saddle, Brax replied after a long pause, "Go ahead."

"I thought you'd want to know I've spoken with Reverend Byrd. He's agreed to conduct the wedding Saturday week."

Brax chewed the crumb of comfort. At last. At long last. "I'll make a point to be back by then." First, though . . . "Claudine, will you take care of the invitations?"

"Of course. Did you have someone in particular in mind?"

"Luke Burrows and his missus, Gertie May." Confident as a peacock, Brax leaned into a relaxed pose and placed a palm on the saddlehorn. "What about a dress? Skylla says her sister can sew. Tell Kathy Ann to look for needle and thread."

"That won't be necessary, I'm sure," Claudine replied.

"We can't have a wedding without a nice wedding dress."

Just how he would get the materials was a horse of a different color, but Skylla would, by damn, put away those widow's weeds. For ever and ever.

"Don't worry about a thing, Sergeant." The widow fluttered her long slender fingers. "I have several lovely gowns that I brought over from Mississippi. Perhaps they are a bit dated in fashion, but they're still lovely."

"I don't want Skylla married in someone else's dress."

The twit bore down. She pressed Brax's hand against her

heart. "You and Skylla aren't meant to be. She's still in love with poor James."

Shoving the woman's hand away, Brax felt a rage run through him. "Who the hell is James? Is he the ensign?"

"Oh, yes. James was Skylla's lover. I suppose you know he died in the war."

When she'd told him about her dead suitor, he'd assumed their courtship had been innocent enough. Thus he'd thought Skylla chaste. Now Brax felt as if a cannon had struck him in the gut. He couldn't stand the thought of another man having touched her.

Get a grip, Hale. What difference does it make that she spread her legs for some now-dead salt? Actually, it was better this way. Virgins had a way of making a sentimental journey out of their maiden voyage. Now that he knew the truth, he could breathe easier when the leaving turned ripe.

"About the wedding," he said, getting back to the business at hand. "It will march on."

Claudine shook her head. "Since Skylla can't bring herself to explain things, it's my place to tell you that you are mistaken." Like a cat, the widow stretched and preened. "You were never, ever meant for Skylla. She doesn't want you. All along she's been adamant about marrying the second candidate."

Cold water rushed through his veins. "Second candidate?"

"We asked Virgil Petry to find two men. One for me, one for her." She wriggled closer. "You are meant for me."

His muscles locked. As if in slow motion, he closed his eyes. *I've been had. Once more I've been had.* Like General Lee at Appomattox Court House, he smelled defeat.

Like hell!

Chapter Nine

Skylla rued the day she and her stepmother had made a pact about husbands. In the dark of her bedroom she forced the motions of calm by slipping a lawn nightgown over her head and taking down her hair. A half-dozen strokes later, she stilled. Thoughts of Braxton had gotten the better of her.

The hairbrush tossed on the bureau next to Electra, who awakened to hiss and paste her ears to her head, Skylla lamented to the annoyed cat, "I have to tell Claudi the truth. Braxton is taking James's place in my heart. I know I'd be going back on my word, but I want Braxton for myself."

Squaring her shoulders, she started for the stairs. Surely Claudine was abed. A door slammed shut somewhere.

Electra ran for cover.

"Stay back, goddammit! I'm warning you, Claudine St. Clair, keep your distance. Turn around and head out that front door. I *am* going to have a word with Skylla. A *private* word."

Braxton.

"He knows." Skylla cringed. "He knows."

Uncertain of how to deal with his temper—in fact, impotent

to fathom the extent of it—she backed against the bureau at the same moment he shoved her door open. It slammed against the wall, matching the furies of betrayal evident in his stance, his face, his eyes—his soul.

"I . . . I'm—"

"You lied to me," he interrupted, kicking the door shut. "I ought to choke you for leading me on. You never said a damned thing about two husbands!"

Her heart pounded. She didn't know what to do, or how to deal with him. Would he wreck the room? Hit her? Do worse?

He took a forward step.

The fingers of one hand clutching the edge of the bureau top, she steeled herself for the worst. "Don't come any closer," she demanded, her voice as even as she could make it under the circumstances. "Not a step closer."

He stopped.

Thankfully.

Her breath came easier, but not a lot. He was in no way appeased. *Stay calm. He has a right to be upset. But don't let him see you cowering.* Straightening, she gathered courage and wits from somewhere. "Braxton, I should have been honest. I knew I was doing wrong, but I couldn't help myself. I was afraid. I was afraid you'd leave."

"So, you were scared your strong back would ride out."

Was there a defense against a grain of the truth?

The pitch of his voice lower than before, he ground out, "You were too much of a mouse to admit a lot of things. While you were stringing me along, you let me think you'd never been touched by a man. You never said you mourn a *lover.*"

She started to defend her reputation. Why not let Braxton know she was damaged goods? When men married maidens, they expected the maidenly. Surely Braxton would wish to be his wife's first man. It was highly probable this kept him from claiming Claudine, the fact that she'd had husbands, and not just one or two. Which unearthed yet another dilemma. What if he wouldn't settle for either of them?

"James was my lover," Skylla admitted with false calm.

"May he rot in hell."

His insult wrought sadness and defiance. Yet the level of his attack caused another emotion in her. She wondered if Braxton felt true affection. How could he? *I want him to.*

"Skylla, I demand to know why you placed a misleading advertisement. I came to Texas with the impression I was going to marry you. *You,* not some relative of yours." He punched the air with a finger. "Petry said nothing—not one goddamn thing!—about a man for your stepmother. He sent me to *you.*"

"There's no need for blasphemy. I won't have it."

"Don't preach behavior." Braxton advanced, threatening her thin grip on composure. "Not after your lie of omission."

Her muscles jerked, and she felt the strength ebbing from her legs as he asked, "What in hell makes you think some man would come all this way to marry a woman who doesn't even hold the deed to the ranch?"

Dead quiet.

It shouldn't have hurt, the mercenary twist to his words. It did.

"Don't stand there like a church mouse," Braxton shouted. "Answer me."

No one would ever mistake Claudine for a church mouse, which hit at Skylla's confidence even more. "You frighten me," she whispered. "Anger is so unlike you."

"How little you know." His chest rose and fell as he blew out a deep breath of aggravation and distaste. He cut the distance between them, stopping close enough to loom over her. The devilish light that so often showed the very life in Braxton was now but a shadow. "What do you think I'll do? Beat you?" He paused. "Or do you fear I'll take you in anger?"

"I'm not quite certain," she managed to utter. "I don't think it'll be pleasant."

They stood staring at each other, both in a blur of doubt about the course of their lives. Braxton began to steer it his way. "That's where you're wrong. When I take you—and I will take you—it won't be in anger. When you and I are beneath the covers"—he nudged his head toward the big brass bed—

"it'll be because we're both hot for each other. And because it's *right*. I want you. I want you for my wife. Marry me, Skylla."

Marry him. Make love with him. How luscious those concepts. She could get over the hurt of losing James. In Braxton's arms, where she would know the joys of passion's culmination. If only the situation weren't complicated.

"I can't marry you." She couldn't meet his eyes. "If you marry a St. Clair, it must be Claudine."

"Not in my lifetime." He emitted a mirthless laugh. "It's you. Or no one."

"But she's so lovely."

His gaze canvassed the thin material of Skylla's nightgown, surveying the woman within. Her prominent ribs and the twisted leg not apparent in the dim light, he replied, "Not as lovely as you."

"All her husbands fought a throng of suitors to win her hand, and they adored her to their dying breaths."

"I'd slay a thousand dragons for you."

All Skylla could do was turn away. "Why must you make this so difficult?"

"Difficult for you? How do you think I feel?" Braxton took hold of her shoulders, turning her to face him again. "You have cast me off like so much refuse."

"Marry Claudine. We'll make it appealing."

"We? What is this 'we'? You own this ranch, you don't have to ask anyone's permission for anything." He squeezed her shoulders, shaking her. "Don't let her run your life. Tell her the deal's off. Or that she can have the next fellow. Better yet, I'll tell her."

"If I marry you, then her husband won't have any incentive to make something of this place. Claudine must marry first. While I still have the power to give over a one-fourth lifetime estate in the ranch."

Braxton shook his head in confusion. "Come again?"

"Mister Petry advised that I must protect the ranch." On sure ground, Skylla found it easier to debate. "Once I'm married, my husband will have legal hold on it. I must protect

Claudine, and her husband, by deeding an interest in the property while it is mine and mine alone."

Braxton's face blanched beneath his tan. "You didn't."

"Already I've given Claudine her part." Yet the document wouldn't be legal until the papers were filed, which made it all the more important for Claudine to marry first.

"So, you've given her a chunk of the Nickel Dime."

"It's not the same as out-and-out ownership. A lifetime estate allows the recipient to live on the property for as long as he or she lives, and it can't be sold without the recipient's permission. As her husband, you'll have the right to stay here for the rest of your life, and benefit from its future success. That should make up for my uncle's debt."

"Clever. Very clever." Braxton took a backward step, then retraced it. Thrusting his fingers through her hair, he curled his hand into a fist. She gave an involuntary yelp. His teeth clenched. "If you've known all along I'm to become your step-father, why did you let me kiss you?"

Stepfather? Her stepfather! *My God, why didn't I think about that?*

His free arm snaked behind her waist and urged her to the hard angles of his body. She gasped at the feel of him, the scent of him, the way he felt when she ventured to flatten her palms on the heated steel of his chest. The room became heated, very hot. Never had she experienced the desire to move even closer to the source of that heat, not until now.

"Shall we share another father-daughter kiss?"

His hard exacting lips captured hers, molding and softening against her mouth; his callused hands cupped her face. His tongue pushing its way past her teeth, he backed her against the bureau. Her arms slid around his waist, moving up the rock-hard planes of his back as her fingers coiled into the curls that brushed his neck. With a groan of desire he pressed even closer, his hands moving to caress her shoulders, her arms, her hips. The feel of his growing arousal sent a heightened surge of excitement through her limbs to settle in her womanly reaches.

He grabbled the ribbons to her nightgown, closing his palm over her breast before he began a kindling exploration of her puckering nipple. The moans of passion that echoed through her bedroom were her own, the scent and feel of desire wafting within her. When Braxton's lips replaced his fingers, he reached to the back of her thighs, lifting her from the floor to bring her closer to his seeking mouth.

"Tell me you like this," he demanded.

It was impossible not to whisper, "Yes, oh yes."

"Does that mean yes, you'll marry me?"

"N-no."

He lowered her to the floor, adjusted her nightgown. Finished, he clasped both her hands in one of his, and said, "Mark my words, I refuse to let another man take the reins of this ranch, because if I did, that would mean he'd have you. I won't stand for that. I will have you for my own. For my wife. And then I am going to make love to you until you forget everything but me. Even your dead lover."

That he had smoothed the mercenary slant of his anger caused her to smile. The ranch was but incidental to him.

Suddenly, Claudine pounded her fist against the bedroom door, "You in there! It's gotten too quiet. Daisy, are you all right? Come out, Sergeant Hale! Right this instant."

"Go away," he shouted after turning his face toward the doorway. "Go away and stay away!"

"I will not. Be warned, Brax Hale. If you don't open this door this instant, I will—"

"Go to hell, Mrs. St. Clair."

Braxton bent his knees, wrapping both arms behind Skylla's knees and lifting her toward the ceiling. As a lumberjack might give a gigantic log a vertical heave, he threw her over his shoulder. Her arms swung over her head, her hair flying free. She giggled. Giggled!

The moment Claudine burst through the door, Braxton feinted to the side and ducked out of the bedroom. Rushing through the house, onto the porch, and into the inky darkness of midnight, he carried Skylla away.

"Where are you taking me?" she managed to ask, her words pumped from her lungs by the motions of his strides.

"To the creek. To take up where we left off."

"Don't you hurt her! Stop right there, bad man!"

Kathy Ann.

Lifting her head slightly, and blowing a lock of hair from her eyes, Skylla saw her sister running toward them, Geoff, Claudine, and Charlie Main a good distance to her rear. Kathy Ann had something in her lifted right hand.

"Oh, my God!" Skylla wailed. "No!"

Her scream caused Braxton to slow his pace, to turn.

Suddenly a shot rang out, the air cracking with the explosion. Skylla felt his body tense; she heard his intake of breath. For a moment he teetered, then slowly lowered her to the ground. He slid sideways. Falling face up at her feet.

Her hot tears of worry and anger spilled as Braxton groaned and rolled into a ball of pain. Instinctively, she scrambled to protect his toppled body with her own, else Kathy Ann might take another shot.

Geoff and Claudine, both shouting, ran forward.

"Did I get him?" Kathy Ann shouted.

"Yes, damn you!" Skylla's voice was a cry, a scream, a lament. Bending over Braxton, she crooned, "It'll be all right, it'll be all right," as he made the motions of bravery.

"I'm okay, I'm okay," he moaned and tried to stand.

Kathy Ann stepped closer, then blew on the pistol's barrel. "He won't be bothering you anymore, Sissy."

Furious, Skylla glared at her sister and let loose with a variation of a threat Papa had employed with her. "Pray to God Braxton's all right, or I'll give you to the Indians!"

One more time, Skylla had let her temper get the better of her.

Chapter Ten

"He's ruint."

Miss Skylla cried out at Charlie Main's pithy statement about her man, while her stepmother dragged the brunette away.

"What happened?" Geoff asked over and over, getting no answer as he and the cowhand lugged Bubba to the first-floor bedroom. The men got Bubba settled on the quilt.

"He's gettin' blood all over hisself." The ranch hand grabbed a folded white garment from the bedside table—probably Miss Skylla's nightdress—and slapped it into Geoff's hand. "Do somethin', boy. Else, he'll die. I need a drink."

The cowboy beat a hasty retreat.

Frozen, Geoff stared at the material, then gaped at his brother's ashen face. He'd seen countless men die for Jeff Davis, and one of them had been his blood kin, same as Bubba, but this was the first time Geoffrey Hale yearned to cry out to The Maker above—and beg for a man's recovery.

"Stop the blood, Geoffie—do it," Bubba ordered, his voice weakening. "Am I ruined?"

It took force of will not to gasp when Geoff gaped at the

crease in his brother's groin. He sat down on the bed's edge to press a cloth against the crimson flow. "You're not ruined, but she like to got you," he joked for the sake of sanity. "An inch to the left and you'd be singing soprano in the church choir."

Bubba's face twisted into the guise of a smile. "Then you think my career as a Romeo isn't over?"

"Heck, Bubba, in no time you'll be flaunting your scar to Miss"—he swallowed—"to the painted ladies in San Francisco."

"Yeah. That's right. Dance-hall girls."

Miss Skylla charged through the door right then.

"Braxton." The crippled girl went around Geoff to kneel beside Bubba, burying her head on his arm. "Oh, Braxton, what have we done to you?"

He put his hand on her head. "You've done me wrong. Make it right, Skylla. Say you're ready to be mine."

She lifted her head, and the look they exchanged was one of two people in agony. In agony from the mess of their lives. Anyone could see that it took a great effort for her not to throw the outside world to the winds and give in to her heart. Why didn't she just do it? Why didn't she give her man the comfort he begged for?

Something died in those pained green eyes. "Go away, Skylla." His voice brooked no argument. "Go away and let Geoff tend me."

Like a wounded doe, she retreated, closing the door softly. Why hadn't she consoled Bubba?

His eyes on his adored brother, Geoff pressed harder on the wound. "Help me," he said, his vocal cords stretched tight. "Tell me what to do."

"You've seen me work on bullet wounds. You've got to take a few stitches to stop the blood. We'll worry about the bullet if I get septic. Get a needle and thread from Piglet."

"I ought to shoot her."

"Don't. She's just a stupid kid. Besides, who gives a damn about her? She's not the problem here."

"Seems to me she is the problem."

"Not hardly. This is a helluva fix we're in."

Bubba's voice hadn't been this hopeless, this dejected, since word had arrived all the girls were dead. They had both cried, grieving for Diana and Susan and Larkin's pretty bride. The baby was newborn when the war started. Lilly had been a cute little baby. Bella said she'd just started being a rambunctious toddler when the malnutrition set in. The Hales were a doomed lot.

One time, in a weaker moment, Bubba had talked about the day Massa John sailed out of their lives—Geoff couldn't remember the day that hexed the Hales. John Hale, a physician trained to save lives, damned his family to hell. His curse was coming to fruition.

Geoff looked at the last of the white Hales. "Don't you dare die on me, Bubba."

"I'm too damned bad to die. The devil is giving me a taste of hell on earth, I reckon." Wiggling, he shoved a pillow behind his back. "Of all my schemes, trying to collect on Titus's debt is the most wild-eyed of the lot."

"Don't talk. I've got to stitch you up."

Ignoring the advice, Bubba said, "Geoffie, they've made fools of us. As soon as I get back in my boots, you and I are hightailing it west. Forget the nosegay of baby's breath."

"What are you talking about, 'made fools of us'?"

"That redheaded twit did more than pick your brain. She's manipulated Skylla into giving her an interest in the ranch. She's worked it so I can't sell the place. Ever."

"She can't do that."

"Wrong. That pansy Virgil Petry had an ace in the hole. I'm pegged to marry Claudine."

It was all Geoff could do not to laugh. That didn't fit. She wasn't the crippled girl possessing the calm temperament and loving nature necessary to deal with a flawed fellow like Bubba.

Geoff had been pushing for California and all it held, but lately he'd had second thoughts. Miss Skylla would be good for Bubba. Very good. And she needed a man to cluck over. That Claudine would never be good for anyone but Claudine.

Warm blood began to seep over Geoff's hand. "I've got to cut these britches off you."

"Yeah, do it. See if there's water in that pitcher over yonder, and don't forget to wash the wound. Fetch the medical supplies from the cookhouse, too."

The wound washed and a fresh cloth over it, Geoff rushed out of the room, nearly knocking Miss Skylla to the floor when he hurried past the staircase in the parlor, where she'd been holding onto the railing for dear life. He righted her.

"What can I do to help him?" she asked, worried.

"Give him time. Keep your distance."

She nodded, wilting to sit on one of the steps.

From the corner of his eye, Geoff saw that redheaded piece of work relaxing in a horned chair, swilling her favorite one-hundred-proof beverage. Like nothing much had happened. "You didn't keep Kathy Ann out of trouble," she charged.

"Neither did you. Ma'am."

Geoff carried on toward the cookhouse. Bubba didn't need the bother of that black-widow spider.

All his life, Geoff had worshiped Brax Hale. As a youngster, he'd been the older boy's shadow, hanging on to his every word. Bubba had seemed as tall as a tree, as solid as its roots. Without being told by a spiteful little neighbor girl, Geoff had guessed they were brothers. Already, Geoff had made a promise to himself. He would follow Bubba wherever he went. Nevertheless, Bubba had left without him, once. When he came here to Texas to search for "Massa John."

By the time the war came around, Geoff had been on the brink of manhood. Thirteen. There had been no stopping Geoffrey Hale when the white Hale men had left Vicksburg with Titus St. Clair, bound for the battlefields. Geoff caught up with them.

He witnessed his brother's valiancy in the theaters of war. He hurt for him when the major let him down. The day General Lee surrendered to General Grant, the same general who'd laid waste to Vicksburg, Geoff stood at Bubba's side as he gave over his sword and rifle. Through it all, he'd been a partner in many schemes and tricks.

Now—by a flea-bitten hound of Jeff Davis's!—he would get Bubba well.

Geoff hurried into the cookhouse. Kathy Ann was there already, shoving something into her pocket. No telling what.

"Where's your needle and thread?" he asked.

"In the satchel." She pointed to the cracked leather bag. Afterward, she took bottles down from the cupboard. "He'll need medicine, too, I guess."

It ought to be anger that he felt, facing the girl who had shot Bubba. There were tears in her eyes, and some had made runnels down her pudgy cheeks. He walked over to pick through the dusty bottles and jars. Concerned she'd cause more trouble, he asked, "You gonna be okay?"

She gave a half-nod, then wilted on a chair. "Oh, Geoff, I'm so sorry! I thought he was hurting her. I didn't want her to end up dead like my real mother. Yvette."

"Da massa, he wouldn't hurt Miss Skylla."

Stepping back, she wiped her nose on her sleeve. "Will he be all right?"

"Shore. He gonna be fine," Geoff hedged.

Without a word she placed bottles and bandages in the black bag. "Soon as I apologize to him, I'm going away."

"Why you wanna do somethin' like dat?"

"All I am is trouble. If I'm on my own, then I won't be trouble to anybody."

Geoff took hold of her wrist. "Doan you be doin' dat. You am trouble, by dat ole mutt Sammy, you am trouble. But you be troublin' dat sister of yours more iffen you leave."

Her old defiant self, she stuck her tongue out. "What do you know, you stupid darkie? I'm leaving soon, and don't you dare tell anyone where I'm going."

Tucking the satchel under his arm, he didn't stop her when

she flounced outside. Nonetheless, he departed the cookhouse to yell, "Doan you forget you promised to stay 'til you say you sorry!"

Stay, she did, although no effort to face her victim was forthcoming. After a long exacting night of tending his wounded brother, Geoff passed her at breakfast. She said nothing. At noon, she held her cat to her chest under a magnolia tree. Once more he reminded her of the·promise, which she answered by turning her tear-streaked face away.

The crisis increased with Bubba, especially by the second day. Never once did he allow Skylla to cluck over him, and when Claudine sashayed in, he threw a bedpan at her. But that wasn't the worst of it. A fever had begun to rage in him.

Skylla kept a kettle of chicken broth simmering on the stove, in hopes that Braxton would accept some of the nourishing liquid. He didn't want anything to do with whatever she had touched. Each time she attempted to see him, he had behaved cantankerously; being uncouth, cross, belligerent, furious, delirious, hateful, sarcastic, or occasionally unconscious.

On the third morning, Claudine entered the cookhouse, where Skylla was squeezing a lemon into a glass. Yesterday she'd gone into Ecru to trade a jug of whiskey for that lemon.

"Brax is especially testy." The redhead plopped an empty enameled bowl down before taking a dishrag to dab at a hank of wet, chicken-smelling hair. "He threw your broth at me."

Skylla yearned to go to him, to soothe his brow, to make it all better. But what could she do, outside of giving in to his proposal? She was on the verge of it. Oh, was she on the verge.

Sugaring the lemonade, she asked, "Will you see that Geoff gets this drink? Have him tell Braxton Charlie made it." Charlie Main, a total wastrel these past days.

"I'll take the lemonade." Claudine stayed put. "Geoff is going to ride into Mason town to fetch the doctor."

"And Brax agreed?"

"Of course not. The numskull thinks that quadroon will

heal him." Claudine smoothed her hair. "Someone needs to watch over the patient. Naturally, Charlie isn't available. He's probably drunk somewhere."

"We can't ask Kathy Ann to sit with Braxton. I'll do it." She expected Claudine to protest.

"If he'll let you, fine. I need a change of scenery," Claudine announced. "A ride into Ecru will do me good."

A glitch in her stepmother's tone caused Skylla to decide: more than an outing was the intent. So be it.

"Before I go, there's something I want to say." The redhead got one of her determined looks on that cameo-fair face. "I'm not liking the way this deal is turning out. His aims are suspect. When a guileless man discovers defenseless women have done something to arm themselves, he'd—"

"Arm themselves? Such as with a pearl-handled pistol?"

"I'm not talking about his injury, and you know it."

"Why should he be expected to come up with a compromise when neither of us has any earthly idea for one?"

"I think he's up to no good. I intend to check him out."

"Fine. Do it."

Claudine started to leave, but Skylla stopped her. "He's done so much for us. Ever since he arrived, life has shown promise. And, Claudi, he has a right to be at the ranch, too. Uncle's debt, remember." Getting no response, she went on. "If you're worried about your place here, you shouldn't. Anyway, we're making too much of this. He'll get well, and we can go from there."

"Really? After he threw that bowl, he had the gall to say he'd marry me when fish wear pigtails!"

Skylla couldn't help but laugh, despite her tormented heart. "Oops. Sorry. He won't be cross, once he's feeling better." *If he ever is . . .*

Taking a step forward, the redhead said, "If I find nothing to concern us about him, I will marry Brax Hale. For the sake of this ranch. You do understand that, don't you?"

"I don't think we should decide anything at the moment."

Blue eyes hardened. "You weren't so mealy mouthed when

the chips were down in Vicksburg. You were so anxious to get out of Mississippi, you were quite willing to let me sleep with that potbellied Yankee official in exchange for free passage to your dream. You said you'd repay me."

Skylla could have gone through the floor, the shame of that bargain with Winslow Packard prowling through her very soul. "You promised we'd never speak of that. You promised."

"And you promised to give me the first husband." A pause. "If Brax meets my standards, you will step back. Understand?"

Skylla may have nodded, yet she couldn't bear the idea of being his stepdaughter.

"Incest. I like the idea of it. Right here in my old buddy Titus's squeaky brass bed." Braxton patted the mattress next to the sleeping calico cat. "Get in bed, daughter. Daddy need some lovin'. Come to Daddy."

At least he hadn't demanded she get out of his sight.

Skylla, setting the lemonade on the bedside table, soundlessly counted to ten, then reached for the pillow he'd tossed to the floor during an earlier fit of temper. Plumping it, she tried to ignore his orneriness. "You seem to be doing fine. You must be improving."

"Right. Geoff's gone for the doctor so we can play gin rummy. Get lost, Skylla. Your stupidity grows tiresome."

Same goes for you. "You're a doctor. You should know a positive approach has a great bearing on recovery. I know from my own travail. So, you see, I wasn't making an idiot's attempt at downplaying the extent of your predicament."

"Always ready with an excuse for her behavior, that's Skylla St. Clair."

She supposed she had that coming. Concentrating on the benign, she noted his appearance. His hair glistened with beads of water and had been slicked back, the teeth of a comb having made a pattern in the curls of old gold. Even sick and filled with the poison of being thwarted and all, he was handsome. "I see you've availed yourself of the water pitcher and towels."

"I got myself dolled up, just in case that big-busted redhead wants to come by to inspect the rack of meat."

In the wake of frazzled nerves combined with being reminded of how the St. Clairs had gotten here—not to mention three nights of lost sleep—Skylla had had just about enough. Her composure slipped. "I was under the impression she brought you a bowl of broth and you threw it at her. You'd do well to collect your wits and recognize where your bread is buttered!"

"Open that window," Braxton barked. "It's hotter than hell in here."

His demand complied with, she handed him the lemonade. "Drink. It'll do you good."

He shoved the glass away. "What I need is the urinal. Some genius set it out of my reach."

She went to the bureau where it sat next to the collection of outdated medicines and paltry sickroom supplies. One item wasn't paltry. Ether.

Braxton, last night, had lamented to Geoff that while this anesthetic had lain idle here, Confederate soldiers had been hacked to pieces without so much as a slug of whiskey to deaden their horrific pain. Then, and now, Skylla prayed that James had gone to a quick and numbed death.

Warning herself off the subject of her fallen ensign, she held the urinal gingerly between the tips of her thumb and forefinger, and carried it across the room. "I'll leave you alone with this."

He grinned nastily. "Why don't you stay and watch? Then you can see how I measure up to Jimmy Boy."

In no mood for crudity or arrogance, Skylla retorted, "What if you come up short?"

"I'll show you my tongue."

"I've no desire to see it. You're beyond insensitive to make light of a sainted son of Dixie."

"What will you do about it? Run me off?"

"You're doing an excellent job of that on your own. Granted, you're the injured party here, but you're not doing yourself the least bit of good by being hateful."

Skylla pivoted around and left the room. Limping to the porch—her leg hurt worse today than it had in ages—she came to grips with a possible solution to the impossible problem of Braxton Hale, provided he survived. He would have to leave.

While the St. Clairs were indebted to him, they could offer to repay the debt in time. This was the only recourse, for Skylla couldn't stand the rift that was splitting her and Claudine, and becoming his stepdaughter would jeopardize her very existence.

In spite of the sense she made from chaos, her heart objected. She wanted him. She needed him, and not just for this ranch, for he'd given her a reason to hope and to dream of something more than a fresh start provided by having a home.

Moreover, he needed her. Her greatest wish, beyond her totally feminine desire to be his, was to help in his emotional as well as physical recovery. If Claudine didn't stand in the way, she could, and would, devote herself to making peace from the disarray of his spirit.

Where did that leave poor departed James? *He's gone. He told you to get on with your life, should he not return.* James would approve. At last she felt free. Free, yet caged.

"Hullo, beauty."

Charlie Main's loud drunken articulation clattered in her ears. Propped against the well, he had a jug tipped to his mouth. When he lowered it, he wiped his mouth on a sleeve and leered. The disgusting sight he presented made it difficult to believe this was the ranch hand who'd been such a good worker. Before his boss got shot.

Standing over Main, she said, "You gave Sergeant Hale your word not to drink during daylight hours." She dabbed her forehead before stuffing the linen cloth back in her pocket. "We are very disappointed in you."

"You sound just like Momma." He took another big slug,

liquor running down his chin. "Poppa choked her for nagging."

"I trust he had an appointment with the gallows."

This path would lead nowhere. Skylla grabbed the jug. With trembling hands, he reached to retrieve it, but he wilted upon getting it through his thick skull that she meant business.

"Get up," she ordered. "Get up and go wash yourself. I have a pot of coffee in the cookhouse. Drink several cups of it. There's work to be done. Get busy."

"I ain't goin' after that snot-nosed sister of yourn."

"What does that mean?" Skylla and Kathy Ann hadn't spoken since the night of the shooting. Which didn't mean she had no regrets about their argument. It did trouble her. Mightily. "Where is she?"

"Don't ask me. She tookened off a coupla hours ago."

Suspiciously, Skylla asked, "Why is it you waited until now to mention this?"

Charlie Main shrugged. "Ain't nobody asked me."

"Disgusting lout! Collect your mule and be gone."

What am I going to do about Kathy Ann? Remorse had eaten at Skylla over their argument. No wonder the girl had fled. *Will a third loved one go to a grave with my hatefulness in her thoughts? I can't let anything happen to her!*

Her gaze turning westward, Skylla made plans. Once Geoff and Claudine returned, the three of them must spread out in a search. The doctor could watch over Braxton. And just what could the misfit threesome do? Hare off on a pair of princely steeds known as Impossible and Molasses? Two displaced Southern ladies and a youth, all new to the West—green, in other words—what could they do in the face of Indians on the warpath?

Since Braxton was once married to an Indian, maybe he'd know how to handle this.

Right then, the curtain of the sickroom moved aside. Liquid from a container got pitched out the window. "Good gracious, he's out of bed! What else can go wrong?" As soon as she entered the front door, she knew what else could go wrong.

Boom!

"Awwggghhhh!"

Skylla rushed into her bedroom cum sickroom, finding what she expected: Braxton, a sheet draped around his middle, had tumbled to the floor. Oh, dear!

Electra peered over the bed's edge as Skylla gave aid. His heavy body put a terrible strain on her leg, but at last he collapsed onto the mattress and dragged the sheet under his armpits. His face held a grayish tint, lines she'd never before noticed bracketing his mouth.

"I'll take care of you," she whispered softly.

"For that I thank you." His expression softened. "And for helping me see the error of my ways." His was a whisper uttered pleasantly. Surprisingly so. Considering his earlier crossness and acute distress. His right hand scooted to Electra, who, now calm, leaned her tricolored chin into his scratching fingers. "Skylla, I apologize for the insults. All of them."

"You were feverish. I have no hard feelings."

He lifted his free arm. "Take my hand. Sit down beside me, sweetheart, and take my hand."

Such a move would weaken her decision to send him on his way, eventually. Yet . . . Relieved at his change, and being weak where he was concerned, she laid her fingers within the much larger glove of his red-hot hand.

"What's the matter?" he asked when he detected her trembling.

"My sister." Skylla curled her shoulders. "She's gone. I'm scared Stalking Wolf has her."

Braxton uttered something, and it may have been, "There is a God,"She'll have them running for cover in no time."

"If you mean to ease my mind, you've failed."

"Then you don't give her her due. If she fought alongside Cornwallis, Yankees and Rebs alike would be subjects of Queen Victoria. If Napoleon had had Piglet's services, we'd all grieve for Wellington at Waterloo. If she'd been at the right hand of Bobby Lee, Unconditional Surrender Grant would have met *his* Waterloo."

"It's generous of you, giving such august credit. But her strengths are beside the point." Skylla licked her lips. "You know Indians ways, you were married to one. What—"

His face became an unreadable mask. "I suppose Titus told you about Songbird, too."

"Yes. I know you married her, for love. And I know you turned your back on doctoring when you couldn't save her life."

"I'd already made up my mind one Hale doctor was enough."

"Your father?"

"Yes. My horse's ass of a father. I won't discuss him further." Brax rubbed a hand down his face. "Skylla, for God's sake, the clock is ticking for your sister. Fetch Main."

"I can't." She made explanations. "There's only me."

"And me. I'll go after her."

"You can't leave this bed!"

A half-dozen heartbeats passed before Braxton admitted, "You're right. I'm in no shape to do anyone good. Skylla, this bullet has got to come out."

As if a gust of winter wind had blown through the open window, she shivered. "Dr. Brown should be here soon."

"No time. Find a jug of good booze. It's hidden behind some old bales of hay in the barn. I'll down half the hooch. You pour the rest in the puncture. Then dig the bullet out."

Panicked, she knew nothing about medical procedures, save what it was like to be a patient. "What about the ether?"

"Forget it. Insensate, I couldn't tell you what to do."

"I'm no doctor. We must wait for Oliver Brown."

"How are you at undertaking?"

A hellish question.

"Skylla, get the forceps and scissors, and clean towels. Find the needle, too, and bring heavy sewing thread. Boil the instruments for ten minutes. Once they're cool, bring them here. I'll cut the bullet out."

Oh, yes. Of course. No problem. Had he gone mad!

He threw back the sheet, exposing the length of his nude body. Skylla had seen a naked man, once. The twilit day she'd given James her virginity. It had been pleasant enough, coitus, although that one time nowhere near matched the heat Braxton generated in her. As well, Braxton would not come up short.

Why try to deny Braxton Hale was the more beautiful specimen? Except for the hunk of wounded flesh on his upper thigh exposed when he peeled away the bandage.

She gasped, realizing the import of his situation. That he was able to talk seemed a wonder. Skylla couldn't count herself a healer, but she knew when a wound had gone bad.

Nothing might be enough.

Chapter Eleven

Skylla sterilizing medical instruments, Brax nursed a question: How much did she know about Songbird? Granted, Titus had ratcheted his mouth, but how much did she know of the whole story? No way could she know about his plot to sell the ranch.

Brax tried to get more comfortable in bed. The moment he moved, pain zigzagged up and down his spine. He gawked at his wound. "Shit." From the looks of it, Braxton Hippocrates Hale would have an appointment with the undertaker before August switched to September, less than a week away. His father's curse was coming to pass. *I pray you never have the satisfaction of knowing your victory, John Hale.*

Whatever the case, Brax would die before he could make love to Skylla in this very bed . . . or on the bed of magnolia blossoms he'd been thinking about for weeks.

Damn, he hated leaving Skylla without a better fight. No. The real trouble lay in the fact that he admired the serene brunette too much. She'd neither collaborated with the enemy to the north, nor hated him for marrying the enemy to both

North and South. She was the kind of woman any man would be lucky to claim until death parted them.

She was hell on a plan.

His thoughts traveled down the avenue to other important personages. What about Geoff? What about Bella? Brax couldn't die right now. He had to see Geoff and his mother settled. As he had many times during the past weeks, he hoped Bella's voyage to San Francisco was pleasant enough.

He had to live. His work wasn't finished here on earth. Including the search for Piglet.

"Miz Skylla," he heard Charlie Main say in a muffled voice from the parlor, "I've been thinking 'bout what you said. I done drunk some coffee. I got Patsy Sue saddled, too. I'm ready to go after your sister, if you're of a mind, ma'am, to give me a second chance. I owe it to your man. He saved my hide back in '60, and I been needing to show him my appreciation."

Brax didn't listen to Main's description of heroism. He was no hero. Anything good he'd ever done, it had been by reflex rather than from a sense of nobility. Braxton Hale had no use for heroes or heroics. That didn't stop him from being glad Skylla had found a rescuer for the pistol-packing brat.

Skylla's good qualities passed in his review. She was too noble for the collection of misfits, liars, and thieves populating this damned ranch.

A collection of admirers, all married or too old to do her any good in bed, circled the seated Claudine St. Clair and chattered like geese. She held court in Emil Kreitz's store. The proprietor hadn't joined the gaggle. Kreitz stood behind the counter, licking a pencil tip and tallying up the purchases of a dressed-up wishbone, the farmer Luke Burrows.

Homer Daggitt, obese as a bear, chomped down on a pickle, squirting juice on the sawdust-powdered floor. "You wuz askin' after that so-and-so Brax Hale." He gifted the circle with a open mouthful of green. "That rascal cheated me outta a hun-nerd dollars, Christmas of '60."

Claudine batted her lashes. "That's the same as calling him a thief. Is that what you're doing, Mr. Daggitt?"

The cluster of men turned their eyes to Daggitt. "That be exactly whut I'm doing, Miz St. Clair. He done cheated ever' man here outta goods and livestock. Ain't that so, boys?"

Luke Burrows spoke up. "You're being a sorry loser is what you're being, Homer Daggitt. He earned that stuff fair and square in poker games."

The cluster mulled the statement, then took Burrows's side. Nonetheless, Claudine frowned. She'd hoped against hope that her disquiet concerning Brax's motives was unfounded. But there had to be fire behind the smoke of Daggitt's charge. Maybe she ought to give up ideas of marrying Brax.

He caused too much friction between her and Skylla.

While she'd always been a woman to look out for herself, Claudine regretted her arguments with Skylla. That lie about Winslow Packard—Never could she admit going to his bed before any mention of Texas had occurred. It had been evil to perpetrate the lie, done to keep the upper hand.

Yet Skylla meant more than any hairy-legged man who just might have ulterior motives when it came to the Nickel Dime. If Claudine couldn't have that golden-haired ladies' man, Skylla shouldn't either. How could she make her think twice?

Skylla watched in amazement as Braxton, a sheet shielding his privates, snipped the stitches in his upper leg. His bravery and courage added to her respect. *You can't send him away. You know you can't.* Somehow, in some way, the dilemma of who would become his bride would come to a natural conclusion.

"Tie me to the bed." He dropped the last stitch in a bowl. "Do it, Skylla."

She tied strips of material around his wrists and the rungs of the bedstead.

"Now pour some of that good alcohol in the puncture."

Not nearly as brave or courageous as the virid-eyed man of medicine, she said, her voice a croak, "Whiskey. Drink some whiskey."

"I've changed my mind. I need my wits."

She forced herself not to look away when she poured the antiseptic into the gaping hole. A litany of disjointed prayers rushed from his lips. The brass rungs molded to his grasp and bent inward.

Her composure slipped. "I—I'm a mess at this."

His face a mask of pasty white agony, he whispered hoarsely, "Undo these straps and hand me the forceps."

She did as ordered. He began to dig into his flesh. She yearned to remove her gaze, but didn't. The least she owed him was a show of bravery.

"Sit on my leg and hold my elbow," he said, his voice hollow. "I'm shaking."

She rested her weight on his leg, and couldn't figure out who did the most shaking, him or her. In shameful awareness, she realized how nice it felt to touch the hard muscles and hair-dusted body belonging to Braxton.

Yet weariness reminded her of three nights of no sleep. Could she hold up to the surgery in progress? She feared if she closed her eyes, she'd sleep the sleep of the dead.

"Get rid of this damned sheet," he ordered. "It's getting in my way. And hold the wound open."

She moved the offender away. When she placed her fingers at the appointed spot, his privates nudged against the heel of her hand. Her heart tripped. His conspicuous sex made her think things she ought not to think at a time like this.

The forceps went still. Brax spoke in the low timbre of a hardy and healthy male when he said, "Someday soon you'll hold those beauties in your hands."

"Don't do this to me. We're in the middle of surgery!"

He chuckled. "Why can't I flaunt my scar?"

"It isn't a scar. And it'll never get to that point if you don't behave." She gathered her wits again. "Set to work on your-

self, sir, else I'll take up your scalpel and divest you of those
items you are so inordinately proud of."

"Good idea."

Again, he bent over his upper leg. It seemed an eternity
passed before he held up a red slime-covered object, pitched
it into a small bowl, then let out a sigh of relief. Calmly, surprisingly, as if he had just done surgery on someone else, he
ordered, "Pour more alcohol on there and then give me the
needle."

Needle and thread in hand, he set to stitching. His long-
fingered broad hand whipped in and out of the mangled hole.
Nausea roiled within her all of a sudden. The last stitch in
place, Braxton looked up at Skylla.

"Don't faint now, sugar. The worst is over."

"I . . . I wasn't going to faint," she lied and gathered herself
up to sit on the edge of the bed. "What do we do now?"

"Think you're up to some nursing?"

"I . . . of course."

"Wet a clean rag with some of that corn liquor. I need a
washing up."

Trembling and weak, she reached for the necessary gear,
and dabbed the cloth on his stitches. But her muscles began
to freeze. "Br-Braxton, I . . . I can't. I am overcome."

He swung aside at the moment she fainted.

It took Herculean effort on Brax's part to get Skylla settled
on the bed, but he did it. Free to avail himself of Titus's best
aged whiskey, he took a big slug of the smooth liquid lightning. Better, he said to himself. Much better. Strong liquor
and soft woman, a damned fine combination any day of the
week, and especially after a shock to the system.

Soon, his toes began to chill. He glanced down to see the
sheet had come loose from its mooring. He tucked it under;
the tips of his fingers struck something between the mattress
and the ropes. A folded piece of parchment left its hidey-hole
by way of his grasp.

He took another sip of whiskey before unfolding the paper. He read the deed of trust once, then twice. It carried Skylla's signature. Dated July 10, 1865, it conveyed a lifetime estate in the Nickel Dime Ranch to Mrs. Ambrose Arthur St. Clair, née Claudine Twill. Brax studied the bottom carefully.

A smile as wide as the mighty Mississippi spread across his face. The deed wasn't legal.

It couldn't be.

There was no county clerk in Mason County on the tenth of July. Deeds didn't require witnesses, not if they were filed with the county, but Petry should have advised Skylla to take that precaution, in view of the unsettled civil situation. Until the Reconstructionists got seated and the deed had been filed, it wasn't worth a red cent.

Hot damn! My luck's changed again.

Mentally, he danced a jig. Physically weak as a kitten, he took a match to the paper. The woodsy scent of burning paper drifted as he angled to toss the offender out the window.

Settled back in bed, satisfied and confident, he slipped his arm under Skylla's shoulders and brought her to him.

"You will be mine, bet your booty on it," he murmured against her dark, dark magnolia-scented hair. Magnolias. He hadn't a clue whether they grew in California, and he decided not to speculate on it. Yet he wondered if Skylla might like that part of the country. What would be wrong with taking her away from here? He didn't want to speculate on that.

When he pulled the sheet over them, he heard the whimpers of her awakening. "Go to sleep, sweetheart. We both need sleep. I'll need all the strength I can get." . . . *To make you my wife in the eyes of God and his witnesses.*

She cuddled against him—thankfully on his good side—and the blessing of a deep sleep overtook her. The feel of her gave Brax a sense of calm, despite his horrendous agony. And he would have to have been dead not to skim his hand along the soft, soft skin of her arm. Fast asleep, she sighed and cuddled closer . . . and he got on with his exploration.

He wasn't dead, but he wasn't in shape for a woman, either,

he realized. His eyes started to close. They flew open when the twit Claudine flounced into the room.

Her mouth fell open, her eyes as big as saucers. "What is she doing in bed with you!"

"Shhh." Brax tapped his finger against his lips. "Don't disturb her. She's exhausted from the workout I gave her."

"Such brag. You're not in any shape to satisfy a woman." Utter malice radiated from the whole of Claudine St. Clair. She advanced to the bed. "I've been to town. I know about your lying and cheating. You're a blight on society, Braxton Hale. You're no better than your lout of a father."

The charge of scoundrel he wouldn't defend, but cold hatred iced his veins at her mention of John Larkin Hale. Thankfully, Skylla didn't awaken. He didn't want her to witness the dirty look he shot her stepmother. Nor did he want her to hear what he had to say. "Watch your words. If you don't, I'll be forced to see you on your merry way. With nothing more than a half-dead horse and a by your leave." He kissed Skylla's head; she smiled instinctively and made the sweet murmur of a woman pleased at where she was. "A supposed female friend can't hold a candle when a woman has found her mate."

"The truth shall set her free of you." Claudine pointed an unladylike finger. "You're on your way out, blackguard."

"Not on your life. I'm here to stay. And I'll stay as Skylla's husband."

Malice watered to a sneer. "I think you're a confidence man out to steal this ranch."

She was bluffing, he felt certain. "Claudine, you're looking for trouble in all the wrong places. We've got enough already. Kathy Ann is missing. Charlie Main's gone after her, but Skylla's afraid the Comanches have her."

Claudine blanched, but recovered. "Leave her to heaven."

"What would Skylla think if she knew you don't care whether her adored sister is seized by savages?"

"Why is it always Skylla, Skylla, Skylla? What makes her so special to you?"

He looked the redhead square in the eye. "For the same reason she's special to you. Because she *is* special."

"All right. You've won this round. But mark my words, Brax Hale, this fight isn't over."

She whirled around, her skirts belling, and beat a hasty departure. Brax knew the fight wasn't over. For now, though, he was out of fight. He fell into a restless sleep punctuated by a redheaded demon welcoming him to the gates of hell.

The specter of Satan appeared to lead Brax into the fiery underworld. With hair of gold and eyes of green, the Lord of Evil had no horns, nor did he carry a pitchfork. He wore natty clothes and carried a satchel. He smiled a brilliant smile that displayed a set of perfect teeth. "Welcome to hell," he intoned. "I've been waiting for you."

"I'm glad you're dead."

"I'm not dead. The pure die young. You and I are still on earth. It's my duty to see that you're never content. Son."

"You've done that, John Hale."

Midday in Austin, Texas—a scorcher in late August of 1865—John Hale, M.D., wore a fine set of clothes as he sauntered into Governor A. J. Hamilton's office in the capitol building. He strolled in triumphant, a conquering hero.

The governor rose from his oversize walnut desk. "John Larkin Hale, welcome back to Texas."

"Thank you, Governor. Same to you."

The bespectacled Hamilton, a Texan of long standing Unionist sympathies, had been newly appointed by President Andrew Johnson. Hamilton had returned to Texas in June from an exile in Mexico. Order was begun. John Hale intended to be part of it.

The governor rested his elbows on the desk and laced his fingers over the buttons of his waistcoat. "We set those seditious slave-mongers on their posteriors, didn't we?"

"That we did."

"You came through the war no worse for the wear, I note."

"I do fine for my age."

He did more than fine for fifty-seven. Few men in middle years had a young wife and two pubescent children. Hell, most men his age couldn't even get it up, much less once a week. If only Harriet weren't tied to her mama's apron strings . . .

"I have my health, my good looks, and I'm never without a superlative tailor. Moreover, I went to the winning side in the rebellion. What more could I ask for?"

Hamilton fiddled with a watch fob. "How's the family?"

John knew Hamilton didn't mean his faithless wife and her miserable issue in Mississippi. Them, he'd been able to keep hidden. They were no longer cause for concern, anyway; word had reached him a year ago that Elizabeth and the rest were dead.

Thank Lucifer.

For the past fifteen years, John had enjoyed a bigamous relationship with a wife who knew nothing of his first family. And he now had a pair of beautiful children whom he knew to be his.

"John?"

"Oh, pardon me, Governor. You asked about Harriet and the youngsters. The climate in the islands has taken—"

"Islands? I thought they rode out the war at her sister's home in Pennsylvania. You don't mean they were with you at your post in the Caribbean Sea? Let's see. You were a major in the medical corps stationed at the prison camp on the Dry Tortugas, I do believe."

John looked down his patrician nose, verily smelling the fruits of disrespect. "President Lincoln himself decreed that my experiences warranted a high rank. I was a *colonel* in the United States Army. I assumed you kept up with my doings."

"John, John, don't get touchy. I had many people to keep up with, from a backwater country without proper lines of communication. Please go on telling me about your family."

"Harriet and the children joined me at Fort Jefferson. They were headed for her sister's in Harrisburg, but stopped their sea voyage for a visit. A detestable place if there ever was one." John brushed the arm of his silk suit, remembering with displeasure his days as prison-camp physician. "Nevertheless, we decided to stay together as a family."

"It brings me joy to see such devotion in a family."

"Thank you, Governor. But the climate in the islands took its toll on young Andrew. His asthma. I thought he might outgrow weak lungs, but he's now a lad of ten, and his lungs, well . . . The drier air in the West should do wonders for him."

"And the little girl, Abigail. How does she fare?"

"Like her mother and brother, she's anxious to resettle in Texas." John was aggravated by the delays that kept his family in those infernal coral islets near Key West. "I'll send for them, as soon as you appoint me to a post . . ."

"Yes, of course." Hamilton picked up a sheet of paper, scanning it. "You've applied for a coroner's office."

"To go along with my medical practice, naturally. I have plans to open another infirmary. We'd hoped for Bexar County."

"Bexar County is yours."

Though he'd gotten his wish, it would be a mixed blessing. John didn't find himself anxious to face Bexar County at all, but Harriet whined to be near her battle-ax mama in that county's seat. There were times John wished he hadn't married a younger woman. They tended to have mothers on the loose.

At least Elizabeth hadn't had a mother to breathe down his neck. But that was her only saving grace. The happiest day of John's life was the morning he had abandoned Natchez—and the adulterous Elizabeth Braxton Hale.

Chapter Twelve

Skylla couldn't believe her ears, for Claudine, now that Braxton's fever was gone, had just said, "I demand you send that blackguard away."

Up to her elbows in soap suds, she scraped discarded bandages against the rub board. "No."

"No?" Claudine used her foot to shove the wash pail away. Water sloshed on the cookhouse floor as well as on the hem of her skirts. "How can you tell me *no?*"

Skylla straightened, massaged her fist against the ache in her lower back, and stuck by her guns. "Blast it, Claudi. How can you stand in this kitchen and argue about Braxton when Kathy Ann is still missing!"

"She's only been gone a day. Charlie is looking for her. And I sent Geoff to help." Claudine elaborated. "I'm concerned about the girl—believe me I am—but what do you want me to do? Drown myself in worry about a disobedient whelp while I see you throwing away this ranch? Brax could well sell this place out from under our feet."

"You have nothing to prove—not even a whisper of proof—

that he has ulterior motives. Claudi, you've jumped to a conclusion."

"Ask Homer Daggitt if you don't believe me. He'll tell you Brax Hale is a cardsharp. Everything he presented to us was the same as stolen. The shoat, the chickens, the food, the supplies. Think, Daisy, think. If Brax cheats men at cards, what else is he capable of?"

"Homer Daggitt is a mean-minded man, and everyone in town knows it."

After pacing up and down the kitchen, Claudine said, "Have you ever asked yourself *why* Brax wants this marriage so much? A man with his appeal shouldn't need to come all the way to Texas simply to answer a newspaper advertisement. He could get a wife of means anywhere."

"Oh? How many rich ladies did we leave behind in Mississippi, Claudi?"

"He could have waited for a Yankee bride."

"He isn't looking for an easy berth. He's wanting to be settled."

"Yes, and green apples are purple. Skylla St. Clair, that man is not—I repeat, not!—right for you. He's going to hurt you. You just wait and see."

"You aren't being fair to Braxton."

"Oh? Daisy, the Hales were déclassé long before the war. And there were rumors, awful rumors about his parents."

"He shouldn't have to pay for the sins of others."

"You should have a look at the strange fruit in his family tree. Take a hard perusal of that colored boy, Skylla St. Clair. You'll see a family resemblance."

"If I looked for strange fruit, I'd look no further than Teddy Twill. Your own kin." Several times Skylla had wondered if Braxton had ties to his batman, since the bond between them was evident. As she'd concluded, she now answered, "Geoff is a fine young man."

"How do you feel about tying in with a liar?"

"Excuse me?"

"I was specific. The age limit was twenty-nine."

"Braxton is twenty-nine."

"Impossible. The strapping blacksmith who served as stud to a multitude of Vicksburg women couldn't be twenty-nine. Not unless he started rolling women in the hay at fourteen."

"May I remind you of a secret you shared with me one stormy evening in Biloxi? A storm—next to a hurricane—had uprooted the chinaberry tree outside my bedchamber window. You and I were scared witless. We got tipsy on scuppernong wine. We—"

"I was grieving for my third husband, Mr. Lewis."

"And I was worried sick over James leaving for the navy. I told you I'd given him my virginity, and you admitted you lost your maidenhood at eleven. And your young man had been *twelve.*"

"Skylla!"

"The point is, Braxton could have been promiscuous at fourteen with those Vicksburg ladies."

"With Joanie Johnson? He did it with Joanie Johnson."

A pair of yucks merged into cackles, and cut the strained moment. Joanie Johnson's daddy had been the richest cotton planter in the Delta, but his daughter was the most repugnant creature in the entire Deep South.

Claudine sobered, grabbing the baton of argument anew. "Furthermore, the next week—*the next week*—Brax's mother took delivery of a piano. It was said the buyer's name was Johnson."

"You're making an awful accusation." Even more awful than Joanie Johnson. "Virgil Petry wouldn't have sent us a scoundrel," Skylla pointed out. "If you heard those rumors long-distance, the lawyer surely would have heard them, too."

"My initial reaction as well. Which is why I've written Virgil and asked him to explain his reasoning."

Incensed that Claudine would go to such lengths, Skylla had to school her anger, else she would have shouted something scathing, rather than reply quietly: "I'm wondering why you waited to make these accusations. I'm wondering why you didn't say something the day Braxton arrived here."

"I should have." Claudine went over to a chair and sat down. "Since it's my duty to protect my stepdaughter, may I have the liberty to point out some other facts? Your cherished Sergeant Hale is not—I repeat *not*—a degreed member of the medical profession. He's just a quack who calls himself a doctor."

"Uncle told me he was a self-taught man, that he'd gotten his learning through books, and by looking over his father's shoulder. Moreover, he studied Indian medicine."

"Quackery."

"Claudi, he doesn't claim to be a doctor with credentials. He was drafted into the practice of medicine during the war. Furthermore, has he ever asked anyone to address him as Doctor?"

The redhead went for the whiskey, downed a shot. A black look speared Skylla; Claudine had not given up. "He's a crook and a liar. He'll have to go."

Skylla's head swam, bedeviled with Claudine's arguments. Was he devious? Surely not. Whatever the case, no one was perfect, and she decided to trust his integrity. "He can't go anywhere. He's got to convalesce." Oliver Brown had given a good prognosis before leaving, but Braxton remained bedridden. Skylla continued her obstinance. "He's not going anywhere until I say so."

"Oh, Daisy . . ."

"I want to know something. Do you really want to send him away? Or are you up to something? Since you've long known of Braxton's past, I don't believe you've given up on him, not on the strength of the idle gossip of a buffoon."

Claudine studied her fingernails. "I can't stop thinking about him." A tear made a path down her cheek. "If he were to say the word, I'd have him in an instant. We're alike, you and me. We're both weak for Brax Hale."

"Whatever are we going to do, Claudi?"

"I just don't know. Trust in the fates, I suppose."

* * *

"I'm back."

Convalescing in bed the afternoon after he'd removed the slug from his leg, Brax pulled the covers over his head and rolled onto his side, away from the returned Piglet. "Just my luck. The Comanches didn't lift your scalp."

He expected one of her usual smart-mouthed remarks, but Kathy Ann sang a different tune. "I'm sorry about shooting you."

"Is that so?"

She stepped over to the bed. Her pudgy hand held up a crumpled sack. "This is for you."

He expected spiders to crawl out of the offering. Instead, stuck-together horehound candy filled the sack.

"I didn't eat any of it. I saved it all for you."

Brax put the peace offering on his lap. "Did you steal this candy?"

"I didn't. I traded Mr. Kreitz for it."

"What did you trade?" he asked and dreaded the reply.

"A couple of topaz stones. I found them in the kitchen the other night. They were in an empty medicine bottle."

Brax recalled Titus squirreling this and that away. Boon surprises weren't the problem. "A trip to town wouldn't take long. Where have you been? Your sister's worried sick."

Reaching into the sack, Kathy Ann helped herself to a piece of candy. "I went to town to sell the jewels, so's I could get money to go to New Orleans. When Mr. Kreitz wouldn't give me real money, I got the idea to come back and give the candy to you. It was dark by then, so I slept under a tree. I was on my way here when Geoff and Charlie found me."

She licked her fingers. "You know what happened before that? I saw Stalking Wolf from a distance. Sarge . . . he acted real peculiar. He was standing on a bluff overlooking the Llano River, jabbering to the sky and stabbing himself with a knife. He scared me half out of my skin."

"He mourned for a lost loved one, Kathy Ann. That's the way Indians deal with loss."

"Indians don't have feelings. They're like wild dogs, doing nothing but going around fighting and acting ugly."

"They're people, just like you and me. On second thought, *few* are like you and me," Brax corrected dryly.

He'd never encountered an Indian as rotten and no-account as the pair in this sickroom. They were a lot alike, Brax and Piglet. Troubled, rootless, opinionated. Merciless.

"They have ways that are unusual to the white man," he said, "but theirs is an admirable race."

"I don't understand why they do the stuff they do."

"They're just as stymied by our ways."

"If you say so."

"Did you know there've been many cases of whites marrying Indians? It's not a bad life, I promise you. You might want to read up on Cynthia Ann Parker. She—"

"I've heard of her." Piglet's face brightened. "What with her, and with your recommendation, why, a girl might find herself a place with heathens."

"Don't get any harebrained ideas. *You* are too young to be away from your family." Topaz not out of his mind, he asked, "Kathy Ann, what kind of getup was Stalking Wolf wearing? Make that, was he wearing any sort of jewelry?"

"I didn't get close enough to tell."

"Nothing flashed in the sunlight?"

"No."

It could be that the Comanche chief hadn't chosen to wear as adornment the topaz stones he'd stolen from Titus. Brax doubted it. Indians had a great respect for beauty and beautiful objects. They would have been fascinated by the bright blue baubles. Brax wondered what had become of Titus's lost treasure.

"What's the matter?" Kathy Ann got a worried look on her face at his silence. "Are you okay?"

"I'm all right. I'm thinking about something."

It suddenly struck Brax. He was conversing with the Piglet. Conversing without antagonism. Strange, he ought to feel more antagonism than ever. She'd nearly killed him; then two men had put their lives on the line to save her hide.

Brax looked her dead in those beady eyes. "Where are Geoff and Charlie?"

"Building the aqueduct, I guess. Last I saw, they were headed that way. Least, that's what Geoff told Charlie to do, help him and Skylla. Claudine's filing her nails."

Being a man who enjoyed having good ideas and having others act on them, Brax was pleased that Skylla hadn't forgotten his mention of an irrigation ditch. But he didn't want her doing men's work. He needed to get into his boots.

If someone had told him in Vicksburg that he'd end up working a ranch, he'd have called the accuser "touched in the head." He remained averse to ranching, and would gladly say goodbye to being a strong back, but he felt good about his efforts.

Did this mean he wanted to settle here? No! While he knew Skylla had a soft spot for this ranch, he also knew she'd be better off once it was no more than a memory.

He'd show her the soft life in California. *That's the sap's way, Hale.* He wouldn't be a sap to set her up properly. Whatever she did, and wherever she did it, she'd be fine.

Nonetheless, his conscience kept nagging him about leaving her to her own devices. He decided to nip it in the bud. Men had been deserting women for centuries—a lesson well learned at his pappy's knee—but . . . But, hell. Elizabeth Hale had had it tough, but she'd lacked Skylla's backbone. And Brax wouldn't leave Skylla with four children and no roof over their heads.

What if she got in the family way while he was making certain the marriage would be legal? Surely once or twice wouldn't hurt. *Didn't you learn anything about conception?* Then again, Songbird, a mother of two, had never conceived with him.

His bullets might be blanks.

The slurp and suck of candy-eating drew his attention. "Planning to leave any of that for me?"

"I'm hungry."

"Then go to the kitchen and get something decent to eat."

She got one of those hardheaded looks on her moon face. "You aren't my boss. I don't have to do nothing just 'cause you say it."

Once he could navigate around, he intended to check the looking glass and see if he'd sprouted gray hair over her. "Could I ask you a favor? Would you please, *please* hand me that rifle over there? Yes, that one. Thank you." Brax took up Claudine's Spencer, got the Piglet brat in sight—boy, had her raisin eyes gotten big—then said, "If you'll move just a little to the right, we won't knock a hole through Skylla's outside wall when I blow your brains out for back-talking me."

Kathy Ann hit the floor.

Brax lowered the scope to her level. "Are you or are you not going to fill your belly with something besides sweets?"

"I'm gonna, I'm gonna," she squeaked, her head covered with her hands.

Brax set the rifle beside him on the bed. "I take it you like the idea of living."

"I-I d-do."

"Then stand up. You and I need to talk." As she struggled to stand, he asked, "Do you understand you could've gotten yourself and two men killed, traipsing off like you did?"

She licked her lips and studied the floor. "Me and Charlie and Geoff, we wouldn't be any loss. We're all misfits."

"If you're fishing for me to say, 'Aw, Piglet, that's not so,' you're in for an overlong wait, because when you hurt Skylla, you hurt me. And I'm the meanest S-O-B in Mason County."

"You are not," she countered, stretching out the words.

"What did I say about back talk? You're on the path to destruction, and I don't want to see that happen."

"Why would you care?"

Brax looked at the brat, clucking his tongue like an exasperated father. Strange girl, this blonde. He reckoned anyone would end up strange, if they'd been reared in the bitter life of a New Orleans whore. Who on the face of this earth hadn't known a corner of hell, though?

Coming up in the Hale household had been no heaven on earth. Nevertheless, when he kept his little sisters in line, it never took threatening them with a shotgun. Come to think of it, his sisters never needed as much as a harsh word. How did he keep the girls—and Larkin—in line? Cards on the table, no aces hidden in a sleeve, and an occasional bluff had made for the winning hand. But Kathy Ann wasn't like his malleable sisters. She was more like Brax himself. She needed someone to give a damn.

Whereas he liked to shirk duties, thanks to his years of having had too many of them, he figured she needed to be useful. Mere asking wouldn't do the trick, though. Extortion might work.

His thigh hurt like a gigantic nail in one's foot when he lifted himself up to settle against the rungs of the bedstead. Poking a pillow behind his back, he inched into blackmail. "You owe me."

"Do not. I brought you candy."

"That's not enough. Candy won't make up for this hole in my leg. Since we don't have a sheriff to keep order in Mason County just yet, I have no choice but to take the law into my own hands. So, I'm gonna give you two choices."

"Two choices?"

"Two choices. You, Miss Kathy Ann St. Clair, are going to help get Skylla to marry me. Or I'm gonna have Charlie Main lock you in the smokehouse until your lard is rendered off and what's left is no more than pig jerky."

Her face had gotten even whiter during his proposal. "Skylla won't let you do that." Bravado switched to common fear. "Please don't lock me away."

A modicum of guilt for summoning her fear of closed places went through him. *Hale, you're getting soft in the heart.* "I won't lock you up. You'll do what's right. I know you will."

"I promise I will."

He hoisted a hand and crooked a finger to bring her forward. "I've got a plan. Let's talk about it."

She moved near enough for whispering. Brax explained his scheme, and when he was done, he asked, "Are you with me or not?"

"I like tomfoolery. But I don't think Claudine or Skylla will play along. And Charlie, gosh, are you sure about him?"

"Absolutely. Now, listen up. And listen closely. If you're out of the game, then I'll have no recourse but to become your *stepfather.*"

"Ugh."

"Right, ugh. Because once I'm your legal father I intend to take over as your guardian. Then you will toe the line. No ifs, ands, or buts."

Kathy Ann scowled, but after enough time to consider her options, she replied, "Okay. Count me in on the scheme."

"Good. Now be a love and go fetch some corn liquor to bribe Charlie with. The good stuff."

Kathy Ann rushed to fetch the whiskey, and the weirdest feeling came over her. The sergeant had made her feel needed. She liked the feeling. Maybe she wouldn't hurt so much with Sarge around to make her feel wanted.

Once in the barn, she caught Geoff snoozing, a saddle for a pillow. He roused up, then pulled straw from his clothes. "Did you tell him you's sorry?"

"I told him."

"Dat be good, Miss Kathy Ann."

She proceeded to the whiskey Charlie had been helping himself to on the sly. Her arms around a jug of leftovers, she said, "You know what? I like your master. For a while there, he talked to me like I'm a real person. Kind of like a good father. Sort of like Ambrose. Then again, your master can be real rotten. Scared the p-waddy outta me, but that's not important right now. He wants me to help with a prank."

"Dat right? What kinda trick?" At the end of her lengthy

explanation, he chuckled and shook his wavy head. "Da massa, he cagey. Real cagey."

"He is. And you know what, Geoffie? I hope he wins."

"Me, too, Miss Kathy Ann. Me, too." The quadroon settled back in the hay. "I think I just ride dis un out. Take me a nice long snooze. I plumb wore out." He began to snore.

"I meant what I said about hoping the sergeant wins," she said to herself.

What was he up to?

Skylla feared Braxton had told Kathy Ann to call everyone together to say he'd be leaving the Nickel Dime, now that his body was on the mend. If he proved Claudine right . . . Well, Skylla didn't want to be proven wrong.

The supper dishes done up, Skylla and everyone but Geoff collected in the sickroom. Braxton lay propped against the brass headboard, a dozing Electra at his hip. Skylla, Claudine, Kathy Ann, and Charlie Main circled the bed.

"Claudine." Braxton gestured toward the cowhand. "Charlie Main has something to say to you."

The ranch hand turned the brim of his grimy sombrero around and around in his hand. He cleared his throat, dancing his meager weight from one foot to the other. The battered hand of a cowpoke who'd lived a thousand years in one lifetime smoothed the heel of his palm across his head of straggling hair. "It's like this, Miz Claudine. I, uh, I"—he shot a help-me glance at Braxton—"I'd like for you to be my bride."

Skylla couldn't believe her ears. Humming, Kathy Ann studied the ceiling. Braxton swiveled his gaze to Claudine; she clutched a handful of material at the bosom of her dress, and worked her mouth up and down. Though she couldn't imagine her stepmother accepting Charlie Main's proposal, Skylla crossed her fingers behind her back.

She wanted Braxton so very badly.

"It's the best solution to our problem, I do believe," said Braxton.

He took the calico pussycat into his arms, holding her close to his chest. Purrs vibrated through the room. For Braxton, Electra had become docile as a kitten and content as a setting hen. His power over women was remarkable.

"Charlie here has been at loose ends, needing a home and direction in life," he said.

"I have," Charlie put in.

"And he thinks you're a fine woman, Claudine. Fine-looking and otherwise."

"I do," Charlie concurred and nodded his head, which caused Claudine to drop onto a chair.

"He'd like to have a fourth interest in this ranch," said Braxton.

"I would."

"He'd be willing to bathe and shave for you."

"You didn't say nothing 'bout—"

"Charlie, don't interrupt me." Braxton smiled at each person in the room. "I'd feel much better about leaving you ladies, were Charlie here to look out for you."

"Where are you going?" Skylla asked quickly, panicked.

"Out west. California, perhaps."

Her heart sank.

"I won't be leaving right away," he clarified. "Not until I get my strength back. By then . . ."

Before she could breathe in relief—she'd do anything to borrow time—he went on. "If I am spurned in my suit for Miss Skylla St. Clair, then I have no recourse but to look out for myself. As soon as a county clerk is seated, I intend to file suit against the estate of Titus St. Clair, deceased." He glanced from person to person, smiling at Skylla. "For my five thousand dollars."

She settled onto a straight chair, crestfallen.

Charlie stepped over to Claudine. "Ma'am, would you marry me?"

"I . . . I'm, I don't think so." Her peaches and cream complexion now resembled chalk. "I wouldn't wish to hurt your feelings, Mr. Main, but I'd guess your age at forty or more."

"Forty-two, ma'am."

"I have had four husbands who were my elders, and frankly, I don't think I'd be happy unless I had a younger man. I fear I'd outlive another husband, and I can't bear the thought of that." The back of her hand had gone to her forehead. She lowered it. "I still think I'm better suited to Sergeant Hale."

The cowhand replied, "I figured you'd say that Miz Claudine. But ya cain't blame a fellow for trying, can ya?"

"No, Mr. Main, I can't." Claudine smiled, though a level of distaste became visible on her countenance. "I am quite flattered that you would want me, but I pray you appreciate my position."

"Yes, ma'am, I can. I reckon."

"Claudine, you aren't playing fair," Braxton said, offended. "You have a chance to marry, but you won't, which cuts me out of marrying Skylla. Each of you has known all along that my heart beats for her, and for her alone."

Warmed by his adamant attentions, Skylla at last believed that, yes, his feelings were true.

"Tell me," implored Claudine, "how would your heart beat, were *I* the heiress to the Nickel Dime?"

"Don't force him into a corner." Skylla straightened her back. "It's unfair of you to ask such a question."

"Claudine, I have an idea," Kathy Ann piped up.

Everyone turned their eyes on her.

Kathy Ann held up a gold coin. "Why don't y'all flip for the sergeant?"

Chapter Thirteen

Everyone in the sickroom gaped at Kathy Ann and her ludicrous idea for the older St. Clairs to flip a coin for Braxton Hale. Skylla had a fifty-fifty chance of winning, but what if she lost?

"Where did you get that money?" Claudine, recovered somewhat, demanded, her lips pursed as she eyed the gold coin.

"I gave it to her," Braxton answered. "It was my last twenty dollars. It's hers for her promise never to run away again, isn't that right, Piglet?"

"Did I? Oh, uh, yeah. Sure. I won't run away again."

Braxton had gotten her to promise *anything*? Astounding. If he had, and apparently that was so, he had influenced her little sister beneficially. True cause for celebration.

"Well?" Kathy Ann said. "What about it? What about flipping a coin to see who marries the sergeant?"

"It just doesn't seem right." Skylla swallowed.

"It's a ridiculous idea," Claudine said.

"True." Braxton put Electra aside. "I never heard of such a thing, truth be known. Yet it's worth considering."

"Seems fair to me," was Charlie Main's comment. "Seems all fair and square."

Kathy Ann spoke succinctly. "I like it."

Braxton smiled the smile of a captain prepared to go down with his ship. "If you ladies agree to the toss, I'm willing to gamble. It's the American way." He nodded. "At least I'll have half a chance of winning Skylla's hand. Are you for it, sugar?"

"T-toss the coin." She waited for her stepmother's response. If Claudine went along with the gamble, then no one could say it wasn't, as Braxton and Charlie Main had pointed out, all fair and square.

"Claudine, do you want heads or tails?" Braxton asked.

"Heads."

Let it be tails. Please, God, I don't ask you for too much. But, please, this time let it be tails. Skylla shuddered.

"You want I should toss that coin for ya, Miss Kathy Ann?" Charlie Main asked.

"That would be nice." Kathy Ann pressed the coin into the center of his palm, then stepped back. "All set, everybody?"

You could hear a pin drop, the room got so quiet. Even Electra seemed intent on the outcome.

Charlie Main cleared his throat, hitched up his dirt-stained britches, and smiled at the gamblers. "Here goes. Uh, hold up. Miz Claudine." He made a fist around the coin. "If you lose, would ya be so kind as to flip a coin over me?"

"No! Now toss that damned coin."

This was the first time Skylla had heard Claudine curse.

The gold piece flew vertically from the nail of his thumb, twirling over and over as it went up, up, up, then down. The bettors sucked in their breaths. The cowboy caught the coin on the back of his left hand, and pressed his right palm atop it.

He stepped over to Kathy Ann.

Skylla quit breathing. Her blood surged in her ears. *God, if you'll see me through this one, I'll never make another selfish request.*

The cowpoke exposed the coin.

"I'll be golly." He seemed shocked. "It's tails."

"Tails!" Skylla jumped from the chair, and it tumbled backward as she bounced up and down. In her excitement she barely noticed Kathy Ann and Braxton exchanging a wink, or Claudine resorting to tears. The redhead rushed from the sickroom, her hoop skirts taking deep bobs as she went.

Skylla's leg didn't hurt. A tomahawk cleaving her scalp wouldn't have fazed her. This was the most exciting moment in her life. She'd won. All fair and square.

It was all Brax could do not to shout for joy. Now that all the pests had cleared out, he eyed his bride-to-be. She stood a couple of feet from the foot of his bed, her dark eyes dancing, her color high with victory.

"Come here, woman of mine."

Skylla rushed to him and threw her arms around Brax's neck. Triumphant, he gathered her close and whispered in her ear, "Welcome, bride-to-be. Make yourself comfortable."

Her mouth covered his in a heated kiss that sent a swirl of blood to a place that took to swelling. And it wasn't his injury. His arms closed around her, then he deepened the kiss by thrusting his tongue into the sweet cavern of her mouth. Damn, he wanted to make love to her.

Right here, right now.

His fingers were aching to touch her, and he led them along her ear, her cheek, the curve of her aristocratically long neck. The hum that she murmured gave approval, and he couldn't stop himself from running his palm along her shoulder. He wanted to get more familiar with her breast, and he began to unbutton the bodice of her mourning dress.

"Pack these clothes away," he uttered. "I never want to see you in black again."

"Whatever you say."

He wanted to say, Let's make love, but good sense finally broke through the cloud of his euphoria. Back off. This wasn't the proper time for lovemaking. When they shared the joy of it, he'd make certain no vindictive redhead or anyone else had an ear to the door. "I'm not up to the likes of you, woman." He buttoned her up. "Not just yet."

Disappointment caused her to start to protest, but he cupped his fiancée's lovely face between his hands, his fingers combing through her hair. "Let's set a date, sweetheart."

She settled down beside him, her side close to his. "You'll need time for a proper enough convalescence. Dr. Brown said you should stay abed for three weeks."

Brax started to get ornery, but didn't. He needed to be ship-shape for their wedding night. "Three Saturdays from now. How does that hit you?"

"Right in the heart."

He kissed her nose. "Go to bed, sweetheart. You're going to need your strength, too."

She chuckled, then returned the nose-kiss. "You win. I'll go upstairs to that lonely old guest room. But I'll be thinking of you."

He caressed her hip. "Believe me, I won't count sheep."

He hated to see her go. And his need for sex protested. But leave she did, throwing a kiss from the doorway.

Her smile warmed him thoroughly. Damn, things were going well. Soon, she'd be his wife. His wife! His hand moved to the part of the bed she'd vacated. If he went to California without her, how would he feel? Rotten. He wouldn't leave her. They were going to California together. By damn, he would never let her out of his sight, not for as long as he lived.

What does that mean? His eyes closed. Did he love her? He liked, admired, and respected her. He couldn't stand the thought of losing her. If that wasn't love, what was it?

It was then that he heard footsteps. Female footsteps.

"I'm going to make your life a living hell."

"I thought that was you, Claudine. Why can't you be a good loser and get lost?"

"I'm not a good loser."

"Try to be. It'll serve you well."

She grabbed the foot rail, shaking the bed. "Damn you. How dare you tell me how to act?"

"Act anyway you please. But take care where you do it."

"If you're trying to threaten me, I won't stand for it. I have as much right to be here as you do."

"Then work for the common good, and you and I won't have a problem." He paused. "Close the door on your way out."

She slammed it.

But he hadn't had the last of his female visitors. Not five minutes after Claudine had huffed off, Kathy Ann turned the doorknob and stuck her head inside. "Did I do good, Sergeant?"

"Sure did."

She eased inside, the click of the closing door accompanying her. "Did I really promise not to run away?"

"Absolutely."

"All right. I won't." She chewed her lip. "Sarge, I'm glad you're marrying Skylla."

"Why is that?"

"I never saw her real happy until you came around. I want her to be happy."

"You're making strides." He recalled his siblings' formative years. "Kathy Ann, it worries me that you're not in school. You need an education."

"You sound like Skylla. She nags me about taking up my studies again. 'Course, she hasn't said much lately. She's been too busy with you."

"We'll both have more time now." Did he mean that? Had he almost promised to take her with them to California? No, he hadn't. He'd deal with the Piglet problem later.

"Sarge . . . you never said, but I need to know. Will you forgive me for shooting you?"

"You bet, Piglet. Everything's worked out just fine."

"Sarge, would you have shot me this afternoon?"

"No, Piglet. I don't want to harm you. A pretty little thing like you, you've got your whole life ahead of you. What kind of S-O-B would I be if I deprived some nice fellow of making you his sweetheart?"

"You think I'm pretty?"

"Pretty as a little piglet," he said honestly.

"They're not very pretty."

"Oh, yes they are," was his quick response.

Beaming, she said, "Thank you. Thank you very much. For making me feel like a real person."

Brax smiled at the smoothness of the situation. Everything would be fine. Mighty fine. Kathy Ann might surprise him and turn out all right.

The future, for the first time in too many years, looked rosy. Skylla would be his. With the exception of Claudine, the combining of St. Clairs and Hales might turn into a happy situation. Hell, if Kathy Ann's recent maturity wasn't a fluke, what would be wrong with her going to school in San Francisco?

"By the way, Piglet. Thank you for the candy."

Skylla gave a thousand silent thanks for Braxton.

As to be expected, though, Claudine left no snide comment unspoken. Her catty, cutting remarks caused Skylla to consider not asking her to act as matron of honor, but she did. Amazingly, Claudine accepted. Perhaps the redhead would grow to accept the inevitable. This pipe dream proved doubtful, though, the coin-toss loser was no sport.

Nonetheless, Skylla packed her mourning clothes and made wedding plans. Never had she had been this full of energy. She lived on love. Additionally, the house had never been as clean or the garden so carefully tended, though housekeeping and gardening ranked way behind the care given to her patient.

He said she ought to have a new wedding dress, but she answered, "Most certainly not," and wouldn't be argued down.

Besides, she anticipated a surprise tenfold better than a new frock. Charlie Main had shared a confidence with her. "Miz Claudine says I oughta tell ya. Your man, he's got a weddin' gift for ya. He and that darkie, they thunk I was asleep one night when they was talking about Brax's Momma's brooch." He opened his fist to show her a cream-colored cameo set in a uniquely filigreed mounting. "He said he's gonna give it to you at your weddin'."

To receive his treasured heirloom—oh, how nice it made her feel!

"Are you gonna give Sarge a wedding present?"

It was bedtime. Kathy Ann, who had spoken, visited Skylla in the bedroom Braxton had vacated a week earlier. This was the first such visit, which thrilled Skylla all the more. Her sister had been making definite strides in social behavior.

"I have a gift in mind," she answered. "I have but one treasure surviving to this September. Papa's emerald and gold stickpin."

"Sarge will like it." Kathy Ann's fingers milled through the things on top of Skylla's dresser. "But didn't Ambrose tell you to save it for his firstborn grandson?"

"Braxton will wear it. Someday he'll turn it over to our son. Eventually, Papa's intention will be met."

Kathy Ann examined the stickpin. "It'll match Sergeant's eyes."

"My thinking exactly." Skylla smiled. "I'm going to find him. I'm going to give it to him right now."

The pin set aside, Kathy Ann shook her head. "You can't. He's gone. He took off with Geoff a half-hour ago. They're going after Oren Singleterry and the stolen horses."

"No. Oh, no!" His health. His safety. Skylla worried for both as she demanded to know: "Why didn't you say something before he left?"

"He told me not to."

Skylla had a word with herself. He'd done fine physically, and he'd been itching to get decent horseflesh for the ranch. Furthermore, she wouldn't quarrel with her sister's loyalty to her soon-to-be brother-in-law.

Kathy Ann spoke. "I almost forgot what I'm here for. Sergeant said you'd need help with a wedding dress. He thinks I'm a good seamstress. He says I'm just about as good as he is."

"We wouldn't want to argue with a surgeon," Skylla commented, not totally in charge of her wits yet.

"Well, what about your dress?"

"Will you help me pick something out?"

Her round face breaking into a grin, Kathy Ann nodded. The sisters dug into a trunk brought from Mississippi. Only one party dress had outlasted the war. Ruffled at its low neckline and beribboned in a deep shade of peach, the gown had short puffed sleeves and was fashioned from white dotted Swiss. It was by far the coolest outfit she owned, yet whimsy was its chief appeal. And the cameo would set it off nicely.

"It needs altering," Kathy Ann said after Skylla slipped it over her head.

"Will you have time? I know you're busy tailoring one of Uncle's suits for Braxton."

"I've got time." Like a Cheshire cat, she added: "I've got something special, too." She reached into her pocket. "Something to sew into the hem of your dress. For good luck." She closed her sister's fingers around something rocklike. "It's a blue topaz."

Opening her hand, Skylla saw a beautiful polished gem. "My gracious. Wherever did you get this?"

"I found it. Up in the attic when I was looking for your uncle's trunk. There's a casket of jewels. And gold coins."

Skylla's initial reaction? "What!"

"You won't have to hoard those four coins you found any longer. I found a fortune hidden in the attic."

Collapsed on the edge of the bed, Skylla reeled. A fortune in the attic all this time? While the St. Clairs had scratched, searched, and plotted simply to survive. A fortune. While Braxton's family had perished.

"Should we tell Claudine?" Kathy Ann asked.

"Of course. Wait. Maybe not."

A treacherous little voice told Skylla not to chance upsetting the wedding plans. What with her bad mood of late, Claudine might do something. Skylla didn't know what, and she didn't want to examine her suspicions too closely. Did she owe Claudine an explanation? Uncle willed his estate, both real and personal, in entirety to Skylla. It was her decision as to how to handle this.

"Kathy Ann, don't say anything to anyone. I want Braxton to be the first to know. It'll be my other wedding present to him, knowing this ranch will prosper."

Chapter Fourteen

"Giddy up." Brax nudged the gelding's flanks. "I said giddy up!"

Impossible continued to plod along. Heading east from Menard County with Geoff on Molasses to his rear, Brax frowned and not only from the frustration of Impossible's impossible gait. He'd failed in his mission.

Oren Singleterry had gotten wind of men at the Nickel Dime, and in anticipation of what was to come, he'd moved on. There were no Nickel Dime horses to herd home. But Brax wouldn't return empty-handed.

"I sold Mother's cameo." Broiling in the late morning sun, he removed his kepi to wipe his brow with a forearm, then eyed Geoff, who now rode abreast on his similarly fleet-footed steed.

"What did you do that for?"

"I had to. Before leaving Ecru, I incurred a wedding expense or two. I need to pay up, once we reach town."

"And?"

"I can't let Skylla be married with no frills. So, I sold the cameo in Menard."

"That explains everything."

"What the hell does that mean?"

"It explains why you've been touchy as an old cook ever since you stormed outta that cathouse."

"Yeah, I'm cross."

No one in Menard town had been able to afford a bauble, he'd learned quickly. Upon hearing a quartet of men compare notes about the local whore, Brax had had a brainstorm. If anyone would have money, it would be a trollop. He near to fainted when Jane Clark opened that door.

She might have cried a tear or two upon learning Brax hadn't returned to Texas for her, but she'd, nonetheless, agreed to buy the cameo at an inflated price. Brax had left Jane's establishment with money in his pocket—probably the first man in history to find his financial situation improved after leaving a whore.

Whatever the case, he hated to part with that cameo. It ought to be Skylla's.

"Bubba. Look to the horizon. Riders."

It didn't take much to halt Impossible. Brax scowled upon getting a gander at six soldiers clad in navy blue. They were U.S. Army troops. Two officers and a quartet of cavalry soldiers, Brax counted as they drew closer, the corporal to the rear in charge of a string of horses, none resembling Army-issue mounts.

The Blue Bellies had arrived.

Brax's hand moved to Piglet's pearl-handled six-shooter that now rested in the holster at his hip. "I'll pick off the enlisted men," he said to Geoff. "You get the officers."

"War's over, Bubba. Time to forget all that picking-off business."

"You're suggesting I not take my foul mood out on Yankees?" Braxton did nothing but stare at the lad's somber coffee-and-cream face.

"Yo there!"

"Bubba," Geoff repeated after that greeting from the nearing Yankees. "The war is over."

Five minutes later, the officer in charge, a major, held up a white-gloved hand to stop his squad. "Greetings, gentlemen. State your business."

"We're on our way home. To the Nickel Dime Ranch, about five miles yonder." Brax gestured southeast.

"Why, you'ns are next to being neighbors," remarked the sergeant, a ruddy-faced man with fire-red hair.

He rode forward and didn't bother to hide his disgust when he caught sight of the kepi as well as Brax's gray britches with military stripes down the legs announcing Confederate issue. "Say, boy." He pointed to Geoff. "Do you know you're free? Is this Reb scalawag holding you against your will?"

"Sergeant Reilly, enough," warned the major, a lanky fellow with dark hair and the airs of breeding, though his flat nasal tones testified to a provincial upbringing.

Brax scorched the sergeant with a glare. "First of all, Geoffrey Hale isn't a boy. And I'll thank you to address him as *Mr.* Hale, if you must address either of us."

The sergeant's hand went to his holster. "You want me to take care of these stragglers, Major Albright?"

The major shook his head, echoing Geoff's earlier words. "No. War's over."

Michigander, Brax decided. He's from Michigan.

The Blue Belly enlisted man retreated, under orders.

"Where you headed?" Brax asked the officers.

"Camp Llano," replied the baby-faced lieutenant. "It's a new frontier outpost and way station for troops headed west. Camp Llano isn't more than a half-day's ride from this spot."

The camp had to be less than a day's ride from the Nickel Dime. Which might mean money. Cattle were on the loose by the thousands, but these soldiers had to eat and they didn't look like they knew their way around a lasso, so the Army might be willing to pay for beef.

"How are y'all doing for rations?" he asked. "I'm in the beef business."

"I'm the quartermaster." The lieutenant removed his hat. "Do you have some for sale?"

"Damn shooting we do," Brax replied.

The sergeant changed his tune. "I'm a butcher. I intend to spend some time smoking meats into jerky."

"How much a head?" asked the youthful lieutenant.

"Two bucks."

The Michigan major took over negotiations from his quartermaster. "One fifty."

Brax shook his head. "One seventy-five."

"Sold."

"How many y'all need, Major?"

"Fifty head."

Brax nodded. "We'll have them to you in, say, four or five days." Which would cut short his honeymoon, but the ranch needed legal tender. "That is if we get cash on the barrelhead."

"Half now, half on delivery."

Over forty dollars! That much again upon delivery. Lord above, forty bucks was the same as the inside of King Midas's coffer. Brax hadn't seen that much money since Second Manassas. If he'd known this windfall was in the air; he wouldn't have parted with the cameo. Regret clamped on him, yet he reconciled himself. The cameo might be gone, but he had the money for wedding fixings and froufrou.

His line of sight kept turning to the string of horses. "Unusual-looking mounts for you fellows, especially the skewbald and that pair of roans."

"We bought them from a horse trader in San Antonio," the major replied. "Fellow named Oren Singleterry."

So, Singleterry had moved south. At least Brax now knew where to find him. He pulled a cheroot from a pouch, his sole extravagance from the recent sale to Jane Clark.

Lighting up, he squinted past a curl of smoke. "Say, Major, how 'bout I bring a hundred head to Camp Llano, providing you part with the eighty bucks and those three renegade horses?"

"Sixty dollars and the three horses."

"Seventy. And I'll throw in a barrel of some of the finest corn liquor outside the Smoky Mountains."

"Liquor? You've got good corn?" was a chorus from the Blue Bellies.

"What do you think, Major?" Brax asked.

"We accept."

"Let's shake on it." Brax rode forward and extended a hand to the major, was met with a firm handshake.

"Webb Albright at your service, sir. What's your name?"

"Brax Hale. Of the Nickel Dime Ranch."

"You wouldn t be the Hale who fought at Chickamauga?" Upon an affirmative reply, Albright leaned forward in the saddle, respect growing in his angular face. "You're the fellow who caught General Hood when he got blown from the saddle."

"How did you have such a bird's-eye view?" Brax asked.

"Word got around." Albright's mount grew frisky. "I'm a United States cavalryman, Hale, but I respect the great fighting men of the Confederate States of America."

"Hale," asked the junior officer, "what are you doing wearing Injun moccasins?"

"No Injun made them. I made them myself."

Webb Albright quirked a black brow. "If you're without decent footwear, I have a pair of boots that might fit you."

Amazed a Yankee would show generosity, Brax appreciated the offer, but declined. "A cobbler in Ecru is repairing my Wellingtons. Gave him the first work he had in months."

Why mention the special-order shoes he'd purchased for Skylla? The telling would have led to other questions, he felt certain, and those slippers were personal. And selling that cameo had made another purchase possible. His pocket held a wedding band. He wouldn't have Skylla getting married without a proper ring.

"I could use a new pair of boots," someone said.

"Me, too," became a round of Northern accents.

The major scratched his jaw. "Army supply wagons are on the way, but we'll have to make do for a spell."

Recalling Skylla's initial plans for bringing revenue to the ranch, Braxton rubbed the corners of his mouth and wished for tannery supplies. (Somehow he couldn't picture the assorted horde of the Nickel Dime gathered to scrape hide, or to rub fat and brains into it, much less carrying out the other tedious details of tanning leather, Indian style.) If they had the white man's supplies, leather could be prepared for shoes, boots, saddles, and the like. If, if, if.

The sergeant spat tobacco to the ground, then scratched himself. "Hale, what did happen to your Wellingtons?"

"I wore 'em running from y'all," he joshed.

"Hell, I wore out two pairs running from you fellows," commented the sergeant. "About got my butt shot, hightailing it in the Wilderness Campaign."

"I'll be damned," Brax joked in the camaraderie of exaggeration. "That was you?"

This drew a round of companionable laughter. The lieutenant added a fish story; the major made a joke about having Stonewall Jackson peppering him with grapeshot and Bible verse.

Then the conversation turned serious, and Brax gave the soldiers the lowdown on Mason County. A strange awareness settled in him. For the first time in years, he got the feeling the war might really be over. It was as if a weight had been lifted from his shoulders.

Now on to getting married.

Tonight Brax would take a wife. He wanted to shout his happiness from the rafters. After the ceremony he and Skylla would have the privacy he'd been dreaming about, since Claudine and Kathy Ann would stay the night at the Burrows farm. He looked forward to all that seclusion.

Wedding guests were collected in the front room of the ranch house, where the hired fiddler played soft sweet tunes, the parlor clear of furniture save for chairs and a few tables. The fragrances of bay rum, lavender toilet water, and candle wax mingled with the scent of the magnolias floating in bowls. The

Reverend Lester Byrd, minister of the gospel and a circuit rider for the Methodist Church, stood alongside Brax in front of the fireplace.

A cool September breeze blew through the open windows. Everyone seemed pleased and relieved, for the wedding guests were dressed in heavy Sunday-go-to-meeting finery gone to tatters. In attendance were the bride's sister, Charlie Main, Emil Kreitz—he had provided a candy dish full of sweets that Piglet had availed herself of—and Luke Burrows and his missus, the plump and rosy Gertie May. Seated in a horn chair, Oliver Brown smiled benevolently. Electra was stationed beneath the kindly physician. The calico complained, hissed, and chewed her claws.

Kathy Ann caught Brax's eye. She raised her hand halfway from her plump hips to wave. He winked back. She looked sweet, standing in organdy and an uncharacteristically shy smile.

The fiddler struck up the wedding march.

Suddenly, Brax's stock got tight. The jitters passed the moment he caught sight of his bride.

Skylla, led by her stepmother, glided past the beribboned staircase and smiling guests. Her head held high, she floated to her bridegroom. That's right, floated. She wore a built-up slipper, cobbled by the Ecru shoemaker. Another tradeoff for the cameo.

His best man whispered, "She's beautiful."

"I know, Geoffie. I know."

She took her place next to Brax. A blush tinted the cheeks of her heart-shaped face. Her hair flowed down her back, a gossamer veil touching it lightly. The peach hue of her low-cut gown set her ivory complexion and dark hair off in their best light. She was a vision, straight from a master's canvas.

"Are you ready for this?" she asked him, her voice a happy whisper.

He squeezed her hand gently. "You bet, sweetheart."

They faced the preacher. Brax couldn't help thinking how the cameo would have added just the right touch to her attire. Somehow he'd get her another one.

Chapter Fifteen

"Get on with the marryin', preacher man," Luke Burrows called from behind the bridegroom, and got chuckles from the other guests.

Brax's eyes slid to his bride again, reveling in her beauty. "Do get on with it, preacher man. I need me a wife."

"Dearly beloved . . ."

The ceremony began.

Minutes later Brax slipped the thin gold band on Skylla's finger. "Don't be nervous," he whispered. "It's almost over."

"Nervous? I'm not. Not at all." She smiled her gentle smile, the one that never failed to warm his heart.

Reverend Byrd cleared his throat to get their attention.

"Wait," Skylla whispered to the preacher. "I have something. A wedding gift."

Her work-worn fingers lifted to the stock Brax had borrowed from Titus's belongings; she stuck something in the center of it. He looked downward, seeing a gold stickpin centered with a green stone that had to be an emerald.

"My father's," she said, making him feel all the worse for selling the Hale heirloom.

"Thank you," he whispered and brought her fingertips to his lips to kiss them. A fist seemed to tighten on his heart. What could it be but love?

She tantalized him with: "I have a better gift waiting for you."

Damned right she did. He grinned smugly.

They got back to the official part of the ceremony. At half past seven, Reverend Byrd smiled and said, "I now pronounce y'all man and wife."

Brax gazed into those expressive dark eyes and tweaked her cute little nose. "Hello, Mrs. Hale."

"You may kiss your bride," the reverend informed Brax.

She tilted her chin up, closing her eyes and parting her lips ever so slightly. Brax brought his mouth to hers to seal their vows. Her bouquet of magnolia blossoms fluttered to the floor.

The minister congratulated the couple, then turned to sign Titus's Bible. Brax and Skylla added their signatures. Back slapping and the usual congratulations followed.

Claudine anchored her arm to the elbow of a bathed and spiffed-up Charlie Main, but she kept her distance. She had agreed to act as matron of honor; Brax knew she meant to keep this promise, but a way to make trouble had to be on her mind. He'd deal with the redhead as the situation unfolded.

He signaled to Geoff, and the younger man crept into the bridal suite to make it ready according to Brax's earlier instructions.

The musician set bow to fiddle, a tune filled the air, and the newlyweds, laughing and smiling, headed to the big dining room, where their wedding cake waited on the long rectangular table. After feeding each other the traditional first bites, the new Mr. and Mrs. Hale sipped wine from goblets borrowed from Emil Kreitz, who'd brought them from his native Germany.

Brax didn't mull the fruitcake's savory taste, his attention being captured by his wife and fantasies about their wedding bed. When the fiddler struck up a waltz, he took Skylla's hand and grinned. "May I have this dance, Mrs. Hale?"

"Most certainly, Mr. Hale."

Making sure he'd be able to catch her should she falter, he guided her to the middle of the room and brought her closer than propriety dictated. She had no trouble following.

"This is a lovely wedding, husband."

"Thanks to the generosity of the Yankee Army." *And to a good-hearted whore.*

"The Army didn't have anything to do with these shoes." She stopped dancing to step back and lift the hem of her dress a couple inches. Kid slippers, one with a built-up sole, peeped from beneath. "You've given me another chance at the dance."

"Same goes for you." Brax kissed her.

"Did you hear the new county officers' have arrived?"

Everyone turned to Oliver Brown. The honest-eyed physician elaborated: "We've got a sheriff and a county clerk. The clerk'll collect taxes, I've heard."

Claudine abandoned Charlie Main. She swept over to Skylla, who glanced at Brax before eyeing her stepmother.

"Since Dr. Brown brought up the subject, there's something you need to know. The Reconstructionists may well void the deeds held by Rebel veterans and sympathizers."

There was a collective response of: "That's what I've been afraid of."

"Do you think they can do that?" Skylla asked.

"Leastwise the Huns will be spared." Luke Burrows's shoulders drooped, as he no doubt wished he'd sided with his Teutonic neighbors. "Mason County's got plenty Huns, but there's a durned sight more of us."

"People could lose their land," Claudine said, as if she gave a damn about anyone but herself.

Brax frowned. "Let's not borrow trouble."

"What is more troublesome than being tossed off one's property?" Claudine inquired. "I've heard stories. These good people will back me up." She nodded at the guests. "Confederate veterans may well be in the same dilemma that plagued the holders of Mexican land grants. Rebels will suffer."

Brax recalled the decency of Webb Albright and his cavalry unit. "The Unionists won't be vindictive."

Emil Kreitz spoke, his accent heavy. "I have studied the history of Texas. After independence from Mexico, the Texians— good Americans—voided many Mexican land grants."

Brax watched his stepmother-in-law hide a grin of triumph. The bitch had orchestrated this tempest in a teacup, had timed it to spoil the evening.

Is the ranch lost? Well, lost or not, don't show this viper she's got you sitting on thorns. Don't let her spoil your wedding night with your wife. However, despite his intentions, he couldn't rid his mind of what the future might hold.

"Thank goodness they're finally gone."

"Amen, sweetheart. Wife."

In the parlor after the last wedding guest had departed, Skylla turned to that deep resonant voice, feeling sweet anticipation as she feasted her eyes on the tall and broad-shouldered form of her new husband. He'd never looked more handsome than in his fine suit of clothes. And he'd never looked more unhappy.

"What's wrong?"

"Nothing." His eyes betrayed his smile. He shrugged his coat off, then pitched it onto a chair. Next came the neckcloth, which he held in his hand. "Thank you for the stickpin. I wish I had something more than a wedding band and a pair of shoes to give you in exchange."

A small voice within Skylla asked when he'd give her the cameo, but she shushed it. *He'll pull it from a pocket. I know he will.* He didn't. She held her beringed hand to her chest. "Don't forget the wine and music. They were lovely."

"Cold comfort."

"Don't belittle your gifts, my darling. I will treasure them until my dying day."

Still, his mind was troubled. The cloud of the Reconstructionists—that had to have troubled him. Unionist officials might indeed turn the Lone Star State on its end, and she prayed that wouldn't occur, for their neighbors would suffer. The Hales and their kin wouldn't suffer. Not with Uncle's fortune found.

A footstep separated them; she took it and placed her hands on his muscled upper arms. "Braxton . . ."

"You look especially lovely tonight," he said in an obvious attempt at disregarding the specter in his mind. He fingered the veil that cascaded down her back, then took her headpiece off, tossing it onto the settee. "I especially like your hair loose." His head bent, and he ran a heavy hank of hair across his lips. "I want more. I want the pleasure of undoing the clothes that keep me from feasting my eyes on you."

Her veins heavy with desire, she inhaled deeply. She'd tell him about the fortune . . . in time. Right now she wanted to savor—and relish—these tender moments. She helped him divest her of the dress. In her chemise she then stepped from dotted Swiss, watching as he set it across a chair.

When his eyes took in her lamplit form, she stood without fear. Once upon a time, not so long ago, his intimate gaze would have given her cause to hide her affliction, but his affection had given her a delicious confidence.

His roving hands on her arms, he bent to kiss her lips lightly and to murmur, "Weddings ought to be conducted in the nude. It would sure save time."

She chuckled at his audacity.

In short order, he undid his shirt, placed it next to her dress. Her gaze riveted to the light brown hair that dusted his solid chest, during which he did the strange dance of a man shucking his boots while standing. Still in britches, he skimmed his hands along her bare shoulders. "Shall we go to the bedroom, or shall we make love in the front room?"

A smile worked at his lips. Once more, she noticed it didn't travel to his eyes. The ranch. That was it. The ranch and its muddled future. It was no way to start a marriage, obstacles separating a husband and wife. "Braxton, if you're worrying about losing the ranch, don't."

She took him by the hand, leading the way to the dining room, where, beneath the linen cloth that had been one of Uncle's concessions to conventional decor, stood a wooden casket. Sturdy, made of mahogany, strapped with wide swatches of brass, the chest compared to a valise in size.

"Your surprise," she stated pridefully, enthusiastically.

Staring first at the case, then at Skylla, Braxton bent down, then rocked back on his heels. His hand went to the clasp, but stilled.

"Go on. Open it." She took a lamp from the buffet to give this special moment the benefit of brilliance. "Behold our rich future."

He unfastened it, lifted the lid. Gold and cut stones gave off a light show of breathtaking proportions.

As if the lid had suddenly gone hot, Braxton let it go. "This is Titus's lost fortune. The Comanches didn't take it."

"Apparently not."

"This was here, while . . ." Levered to his feet, Brax had a bleak countenance. "What in the hell is going on? Why did you pick this particular night to show this off?"

Her excitement deflating, she explained about finding the treasure, ending with: "Our ranch is secure. We needn't worry about anyone taking it from us. We can pay whatever it takes to keep the Nickel Dime in our family."

"Are you crazy?" His fingers locked on her elbows. "To hell with this place. We can pack up and be out of here by sundown tomorrow."

Her voice seemed to come from a distance as she replied, "You can't mean that."

"I said it. I mean it. Skylla, California is a wondrous place. We can live there, be the toast of San Francisco."

San Francisco? San Francisco! That he would mention such a place meant that it had been on his mind. Who was this man she'd married? Where was the rancher who'd worked like a slave to keep them afloat? Was Claudine right about him?

"Does our land mean nothing to you?" Skylla asked, hoping against hope he'd put her mind at ease.

"This ranch is the devil's backyard."

Her illusions were shattered. Her confidence ebbed. She backed away, shod in the shoes she'd prized only moments ago. Her hips bumped against the table on which were the leavings of the wedding cake. Since she'd been wrong about his feelings for a home they both had a stake in, how wrong was she about his feelings for her?

"Skylla? Skylla, talk to me."

"You're a stranger, Braxton Hale."

"I'm the husband who wants a good life for the Hales."

"I thought you wanted all that was offered here. Including the crippled woman who owns the place."

He stepped forward to lay his fingers against her chilled cheek. "You know I want you."

"I don't know anything anymore."

"Then let me show you what to think." He reached for her, but she drew away. Tasting bile at not getting his way, he cursed. "You're my wife. I mean to have you. Come here, Skylla."

"Save your charity."

Eyes closing, he lifted his head toward the ceiling, then leveled his green gaze to take in the uncertainty and crushed dreams evident on her face. "I've never considered you with *charity.*"

Oh, how she yearned to believe him. But she wouldn't allow herself such folly. What should she do, and which way should she turn?

He soldered his grasp to her elbows. "I'm going to ask you again, Skylla. Come away with me."

The terrible temper that she had carefully guarded for so long snapped. "Never! I will never, ever leave this ranch! And you're mistaken if you think you'll change my mind!"

"You'll by God do what I say."

"You've never been more wrong." She pried his fingers away. Her hand raked into the wedding cake, and she threw a big wad of it at him. The mass oozed through the hair of his chest.

Wiping his hand down the offensive pastry, he said tightly, "What's wrong with you that you'd want to stay five minutes in this abyss of hard work and little reward?"

"It's my home!" She whipped around, meaning to seek out her bedroom and the comfort of solitude.

A roar like a lion's shook the rafters; then a huge chunk of white icing and fruitcake flew in front of her advancing form, causing her to stumble into what was left of their wedding cake.

One foot flew out from under her; she slipped in the slickness. Falling backward, she felt strong hands grabbing her. No! She wouldn't tumble into the well of his demands.

Yet he turned her into his arms, and then they were both on the floor, him above her, amid the destroyed cake. Their destroyed dreams.

"I'll show just how much charity I have for you." His mouth descended as if to kiss her, but she ran her nails down his jaw, scratching him.

At feeling blood under her nails, she heard another leonine roar, this one reverberating in her skull.

"Get off me," she moaned.

But he didn't. His fingers clamped her shoulders; he held her to the floor. The sheer weight of him nearly smothered her, and she wasn't strong enough to stop the onslaught of his lips. His tongue, harsh and cruel, invaded her mouth. The punishment should have caused her to fight him all the more, yet the torture became tinged with sweetness as his hold on her shoulders lessened and his tongue began to slide along her teeth in an action not unlike the primal motions of mating.

Mindless, she moaned. Her arms closed around his back as he writhed against her. He murmured her name into her mouth, and she met his undulations with her own. A cry of passion on her lips, she dug her fingers into his back and arched against him. It was then that he rolled to the side. They were a mess of cake and icing and the trickles of blood from his jaw.

"I'm going to take this chemise off you."

When she was naked below him, he ran his hand along the indentation in her calf. She tried to move away, could not. When his mouth settled on her scar, she bit her lip.

"This is the charity I feel for you, Skylla Hale."

His tongue slid along the mess of cake and the damage war had done her limb. A gentle massage followed, one that slew her insecurities about her appeal. He murmured words of reassurance and affection that went straight to her heart.

His gooey hand traced a path to her hip. His lips then replaced it. When she forced herself not to respond to his touch, he brought her atop his long, hard body. He reached behind her head to cradle her nape. "I love you, Skylla Hale. I love you with all my heart."

"Don't say things you don't mean."

"You *don't*. I've yearned for you since the day I first saw you standing beside that magnolia tree, a butterfly on your finger. I love you, you're my wife, and I aim to claim you."

"You lie about your feelings."

"Yeah, I'm a liar. I'm a lying son of a bitch. I'm not worth the soap to clean your shoes, but I'm your husband. A husband whose blood is afire for you." His lips ascended to her throat. "Don't ask me to stop, because I won't. I've lain awake too many nights wanting you. For tonight, for now, don't let anything stand between us. I need you so badly I don't know what I'm capable of if I don't find out what it's like to put myself deep inside you."

Her arms closed around him again. Tomorrow, she could cry for shattered illusions.

Chapter Sixteen

Their mouths met with a fevered passion befitting to lovers. Rearing above her, Braxton curved his palms around her breasts, his thumbs and forefingers teasing her nipples. Skylla combed through the curls of his hair, while with a masterful touch he caressed her. She responded to his touch, from her toes to the top of her head, feelings settling deliciously into her womanly parts. She must have moaned in delight, for he laughed softly, bringing her fingers to the prickly, sticky hairs on his chest. To doubt his passion would be idiotic. He wanted her. She didn't doubt that.

The lamp that had illuminated a king's ransom flickered, then died, leaving the dining room in shadowy moonlight.

"I've got to get these britches off." He left the floor to stand above her, his gaze never leaving her face. His torso was limned in silver as she watched him.

"On second thought . . ." Stretching out beside her, he brought her hand to the top of his trousers. "Take them off me."

Sticky fingers fumbled with the buttons; her attention centered on the bulge of his sex, swollen and straining against the material. His hand clamped over hers, and pressed her palm against it. "Touch me, Skylla. Touch me."

Her fingers slipped beyond his waistband, and she sucked in her breath at the feel of velvet-covered steel. But he then countermanded his own order. Saying he needed more, he rolled onto his back, lifting his slim hips to shove the last of his clothing away. Naked, he brought her into his arms again.

Yet terrible thoughts raced into her mind. What if this turned out to be their only night of marital congress? What if he left her for the greener pastures of California?

"You're pulling away from me," he said.

"I'm not."

"You are. Stop, Skylla. Stop it right now." Aligning himself with her nude body, he brushed hair and goo from her temple. His voice troubled, he asked, "Am I losing you?"

"Have we lost each other?"

"Never. We'll work something out. I promise we will." His gaze gripping hers, he ordered softly, "Open your legs, sweetheart. Let me into your body. Let me stay in your heart."

Appeased, she let him nudge his knee between her legs. Oh, how she relished the feel of him. Levered above her, he dipped his mouth to hers, his hands encircling her face. She felt his long and thick member settle at her womanly crevice. Her legs spread wider. And with one magical thrust he sealed their marriage.

She moaned her pleasure. He moved slightly, then, with a forceful lunge, caused her to gasp for air. He withdrew and plunged again, and her arms closed around him, gripping him. Even before she reached the shattering climax that left her panting for breath, she knew he was her husband for all the days of their lives.

And beyond.

She was Mrs. Braxton Hale.

Completely, unequivocally.

Mrs. Hale of the Nickel Dime Ranch. The property that

would remain in this family beyond the time she and her husband were in their graves. She would accept nothing less.

Somehow she'd talk him out of California.

The place stank in more ways than one. Claudine scorned
her poor excuse for a lover, as she did their chicken-coop
meeting place at the Burrows farm. "Get dressed, Charlie."

In the dark and amid the roosting chickens, he stepped into
his britches, then snapped his suspenders. "Pumpkin, ain't
you gonna say nothin' about me not bein' too old for ya?"

"You're wonderful." Her lie flowed smoothly.

"Don't ya wanna hear 'bout that Menard whore?"

"What about her?" Claudine bundled up their pallet.

"I was over to Ecru yesterday. That good-looking gal what
lived there 'fore the war was in town—Jane Clark—be wearing
the cameo I seen here at the ranch."

In Claudine's estimation, Charlie Main had no eye for the
finer things in life. To her, he'd mistake a toad for a cameo.
And anyway Skylla would never believe the story. Unless
Claudine could get some hard evidence against Brax Hale, the
cameo tale wasn't worth looking into.

If it proved true, the marriage between Brax and Skylla was
done for. Skylla might not believe gossip, but she'd have to
believe her own eyes.

"You'd best get back to the ranch, Charlie. You're supposed
to round cattle up in the morning." Claudine left the coop
and crawled back into the bedroom window of her temporary
room at the Burrows farm.

In the still of night, Braxton carried her to the room that
had been laid out for them, and Skylla marveled at the magnolia blossoms that carpeted their bed. He set her onto her
feet, those blooms filling her nostrils with the rich scent of
their oils.

"There's wine," he whispered. "Let me pour you some."

She nodded, speechless. Though he might not love the Nickel Dime, love for her was evident in the attention given to making their wedding night special.

They sipped from the same glass, smiling and kissing between swallows. When they had finished, he broke away, saying, "I think we should avail ourselves of the pitcher and bowl."

"We are a sight," she returned with a small chuckle.

He ran a soft wet cloth over her body, his lips checking the result. Anew, her passions built. And she gave the same ardent care to his sinewed flesh. Once more, he lifted her into his arms to settle her on the heady blossoms.

And they made love again, this time with even wilder abandon. At some time before dawn, they fell asleep, locked in each other's arms. Never had she slept with a man, and her dreams were involved with the joys of this new experience. When she awakened, the scent of magnolias clinging to her skin, she burrowed into his warmth.

Yet California whirled into the forefront of her thoughts. How could she talk him out of such an idea? How could she make him love something he didn't love?

The parlor was a mess. Skylla glanced toward the closed bedroom door. Should she awaken her husband and ask him to help with the cleanup? No. She needed quiet time to amass her strategies to keep Braxton here at the ranch.

With no clear plan in mind, and determined that no one would see the evidence of last night's argument, she scooped up dollops of mashed cake and threw it into the pail collected from the cookhouse. As well, she carried well water indoors, and was scrubbing the floor when Geoff tapped on the front door.

She gave silent thanks that it wasn't Claudine returned.

Rather than invite him in, she walked onto the porch. "I thought you and Charlie were rounding up cattle for the Army."

"Dey rounded up. He watching dem at dat ol' Safe Haven

Canyon. Me, I gots to go to town. Gots to get da saddle fixed,
'fore dat ole skewbald throws dis darkie into da cactus patch.''

"I'll tell my husband to meet Charlie Main at the canyon."

Geoff's canny gaze assessed her. "Are you all right, Miz
Skylla?"

Gone was his usual uneducated voice, which she wondered
about. "I'm fine."

"Where's Bubba? Did he hurt you?"

"Certainly not."

Geoff collected his wits. "Da massa, where he be?"

"He's asleep."

"I off to town, then." Geoff swung to alight the stairs.

"Wait just a minute, please."

He turned his face up to her.

"Geoff, where's your family?" she asked.

"I gots none. 'Cept for da massa and Bella."

"How long have you known Braxton?"

"My mammy, Bella, been wit' da Hales befo' I borned."

"I've long suspect your ties were of long standing." Skylla
moved to the top of the stairs. "I suspect you've known all
along about his plans for California, too."

"What's Calibornion?" he replied guilelessly.

Skylla exhaled, yet . . . "Tell me something, Geoff. Are you
brother to Braxton?"

His toast-tinted complexion went pale. "Dat Miss Claudine
been talkin' to you. Doan you believe her, Miss Skylla. Ain't
no way dis darkie be brother to your man."

He was lying. But his was an understandable lie. Skylla
turned away from the boy, then stopped to say over her shoulder, "Take care what you say about Mrs. St. Clair. And don't
ever lie to me again, Geoff."

Skylla finished cleaning up the parlor, afterward going to
the cookhouse. Within minutes she had a cookfire built, the
coffee brewing, and sausage, cheese, and bread sliced. Idly,
she wondered why Electra didn't arrive to beg for a portion.

As she took biscuits from the oven, she heard her husband
enter the kitchen. She faced him. His hair tousled and a morn-

ing beard poking through his strong jaw—and with livid scratches that gave testament to her former anger—Braxton yawned and scratched his biceps. "Mornin', wife."

"Good morning." She slapped a plate on the table.

Ignoring the repast, he took a giant step to take her in his arms. He might not have shaved or brushed his hair, but his breath had been attended to. And he wore bay rum. Such a normal scenario. A man greeting his wife on the morning after their marriage. If only California didn't stand between them . . .

"Don't you want coffee?" she asked, needing to settle matters and not in his arms.

He read her mood. "Skylla, about last night—"

"I don't want to discuss it on an empty stomach." Yet she had no appetite for food. "The men have the cattle rounded up. Geoff's had to ride into town, though. Something about seeing the saddlemaker. You'll want to help Charlie. Won't you?"

Braxton let her go to step back. "Forget the cattle drive."

"You promised Major Albright you'd deliver at the earliest possible time."

Silence fell.

"Are you planning to go back on your word?" she asked.

"We don't need a few measly Yankee dollars."

She scrutinized her husband's expression and didn't care much for what she saw. "You took Yankee dollars and Yankee horses. And you spent Yankee dollars. We owe Major Albright."

More silence.

Braxton gave in. "I'll make good on my debt."

"And then what?"

"I'll hightail it back here, what else?"

California was on the tip of her tongue. She swallowed her comment. Turning away and pouring Braxton a cup of coffee, she yearned for him to say he'd given up the idea of leaving.

Even before he walked up behind her, she sensed his presence; tiny hairs lifted on her neck.

"Skylla, I want you. Again."

He nuzzled her shoulder, eliciting a shiver of desire, and caressed her hips. His britches-covered shaft pressed against her backside, and she did nothing to hide her sighs. He swung her into his arms and smothered her sighs with a kiss hotter than a cookfire. They were on the dirt floor in no time, her skirts in disarray around them. His lips and hands began another conquest, yet the conquered railed.

She held him away. "You and I need to talk."

"Later."

When he fumbled with the buttons at her bodice, she tried to roll away. "Damn you, Braxton. Damn you!" She beat her balled fists against his shoulders. "We've settled nothing. Don't do this when my mind is troubled!"

He stilled. "What do you want, Skylla? For us to stay here the rest of our lives at this hellhole of a ranch?"

"Yes."

"Don't force me to promise something in passion—something that I'll regret later."

"You won't regret it. We'll have a wonderful life here, Braxton. We have money for everything we want and need. This ranch will prosper. For us. And for our children."

"I'd love to have children with you. But . . ."

"Then let's build a firm foundation for them. Let's create them a legacy that will sustain and support them—and their children. Let's give them what you and I were torn away from."

"Is this damned place that important to you? Is the Nickel Dime all that's tearing us apart?"

She recalled all the things he'd never told her about himself, including his ties to Geoff, yet she answered, "Yes."

His eyes closing, he swallowed. With a ragged voice, he replied, "Then you've won. We'll stay here. Forever and ever. This land will remain ours."

Pure joy filled her breast. He loved her enough to make a huge concession, so what else could she ask for? "This land will be ours. And our children's."

Yet their conflicts weren't settled, for he said, "Skylla, I may be sterile."

"Whatever makes you think that?"

"I never got a child on my first wife. She had two babes from her first marriage, so I know the problem wasn't Songbird."

Throughout her life, Skylla had dreamed of being a mother. Could she go to her grave childless? Yes. Yes, she could. While she hoped he worried for nothing, she, too, could make concessions. "I didn't marry you for children, Braxton. I married to spend the rest of my life with you."

The clouds over his face lifted. "Then let me make love to you before I leave to settle my debt with Mr. Grant's army. If you'll allow me."

"I will let you. More than willingly, I will let you."

He smiled. His fingers brushed the material away covering her breasts. He took her nipple into his mouth. Once more he made luscious love to her. With his mouth, his words, his hands. And when he reared up to unfasten his britches and say, "Take me out so that I may finish our lovemaking," she went to the task without haste. His whisper as sweet as their wedding wine, he enjoined, "Now guide me in."

She did.

It had been a stupid mistake, his blabbing about California, one that could have cost Brax his wife. In the aftermath of backing down, and in afterglow of making love to her in the cookhouse, Brax came to grips with the future. San Francisco would be nothing more than a concept.

He could live with that. As long as he had Skylla at his side. A smile traveled across his face. Damn, he loved that woman. And he'd never had better luck than to find her, then marry her. An added bonus was the wonderful lover she'd turned out to be. The finest woman in the world and with a fortune to line their nest. Was there a luckier man on earth?

In the bedroom—she was outdoors—he dressed for the cattle drive. A thought chipped into the crevices of his mind.

Geoff's mother had to be halfway to California by now. How could he get word to Bella about their changed plans?

He mulled the problem while exiting the bedroom, then stared at the treasure that could have saved Diana and the rest. He threw the lid back. How much worth did it encompass? A great deal. What else had Titus hidden? Who gave a damn?

He scooped up a handful of coins and topaz. Riches with which to buy his wife a cameo as well as a few creature comforts. Was it wrong to help himself to Skylla's fortune? No. At least five thousand dollars of this lucre belonged to him.

Did Claudine know about the gold and jewels? From her actions of late, Brax doubted it. *Don't let her get her paws on it.* The cameo money got shoved in his pocket. Calling up his strength, he scooted the heavy chest to the bedroom. Chances were, it would fit under the bed until he and Skylla could find a better hiding place. When he pushed the bedstead aside, dust motes swirled. And he got an eyeful of a trapdoor.

He lifted it. The dank awful smell reminded him of the Vicksburg jail. Rats skittered about on the ground below, which caused him to shiver. This was not a hidey-hole he wanted to make friends with, but it would do until he and Skylla decided where to deposit the casket's contents. The muscles in his arms were strained as he wrestled the whole chest down below.

Finished, he rearranged the room and wiped his hands.

A commotion and a woman's scream from outside drew Brax's attention. He rushed to the window to see Claudine, her chignon askew, pulling Luke Burrows's buckboard to a grinding halt in front of the house. Dust devils whirled, the horse whinnied, and Claudine continued screaming, "Someone come quick!"

Brax grimaced. *What kind of witchery is she up to now?*

Skylla limped from the cookhouse, in her stepmother's direction. Brax strapped a gunbelt around his hips, just in case Claudine wasn't the problem.

Chapter Seventeen

The Comanches had captured Kathy Ann.

Claudine sank onto the settee in the parlor, took a restorative swig of last night's wine. "We were riding home this morning. She saw that cat of hers run into the woods. Kathy Ann jumped down from the buckboard and rushed after Electra."

"Oh, no." Skylla blanched.

Brax gave her hand a squeeze of assurance that he in no way felt. It had taken a good while for his impression of Kathy Ann to change, but that had come about.

Claudine, her face broken into welts, blew her nose into a handkerchief. "She said she wouldn't let savages get Electra. She caught the cat." Tears came. "It was awful. She wasn't fifty feet from me when a half-dozen redskins surrounded her."

For a moment Brax wondered if this was a hoax dreamed up by a woman in fear of her fate, but he gathered that wasn't so. Claudine might be a witch, but she wasn't without some heart. He loaded the Spencer as well as Kathy Ann's six-shooter.

Red-rimmed blue eyes turned to him. "What happened to your face?"

Skylla did the answering. "Mind your own business."

Brax agreed. Besides, there was a more important matter here. Did Stalking Wolf know the Army had arrived? Did he know a measure of the white man's law and order was on the horizon? Brax doubted it. Unless the Comanche chief looked to get his people obliterated, he wouldn't be making trouble if he knew white soldiers and lots of them would come after him and his. Of course, the presence of the white force might be what was prodding the chief to move deeper into the Comancheria before trouble broke out . . . and to take a young blond captive along?

Skylla placed her hand on Brax's arm. "Braxton, what's happening to her?"

"Unless they're planning to move out, I doubt they'll want her scalp. I reckon they'll use her as ransom. Or . . ."

"Or what?" Skylla asked.

"I figure he's lost a loved one recently. Maybe a wife. He may be looking for a new one. I'll bet all that blond hair looks mighty good to him."

"Kathy Ann as wife to some redskin?" Claudine made a gagging noise. "Why, I never heard anything so absurd. Besides, she's only fifteen!"

"Which was your age when you took your first husband," Brax pointed out. His eyes went to the dining room, where a slab of wedding cake had been recovered, no doubt by the bride. "Skylla, slice and box up the rest of that cake."

"What for?" she asked.

"For Indian children. They like sugared treats."

The cogs in his brain turning, Brax made a list of other handy items. One of these he could get from the medical supplies.

He said, "I'll be back soon as I can."

A biscuit tin of leftover cake held close to her chest, Skylla looked up at him. "I'm going with you."

"If you feel a need to help, fetch Main." Of course, his

leaving would set free the gathered cattle, but this was no time to worry about a promise to the Army.

Claudine nodded, disturbing the last trace of her chignon. "Yes. Go for Charlie."

Skylla stuck to her guns. "I said I'm going after my sister. And I won't bend."

Claudine hopped up from the settee. "We've got to form a search party. We must get in touch with the new sheriff."

Patting the air, Brax said, "No. If there's anything I learned during my time with the Comanches, it's that they are proud people. Their culture isn't ours, but, like all men, Stalking Wolf won't stand for being cornered. He'll come out fighting. Kathy Ann and her cat won't be the only victims."

"You don't know that Indian," Claudine pointed out with open hostility. "You have no way of predicting his behavior."

They did need a safeguard. "Claudine, can I depend on you to drive Luke Burrows's buckboard to Camp Llano? The army will help us. If necessary."

She nodded reluctantly. "I'll need a map."

He gave directions to the new outpost, ending with, "Ask for Major Albright. Major Webb Albright. Tell him . . . if I'm not returned by tomorrow noon, come after me."

"Us," Skylla corrected. "Tell him to come after us."

The tin of cake in her hand, she hobbled toward him. She'd turned into a feisty thing, his wife. If he rode out alone, she wouldn't be far behind. "Let's go, wife."

She smiled, taking his hand, and they rushed to saddle their mounts. They reached the stable and got a shock. Geoff and Charlie had the skewbald and one of the roans, horseflesh traded from the Army, but the other roan was gone.

Impossible and Molasses remained.

Brax broke into laughter, not feeling half as amused as he sounded. Perhaps Stalking Wolf really did want Kathy Ann for his woman, and considering the missing horse, Brax figured the Comanches were on the move. Considering the late hour, he nixed any idea of changing mounts with Charlie Main. No time for it. "We'll ride the geldings."

I hope to hell we can catch the Indians and Kathy Ann on these candidates for the glue factory.

Kathy Ann heard the Indians laughing even before the riders arrived in the Comanche village that was in the beginning stages of being dismantled. Well, they were funny looking, Sergeant and Skylla galumphing in on elderly geldings.

Already she knew her captors had stolen the roan. That had to have Sergeant mad. Kathy Ann wished she could get a better look at her saviors. Saviors? They could be here solely to reclaim horseflesh. *Sergeant wouldn't be that unkind. He must be here to help me.*

Naked as a worm—except for moccasins and a breechclout—Stalking Wolf left her side to meet the riders. Strapped to a tree and with a quartet of elderly squaws, all with mutilated fingers, circling her, Kathy Ann couldn't do as she pleased.

Little good it had done to rescue Electra. Already those hags had laced the calico cat inside a wigwam and were boiling a bag of weeds to make some sort of witch's brew. It looked as if one of the squaws was sharpening a knife.

Probably to butcher Electra.

Kathy Ann wasn't one to cry. But she had to sniff back tears. She couldn't stand the thought of Electra becoming anyone's feast. As for herself, she didn't feel any fear. Matter of fact, she'd hoped Stalking Wolf and his braves would find her. It was time she got her own man. Here lately, her dreams had been filled with a black-haired warrior who sashayed around, naked as a worm.

Her gaze followed him. Wow, he was a well-muscled worm, and she liked the looks of his coppery skin. A fellow like Stalking Wolf would never have the anemic look. And he'd talked about Cynthia Ann Parker. Trouble was, Kathy Ann had never gotten around to asking if the white girl had owned a cat.

She lost sight of him, thanks to one of the squaw guards stepping into her line of sight. Thankfully the old biddy and a couple of others got interested in the visitors; the trio, jabbering in their unintelligible tongue, walked toward Sergeant and Skylla, who were no more than ten yards from Kathy Ann.

Raising his right hand to shoulder level, Brax spoke gibberish to the chief and his clutch of followers.

"Stalking Wolf speaks English," Kathy Ann called out, wanting to hear and understand every syllable that got uttered.

One of her guards shook some sort of rattle to shut her up. If Kathy Ann had been inclined to talk, no dumb rattle could stop her. She stuck her tongue out at the stupid old squaw.

With interest, she noted her sister and new brother-in-law as they began to haggle for her release. They weren't after horses alone. A comfort. In truth, though, she didn't want to be returned. If Electra didn't turn up in someone's cooking pot.

A dirty Indian girl of three or four walked up, staring solemnly. Her eyes, strangely, were hazel. A swarm of flies accompanied her.

"Get away," Kathy Ann ordered. "You're making me sick to my stomach."

Naturally, the girl didn't budge.

Kathy Ann pulled a face and made a rude noise, which got rid of the pest. *She's kind of cute, though.* Someone ought to see after that kid, clean her up. *Not my problem.*

Free to ruminate over her captor, Kathy Ann smiled despite her bonds. Back in the woods, Stalking Wolf had treated her royally. And he'd handled Electra gently, even after the cat scratched him. He'd tickled her chin and said something in a sweet tone, before passing her to Head Too Big for the trip here.

When Stalking Wolf had pulled Kathy Ann up in front of him on the paint pony and had ridden west, she hadn't sensed a meanness in him. She hadn't fought the Comanche chief, either—the pony had protested her weight, though. The rough-rock crags of Stalking Wolf's handsome face intrigued her.

Stalking Wolf's unbound hair whipped in the breeze, now

and again whipping forward into her face. The other men wore braids, but Kathy Ann liked Stalking Wolf's look better. Then the red man touched her tenderly and spoke gently, in English.

"Sun In Her Hair," he'd announced. "That is what I will call you."

The sway and dip of the horse rocked Kathy Ann against him. "Say, Wolf, have you ever heard of Cynthia Ann Parker?"

"She was the white-eyes woman of Peta Nocona."

"Did she like being Peta Nocona's wife?"

"It has been said that she loved him. I do not know for myself. Peta Nocona and his tribe live to the land of the dawning sun. The drums say she is mourned."

Kathy Ann leaned back against the chest of her captor. "I wouldn't let anyone take me where I didn't want to go."

"You do not behave like other white women."

"I dance to the beat of my own drummer."

"Yes, Sun In Her Hair, I sense that." His arm moved against her midriff. "I would like to know . . . have you visited the inside of a man's tepee?"

"Nope."

"Have you followed a man to a place by the stream?"

"Are you asking if I'm a virgin?"

"A virtuous girl is a prize to behold."

"Behold the prize. I'm a virgin."

She could feel his smile against her hair. "I would be honored to break the trail for you and allow you to carry my possessions on your back."

While pleased at his interest, Kathy Ann had to think about that offer. Carry his stuff on her back? What kind of deal was that? Moreover, she hoped she heard him right—he was kind of broken-spoken—about that breaking-trail business. She hoped he hadn't said he'd do her the favor of breaking wind.

"Will you not speak to me, Sun In Her Hair?"

"A gentleman carries things for his lady."

"Such a shame for white women." Stalking Wolf kneed the mount, and turned the sleek pony in a westerly direction.

"The women of my tribe are honored to carry their men's bundles and cook their meals, and make the tepees warm. It is a greater honor for the braves to protect and cherish these fine women."

"I can think of worse things to happen, I suppose. Like, one time I had a tooth pulled. That's worse than cooking and hauling and making a tepee into a castle."

"Have you lost many teeth?" he asked, worry in his tone.

"No, why?"

"If an Indian cannot chew pemmican, nothing can be done. That person must be banished to meet the Great Spirit."

"Ugh."

"Tell me, Sun In Her Hair, if the men carry the belongings, who saves these women when they are attacked?"

"The men do."

She felt his nod of head. "That is why we are able to take many white captives," he said. "The white man must put down his woman's work before he can pick up a long-knife."

"Personally, I think your way stinks."

"There is nothing wrong with the way we smell, unless the buffalo fat turns rancid." He leaned his mouth close to her cheek. "Do I smell bad to you, Sun In Her Hair?"

"You might try a splash of lavender water behind the ears and under the arms." She giggled. "No, Wolf, you don't smell so bad. You smell nice."

At least a half-dozen minutes passed before he said, "I have need of a woman to carry bundles for me and my daughters."

"Daughters?" Darn, he was married.

"I have two strong daughters. One is four summers, the other is in her second summer."

"Just a doggone minute. You ought to be ashamed. What do you think you're doing, making sweet-talk with me? What would your wife think if she knew you'd asked me to carry your junk?"

"I am entitled to two wives."

"I know she'd love to hear that. Your poor wife is at home—uh, at your tepee—breaking her back lugging your stuff around, slaving over a hot cookfire, getting ready to welcome you, when you yammer about taking another wife."

"She has gone to the happy hunting ground."

"Is that far from here?"

"Very far. She is dead."

Goody! "I'm sorry, Wolf. You must miss her."

"Yes, my daughters and I miss her. She had no sisters for me to take to wife. And I cannot marry any woman in my own tribe. I must look outside my village for a wife."

"Oh."

"My daughters . . . In truth, Sun In Her Hair, they belong with my wife's people. It is against our customs for me to hoard them. But I would miss my little daughters if they were no longer around to toss in the air and kiss on the cheek."

"Seems to me your in-laws would be willing to let you keep the girls, if you asked nicely."

He laughed sadly. "I am in no danger of losing my papooses. The family of their mother does not want them."

"That's awfully cruel of Indian grandparents. Those babies need someone to look out for them."

"Enough about my daughters." He leaned his mouth close to Kathy Ann's ear. "I have watched you many moons, since you came to the land the white man calls the Nickel Dime Ranch. It has been only since my wife went to the happy hunting ground that I have stared at you as a man stares at a woman."

"I knew you were watching me."

"I know you knew." The hand that held her midriff moved up to her breast. "I need you for my wife. I want sons from you, too. Will you do this?"

Despite her thrill, Kathy Ann knew Skylla would pitch a fit if she got married. Fifteen might seem too young to some people, but Kathy Ann felt older. She hated being trapped in a kid's age. She needed someone to love her. And she needed someone to love, and not a sister or a brother-in-law, no matter how nice the latter had become.

As for the Indian chief's proposal, she'd better get a few

matters straight. "I won't have a husband whose idea of a happy hunting ground means looking for a second wife."

"If you please me, I will not take a second wife."

"Well, I have a different idea of marriage. I have no intention of becoming some household drudge. I've dreamed of a husband who provides the bonbons and spoils me silly with gifts galore." That wasn't quite true, but it sounded good to her.

"What is this you speak of, bonbons?"

"Candy."

He squeezed a thigh. "You eat plenty bonbons already. Meals of buffalo-eye stew will make you sleek as a mountain lion."

Her stomach turned over. Given that menu, a girl in an Indian village could surely stick to a reduction diet. "Take my word for it, Wolf. If you want a white woman, you'd best give her what she wants. I can't imagine any of my white sisters going for that stew."

"You would waste useful food?"

"Those eyeballs ought to have the chance to go to their own happy hunting ground. Intact."

"I do not understand your logic."

"You sure are stupid for a guy who can speak fair English. Where did you learn it?"

"From my wife. She was of your race."

That made the cruel grandparents white! Kathy Ann was suddenly embarrassed for white society. Not being a civic light, though, she had more thoughts. "Wolf, you've been teasing me. You've known all along about white ways, haven't you?"

"It is fun to tease."

"I'm surprised your wife didn't set you to rights about that hauling and toting business."

"That was not Sweet Spirit's way."

Sweet Spirit. Gads. It was just Kathy Ann's luck to get captured by a guy who'd been married to some sort of saint. "Wolf . . . what would you do if I was naughty?"

"You will not be naughty. I will make you happy. I have need of you, pretty white eyes."

He needed her. Good. She wouldn't mind hauling his junk all over Texas. "Tell me something. Those wigwams of yours, they don't have closets, do they?"

"What is a closet?"

She smiled.

By now they had reached his village, peopled by about fifty men, women, and children. While the women offered to beat Kathy Ann for him, Stalking Wolf declined their invitation. He didn't protest when they tied her to a tree, though. Neither did Kathy Ann, since she was out in the open.

She rather liked the idea that he would go to lengths to make certain she didn't leave. He was quite a man, that Stalking Wolf. Everything would be great, if only his cohorts wouldn't make some sort of cat-eye soup out of Electra.

Skylla and Braxton sat on the ground, facing the ashes of a campfire and opposite the young Comanche chief. With a dozen armed braves flanking Stalking Wolf, Skylla shivered, both fascinated and repulsed. Even though Braxton had sworn these were orderly people who wouldn't make war without provocation—Skylla cast a glance at her trussed sister, who hadn't provoked an abduction—this was a savage place.

Half-dressed natives with feathers stuck in their long black-as-a-pit hair. Spears, arrows, rifles. Dead animals in various stages of evisceration. Women dismantled tepees while doing the gutting, the cooking, and keeping an eye on the children. A young brave, scars where his eyes had been, beat a strange tune on a drum made of leather. As well, Skylla noticed a particular piglet, no doubt the one stolen in July.

Braxton and Stalking Wolf spoke in the Indians' tongue and shared the smoke from a long clay pipe. He seemed right at home, her husband. Wasn't that natural? He'd lived among the heathen and had married one. His mastery of the Indian culture gave Skylla a dash of confidence that all would be well.

Still, despite her confidence in Braxton, it was unsettling to be here. Antebellum Biloxi, this was not. Biloxi. Her skin crawled. If she lived to be a hundred, she'd never forget the night vigilantes—many a "friend" of long standing—hanged her father. What was more savage?

Braxton held the pipe aloft to study the smoke that rose toward the heavens. A devilish smile eased across the angles of his face as he eyed his wife. "You must feel left out, since we haven't passed the pipe. We can't share such a *tasty* smoke. Tribal customs, you see. Ladies don't smoke peace pipes."

"Women aren't allowed a voice in peace? We're only meant to keep it. How very modern," she added dryly. "How very civilized."

"Would you mind if we speak English?" Braxton asked the warrior chieftain. "My wife feels left out."

"You respect your woman's wisdom and counsel? That is good for a white man. I didn't know such was done in your society." Stalking Wolf nodded at Skylla. "Comanche men know the Great Spirit makes women wise and clever."

Braxton took another drag from the pipe. "This I know. I learned your customs when I lived among your brothers in the direction of the rising sun. I am Yellow Hair of Good Medicine of the band of the great chief, Night Fire."

"Ah." Stalking Wolf smiled, showing strong straight teeth. "Night Fire's drums told of a white man. A holy man. That was many moons in the past. Night Fire went to the happy hunting ground two winters ago."

Holy man?

A tiny Indian girl with hazel eyes wandered over to stand by the chief, but a gray-haired woman took the girl's hand to lead her away before Skylla could hold her arms out to the tyke.

"My first daughter, Eyes Like A Leaf," Stalking Wolf said. "Do you have papooses, lady?"

Skylla shook her head. "No, sir, we don't. We were married just last night."

He nodded and tapped more tobacco into the pipe. "Last night. You may have a papoose on the way."

While Skylla blushed, Braxton looked as if he'd swallowed a frog. It hurt her that he had been reminded of his sterility.

He said, "We have a gift for the children."

"Cake." Skylla lifted the rectangular tin.

Stalking Wolf smiled. "They will like it."

"I want some, too!" Kathy Ann shouted.

Skylla expected to hand the treat out, but a wizened woman took over the task. It would have been nice, getting close to the children. And to Kathy Ann. Skylla wished for a private word with her sister. All she could do was smile in Kathy Ann's direction and pray the girl was okay.

The children were now gathered around the older woman, who must have understood Kathy Ann, for she fed the captive a slice of cake. Conversation between the men turned to great buffalo hunts of yesteryears, then they lamented the dwindling herd. Next, they discussed the lack of rain and a goodly many other lackings. Truth be known, Skylla had grown restless with small talk. She wanted to poke Braxton in the ribs and say, Hurry, please. I want my sister out of here.

It seemed forever before Braxton said, "Stalking Wolf, you have my roan."

"I do."

"I want him back."

"That I cannot do." Stalking Wolf planted a hand on his knee, leaning forward. "The white man called St. Clair stole horses from my people. I saw that the debt was repaid."

Braxton mumbled something under his breath. He then took another drag from the pipe. The smoke curled skyward. "I wonder . . . did you know the Army has returned to this area? And the law has been installed, as well. Is this why you are breaking camp?"

From the look on the chief's face, Stalking Wolf hadn't known.

"It's my guess then," Braxton said, sending his wife into a cold chill, "you intend to keep the blonde."

"That is my plan."

"This woman you hold is the sister of my wife. We are here to take her home."

The Indian shrugged a shoulder. "Sun In Her Hair pleases this chief of the Comanche people. I will provide her home."

Braxton handed the pipe to the chief. "She needs to finish her education."

"I will teach her what is important."

Skylla spoke. "Sir, she isn't of marriageable age."

Stalking Wolf glanced at Kathy Ann, who watched with mute interest. Swiveling his eyes to Skylla, he asked, "How many summers is she?"

"Fifteen."

"That is old enough." The Indian took some sort of amulet from around his neck; it looked like a long fang. "She will be my only wife. You may take this in payment for her."

"A charm for a healthy girl such as the sister of my wife? You place her value too low. And you insult her family."

Stalking Wolf stood and took three steps away from the dormant campfire, then retraced his path. "I will give you the roan. I will give you a buffalo hide for your marriage pallet. I will promise not to raid the land you call the Nickel Dime."

"That is a generous offer. But we cannot accept."

"What do you want for her?"

"We won't barter for her."

As if he hadn't heard, the chief repeated, "What do you want for her? I am willing to give whatever you ask."

"Kathy Ann is not for sale or trade."

The Indian's eyes turned hard.

"On the other hand," Braxton said evenly, "my wife and I offer you many riches for the white girl's release."

He reached into his pocket, throwing a handful of golden coins and brilliant blue topaz stones on the ground in front Stalking Wolf. Skylla gawked at the bonanza, then gave a mental, "Oh, no." They had abandoned the treasure chest in the open light of the dining room! Would they return home to nothing?

Braxton straightened, drawing her attention. "I won't ask for our horse. And I will give you a barrel of firewater."

"Firewater?" echoed the braves, all understanding this white man's word. They took an eager step toward the offerer.

"No!"

Everyone went still at the chief's shout. He bent to slash the heel of his hand along the ground and send the riches flying. His face hard as granite, he looked up and said through gritted teeth, "I will have Sun in Her Hair."

His braves moved forward, their weapons pointed and their faces tight with menace and enmity. A frisson of fear went up Skylla's spine. Braxton had been wrong—very wrong! He didn't know the best ways to negotiate with this savage beast. No white person would leave here today. Not alive.

Chapter Eighteen

Skylla steeled herself for imminent death.

The braves, their spears pointed, shouted a war cry and lunged for her and Braxton. A certain tranquillity came over her, as if God were cushioning the blow. She had one terrible thought, and it had nothing to do with a fortune possibly lost. She'd never told Braxton she loved him.

He, meanwhile, had hurtled to his feet. Ready to take a spear for his wife, he jumped in front of her. In a voice that rumbled through the Indian village this autumn afternoon, he shouted something in the Comanche tongue.

The warriors froze, then raised their war lances. They backed away, wary, and glanced at one another. Their chief folded his arms over his broad, bronzed chest.

"You cannot do that." Stalking Wolf glared at Braxton. "You cannot bring the dead back to life."

"If Yellow Hair of Good Medicine can perform this miracle, shouldn't an honorable chief of the Comanche people be honored to free the miracle maker?" Braxton's arms were set akimbo. "Surely he would allow that miracle maker to take what he requires from this village, including his women."

Stalking Wolf met all this with a scowl.

Braxton continued. "Surely that great and noble chief would keep his distance from the miracle maker, his land, and his possessions. And he would not seek repayment for any more debts made by Titus St. Clair." Receiving nothing in reply, he added, "Naturally, the miracle maker feels obliged to gift the great chief with wampum."

"Wampum?"

"The miracle maker would leave the blue stones and the gold stones, plus the fine horse. And he would be pleased for the chief to help himself to cattle within the boundaries of the white man's ranch. He could have as many head as needed to feed the women and children of this village for their journey deep into the Comancheria." Braxton looked his adversary in the eye. "Does this sound fair to Stalking Wolf of the Comanche?"

"What about the firewater?"

"That, too."

Studying the ground, then the sky above, the Indian pondered the offer. At last, he answered, "If Yellow Hair of Good Medicine cannot bring the dead back to life . . ." He made a slashing motion across Braxton's forehead. "His scalp will decorate the flap pole of my tepee."

"Fair enough."

A gush of exasperation rushed from Skylla's throat. *Heaven help us, Braxton. Whatever is wrong with you that you would make such an outrageous claim?*

"With one condition," Brax added. "If Yellow Hair of Good Medicine fails, his women will have the freedom to leave this village and return to their home."

Her heart skipping, Skylla listened to her husband barter. Her gaze swept to her sister, still trussed to a tree. The girl's mouth had dropped; she didn't move a muscle. Skylla's gaze shifted back to Braxton. He had wagered his very life—to save the St. Clair sisters. He would have taken spears meant for his wife. Skylla loved him all the more for his selflessness.

"I will need a volunteer." Braxton repeated those words, this time in the language of the Comanche.

All the Indians retreated, except for their chief.

"Your woman will be the volunteer," said he.

Without missing a beat, Braxton replied, "Unacceptable. If my medicine goes bad, I will not have my woman suffer for it."

The green-eyed tyke tiptoed forward. She held Electra at her side, at an uncomfortable-appearing angle. The calico, for some odd reason, didn't protest being held thusly.

Braxton smiled. "I will kill the cat, then bring her back to life."

"You will not!" screamed Kathy Ann.

"Quiet!" Stalking Wolf turned to the blonde. "This is a pow-wow, not a time for womanly advice."

Skylla didn't have a taste for cruelty to animals, but when it came down to a choice between a human's life and a feline's, there was no question in her mind. Let Braxton perform his wild stunt on Electra. Poor Electra.

"If my lady would hold on to the cat . . . ?" Braxton lifted a sandy-gold brow.

Somehow Skylla was able to nod in agreement. He took the cat from the little girl, leaned over to whisper something that sent her scurrying into the tepee she'd unlaced to fetch the cat, then handed Electra into Skylla's shaking arms.

He turned and sauntered over to Impossible, began to search through his saddlebags.

Not a woman to kiss cats, Skylla nevertheless held Electra close and pressed a hard kiss to the top of her flat, furred head. The cat lay purring. A lamb in calico coat, she looked up with trust complete and replete.

Traitor to that faith, Skylla started to pray for a good end to this ploy, but stopped. She couldn't ask Him for another favor. During the coin toss, she'd promised Him she wouldn't.

"Sit down, please, lady of mine." Braxton patted Skylla's shoulder. "Hold Electra on your lap."

She sat. She held fast. But when she got a look at what he held in his hand, she had to swallow her smile of relief. Braxton, infinitely resourceful, gripped a cotton-stuffed cone with a hole at the top, a short glass tube fitted with a pliant bulb, and a bottle of what she knew to be ether.

"Hold her steady," he ordered Skylla.

He took the stopper from the ether and drew liquid into the bulb. While holding his breath, he settled the cone over Electra's muzzle, dripped a small amount of the anesthetic into the cone, then rushed to push the cork back in the bottle.

The smell of ether swirled. Skylla, too, held her breath. Electra squealed, yowled and fought, then went limp.

In the blink of an eye, Braxton shoved the large end of the cone into the dirt. "She is dead," he announced.

Kathy Ann cried out.

Subsequently, all eyes moved to the inert cat in Skylla's arms. Electra's mouth lay slightly open; her beautiful tricolored coat was now clumped and ugly, her limbs slack and her eyes glassy. Still and all, Skylla sensed a slight breath in Electra, an ever so slight sign of life. She glanced up to see if the Indian chief noticed. He hadn't.

Stalking Wolf was walking over to the sobbing Kathy Ann. He touched her cheek and said something that calmed her.

When he returned to the spent campfire, he directed an order to Braxton. "Bring the cat back to life. It troubles Sun In Her Hair to see the carcass."

"The cat must stay dead for some time."

"Stalking Wolf says bring the cat back." He reached for a knife sheathed in the waist of his breechclout. "Now!"

"If the spell is interrupted," Braxton replied calmly, "bad medicine will hail upon the peaceable Comanches."

Stalking Wolf bent a skeptical eye on him.

"You must have patience, great chief."

The minutes turned to an hour. An hour turned to two, then three, then four. The sun settled in the western horizon.

Skylla's arm had gone to sleep from holding the cat. The blind drummer began to beat the drum with bone drumsticks and to sing a mournful song. A restlessness pulsed through the village.

A lovely young woman stepped between Skylla and Braxton, offering Skylla a drink from a gourd of water. Nothing had tasted better on her parched tongue. "Thank you," she said.

"You are welcome." The Indian woman ducked her chin.

"You speak English?"

"A little." Sloe eyes looked up at Skylla. "I am called Pearl of the Concho. What are you called?"

Skylla answered, then asked where Pearl of the Concho had learned to speak English. "From the first wife of Stalking Wolf. Sweet Spirit came from a land called Eng-land. We cry for the loss of Sweet Spirit. We pray for a new wife to bring the sunshine back into our chief's eyes."

Skylla studied the man. There was nothing dull in his eyes, especially when he turned them to Kathy Ann.

Stalking Wolf then gave a terse order that sent Pearl of the Concho rushing away. Skylla was sorry to see her go. She would have liked to ask many questions about these strange people known as the Comanche.

"You want? You want?"

Skylla turned her face to an aged woman holding a pot of some sort of stew.

"You want?" The Indian held the iron pot up. It was not unlike the one stolen from the ranch in March. "You want?"

Shaking her head, Skylla watched the frail woman moved to Braxton and make the same offer. Like the Indians, he tucked into a gourd filled with stew.

By the time the moon was high in the sky, the almost imperceptible movement of Electra's chest under Skylla's fingers began to still. Skylla telegraphed a silent and frantic question to her husband: *Did you give her too much? Have you killed her!*

Stalking Wolf ran out of patience. "You lie, Yellow Hair of Good Medicine. You lie!" He shook his finger. Gesturing with his head, he called his braves forward. He spoke quickly, in words that had to mean, "Tie up the charlatan!"

Fear got the better of Skylla. She did something she'd promised not to do. She asked the Lord above to grant one more favor. *Help us!*

Braves grabbed Braxton's arms, pinning him to the ground, while another hit him twice on the shoulder with a primitive club. Also restrained, Skylla dropped the cat—and wailed for her husband's life.

Then it happened.

Electra reared her head. She got to unsteady paws, moving drunkenly, before stopping at Stalking Wolf's moccasins to retch and vomit.

Stalking Wolf barked orders to his braves.

They let go their holds on Braxton and Skylla.

A great shout went through the Indian village. The blind brave beat the drum faster. The women began to dance, sing, and shake rattles decorated with feathers and beads. Before it was over, the villagers prostrated themselves at the mighty Yellow Hair of Good Medicine's feet.

Yellow Hair of Good Medicine had been sent by the Great Spirit was the general consensus. A holy man.

Home. It had never been sweeter, given their brush with death. And given that Braxton had eased Skylla's mind on the treasure issue by saying he'd hidden it.

Kathy Ann, though, didn't celebrate their return. The moment they arrived, she headed for her upstairs room, sullen at being rescued. The girl just didn't know what was good for her. On the parlor's settee, Skylla took comfort in the warmth of her husband's arms.

"She can't be serious." Skylla snaked a hand around to his muscular back. "How could she wish to stay with such savages?"

"It's not the worst life in the world. It has an elemental

order to it that can bring a certain peace to a troubled individual."

Skylla sensed that he referred to his own years with the heathen. Curiosity about her husband crowded to the forefront of her thoughts, but she did not wish to wait any longer to tell him of her feelings.

"You were wonderful out there." She lifted her eyes to his. "I love you, holy man."

"Say it again." He waited with bated breath.

"Holy man," she teased.

"Not that. The other."

"I love you!"

His eyes now glowing in the reflected lamplight, he smiled. "I love you, too. With all my heart, Skylla Hale."

Those wonderful words caressed her heart. She wanted him to be as content. She wanted and needed to understand everything about him. "Braxton . . . I know you don't like Texas much, but please know I'll do everything in my power to make you happy."

"I am happy." He touched his forehead to hers. "What pleases you, pleases me. You love this place, so I'll learn to love it. Which calls to mind priorities. Getting those cows to the Army. I'd best ride out to the canyon. The boys will be wondering what happened to us. Furthermore, I've got to get to Camp Llano on the double, else Major Albright and his Blue Bellies will be charging the Comanches."

"Braxton, it's midnight. You mustn't do anything until you've rested. You need it, with that shoulder."

He chuckled. "I'm bruised, wife, not broken. I fought four years in a war. That was worse than a mere clubbing."

"You win. Take off." Not before they could spend a few minutes in the bedroom, she hoped. "Husband, where do we start spending our money?"

"On food and horseflesh. Then we've got to deposit the rest in a bank. They have some good ones in San Antonio."

"In the meantime, why don't I call on the county clerk?"

"We do need to know where we stand on the land issue."

It was then that Skylla noticed the handkerchief Claudine has discarded after her tears of the morning. "Braxton, there's something else. I know you and Claudine have been at odds. What can we do to make her happy?"

"Set her up in an establishment somewhere else."

Stunned that he would send Ambrose St. Clair's widow away, Skylla inched away from the warmth of his arms. "This is her home. I owe her a home, and if you think I'll turn her out, you are mistaken."

"Turning her out and setting her up are two different things altogether."

"You sound as if you had this planned out for a while." Skylla swallowed. "Would I be wrong to say you had California planned in advance, too?"

"Not on your life," he answered smoothly.

Should she believe him? She must! To continue doubting his purposes would play havoc in their marriage, and why start out with conflict between them? Still, while she wished to settle the matter of Claudine, Skylla needed to settle her curiosity. "What made you think of California in the first place?"

"A fellow I served with in the Confederate Army had done some prospecting out there, ended up in San Francisco. It always sounded like a good place to make a fresh start."

If the far West was so appealing, why did the man return to the South in the first place? Skylla wouldn't ask. Some nebulous soldier wasn't the problem here. "Braxton, in the beginning, you told me not to press you about your past. But as your wife, I'd like to know more about you."

He left the settee, going over to the liquor bottle Claudine kept handy. "Look, it's after midnight. I need to hit the trail. It'll take me a good while to get to Camp Llano, especially since I've got to stop by Safe Haven Canyon."

As he downed a shot of whiskey, Skylla said, "If you must go, fine. I understand. But I'd like to know one thing. Uncle said you first came to Texas to look for your father. Do you have some reason to believe he's in California?"

"No."

"Did you ever find him?"

"No."

"That bothers you, doesn't it?"

"Yeah, it bothers me." Braxton crossed to the hearth, placing his hand on the mantel and staring into the fireplace that held no flames. "I guess it isn't in the cards for me to find out why my father damned his family to hell."

Damned his family to hell? How could any father and husband do such a thing? She went to Braxton, placing her hand on his shoulder. "Now that we have money, why don't we hire a detective to find him?"

"I know where he is. Or was. I got a clue from a Yankee soldier, the one who took charge of my weapons at Appomattox. 'I know a Hale from Mississippi,' he told me. 'A sawbones. He's with our Medical Corps, down in the Dry Tortugas.' A strange coincidence, but it didn't take much to deduce Dr. John Hale, late of Natchez, was one and the same with the Unionist doctor."

The rank hurt in her husband's admission tore at her. "How frustrated you must feel, knowing where to find him, but not being able to do it."

"There was always something to hold me back. Raising the younger Hales, at first. Then being held in captivity by the Indians. Then my marriage to Song of the Mockingbird. After she died, I thought I could make my search, but my mother needed money. So I took a job with Titus and sent my salary home. You probably know all this."

"Uncle did mention your search." The pitched battles from 1861 to 1865 had deterred him, she knew. "Why didn't you go after John Hale, once the war was over?"

"Hell, Skylla, I was in shreds. General Lee's defeat, you know. And I had to get back to Vicksburg. Geoff's mother was there. We needed to make certain Bella was okay, which she was. By then I'd decided to hell with John Hale." His smile didn't reach his eyes. "I'd decided I needed me a wife."

"That you have." Her hand moved to his chest. "I pray your heart will heal, now that you have a home and family."

"We're a family all right. But we've got a troublemaker in our midst. Claudine."

"Braxton, we're her family. Can you accept her as such?"

He took a long time answering. "She can stay. As long as she doesn't cause trouble."

Claudine should have been content. In the hour before dawn, she eyed the handsome Yankee who snored softly in her arms. They rested on a pallet in the log cabin that was quarters for Major Webb Albright. While Webb knew how to make love to a woman, this particular one wanted more than that satisfaction.

She hoped the Indians hadn't raised Brax's scalp. She wanted the pleasure of doing it.

Recalling those red demons, she shivered despite the warmth of her lover. It was good that she'd shown concern over Kathy Ann, but what about Skylla?

Claudine would have gladly choked her stepdaughter for demanding to go into the Comancheria. If something happened to Skylla, where would that leave Claudine? Once more, she'd know profound loss. And once more her future would be shaky. A lifetime interest in the Nickel Dime wouldn't mean much, should Skylla go to a grave, especially with a surviving widower.

She yearned for word to reach Camp Llano before the major and his men were forced to fight the Indians. If anything happened to Webb Albright—well, it just couldn't. Her eyes settled on him. He'd be her salvation. Salvation in marriage would give Claudine a firm foundation to stand on as she made trouble for Brax Hale.

Chapter Nineteen

It was just one thing after another keeping Skylla from town. First, Claudine returned home, flushed with romantic interest and filled with plans to marry a stranger! Skylla tried to reason with her, tried to make her understand there was no need to rush into anything. By late afternoon—too late to call on the new county clerk—she even confessed that luck had come their way.

"We'll have everything we need," Skylla said brightly. "We'll never wish for a thing. You can take all the time in the world to find a proper husband."

"Webb Albright is proper enough. And at least he's marrying me for myself instead of a ranch and resulting dowry."

"I got my man by a coin toss. Fair and square."

"That's not what Charlie says."

Skylla wondered what Charlie would say now, once he'd found out Claudine's head was turned by another man. The bedraggled cowhand had been encouraged by her, and encouraged plenty. And who could guess how he would react to losing out?

"Brax used a trick coin," Claudine elaborated on her theme. "The whole toss was a setup."

"Which only proves the lengths my husband would go to to win my hand."

"Which only proves he wanted the ranch enough to cheat for it. If you're smart, you'll watch your purse, or he's liable to start picking it."

The nastiest thought popped into Skylla's mind. Braxton *had* helped himself to the stash, though Skylla couldn't fault the result.

"Daisy, a decent fellow would've at least brought you a box of chocolates when he showed up to marry your ranch. Brax didn't even give you that cameo."

Why ask how she knew about it? Charlie Main had been talking. But that was beside the point. Why *hadn't* Braxton given her the cameo? What was he saving it for? Skylla hated all the questions that chipped at her trust.

"If he didn't give you the brooch, what could have happened to it, hmm?"

"Maybe he sold it to put food in your mouth."

"You'd like to think so," Claudine came back. "Well, I have no choice but to make certain my interests are seen to." She poured a snifter of whiskey, then sipped it. "When do you plan to file the deed of trust in my favor?"

"For heaven's sake, Claudi, I must deal with the Reconstructionists about the ranch before I file the life-estate papers."

"What if those papers are null and void, since we didn't have a government at the time you signed them?"

"Will you settle for money?"

"You insult me by asking to buy me off. I suppose that was Brax's idea. He's ensconced in your bedroom, and I'm to be parceled off with a fistful of coins."

Skylla studied the floor, recalling his suggestion and realizing home life would be easier were Claudine to go away. *Have you no shame?*

"Daisy, I'm entitled to part of this property and its resultant profits from here on out. I did—need I remind you?—force myself into sin with Winslow Packard for your benefit."

"Is this the way it's going to be?" Skylla asked, falling victim to a headache. "Every time a disagreement arises, you'll throw that up to me?"

Contrite, Claudine set the snifter down to glide over and take Skylla's hand. "Forgive me. I don't want to hurt you."

"And I don't want you hurt. Please don't rush into marriage. We have so many things to settle. Once they are done, then you can make a decision."

"If you wish, I'll wait."

The women had made a stab at peace, yet Skylla's headache didn't go away. The pain should have passed by the next morning. It didn't. In fact, it got worse, thanks to Claudine's driving away under the auspices of returning Luke Burrows's buckboard. Skylla sensed that wasn't her only task. Would she elope with the Yankee major?

The best thing to do, Skylla decided, was to get legal matters in order. Once the deed of trust had been filed, then she would have ammunition to keep Claudine from making a mistake. She began her search, paying little mind to outdoor sounds, although she did hear Kathy Ann's laughter a couple of times.

Skylla threw off the bedclothes to shove her hand between the mattress and ropes. Nothing. She lifted the mattress, taking a quick look. Again, nothing. The document wasn't in its hiding place. There was nothing save dust and lots of it.

What could have happened to the deed of trust?

Dressed for her trip to the courthouse, Skylla stopped short. Clothes littered the parlor, Kathy Ann's clothes. The girl preened in the remnants, twirling around barefoot. Agog, Skylla stared at her sister, who wore a buckskin dress, large in size and decorated with paint along with bright blue stones.

"Isn't it lovely?" Kathy Ann gushed. "It's a gift from Stalking Wolf. His braves delivered it a few minutes ago. Oh, by the way, he's not moving his village just yet. At least that's what I gathered from Head Too Big. He and another brave took the firewater Sergeant promised them."

Skylla was in no mood for chitchat. "Take that dress off. I won't allow you to accept gifts from an Indian."

"I'm not taking it off. I'm keeping it." Her hands smoothed down the soft leather. "Unless . . . unless Sergeant says I oughtn't to."

All Skylla could do was try to reason. "Lovey, that Indian will think you're interested in becoming his wife."

"I am interested."

Land's sake! Whatever was Skylla to do? Now she had two relatives with marriage in mind. "You can forget it."

Pudgy fingers fondled the dress's ornaments. "If you're talking about these blue rocks, you needn't worry. They aren't real topaz. They're some of those fakes ones Sergeant had in his saddlebag a while back."

"Excuse me?"

"He and Geoff had a bunch of colored glass when they first got here."

Skylla couldn't imagine what they had had in mind, but she intended to question her husband about it, once he returned from delivering cattle to Camp Llano.

At the same moment she had this thought, she heard a noise from outside. She collected Kathy Ann's pistol and went to the bedroom window, disturbing Electra on the sill and drawing back the curtain to see a pair of men tying fine-looking mares to the hitching post. One man wore a Rebel kepi over regular clothes, the other the faded uniform of the Confederacy.

Skylla opened the window. "State your business, men."

They raised their hands to show they weren't armed. The taller of the two, a fellow with dark hair and blue eyes, ambled toward her. "Would you be Major St. Clair's niece?"

"I am. I'm Mrs. Braxton Hale."

"Brax Hale! I'll be dipped in snuff. Congratulations!"

"Who are you?"

"I be Luckless Litton, ma'am." He pointed to the other man. "That be Snuffy Johnson."

As soon as she heard the names, she recognized them, and laid the pistol on the windowsill.

"We used to cowboy here at the Nickel Dime," said Snuffy, a slim fellow with a head of riotous carrot-colored curls.

Two of Uncle's ranch hands had returned. Thank goodness.

She waved them indoors, smiling and teasing. "What took you so long?"

Immediately, Uncle's returned cowboys set to work to complete the fence at Safe Haven Canyon. Working men needed substantial food, and Skylla had to find the new county clerk.

She borrowed Luckless's fine mare and rode into the county seat, Mason town, where she asked after that official, but was told Mr. Packard had business in Ecru.

Mr. Packard?

She shuddered, hearing the name. Surely not Winslow Packard. The boardinghouse lady didn't know his given name, so Skylla tucked her fears away and backtracked to Ecru.

She reached a near-to-deserted town, this not being the usual marketing day of Saturday. No one had seen the new county clerk. Darn. She'd so hoped to get his advice.

At least she could buy a few groceries. Herr Kreitz was the only person in his store when Skylla walked in.

"This is a nice surprise, Mrs. Hale." Wiping his hands on an apron, the Prussian stepped from behind the counter that was sparsely stocked, thanks to the hard times after the war. "How can I help you?"

"I have a long list," she said proudly, thankful she had plenty of money, for once.

The good-natured grocer couldn't provide everything, but he had several key items. Before long, she was enjoying, compliments of Herr Kreitz, a huge and briny pickle from the barrel in the middle of the rectangular store.

"Please fish me out a dozen of these," she said. "We have new men at the Nickel Dime, and they'll be looking for a nice dinner in a few hours. Actually, they aren't altogether new. They used to work for my uncle. Do you remember Snuffy Johnson and Luckless Litton?"

"*Ja,* I remember." The proprietor smiled. "They are good men. You and your husband will not regret their return." The last of the requested pickles packed in a large jar, he walked to a line of sausages strung behind the counter. "The boys, I recall, liked this kind of sausage." He took down a half-dozen strings. "Would you prepare them for your supper? And tell them Emil Kreitz sent the sausages as a welcome home gift?"

"How very kind. Thank you. I'm sure Mr. Johnson and Mr. Litton will enjoy them immensely."

"They are for everyone at the Nickel Dime." The grocer had pickled eggs and red cabbage on hand, which he suggested would go well with the sausage.

"How about fruit?" she asked. "I think a nice pie would be in order."

"*Nein,* no fruit." He shook his head. "A lady in Fredericksburg will send canned peaches. Next week."

A while back Luke Burrows's wife had mentioned vinegar pie being delicious—a Texas staple—so Skylla purchased a small jug of vinegar, then asked the grocer to total her bill.

She laid the money on the counter, and said, "Have you met the new county clerk? I heard he was here in Ecru today."

"I have met him." The Prussian's square face twisted. He motioned toward the street. "The jackal is out there."

"Thank you."

She picked up her marketing bag, made for the boardwalk, and came up against the stare of a silver-haired portly man wearing a fine suit of clothes. Winslow Packard.

"Fancy meeting you here, Miss St. Clair," he said as her bag slid to the boards. "But then, I did have the advantage of knowing your destination." He picked up the fallen goods, holding them. "Where is Mrs. St. Clair?"

It would have been easy to despise Winslow Packard, for great shame is known to rouse such animosity. Yet Skylla found her feelings at cross purposes. Packard was the evidence of the means for the trip from Vicksburg. If not for him, though, how would she and her kin have gotten to Texas?

"Might we sit down?" she said. "I find my leg is sore." A couple of chairs were lined against the storefront. Gathering her groceries, she limped to one, seating herself. "I never expected to see you again," she declared, an understatement.

Packard pulled a chair out so he could look straight at her. Seated, he dropped his laced fingers between his spread legs and raised his gray eyes. "I always expected to see the St. Clairs again. I used my clout to garner the clerkship of this county. My intentions are to marry your lovely stepmother."

Great Scott!

Two suitors in a row for Claudine.

Where had all these men been a few weeks ago?

You can't be serious. Claudine would no more marry you than she would Charlie Main.

Skylla spoke up. "I'm afraid you're too late, Mr. Packard. Mrs. St. Clair is engaged to a cavalryman."

Packard's face clouded.

Which caused Skylla to groan inwardly. Just what she needed, to alienate the official. Marshaling courage, she elevated her chin. "I've been meaning to speak to you, Mr. Packard. There are rumors hereabouts. Rumors that you will invalidate land titles held by former Rebels."

"The issue hasn't been decided," he answered tersely, rising to his feet. "If Mrs. St. Clair would like to discuss the matter, have her meet me at my office. Or better yet, my boarding-house quarters."

The innuendo wasn't lost on Skylla. She wouldn't allow his blackmail to break her spirit. "The issue isn't for Mrs. St. Clair to discuss. I own the Nickel Dime Ranch. That is, it belongs to me and my husband. We are ready and willing to pay our taxes. Mr. Hale and I will call on you at your office, unless you're willing to discuss official business *now.*"

Herr Kreitz had been right in calling Packard a jackal, for a feral meanness shot into the man's eyes. "You weren't so prissy when you were begging to get out of Vicksburg."

"You weren't too good to take my stepmother up on her offer, either. I should imagine one night with Claudine St. Clair more than covers our debt."

"One night?" He sneered. "Do you honestly think I'd compromise a United States naval vessel for *one night* with any woman? I wonder how Mrs. St. Clair's fiancé would feel, should I mention that she'd been crawling into my bed for two weeks?"

"That is an ugly accusation, Mr. Packard."

Skylla didn't look back as she limped to her borrowed mount. She had just gotten into the saddle when Packard took hold of the pommel, and said, "I make no accusations, Mrs. Hale—or whatever you're calling yourself. I speak the truth. Claudine St. Clair was my lover. And if you're wanting to keep that ranch of yours in the family, she will be again."

It was true. It was all true. When Claudine got back to the Nickel Dime that night, she admitted that she'd been sleeping with Winslow Packard.

"That means you chose to play on my guilt, to make me beholden to you."

"Don't be silly, Daisy." Claudine fluttered a hand. "I did what I had to do. Surely you can't fault me for that."

"I most certainly can."

Their friendship, their familial and business ties—the invisible cord that had tied them together—came loose. "You blackmailed me," Skylla accused, her heart breaking. "Time and again, you blackmailed me."

Blue eyes turned to steel. "So what if I did? I had to look out for myself. If your father hadn't been a slave-monger, we wouldn't have been in a fix to start with! But no! Ambrose had to get himself lynched for taking in a stupid runaway slave—which lost us everything!"

"You would even insult my father and his values. You have already insulted your adopted daughter. You have insulted me, my husband. And now you expect my sympathy." Skylla rushed as fast as her uneven legs would permit to the door. She opened it, flourishing a hand toward the road. "Get out, Claudine. Get out now."

Claudine lifted her nose imperially. "I'll be glad to. I've had enough of watching you lurch around. And I certainly don't want to see that roué of yours cheat you out of everything you own."

Sweeping to the door, the redhead fired a parting shot. "I don't need you. I have Webb Albright. And a cameo that—"

Skylla slammed the door on her and her words. If she never heard of that cameo again, it would be just fine. Yet she had a sneaking suspicion she had not seen the last of Claudine St. Clair.

Chapter Twenty

Although she didn't regret her parting words to the hateful and malicious Claudine, it didn't take Skylla long to have a change of heart. Just because they didn't see eye to eye about Braxton didn't mean a St. Clair should be turned out in anger. Without a dime. With this in mind, and praying the subject of Stalking Wolf wouldn't come up, Skylla went to her sister. "Kathy Ann, I need your help."

The word "help" captured the sulking girl's attention. "What do you want me to do?"

She told her to borrow Mr. Burrows's buckboard, then carry money to Claudine at Camp Llano. Kathy Ann set off on her errand, and Skylla busied herself while waiting for her husband's return. The hours ticked by. Then the girl returned home, saying, "She did it. She's married. She took the money, anyhow."

"Is she . . . ? Did she say anything about me?"

"Said she was sorry y'all had a fight."

Skylla dried the last of the supper pans, then put it away. "I'll give her time to cool down before I pay her a call."

After sucking a pickle, Kathy Ann asked, "What are you gonna say to Charlie about her getting married?"

"Why say anything to him?"

"Because they've been meeting in the barn. They even met on your wedding night. In Mr. Burrows's chicken coop."

"Have you been spying on her?"

"Nope. Those chickens were making such a racket, I couldn't sleep. It's a good thing the Burrowses are old, else they would have heard the commotion."

Could it be true about Claudine and the scruffy cowboy? Skylla had suspected as much, but the confirmation made her feel all the worse. She had had everything, while Claudi had been desperate.

Skylla needed time to deal with the problem.

It took three days to move cattle between the northern border of the ranch and Camp Llano. While the roan and the skewbald mare had made the work easier, Charlie's mule, Patsy Sue, had bitched and complained about pulling the wagon of whiskey. Now that the men of the Nickel Dime were headed home—this afternoon of the fourth day—Braxton took pride in their accomplishment.

Furthermore, he had plans. Webb Albright had put a bug in his ear about money-making. It wasn't a bad idea.

Charlie Main doffed his sombrero to wipe his brow with a shirtsleeve. From the driver's seat of the empty cart that had hauled whiskey to the army, he announced, "I'm plumb wore out."

"Say it again, partner." Geoff nodded. "Dis ole boy, he could use a few minutes of dat ole shut-eye."

Both men had their eyes on the grassy banks of Topaz Creek. It did look inviting. Tired, sweaty, horny for his wife, and favoring his bruised shoulder, Brax saw no reason not to rest up a bit. He cottoned to the idea of not showing up at the ranch too tired to hold his own . . . or Skylla.

Besides, he needed to talk something over with Geoff.

The men climbed from their perches, each lending a hand to unhitch the cart. They watered the animals, then hobbled them in the grass. Patsy Sue joined the equines to munch hungrily.

"I shore could use a shot of that hooch we left them Blue Bellies."

"Have some water, Main," Brax said. "You never know. It might do you some good."

"Water? That stuff'll rust my pipes." Charlie Main guffawed at his own joke, then yawned.

He hadn't been drinking much lately. Matter of fact, he looked and acted a lot healthier. It was love.

After washing his face with a bandanna, the cowpoke took a long drink from the creek, then stretched out on the ground. He had no more than dragged his sombrero over his eyes before loud snores sawed the air, disturbing a nest of sparrows in an oak tree nearby.

Geoff and Brax drank their share of water, then lay down a good fifty feet away from their partner. "What's the first thing you're going to buy with all that money?" Geoff asked out of the blue.

"Soon as I get to town, I'm buying a cameo for a pretty little dark-eyed gal answering to Mrs. Hale."

"I know. A farewell gift."

"There won't . . ." Brax knew Geoff had his heart set on California. How could he ease into his plan? "I'm buying a big ox and a bigger string of cutting horses."

"Cutting horses? What's the use of workhorses? We need a pair of good travelers to get us to California."

Brax listened to the gurgling creek. Coercing a yawn, he pulled his hat over his eyes. "Get some sleep, Geoffie."

That was not to be. Geoff said, "Miss Claudine sure made an impression on Major Albright."

Surprisingly, Charlie Main hadn't noticed all that billing and cooing. Any fool could tell he'd had been keeping himself clean for the redhead. Damn. No doubt that dumb old cowpoke would be getting the mitten instead of the hand.

Brax notched his hat up on his forehead. "With any luck that hussy will run off with Albright. Let's hope she makes a clean cut, for Main's sake."

"If you and I are heading out any day, now that you've got loot, why do you want Miss Skylla's stepmammy to leave her?"

"Uh, um." Brax ran a palm over his mouth. "I've been wanting to talk to you about California. I sent a letter to Bella by way of those cavalry soldiers who were headed west." There had been five of them at Camp Llano, preparing for the next leg of their long land journey. "They were happy to oblige."

"What did the letter say?" Geoff asked slowly.

"That I've changed my plans." Brax sat up to rub his shoulder. "I won't be seeing the inside of any San Francisco gambling hells."

"I suppose you've thought through what all that means, haven't you, Bubba? Could be you'll ranch 'til you die."

"We can get help for the hard work. If not, well, I've got a good feeling. Besides, I'd sure hate to miss the bluebonnets next spring."

"You were always more for the settled life than you made out."

Why argue? For once, Brax accepted the truth about himself.

"You seem pretty sure of your wife, Bubba. What're you going to say to Miss Skylla when she finds out you were planning to sell the ranch out from under her?"

Brax got sick to his stomach, just thinking about what all could happen should she find out her husband was no pillar of society, propriety, or fair play. *Be reasonable. Don't panic.* "How would she find out?"

"That Jane lady knows. You told her."

"Jane knows I was looking for a buyer, that's all. Anyhow, she won't say anything to make trouble. Jane's a good gal."

"Me," said Geoff, pointing at his chest, "I think you're putting too much faith in a lady you loved and left."

"Don't worry about Jane."

"Your wife is no dummy. I can't help but wonder what your

wife would say if she found out you made a deal with a whore—selling Miss Elizabeth's cameo—no more than a couple of days before your wedding day."

Damn, double damn! "Let me worry about my wife."

"Best of luck to you, then." Geoff pushed to stand, walked over to the creek, and scratched his head. Turning back toward Brax, he said, "What did you say about me to Bella?"

"That you might be coming out there to join her."

The youth crouched on his heels to snap a blade of grass at the root. "Are you wanting me to leave?"

"I'm not wanting to hold you back. You're a grown man now. Almost eighteen. It's time you made your own decisions."

Brax would never admit how much it hurt to give the boy his freedom to be a man. He glanced at Geoff, whose brow had furrowed. When Geoff got that look on his face, he so resembled Larkin Hale, Brax's dead brother, that it hurt.

"I wouldn't know what to do if we split up."

Uncomfortable, Brax squinted at the sky. A storm was brewing. "Geoffie, if you choose to leave, you'll have the money for a proper start."

"I have a choice?"

"You do."

"I suppose I can find some sort of job. I never was too keen on cheating folks."

"It's a sorry life, grifting around."

"I'd like to be respectable. That would make Miss Elizabeth proud. She always worried about me."

"Yeah, Mother would be proud, Geoffie. Real proud. She loved you like a son. I'd be proud, too."

Geoff smiled. "You know, I've been thinking. I'd like to get me a nice little wife."

"I saw a good-looking gal in Stalking Wolf's village. Pearl of the Concho is her name. Maybe you ought to find an excuse to trail Stalking Wolf. He'll let you bring her back, provided he knows Yellow Hair of Good Medicine said it must be."

"Think so?"

"I'd like to see you settled with a wife of your own."

"If I were white, I could have all kinds of choices."

"Won't do you any good, wishing for the impossible." Not for the first time, Brax thought about how accepting Skylla had been about Geoff's color.

"I'd like to court Miss Kathy Ann."

"I figured as much. I've seen you ogling Piglet. Has she given any indication she might be of a mind to accept you?"

"No. She treats me like dirt. Not black dirt, particularly. But dirt."

"She treats everyone like dirt," Brax answered with a chuckle. "Pretty much."

"Do you think I might have a chance?"

"Honestly, no." He had to give it to Geoff straight, though Brax hated to discourage the lad. "Her interest lies in Stalking Wolf, I'm afraid. On the way home the other night, while Skylla made a nature call, Kathy Ann let me know she wasn't too pleased about being rescued."

"Damn. Damn, Bubba, damn."

"I'm sure you voice her mother's and sister's sentiments—if Kathy Ann decides to go back to Stalking Wolf." Brax looked with concern at Geoff. "Are you in love with her?"

Geoff shook his head. "No. But I've had lots of fantasies about getting experience with a woman."

Nothing more was said for a good five minutes, then Geoff asked, "What in particular did she say that makes you think she'll run off to Stalking Wolf?"

"She asked me if I liked the taste of eyeball stew."

"What did you tell her?"

"I said the juice wasn't too bad. That if a body got hungry enough, anything would taste good. She, uh, she said they'd eaten anything that crawled. In Vicksburg."

Kathy Ann had started to explain the siege that ended on Independence Day, 1863. Brax had shut her up. He'd refused to hear it. Still hurting for his two sisters, for Larkin's widow, and for his young niece, he hadn't wanted a mental picture of their suffering.

"Kathy Ann said something interesting about Virgil Petry,"

he now commented to Geoff. "She told me why he put up the traveling money for the husband-wanted deal."

"Is that so?"

"There was a personal tie between Virgil and Claudine's bachelor uncle, which I knew all along. To put it mildly, those fellows had eyes for each other. It was all hush-hush."

"I always figured Massa Petry was sort of odd."

"I never told you what Virgil did to spring me, did I? Virgil said yes to the captain of guards. The Yankee had been after Virg's lard-ass for a while, but Virg didn't like his looks. He gave in to get his former lover's niece a husband. Me."

"But how did you get him interested in you?"

"Blackmail."

"I should've guessed."

"I told him if he didn't get me out of the stockade and give me a recommendation, I'd slander his name all over the Delta. I took a wild guess and said I'd let it be known that he'd been buggering little boys. I must have guessed right. He jumped right on that repulsive Yankee he'd been avoiding."

"Dat may be right, but dat ole lawyer had da last laugh. He sent you to Miss Claudine."

"Who's laughing now?"

The wind kicked up all of a sudden, bringing the scent of rain with it. It was time for the autumn rains. The Nickel Dime could use some of it. But why did he get the impression the storm wouldn't be limited to the heavens opening up?

"Bubba, tell me more about Pearl of the Concho."

After Brax launched into a description that didn't need inflating, Geoff said, "If we found a mutual interest, where would I take her to live? Truth is, Bubba, I never hankered for California. That place was your dream."

Brax went still. He allowed himself the liberty of butting into Geoff's decision-making. "The Nickel Dime has enough land for a bunch of Hales. . . ."

"Now that you mention it, Mason County has kinda grown on me. I could see spending a lifetime here."

A grin lightened Brax's face. He reached out to rub his

knuckles across the naps on Geoff's head, then did something he hadn't done in years. He gave the boy a bear hug and a big slap on the back. "Glad to hear it, Geoffie."

He'd been hoping—hell, praying!—Geoff wouldn't say his goodbyes. Never had he been able to announce, or even to acknowledge, that Geoffrey Hale was blood kin. They had never even discussed it between them. Still, he loved Geoff like a brother. Geoff was his brother. The last brother Brax had to lose.

Elizabeth Hale, wraithlike on her deathbed, had whispered to her firstborn, "Take care of little Geoffie. Don't ever whisper a word of it, but . . . he's your blood brother."

The saintly Elizabeth expired then, still concerned for her demon husband's by-blow. There had been no end to the dirt John Hale had piled on the family. *Forget him and his dirt.*

A good washing was what he needed.

Arriving at the Nickel Dime headquarters in the midnight hour, Brax waved good-night to Geoff and the grizzled ranch hand; they headed for the bunkhouse. Damn, Brax felt good. Geoff wouldn't be leaving. He would stay.

While it was tempting to make a beeline for his wife, he wouldn't go to her smelling like cows and three nights on the road. He headed for the well to draw a big bucket of water.

That he lugged into the cookhouse; he didn't bother with a lantern. He built a fire in the stove, setting the bucket atop it. The heavy table shoved aside, he dragged the hip bath into the middle of the dirt floor. A good washing and some dental sprucing up, and sure as shootin', he'd be ready to hike into the house and pull his beautiful wife into his hungry embrace.

Using baking soda on his teeth, then a mouthwash of whiskey, he took care of half the problem. Settled as a tall man could get with his legs drawn up to his chin, he savored the warm water and the joys of a cake of soap. All the while he went through his ablutions, he kept an ear peeled. Surely Skylla knew he'd gotten home. Would she visit? This cookhouse seemed the best spot for a reunion, since the main house would be cluttered with big-eared women with no men to call their own.

"Braxton?"

His wife.

He smiled toward the door she opened, his smile widening when he got a gander at her. He let himself drink in her womanly curves and the luxurious fall of her hair. He liked it down. But his smile faded when he got a good long look at her outfit. She wore britches and a shirt. Shoot, he'd hoped for her naked, and would have settled for a nightgown and wrapper. Fully dressed said something's up and it ain't good.

Chapter Twenty-one

"Hello, Braxton."

Upset but doing her best to control it, Skylla refused to gaze at her husband's naked shoulders and knees, evident in the hip bath. She centered on his face. Was that a wise choice? His eyes, so alluring in the dim light, so intense with obvious desire, aroused her passion.

His lips beckoned. "I've missed you," he said in a voice hoarse with longing. He lifted his arms in invitation.

"We've got trouble," she announced.

His elbows settled on the rim of the tub. "I was hoping for good news."

"There's been some of that." She told him about Titus's cowboys returning, then sat down on a chair and spoke of her problem. "Kathy Ann is in love."

"Let me guess the lucky fellow. Stalking Wolf."

"Yes."

Braxton ran a hand down his face. "Has he shown up?"

"No. He sent messengers. With a gift."

"It sounds serious."

Skylla could have bopped him on the head. "I'd like to know why you aren't upset."

"Stalking Wolf is a good man. And you and I both know he has more than a passing interest in Piglet."

"I don't want her taking up with a dirty, thieving savage. Besides, she's just a child, fifteen or no fifteen!"

"It's not your decision to make. She'll do what she wants, and no one will be able to stop her."

"You can be blasé. She's not your sister."

"That's a low blow. I've done my best for that girl."

Skylla lowered her gaze. He had. He'd done his best for everyone and everything connected to the ranch. Claudine, forever crying wolf, had been nothing but mean-minded. *But what about the "fake" topaz? What about his helping himself to the treasure trove?* It would be petty to mention those things.

"By your silence, I take it you don't think I've done right by Kathy Ann."

"You have been good to her. Moreover, you're right. She'll do her own choosing. After the unhappiness of my sister's younger years, I ought to be pleased at their love match. But life with the chief of a nomadic and savage people? No!"

"What does Claudine have to say about the girl?"

"This brings up another problem. Claudine got married this afternoon. To Webb Albright."

"There is a God."

"I wouldn't get too tickled if I were you." Skylla launched into the whole story, including the awful truth about Winslow Packard. "I think there's going to be trouble."

"Let it rip. I'm not scared." Before she could open her mouth, he murmured, "I've missed you. Missed you like crazy."

"I've missed you, too."

"This water's getting cold. Mind if I get out? Would you mind drying my back?"

She knew what that would lead to, and though she wanted it as much as Braxton did, she admitted, "I have a headache."

He exhaled in exasperation. "Skylla, we've been married less than a week. We made pretty good love, more than once.

And we made pretty good partners, dealing with Stalking Wolf. Those things ought to count for something." Impatience filtered into his expression. "Is this the way it's going to be with us? You let your family give you a headache, then you don't want to make love with your new husband."

"They didn't give ·me a headache. You did. All along I've tried to have faith in you, but all along I get clues that you're not to be trusted." She inhaled. "I want to know something. How old are you?"

His answer was slow, hesitant. "Thirty-one."

"You claimed to be twenty-nine."

"I did."

"Did Joanie Johnson's father buy your mother a piano?"

"He did not. I worked eighteen hours a day at Woody's to buy that piano. Who put such a notion in your head, anyway? Don't bother answering. Claudine did it."

While Skylla felt relief over the piano, she would have *all* her questions answered. Her eyes closed. "Braxton, the topaz you traded to Stalking Wolf. It was all glass. Fakes."

"Not true. Not true at all."

A giant whoosh of water accompanied Braxton's departure from the bath. She heard him making the motions of drying off with a towel he must have gotten from the cupboard. Even before he put his hand on her shoulder and turned her to face him, she felt his imminent touch.

She meant to look into his face and demand a better explanation about the topaz. It was then that she noticed the deep-purple bruise on his shoulder. How it must hurt! It hurt her just to recall that Indian brave battering Braxton with a club.

"It's not painful, if that's what you're thinking," he said, reading her mind.

"Skylla, about those gemstones . . ." He bent at the knees to sit on his heels. The towel broke loose as he shifted, the material pooling at his privates. "I can't imagine Titus burying *glass*. There'd be no reason for it."

Heartened by the rank honesty in her husband's face, Skylla exhaled in relief. The guileless look in his eyes gave her further comfort. She placed her hand over his. "Thank goodness for you. I—I . . . well, I'll admit I've had awful thoughts. Please forgive me for doubting you."

"Let's don't start that forgiving business."

She stood, invitation in her tone as she said, "It's late. We should turn in."

"Best offer I've heard lately." He, too, got to his feet. One hand holding the towel in front of his manly equipment, he appended in a voice heavy with ardor, "The best offer . . . ever."

The moment he took her fingers with his free hand, a clap of thunder rent the air. Lightning pulsed, casting the cookhouse in a gray light, and rain beat a tattoo on the tin roof. Immediately, the clean crisp scent of nature washing the earth mingled with the nice scent of a freshly washed husband.

"Autumn rain," he said quietly. "Overdue. But welcome, wouldn't you say?"

"Oh, yes."

"Should we make a dash for it?"

"We'll catch our deaths if we do."

"That's what I was thinking." He lifted his hand to trace his fingers along Skylla's cheek. "We wouldn't want to catch our deaths, would we?"

She shook her head, smiling up at him and luxuriating in the tingles that his touch elicited. "It would be wise if we waited out the storm here."

"Sounds reasonable."

"Do you like rain?" she asked, realizing how little she knew of his likes and dislikes.

"Yeah, I like it. Especially when it's just you and me and the rain beating on the roof. What do you say about us making a pallet on the table . . . ? We could sit on it. And watch the rain through the windows."

"I'll grab a tablecloth out of the drawer." As soon as she finished spreading it across the oaken table, she felt the tickle of his breath on her neck. She shivered. Deliciously.

"Skylla . . . I want to do more than watch the rain."

"I know."

The towel slipped when he wound both arms around her. Her fingers climbed to curl into his hair. Feeling his growing erection, she pressed against it.

"I want a kiss," he murmured.

Her lips parted as he angled his mouth to hers. For a splendid moment he explored her lips, drawing forth shivers along with a moan of desire. Then his tongue dipped between her teeth to explore the core of her mouth. He tasted of whiskey, not a bad taste. Her hands moved to the sides of his face, and she held him as he now held her. The need for more than a kiss roared through her, like the thunder outdoors.

When he ended the kiss, he nipped her bottom lip with his teeth. "We're not doing a very good job of watching the rain," he said silkily. "And I think you'd get more out of that if we got you out of these clothes."

"Such wisdom. Such good advice."

Without so much as a fumble, he unbuttoned her shirt and slipped his hand inside her camisole. The calluses on his fingertips gently abraded her breast and its now-puckered tip. As he slipped the shirt off her shoulders, his lips enticingly touched the dip of her throat, then trailed provocative kisses to her shoulder and down her arm.

After untying the camisole and slipping it over her head, he reverently folded her shirt and undergarment. With lightning illuminating the kitchen, he laid her things on the chair. She gazed with appreciative eyes on the play of his back and arms as he moved. It became a yearning, the need to run her hands along those bunched muscles.

Not another moment passed before she got her chance, and he felt so wonderful, so strong, so . . . capable. Eagerly, her hands swept over the hard lines of his hips, and she chuckled with pleasure upon scooting her fingertips to the satiny yet unbelievably rigid part of him.

In a voice barely detectable under the staccato beat of the rain, he said, "Skylla . . . oh, sweet baby, see what you've done to me."

Without modesty, she looked at him . . . there. "You're beautiful," she stated without hesitation. "Truly beautiful."

He chuckled. "You're too kind, sweetheart. I'd say it's more along the lines of it's-so-ugly-it's-cute."

"You are mistaken. Only true beauty could rouse such a heat in my private parts."

This drew a peal of laughter. "You, my wanton little wife, are quite a woman. Quite a woman. And I'm getting more impatient by the moment to . . . watch the rain."

His nimble fingers worked the buttons of her britches, then slid them and her drawers down her legs. She felt as if she were ablaze, so heated was her blood. Would she be transmuted into an inferno of passion? Oh, yes. She did believe so.

"I don't think I want simply to watch the rain," she whispered, gazing up into his marvelous eyes.

"What do you want?"

"You."

With that he lifted her onto the table. Letting her legs dangle freely, he spread her thighs, stepping between them. His thumbs at her armpits and his hands spreading to support her ribs, he began to finish what they had started. He cherished her breasts, her belly, her navel—each with hot and ardent lips. When the fingers of one of his hands covered her naked mound, she whimpered. That whimper turned to a gasp at the same moment he delved into the cleft of her womanly place.

"You feel so good," he uttered. "Perfect."

"In the vein of it's-so-ugly-it's-pretty?"

Gently, he nipped the tip of her nose with his teeth. "You would have made a good strumpet in some bawdy alehouse of old, my love."

Feeling saucy as a wench and paraphrasing Shakespeare, she winked at her adored husband. "Milord, you make much ado about nothing."

"I'll teach you to call me a liar!"

His finger found her most sensitive nub, and he knew exactly how to exact passion. The ability to stay upright departed her, and she fell back on the table, bracing herself on her elbows. She looked down at him; he was smiling a wicked smile. She started to lean forward . . . but there was no doing anything beyond giving in to her wondrous feelings, for he had lowered his mouth to that place where his fingertip had been. His tongue made a slow and masterful foray. Never too rough, never too gentle, always with a proficiency not to be improved upon, he laved her. Was there no end to the wonders of him?

Suddenly, flashes of heat singed her every pore, her every cell, her every vein. And like a burning leaf as it curled in a fire, her muscles drew inward. "Stop! For God's sake, Braxton, stop! I can't take it!"

He stopped.

Yet she hated herself for asking.

That emotion lasted a fraction of a second. His long and thick erection slid into her wet portal. She moaned. And then he had her in his arms, her behind leaving the table.

"Wrap your legs around me," he commanded in a hoarse voice. "Put your arms around my neck."

She did as bade.

His strong legs planted to the earthen floor, he pushed deeper into her, and lifted her from the table. She gasped at her response. Her nails dug into his back, her teeth into his shoulder. Was there anything better than making love to him?

"Am I too rough for you, my precious wife?"

"Not in the least."

Unconvinced, he added, "I can make love to you gently. Or I can give you the wildness of my loving. Which will you have, wife?"

"I-I'm not sure."

"Know your power. Use it. Tell me what you want."

They went still, still as a calm night. This wasn't a clement night. She didn't want tranquil. Her half-lidded eyes blazed a trail to his fixed gaze. "Hold nothing back, husband."

He didn't.

Her moans of ecstasy, not one but several, filled the cook-house. He rubbed raw her ability to make sense of anything. Yet there was a certain clarity to her feelings. Her mouth rushed to his shoulder again as he pumped wildly into her, and she couldn't help but nip at his skin.

He yelped. He yelped at the same moment that his primal groan drowned the beat of the rain. The pulse of his release shot into her—she felt it in his every action. A calm, a celestial calm, settled through her. She knew, as women have known throughout the ages, that she and her husband were forever cleaved, the one unto the other.

He went still. Too still? She had hurt him.

"I . . . I'm sorry. Oh, Braxton, my darling, I am so sorry. I didn't mean to hurt you. This is the shoulder the Indians at-tacked, isn't it?"

Holding her tight, he let his lips hover over hers. "I'm man enough to take it."

"Is there anything to eat around here?"

The night storm having softened to rain outside the cook-house, Skylla smiled at her naked husband. She had to pinch herself in this, the afterglow of lovemaking, to make certain she wasn't in the throes of a wonderful dream. Marriage more than agreed with her. If only she weren't troubled about fam-ily . . .

Glancing to the cupboard, she finally answered, "I could fix you a plate of leftover sausage and pickles. And there's pie for dessert. Vinegar pie. Interested?"

"Vinegar. Sounds awful."

"Try it, you might change your mind. It tastes a lot like lemon pie. Mrs. Burrows swears by it. And it made a hit at dinner tonight, um, I mean last night. It was all I could do to save you a piece."

"You're wonderful, Skylla Hale. Flat out wonderful." He pulled her into his arms and began to nuzzle her neck. "For-get the food. I'll just feast on this sweet piece of pie."

"Later, you insatiable beast," she murmured, shivering with delight yet pulling away. "You wanted food. I'm going to provide it."

"Killjoy." He swatted her bare behind, but let her go, sitting down on the cloth-draped table, his back resting against the cookhouse wall, while watching her fill a plate with food. When she handed it over, he asked, "Share it with me?"

"By all means."

"Then get your butt up here, woman." He spread his legs and patted the area between them, gesturing for her to sit there. "I'm so hungry I could eat the south end out of a north-bound jackass."

"That's not much of a testimonial to my cooking."

"Get up here, woman, and now," he ordered with affected gruffness. "Else, I'll tell everybody that you can't even boil water without burning it."

She made a face at him. He returned the gesture. Then they both laughed as she levered up to her appointed place, leaning back against his shoulder—the one without the bruise—and just plain relaxed. Relaxed, and luxuriated in the warm cocoon of Braxton.

He fed her bite after bite, until she realized that he had been the one to cry hungry. "My turn to feed you," she said, scooting around to lift a slice of sausage to his lips. Mesmerized, she fed him pickle, then pie. The way his mouth moved when he chewed, it had a sensuality to it. And she hummed low in her throat upon recalling the vast talent of those lips.

At last he licked his lips. "Mm, mm. You're right. The pie was delicious. Will you make it again some time?"

"With pleasure." It did please her to do for her husband, even though she had the idea to hire a cook.

He reached for his denims and dug into the pocket, saying, "I brought you something." Proud as a youngster presenting his mother with a frog, Brax handed over an amber bottle. "Liniment."

Liniment? Neither liniment nor a pair of corrective shoes

was a box of chocolates—or a cameo—but his offering pleased her. "I'm sure it'll help. Where did you get it?"

"From the quartermaster at Camp Llano. We got in a card game, and rather than take his money, I told him I'd settle for some of his horse liniment. Now, you'll want to use it three times a day, first in the morning, then at noon, and before you go to bed." His wiggled his brows. "I'll do the rubbing-it-in."

"Yes, Doctor." She reached up to hug him. "Thank you."

"Let's give some of it a try." He poured liniment onto his palm, rubbed his hands together, then smoothed the cool-hot liquid along her twisted calf. Brow furrowed, he said something entirely off the subject. "While I was at Camp Llano, I talked to Webb Albright. He says there's a railhead up Kansas way. The railroad goes to Chicago. The stockyards of Chicago. Albright says beef is selling for forty dollars a head up there."

"Forty dollars? For one cow?" Her eyes widened.

"What do you think about a cattle drive to Kansas, come the first of the year?"

"What's wrong with now?" she retorted, giddy with the thought of forty dollars a head.

He shook his head, made a couple of kneading rubs to her flesh, then replied, "Winter will be here before we know it. Winters can be tricky up that way, I understand. We need to cull and brand all the stock we intend to send to Kansas. Which means we need more cowboys and good horseflesh."

"The first of the year will be fine, then."

He landed a peck of a kiss on the tip of her nose. "In the meantime, now that Snuffy and Luckless have shown up, I say we send down to San Antonio for some tannery supplies. Those fellows are crackerjack tanners. We'll get in the tanning and hide business, like you suggested. There's a market for hides closer than Kansas, sure as shootin'."

"I'm for it. But what's this 'send down to San Antonio'? We need all kinds of things for the ranch. I need all kinds of things. To tell the truth, honey, I've got a hankering to go shopping. Let's me and you go to town."

He moved behind her, pulling her to him. His arms crossed under her breasts, he said, "You called me honey."

"Why, I guess I did."

"That's the first time you've called me a sweet nothing."

"There's a first time for everything—honey."

He nuzzled her nose. "Yeah. And there's time for something else. . . ."

"Oh?" she teased. "You want to get an early start on helping the boys build your precious fence?"

"That is *not* what I've got in mind."

They stole naked through the night, ending up in their bedroom. He put Electra out, then turned to Skylla. Her eyes were on the bed. "Braxton, honey, I've misplaced something. A legal document. I'd stuck it between the mattress and the ropes. You haven't seen anything of a folded piece of paper, have you?"

Suddenly he began to cough. And cough.

Chapter Twenty-two

That deed of trust was going to be the death of him.

Three hours after she'd questioned him about the deed's whereabouts, Brax still had a headache, a giant headache that had penetrated his skull to pound on his brain.

Luck had been his until this morning. Boy, had he been lucky. Matter of fact, he'd considered himself the luckiest man alive. A happy marriage; Piglet with her eyes on a husband; Claudine having one. Neither that business with the new county clerk nor the redhead's vague threats had had him ruffled. Luck's name was Brax—until Skylla had reminded him of his harebrained scheme.

The headache didn't go away all morning, even when he busied his mind. He figured to sell the topaz gems and bank the proceeds, plus Titus's gold, in San Antonio. There, he would buy a wagon to haul supplies back to the ranch. He intended to talk his wife out of making the trip, even though as brother to two sisters who had delighted in shopping, he knew his wife thirsted to sail from millinery shops to dress shops and back again. Next trip. This trip, he had unfinished business with the horse thief, Singleterry, and he didn't want her in the middle of the showdown.

With his head pounding, he couldn't deal with composing an argument to keep her down on the ranch. Nor could he decide, how to get out of the trap of his own making: the deed of trust.

The sun on his aching head, he rode to Safe Haven Canyon and got reacquainted with the cowpokes, Snuffy Johnson and Luckless Litton. Talkative fit Luckless. The most distinguishing feature in the laconic Snuffy was wild red hair, so bright it looked as if a bolt of lightning had struck him.

"Never figgered to see the likes of you agin," Litton said, pounding a post into the ground. "Me an' Snuf, we figgered yew was in the good life, since ya tied in with Gen'l Hood."

Snuffy nodded and spat a stream of tobacco to the ground.

"I fared well enough. Better than most Rebels." Brax wiped his brow. "I didn't finish the war with Hood. I got separated from him a few months before Lee surrendered. Hood was doing all right, and my services were needed at the front."

Litton nailed a cross tie into the fence post. "We heared the gen'l went down to Nawlins, got marr'd up down there. Marriage shore does agree with ya. We ain't seen ya so fat and happy, never. Ain't that right, Snuf?"

Snuffy nodded. Then spoke. "How come you come back to the Nickel Dime? Did ya reckon to squat on the place?"

Brax answered with a question of his own. "Did you two reckon to squat on the place?"

"Ta tell the truth," said Litton, "that be 'xactly what we bet on. Didn't know nothing about no heiress, but figgered she be the major's niece. She be as purty as he let on."

Brax wished he'd listened closer to Titus.

Litton hitched up his britches. " 'Course, now that we be here, we ain't too upset to hire out as hands, are we, Snuf?"

"We ain't riled."

"That be a right nice lady ya got, that Miss Skylla." Litton dusted his hands. "We be happy to work for y'all."

Brax pulled on gloves to lend a hand with the fencing. "We

could use a coupla dozen fellows like you. My wife and I have big plans for the ranch. Anyone who stays loyal to the brand, there's gonna be nothing but good coming to him." Brax launched into a monologue about a cattle drive and a tannery.

"Sounds good, don't it, Snuf?"

Snuffy nodded.

"I'm thinking y'all might be due for a raise. How 'bout thirty a month?"

"Oh, boy, I can hire me a whore," the normally quiet Snuffy exclaimed. "A purty whore what dudn't stink like piss nur fish. That's what I been dreamin' about durn near all my life."

Every man was entitled to his own idea of heaven.

After his jawing with the restored cowhands, Brax had back-tracked to headquarters and a thankless task. His wife at his side, he approached Kathy Ann in her room. "Piglet," he said, "that dress has got to go back."

"If it goes, I'm going with it."

He read her look, and it was determined. It dogged him, cutting into her happiness, though he doubted Skylla would change her mind. "Kathy Ann, we'll buy you a dozen dresses. A hundred dresses. Whatever you want to make you happy."

"I thought you were my friend."

"I am, Piglet. I am."

Skylla stepped toward her. "Lovey, would you like to go away to school? We could send you back East. Or to Europe. Or we can tutor you here."

Her eyes filled with tears, she asked, "Is that what you want me to do, Sergeant?"

"Your sister and I want what's best for you." He wouldn't mention their diverse views on "best."

Kathy Ann turned to her bureau, removing her adored buckskin dress from a drawer. Not facing them, she thrust it out behind her. "Take it."

Brax couldn't. Skylla did. It broke his heart to hear Piglet's plaintive sobs as they left her. "I hope you're happy," was all he could say to his wife.

He found that he didn't want her around as he tackled the next dirty job. Thankfully, Skylla didn't press the subject. Brax approached Charlie Main, who was collecting a saddle from the tack room. "Main, why don't you sit a spell?"

"Whut be the matter?"

"Claudine got married."

His sun-battered face went white, the light collapsing in his eyes. "I wanted her for my own."

"I know you did, ole buddy. I know you did."

The cowpoke dropped the saddle. "I'm gonna do whut I shoulda done, long time ago. I'm taking Patsy Sue, and we're leaving."

"Main, don't rush off. We need you here. But if you're set on going, my wife and I want to give you a grubstake."

"I won't need a grubstake where I'm going."

If Main's next moves were in character, he'd no doubt get drunk, tear up Leander's Saloon, pass out, then get up and start over again. Nickel Dime money could put the saloon back in shape. Besides, if ever a man earned the right to tear something up, it was Charlie Main.

"You're just tearing my heart to itty-bitty pieces, Winslow." Ten minutes ago, Claudine had stepped into his office, and was proceeding to win him over to her side. "Kiss me."

"Go home, Claudine."

That was exactly where she intended to go after she got through at the Mason County Courthouse. And after she got through with her mission at the Nickel Dime. In the saddlebag of the fine mount her new husband had provided was a beautiful cameo brooch once the property of Elizabeth Hale.

Winslow Packard would be her insurance, in case Skylla proved too obtuse to see the light.

Claudine batted her lashes at the fat Yankee's frowning face. "Surely you're not mad at lil ole me for getting married. I waited and waited for you, sweetie pie. Waited until I just couldn't wait any longer." She patted his jowls. "How about I prove just how sorry I am I didn't wait a tiny bit longer? Hmm?"

Packard stepped back to pull the window shades. He asked over his shoulder, "What would your husband say to all this?"

Plenty. But Packard held the key to her revenge, since the Mason County records were in his possession. If there was any way to get back at Brax and his traitorous wife, provided the cameo didn't do the trick, it was through the county clerk.

She swayed over to her prey. "Don't you worry about Webb. He's out playing soldier with his Army chums." Her hand moved down Packard's mountainous gut, stopping where she knew she could get the better of him. "Has Peewee missed me, hmm?"

Now that she was playing with his toothpick of a pecker, Packard got that dumb look of men ruminating on their own satisfaction. His fingers moved swiftly to disengage the prize from his trousers. "Kiss it," he groaned.

She played with it instead. "I'll kiss it. I'll kiss it anytime you like. Provided you do me a favor."

"Anything, anything," he croaked.

"Find where title of the Nickel Dime Ranch passed to Titus St. Clair. Then I want you to burn the whole record book."

He pressed her nose to Peewee.

He was no Webb Albright. The sight and smell of Packard revolted her. She wrenched away, sickened at the act she'd fallen to.

"What's the matter with you, Claudine?"

"I-I can't, Winslow. Please forgive me, but I can't continue with this." How could she have fallen so far? Blaming it on the events of wartime and afterward, she examined her soul while Packard bellowed his discontent.

Once, she'd been the decent person Skylla had always believed her to be. She could be that person again. The war was over, the aftermath following its natural course. With the goodness of Webb having come her way, why hadn't she accepted with good grace her fifth chance at love?

"Forget the deed book, Winslow."

His face got mean. "Believe me, I wouldn't have compromised public records for a piece of Southern trash." He buttoned himself up.

"You're right. I've been behaving like trash." She gathered her gloves from his desk. "Goodbye, Winslow."

"Planning to sneak back to your hubby?" He sneered.

"Actually, I'm planning to atone for my trashiness," she answered, not that he'd care. "I'm going to call on my daughter and her husband. It's time I offered best wishes for their long and happy life together. And begged their forgiveness."

On her way, she'd toss that cameo in the Llano River.

"Clawdeeen!"

Startled by the opening of the door as well as that plaintive cry, she whirled around to see a gun pointed at her head. "No!"

Charlie Main pulled the trigger.

The bullet struck her in the face. For a split second she felt horrendous pain. Then she felt nothing.

The bleak and drizzly day of the funeral matched the dark clouds in Skylla's heart. Throughout the service at the Ecru cemetery, witnessed by the departed's family plus the county clerk and a throng of busybodies, Skylla tried to keep her composure. As if they were lifelines, she clung to Braxton and Kathy Ann, yet she couldn't stop her tears.

It was a Southern tradition for friends and family to gather after a funeral, yet Webb Albright, too deep in shock for tears, declined Kathy Ann's invitation to visit the Nickel Dime. His eyes never turning to the jail where Charlie Main awaited the hangman, he rode hard for Camp Llano.

Few people gathered at the ranch, the scandal keeping them away, and that was fine with Skylla. She did appreciate the kindness of Oliver Brown, the Burrowses, Emil Kreitz, and the ranch hands, Geoff as well. Yet she appreciated it more when everyone left.

They sat on the settee then, she and Braxton, Kathy Ann serving cup after cup of coffee. "Sit down, lovey," she said. "I need to hold your hand." Already Braxton held one of her hands. His strength and Kathy Ann's flowed into her—mere touch could do so much. Would she ever be herself again? Or must she live with a guilty conscience for letting a loved one die with a rift between them?

Into the quiet, Kathy Ann spoke. "I wonder what she was doing in the county clerk's office?"

"She must have been checking to see if I filed some papers in her favor." Claudine's repute had suffered enough from her getting shot by a spurned lover. Skylla wouldn't add to it by mentioning the affair she'd had with the Yankee. Braxton wouldn't mention it, either, she was sure.

"Skylla," he said, "Packard called me aside."

"I know. I saw him."

"What did he have to say?" Kathy Ann asked.

"He told me why Claudine was in his office. He said she dropped by on her way to visit us here at the ranch. Skylla, she was going to wish us well."

"Really?" Kathy Ann said, aghast.

Braxton nodded. "She intended to 'beg' our forgiveness."

"What was she telling him for?"

"Lovey, no more." Skylla brooked no argument. Tears welled; she leaned her head back, yet some of the awful weight lifted from her heart. "I'm glad Mr. Packard spoke with you, Braxton. It reinforces what she told Kathy Ann. I couldn't live with it if I thought she wouldn't let go of hard feelings."

"Too bad that old drunk killed her."

"It would be easy to hate Charlie," Skylla replied to her sister. "We mustn't. Life is too short for hate."

"Here, here." Braxton put an arm around her.

Kathy Ann sniffed back a tear. "But I wanted you and Claudine to kiss and make up. For your sake."

"That cannot be, though I'll always regret that we didn't

make amends with each other." Skylla would forever grieve
for her stepmother and the end of their lengthy friendship.
"But, lovey, if she was on her way here, then she'll rest in
peace."

"Amen."

The funeral and resultant hanging got in the way of everyone's plans. Thus, Geoff Hale was two weeks late leaving for
the Comanche encampment. The sun beating down on his
old cap, he hummed as he rode the skewbald through the
grasses, in the direction Bubba had given to Pearl of the Concho.

Geoff had left the ranch in good hands.

Here lately, more men had shown up, eager to hire on. Re-
bels mostly, but three Yankees, a couple of freed slaves from
Alabama, and a vaquero from the brush country. Three of the
Johnny Rebs were skilled cowboys. Bubba figured to train the
others. A Frenchman with experience as a trail cook got a job.
That René fellow lived up to "touchy cook."

With the extra help, the cattle drive was taking shape.

And that redheaded piece of work was gone—good rid-
dance. Geoff recalled her burial. No one shed a tear, except
for Miss Skylla. Frankly, he'd been surprised when Claudine's
widower showed up.

The Yankee major had even witnessed Charlie Main's hanging—justice was swift on the frontier. Some real tears had been
shed over Charlie. Geoff had cried for the stupid, gullible cowboy who'd thought he could love above his station.

Was an Indian girl above a quadroon? Some people might
think so, but Geoff intended to let Pearl of the Concho make
that decision. Raising his chin to the buttermilk sky and giving
Molasses a nudge, he burst into song. Here he was, going on
eighteen, and on his way to get a wife.

"Geoff! Geoff, wait up!"

He turned in the saddle, in the direction of that feminine
voice he didn't have any trouble recognizing. On Luckless Lit-

ton's bay mare, Kathy Ann headed straight as an arrow for Geoff. Riding abreast, she patted a burlap sack that jumped in her lap. Her cat, no doubt. "I'm going with you."

"Uh-uh. You da bad girl, wantin' to upset your sister when she in mournin'."

"Sarge will make it all right with her. He knows I'm leaving. He gave me his blessing."

"Da massa love you, Miss Kathy Ann."

"I know. And I love him, too. But enough about that." She hitched up a brow. "You can stop with that silly accent stuff. I've heard you talking with Sergeant when you think no one is listening. You're no field nigger."

"I don't like that word. It's a mean word, Kathy Ann."

"Don't get your feelings hurt, Geoff. You're all right for a colored boy."

"A left-handed compliment to be sure."

"Oh, don't be so touchy."

"You'll know what it's like to have people look down on you, if you don't turn back. White people accept a white woman married to a savage just about as well as they accept someone who's got ancestors hailing from Africa."

"Stalking Wolf is a fine man. I'm going to marry him. I'll never look back."

"Good for you, Kathy Ann. Good for you."

Chapter Twenty-three

San Antonio, Texas
November 29, 1865

With trouble in his heart, Brax watched his wife crumple Kathy Ann's letter, her shoulders wilting. Why hadn't he told that French cook not to forward correspondence to their temporary address, the Menger Hotel? Skylla hadn't recovered from losing Claudine in such a tawdry fashion, nor was she reconciled to losing Kathy Ann. And now, the letter.

Alone in their suite, Brax took hold of Skylla's shoulders. He knew she wanted to lash out at him for permitting Kathy Ann to follow her heart, but he knew something else. His wife was trying to control her temper, and in the aftermath of the loss of Claudine, she was ever so much more circumspect.

Not a man to shun an advantage, he said, "Be happy for your sister. A babe is a cause for joy. Just think, you're going to be an aunt."

"I suppose I should be happy for Pearl, too."

Yes, there were two babes on the way. Geoff had returned

to the Nickel Dime with an Indian wife, now known simply as Pearl. They expected their child next summer. So, apparently, did Kathy Ann. Each couple had a child except for Brax and Skylla.

My fault. My damned fault. Another sign of damnation. When John Hale damned his family, he covered all bases. This, however, was nothing Brax cared to explore verbally.

His fingers slid into the luxurious silkiness of Skylla's dark, dark hair, and he angled his head to kiss her tears away. In a gentle yet firm tone, he tried to reason with her. "You're going to make yourself sick, getting upset. Yes, your sister has married a savage. Yes, she's carrying Stalking Wolf's child. People get married and have babies." *Everyone but us.* "Skylla, we'll lose Kathy Ann forever unless you're willing to bend. If you accept Stalking Wolf, she'll come back to us. Not alone. With her husband. Someday with her children. But she'll come back."

Skylla stared up at him, and from the look in her heart-shaped face, he knew she wavered. Wavered, but did not give.

When she slipped out of his arms, she padded barefoot across the suite's lush wine-red rug, going to the window to let in the crisp air of late autumn. A breeze lashed her unbound hair, whipping it behind her. Her shoulders, usually so proudly straight, slumped. She said in a strained voice, "I thought she'd return to us. I can't imagine Kathy Ann content in a savage world. I thought she'd be home by now."

"Sweetheart, you never gave her her due. She's a clever girl. A clever girl becoming a clever woman." He knew this for fact; he'd made a trip to the Comanche village. Kathy Ann had blossomed. "She's happy."

"You make it sound so right."

"I hope I'm getting through to you." He crossed the room to help his wife accept reality. "Write her a letter. Luckless will deliver it. Tell her how happy you are she's found happiness. Dollar to a donut, she'll call on us in no time."

"You're right. You're always right." Skylla slid her arms

around him, leaning her cheek against his chest. "Every night I say a prayer of thanks that you rode into my life."

Brax had his own prayer of thanksgiving. The ranch had adequate help, was sailing along in preparation for the cattle drive. A goodly amount of money had been deposited in the bank, both from Titus's bounty and the proceeds from the sale of tallow and hides. And from the sale of topaz stones. Further, the drive to Kansas had taken shape. Safe Haven brimmed with five hundred branded longhorns fattening up for the trip.

Everything should have been rosy.

Except that Brax hadn't been able to even the score with Oren Singleterry. He'd given in on the first trip to San Antonio, had agreed not to pay a call on the horse thief. She'd argued that he should forget a few head of horses. He hadn't been of the same mind. "Go on home, sweetheart," he said. He kissed her forehead. "Let Luckless escort you to the ranch."

Her arms tightened around him, her sweetness seeping into his being. "Let the law take care of Singleterry," she said. "You have a good case. Webb and his soldiers will testify on our behalf. They'll say they saw where a running-iron had been burned over the Nickel Dime brand."

"It could take months for the law to settle the dispute."

She looked up with those huge brown eyes that now held the glint of reason and common sense. "We've waited this long to get the horses back. What's a few more months?"

Her arguments were getting to him.

Using her fingers as combs, Skylla brushed long hair behind her ears, again looked him straight in the eye, and said, "If I can give up my sister and make peace with myself over Claudine, you can bend on this quest of yours."

"We need help." Brax, his wife to his right, held his oyster-colored Stetson in his hand, facing the sheriff. "We're here to lodge a complaint against a horse thief."

In his office in the Bexar County Courthouse, Sheriff Hermann Klein pared his fingernails with a butcher knife, blew his nose into a handkerchief that might have once been clean, and sniffed mucus back into his sinuses.

Brax said, "Oren Singleterry, now a resident of Bexar County, stole those horses."

"We hanged that varmint last month."

"What?" Brax and Skylla said in unison.

"We hanged that varmint Singleterry last month. For horse-thieving."

Damn. Double damn.

"What did you say your name was?" inquired the lawman.

"I didn't. But it's Hale. Brax Hale. This is my wife, Skylla Hale. She inherited the Nickel Dime Ranch in Mason County from her uncle, Titus St. Clair. We want Singleterry's horses."

"You cain't have them. We sold them at auction."

Foiled again. And it had a nasty taste.

Klein screwed up an eye. "Did you say your name was Hale? I know a fellow named Hale. Used to live here before the war. Came back a few months ago." As was ordinary around these parts, he asked a question not to be expected in that vast and spread-out region. "Would you be kin to Dr. John Hale?"

Being gut-shot couldn't have hit Brax harder than hearing his father's name. The sheriff's office seemed to ebb and recede, a surging in his ears wreaking havoc with his balance. He planted his palms on the desk and leaned forward to catch his breath. Skylla's fingers wrapped around his biceps, squeezing his flesh to show support. She stepped to the left and settled closer to his side.

"You okay, Hale?" asked Sheriff Klein.

"He's fine," Skylla lied. "A touch of heart trouble."

"You ought to take him to John Hale. If anyone can fix a bad ticker, John Hale's the one."

Brax swallowed, or tried to. After all these years of wanting answers and being thwarted in getting them, he was in the same town as his father. How could that be? John Larkin Hale, Unionist doctor, was supposed to be in the Caribbean.

"Repeat that name," he ordered.

"Dr. John Hale. He's the coroner here in Bexar County. Right nice-looking fellow, about fifty. A dandy if I've ever seen one. Fact is, y'all look enough alike to be father and son."

Brax choked out, "Where can I find him?"

"Prob'ly at his infirmary." The sheriff looked up at the clock on the wall reading one P.M. "He ought to be in. Does his doctoring over on Burnet Street, a couple miles from here. Big clapboard place. Porch running all around it. You can't miss it. He's got a sign hanging in the front yard."

Brax patted his gunbelt. Skylla took his hand, which prompted him to turn to her. Understanding and a silent message to be cautious met his gaze.

Her eyes torn from Brax, Skylla then faced the lawman. "Thank you, Sheriff. We'll be on our way."

"Right," her husband muttered. "Let's go."

Brax Hale had fifteen years' worth of answers to get.

"Are you sick or hurt?"

Skylla held her husband's hand as he bared his teeth at the clinic attendant, a balding man wearing spectacles who stood behind a tall counter that separated this spartan, empty waiting room from the main part of the infirmary. "Do I look sick?" Braxton asked.

The man blinked, then closed a small case containing surgical instruments. "Doc doesn't cure sour dispositions."

"Then the sheriff's been spreading lies. Said your man was good at healing broken hearts."

"Weak hearts. The Almighty works on the broken ones."

From studying her husband, Skylla knew he was about to say God ignored Hale hearts. "Is the doctor in?" she asked. "My husband needs to speak with him."

"He isn't here. Is your man a patient of his?"

"I'm his— I'm an acquaintance from Mississippi."

The diminutive man bent a skeptical eye on Brax. "Acquaintance, you say?" A spark akin to recognition glinted in his eyes. With an owl-eyed smile, he offered the olive branch of down-home friendliness. "Come to think of it, I'd guess you a relative. I sure would. Welcome to Texas, y'all."

"Where is he?" Braxton snapped.

The man swept a hand toward a line of straight chairs. "Have a seat. Dr. Hale is making house calls. He'll be back directly. How about a cup of coffee? Got a fresh pot in the back. It's lip-smacking good. Beans came out of Vera Cruz."

"Thank you, no." Skylla let her husband take her arm.

He led her to a pair of chairs. Wordlessly, he plopped down, his face an unreadable mask to the casual observer. He closed his eyes, crossed his legs, and rested his fingers over his stomach in a semblance of casualness.

Her gaze traveled across the room, where a vacant invalid's chair stood, a peg leg lying across it. Almost, she had been doomed to such bondage. She closed her eyes to the memory. From somewhere deep in the bowels of the place, a man cried out, his sob echoing in her ears. She then noticed the stench of sickness and dying, similar to that in the Vicksburg infirmary, though the ailing of 1863 weren't afforded the sharp scent of antiseptic.

She shuddered. Not from thoughts of her own problems. Out of fear of trouble with Dr. John Hale, and of what measures her husband would go to with his long-absent father. She prayed Braxton would leave here with peace of mind. He deserved to know why his father had deserted the family.

And he needed the peace of mind he'd given her.

"You say you knew the doc in Mississippi." The attendant parked an elbow on the counter, misreading—or disregarding—Braxton's surliness. "Comes as a surprise. Never heard Doc say anything about that neck of the woods. When was he over there?"

Braxton opened one eye. "Most of his life."

"I sure never knew." The man took his spectacles off to clean them with a rag. "I bet he'll be tickled to see you. He's sure a good man. Been good to this town. I— Did I tell you my name? It's Luther Mullin. I'm head orderly at the clinic."

"Pleased to make your acquaintance," Skylla put in.

"Yeah, real pleased."

"Goes for y'all, too." Mullin smiled. "As I was saying afore I so rudely interrupted myself, ever'body in San Antonio was pleased as punch when the doc came back here. He sure does a lot for the community. Even takes care of Mexicans."

"A saint to be sure." Braxton's voice dripped sarcasm.

"We sure missed Doc when he served in the Army. Lots of people resented him signing up with the Union folks—not the Germans around here, naturally, since they never believed in slavery—but they tend to change their minds when the doc gets 'em well. Usually for free. Sure enough, it's good to have him back. Him and his pretty little wife and kids."

Braxton tensed. "Wife and kids?"

"Harriet and the younguns, Abigail and Andrew. Those are sure cute younguns. Abigail, she's a cotton-haired peach. 'Course, the boy could stand to put on some weight."

His face going pale beneath his tan upon digesting news of his father's second family, Braxton straightened in the chair. Skylla put a hand on his wrist at the same moment he said, "I thought his wife's name was Elizabeth."

"No. It's Harriet. Harriet Rourke, she used to be. Her widowed mama's been here in San Antonio since the days of the Republic. I've known Harriet since she was a tyke. Harriet Alice Rourke was her name. Now it's Mrs. Hale."

Skylla stepped into the conversation. "I'm sure they're a lovely family," she said. "I could use a breath of fresh air. You *will* escort me outside, won't you, husband?"

Before they could exit the infirmary, a buggy pulled up, visible through the window. Braxton's breath hissed through clenched teeth. A tall man, white streaks in the burnished gold hair at his temples, stepped out of the conveyance and turned to pluck a black satchel from the seat. Even from this distance, Skylla saw the resemblance between father and son. As well, she saw a striking difference.

Loose-limbed, the middle-aged man strode up the walk,

climbed the infirmary steps, and rushed inside. "Afternoon, Mullin. Old Mrs. Pruitt—"

Braxton stepped in front of his father. "Remember me?"

The doctor dropped his black bag.

Chapter Twenty-four

John Larkin Hale took a backward step from the past he'd tried to forget.

The muscles in Braxton's face were tight, his eyes shooting verdant bullets. This was trouble John Hale didn't need. "Step into my office."

Striding into the room that sported numerous diplomas and awards, signs of respectability and acceptance, John closed the door. He motioned for Braxton and the pretty brunette to sit down. She complied. Braxton—it came as no surprise—remained standing. Ready to vent his spleen.

John went around the desk to sit. Leaning back in his chair, his elbows propped on the arms and his fingers steepled, he scrutinized a part of what he'd tried to forget. The first of Elizabeth's brats. Her visage should be hovering over Braxton's face, as it had in John's memory. Instead, he saw himself a quarter century ago. Not a comforting thought.

"I thought you were dead," he said.

The woman's gaze shot up to Braxton. It was easy to detect

her loving concern. Harriet was like that, loving and concerned.

"Hello to you, too, Father."

John eyed his begotten son. Since Braxton hadn't gone to
a grave, what was the chance of more Hales waltzing into town,
expecting a carriage ride around the Alamo and a picnic along
the San Antonio River? If Harriet found out . . . trouble. If
battle-ax Bertha found out he was a bigamist, she'd skin him
alive.

"What do you want?" he demanded. "Money?"

"Answers."

With a smile displaying his teeth—he prided himself of having a perfect set of thirty-two—John turned his attention to
the woman. "Excuse our ill manners. Who might you be,
ma'am?"

"His wife."

"More's the pity."

"My husband is the finest man in the world. Which you
would be fully aware of, if you'd been a concerned father."
Her bosom rose and fell as she went bear-hunting with a
switch. "You've been the loser in this situation—you've
cheated yourself out of the joys of knowing Braxton!"

"Little spitfire, isn't she?" John said to his son.

"Not in the least." Braxton slapped a hand on the desktop.
"We didn't come here for chitchat or summations. I won't be
ignored, Father. I want to know why you did it."

There was no mistaking his son's question. "I've spent fifteen years trying to forget Mississippi. If you have come here
to cause trouble, know something and know it well. I won't
allow you to spread poison." John decided not to get too specific.

"I didn't come here to bust up your cozy little home with
your young wife and those little woods' colts of yours. I said
I want answers." Braxton paused. "Why did you damn your
children to hell?"

His wife laid a gloved hand on the desk. "Dr. Hale, they did
suffer greatly."

John studied the sorrow on his son's face.

Braxton stared downward, then fastened his gaze on John. "Why couldn't you find it in your heart to support your family? Do you know how hard it is to keep a log cabin warm, to tell a barefoot child there's nothing to eat but bean juice? How do you tell a kid that Father isn't coming home?"

Making its debut, guilt went through John for not looking after his son. But it was a fleeting shame. Braxton didn't look any the worse for the wear. Matter of fact, he looked healthy as a horse and prosperous to boot. "Deprivation builds character."

"And milk builds strong bones. Something my sisters didn't have." Braxton, with a gavel-like fist, banged the desk once. "What have you got to say for yourself?"

"You don't want to hear it."

"If it pertains to the Hales, I *demand* to hear it."

John searched for what to do next. He decided to take the blame. "I was a louse. A louse who skipped out on the marriage. I had a wanderlust that wasn't quenched until I reached Texas. Here, I found my peace."

"I reckon you have. Running a charity hospital. Forgetting charity starts at home. Yeah, you've got your peace. By committing bigamy and fathering a couple of bastards."

"Yes."

"Have any plans to desert the new family?"

"No."

"I wouldn't be too sure about that, if I were them."

"Son, belligerence rarely wins an argument."

Braxton turned that distinguished Hale nose in his wife's direction. She murmured something to him. They were a fine-looking pair, John decided. Good-looking children would spring from Braxton and his missus. Did they have children already? Verbalizing this question would indicate interest, which was the last thing John Larkin Hale wished to convey.

Yet he had no control over the memories that flashed into his mind. As if it were yesterday, he saw his son toddling after him, wanting to play doctor. The toddler became an even more inquisitive youth, never missing a call on a patient or an afternoon in his father's office. By the time he was twelve, Braxton had read every medical book in John's library, and was assisting in surgeries. Had he continued his studies?

Braxton said, "Will you let me tell you about the family you left behind?"

John would just as soon turn old Mrs. Pruitt over her kitchen table and lance another half dozen boils on the acreage of her fetid behind. Mrs. Pruitt not being the option, he decided to listen. "If you wish."

"Your legal wife is dead. Thankfully, she was spared the war. Not so your daughters. They took shelter in a cave. Diana and Susan were killed when it collapsed. Diana's little girl died of scarlet fever—Lilly already was malnourished. Larkin's widow took enemy fire."

John stole a look at the tearful brunette. It was as if she heard this gruesome tale for the first time.

"As for Larkin"—Braxton swallowed; his wife placed her hand over his—"Larkin's head got blown off in 1862. He fell dead in my arms. Geoff and I buried him in Manassas, Virginia."

As a physician John Hale agonized for the pain and suffering that had befallen the family carrying his name. As the patriarch of that hapless clan, he experienced a wave of nausea. Yet he despised his weakness, for it was easier to deal with the past when girded with indifference.

The brunette put an arm around her husband. "Let's go, honey," she whispered. "Let's go."

"No! The bastard has explained nothing. Nothing!"

"You need to get rid of your bitterness, son."

"By God, I'm trying to make sense of you. You're devoted to this new family. What's so special about them? We were good children. Even the last one—the one you had with Bella."

Braxton turned to his wife as if to explain himself. Her heart-shaped features didn't show shock. Undoubtedly, she'd known about the boy, but her husband hadn't done the telling.

So, he has his own secrets.

Braxton again glared at John. "Why did you damn all of us to hell?"

"Damn you to hell? If I did, it was in the throes of anger." What could he say that wouldn't destroy the son who had adored his mother? Plainly, Braxton wouldn't let up until the rotten truth came out. Regretfully, John admitted, "You were my only child with Elizabeth. She wasn't faithful. She stepped out with this man and that one."

"A lie!"

"The truth. I tried to put up with cuckoldry. I did my best to turn my eyes. Then a fellow from New Orleans came to Natchez. Dark-haired, black-eyed, quite the swain. Your mother was smitten. When she gave birth for the last time, she had to face up to her infidelity."

Braxton came across the table to grab John by the collar. "Don't you dare slander my mother!"

Gagging and choking, John forced his son's fingers from his throat. Free, he sank back in his chair and sucked in oxygen. Braxton hovered, waiting to strike again.

"You wanted answers," John said. "I'm trying to give them. If you want to call me names, go ahead. If you wish to curse my mortal soul, do it. But if you want to learn of the past, sit down. What you do after you get your answers is your business. As long as it doesn't affect Harriet or Abigail or Andrew."

For a time, Braxton grappled with deciding on his next move. Finally, he took a seat next to his ashen-faced wife.

John slammed his eyes shut. "Elizabeth gave birth to a throwback. A throwback to African ancestors. It seems her New Orleans man passed as white. The babe appeared a quadroon."

No hot rejoinder met this testimony, so John went on. "As it were, Bella delivered a stillborn child a few days after Elizabeth dropped her cur. Bella's child wasn't mine, I'll have you know—no matter what everyone in Natchez thought." John pinched the bridge of his nose. "The women concocted a story, telling busybodies Elizabeth's son had died. She slipped the light-skinned boy into the slave quarters. I tried to ignore it all. I stuck it out for another two years."

"I don't believe you."

Opening his eyes, John frowned. "If you can't see the truth, then you are wasting your time and mine."

"Tell me why you saw fit to leave with every dime, including the proceeds from a loan on the family home, a place her father built at the turn of the century."

"I waived my rights to Braxton Grove."

Braving his son's skepticism and hostility, John told about an incident that occurred in the summer of 1855. He happened upon the cotton merchant Harry Braxton, who had business in Galveston. Elizabeth's brother remained furious with her, vowing never to give her a red cent. First, for her affair with an unsavory character. Lastly, for her extreme bad judgment.

She'd mortgaged Braxton Grove to set her lover up in the cotton-factoring business in New Orleans. When the loan wasn't repaid, she'd lost the family home. She hadn't let Harry know about it until the property had slipped out of family hands.

Obviously pierced to the marrow, Braxton had whispered, "I remember when the bank foreclosed on the house. But not for the reason you claim. I can't accept your story. My mother would never have jeopardized the roof over her children's heads, and she *never* committed adultery."

"Ask yourself something. Could a quadroon have come out of Bella? I bought her straight off a slave ship from Africa. Her skin is like ebony. And she's too fine a woman for the nastiness Elizabeth pulled her into, I might add."

"You're making excuses."

"Then use your head. Think back on your brothers and sisters. Did they resemble the Hales? What about the quadroon? Is he tall like Bella, or short like Elizabeth? Do you see your mother's nose and mouth in Geoffrey's face?"

The brunette gasped.

Braxton looked as if he'd been dragged along a path covered with cactus and rocks, which distressed his father. John hated feeling anything for the son he'd left behind, yet he didn't falter in dealing the final blow. "Next time you're in New Orleans, call on a wealthy cotton factor. He lives in the Vieux Carré, or did last summer. Read him the riot act for skipping out on your mother. His name is Geoffrey Bain."

Braxton brought one hand up to drive his fingers through his hair, dislodging his ten-gallon hat. His wife hovered over him. Another sharp pain of regret went through John Hale; it had to do with hurting his son.

Speaking to Braxton's companion, John said, "Ma'am, take him home. Wherever that may be. Take him home and make him forget."

She glared. Her pretty brown eyes turned hard and mean. Protecting her man like a mama cat did a kit, she ground out, "May God damn *you* to hell, John Hale."

"Ma'am, I've been in hell for thirty years."

Halfway between purgatory and someplace worse, Brax brooded in the suite at the Menger, trying to make sense of life. Impossible. He couldn't move, speak, scream. Or cry. His eyes slammed closed. He was too numb for tears.

Skylla knelt at his feet. Dear, precious Skylla. A woman too good for a wretch.

"Drink this. It'll make you feel better." she placed a glass of something in his hand. "Down the hatch, honey."

He quaffed it. Bourbon. Fiery bourbon that settled like a bomb in his twisted stomach. "Another." He held the glass out. He downed it. And another. Somewhat collected, he opened his eyes to all the sweetness in the world.

"Everything fits into place," Brax whispered. "He told the truth. I remember Geoffrey Bain. Now I know why Uncle Harry turned cold about the time we moved to Vicksburg.

Callous bastard, making the children pay for their mother's
sin. I sprang from a collection of devils."

His father might be Lucifer incarnate, but Brax had seen
something else in the clinic office. He'd seen a mirror of himself. The evil part of him, he came by naturally. Thus, he despised himself as well as the father whose corrupt blood had
carried down a generation.

"Think on something." The no-nonsense in Skylla's voice
caught his attention. "Your mother wouldn't turn to another
man unless she had good reason. As for mortgaging the home,
who among us hasn't made a stupid mistake of the heart?"

"Yeah. Who among us."

"Furthermore, *she* never neglected her children. She could
have parceled Geoff off somewhere much farther away than
the slave quarters."

"I should have told you about Geoff."

"Yes, you should have. It hurts that you didn't have enough
faith in me to share your secrets, especially since I'd guessed
it. But Geoff isn't the issue. This is about your mother. She
looked after each of her children, even without a husband's
help. Without anyone's help but yours and Bella's."

"Mother worked harder than me—or even Bella—at least
where the children were concerned."

Reverting to the times he'd seen his mother bent over a
washtub, a stove, a schoolbook, or doing the hundreds of
other tasks she'd performed for her family, he allowed some
of his resentment to ebb. The loving respect he'd always had
for her began to return. Thanks to Skylla's reminders.

She took the empty glass from his hand. "Come to bed,
Braxton. It's late. Near midnight. You've been in that chair
for hours. We've got to get a night's rest. We'll need our
strength for the trip home."

"Yeah. All right."

On leaden feet, he trudged to bed, threw off his clothes,
and slid between the sheets. Already Skylla was there. All sweet
and soft and comforting. He rolled to her, levering up to take
those wonderful lips in desperation. As happened every time

he touched her, he got hard as a pistol. He knew women needed foreplay—maybe she'd forgive the selfish act of a husband who needed her with every cell of his being. "Take me into yourself," he groaned. "Make me forget how much I resemble that bastard."

A tear slid from her eye. As Brax lifted it onto his tongue, she said, "You're nothing like that man."

How little you know, sweet wife. His fingers clamped on her silken shoulders. "Make me forget everything but you."

She opened her legs to him.

He loved her as if there were no tomorrow. The blessed softness and tenderness of her body and heart enveloped him, giving comfort, love, and ultimate surrender. She was so tight around him, so giving of herself in every way—so responsive, their lovemaking fanned by passion gone wild. From deep in his lower spine, he sensed the climactic explosion, and it was oh so good. Yet he gave a silent prayer that his seed was benign.

The world would be better for the Hale line dying out.

Chapter Twenty-five

"You're a sawbones. Do something afore the lad dies!" On the crest of her demand, battle-ax Bertha bore down on John Hale in the upstairs drawing room, where he'd tried to escape this hell of his own making. The quarter-ton mule-skinner twisted his ear. "Andrew's dying. And you're ignoring him."

"I've done all I can. He's resting. He needs rest."

A week into December, the boy's asthma had gone into pneumonia. The prognosis was bleak. John prayed for a miracle, but would have settled for a dance with the devil. This was the price he paid, he supposed, for deserting his firstborn son. What about the other Hale children? They hadn't been his, but they had believed they were. He shouldn't have made them pay for Elizabeth's transgressions. If he did something to right his wrongs, would God be merciful with young Andrew?

John left his chair, shoving his corpulent mother-in-law out of his path, and hiked to Andrew's room. Harriet was there already. A petite brunette, she sat at her son's bedside. Her gentle eyes turned up to her husband, and he couldn't help thinking how much she resembled his daughter-in-law.

"John." Harriet rose from her chair.

"Papa," was Andrew's faint greeting.

"He's so sick." Abigail left the opposite side of the bed. Tall and thin at twelve, yet beautiful by Hale standards, she looked up with big green eyes. "Make him well, Papa."

"Wife, daughter, come sit beside me in the bay window. I must bare my soul." He led the way to a spot overlooking the lights of San Antonio. Abigail crawled onto his lap, burying her cheek against his shirt. Harriet knelt at his knee. "I left a family back in Mississippi . . ."

After he'd cleansed his soul, his wife and daughter still loved him. And Andrew rallied. John was blessed.

Despite his many blessings, Brax Hale wished to hell he'd never run into John Larkin Hale. Comfort didn't come from the understanding wife who hovered over him. Many times she'd said, "I wouldn't be a wife if I didn't want to help you," but he wouldn't allow her to intrude upon his darkness.

"You're one dumb hombre," Geoff pointed out, a week before Christmas. "Pull yourself together, or you'll lose the best thing that ever happened to you. Miss Skylla."

"She'd be better off without me."

"You may be right." For the first time ever, Geoffrey Hale looked at his brother with disgust. "You're a fool."

"I'm a liar and a thief. I'm a no-good bastard. I am John Hale."

"Yes, Bubba. That is exactly who you are."

One late afternoon in the cookhouse, while Brax enjoyed the product of the distiller's art, the French cook announced the county clerk's arrival. "Monsieur Winslow Packard wishes to see you."

"What does he want?"

The cook lifted his palms. "How do I knowing? He say get the boss, and I am here to got him."

Brax went to the rotund Yankee not seen by any member of the Hale family since Claudine's funeral. "What do you want, Packard?"

"I'm here to explain a few facts. You're disfranchised, Hale. You're no longer a citizen of the United States."

"Breaks my heart."

"This ranch could revert to the government."

Not for a moment did Brax buy into the bluff. "How much money are you after, Packard?"

"Back taxes, for one. But loyalty to a flag is my purpose. Are you prepared to sign an Oath of Citizenship?"

"Hail, hail the bonny blue."

"No wonder the South lost the war, with your drunken sort fighting for it."

"I could name a few disgusting bastards on your side, too. Like you, Winslow Packard." And John Hale. Brax raised his fist. "Get off this land. Before I knock you on your lard-ass."

Packard drew back a fist, landed a hard blow on Brax's jaw. Brax reeled, stumbled, then fell, nose to the ground.

Christmas Eve should have provided the perfect occasion for telling Braxton, who considered himself sterile, that he was going to be a father. The parlor had been decorated with garlands, holly; even a spray of mistletoe hung above the archway to the dining room. Popcorn and baubles decorated a cedar tree cut this morning; wrapped presents rested under it.

In the cookhouse, Pearl helped with the wild turkey dinner that the trail cook had been preparing since before the crack of dawn. The table lain, guests would arrive in an hour or so for the feast. Alas, Webb Albright had demurred.

While Skylla grieved for Claudine and the hell her widower knew, she wouldn't allow this holiday to be ruined—the first Christmas in years not plagued by war.

Taking pains to fit candles on cedar limbs, she glanced at her husband. Dressed in a natty suit, its frock coat trimmed in velvet, and with her father's stickpin centered on a striped neckcloth, he brooded into his third eggnog.

Patience would win him over, she felt certain. If she could recover from her many losses, so could he. In her heart lived confidence: he would come around to prospective fatherhood. As soon as he slew the dragon of John Hale.

Tolerance was the magic word. It was going to take more than a few weeks to heal that visit with his all-too-frank sire, but she didn't have enough patience. "It's too bad so many of the boys had other plans," she said to make small talk. "What with this mild weather, I'd hoped to set up picnic tables so we could all enjoy dinner together."

"The boys wanted whores, not turkey."

"I'm pleased Snuffy, Luckless, and René prefer turkey."

A grunt answered her statement.

Skylla watched Braxton reach for the ladle and pour another cup of eggnog. "Are you going to save any of that for the guests?"

His lip curled. "I'll let you know when they get here."

"I'm looking forward to our visit with Kathy Ann and her little stepdaughters. And Stalking Wolf, too."

"Reckon he'll be wearing a Santy Claus suit?"

"Is that supposed to be funny?"

Braxton put down the empty cup. His hand spreading on the top of his thigh, he answered, "Yeah. Funny as a dead baby."

She stumbled away, lest she faint and knock the tree over. "Don't jest."

He shot her a disdainful look. "Your dander's up because you've been cheated out of children."

Plumbing her back, she marched to him, thankful for the steadiness given by the padded-sole slipper. "I have a child already. Heaven knows you're acting like one."

"My father was right. You are a spitfire."

"I'm going to ask something before the guests arrive. Will you *not* allow John Hale to spoil Christmas?"

"He's spoiled a bunch of them. Why not this one?"

"Why not?" She settled onto Braxton's lap. "I'll tell you why not." She clasped his ear to give it a loving yank. "Because this is our first Christmas as man and wife."

He swatted her hand away. "Why don't you give it up? I'm beyond redemption. No devil deserves an angel."

"Let me be the judge of that."

"You never give up, do you?"

"Not where you're concerned."

He exhaled. His arm settled on her legs, his fingers pressing her ribs. "I have been an ass. I'm not proud of it, but it seems to be the only way to handle myself."

It wasn't much, but it was a beginning. "Can you understand that everyone makes mistakes? Honey, to err is human."

"You've never made a mistake. You're an angel."

"No one is an angel. We all make mistakes. Haven't you ever done something you aren't proud of?"

His head lifted; he rested it against the chair back to study a faraway spot. "I'll never forget what he did."

"I'm not asking you to forget. I'm asking you to step into his shoes, then decide how you feel."

He paused for contemplation, at last answering, "You do know how to break a man down."

"Then you're not going to let him ruin your life?"

A sigh got rid of the last of his blues. "I can put myself in his shoes. It's easier to make mistakes than own up to them." His voice dissolved to a whisper. "Thank you for making such a difference in my life." He eyed the packages awaiting the family. "What do you say about opening your gift before the tribe—literally—gets here?"

"A cameo! How lovely!"

Cameolike herself in satin and wearing a choker of topaz, Skylla sat next to Brax by the Christmas tree. She held the gift aloft. More than an inanimate face carved in relief, however, she was a living, breathing angel come down to save a blackguard even the devil wouldn't want.

Thank God, she had finally chipped the ice from his soul. Why was tonight different from any other? It was Christmas, she was the most virtuous of angels, and he was tired of fighting the demons of resentment, frustration, and relationship.

"I love you, Skylla Hale." He hungered to make love to her under those fragrant cedar branches. "Enjoy the cameo." It looked very like the one he'd sold. He wished he could buy back the original, but however pure his intent, a good gambler always knew when not to press luck.

Skylla took the brooch into the center of her palm. "How very sweet of you."

What was that funny catch in her voice? It worried Brax, and he didn't want to be worried, not in the aftermath of coming to grips with bygone days. When Skylla had made him think about all that forgiveness stuff, he'd realized that if push came to shove, he hoped she'd forgive his trespasses.

He watched her run a finger along the face of the cameo. "My love, I've been wanting to give you a cameo for a long time."

"This is your mother's cameo, isn't it?"

"Elizabeth Hale had a fondness for pretty things," he hedged, sick to his stomach suddenly.

"Before our wedding, Charlie Main showed me this cameo. He said you intended to give it to me during the ceremony. With everything that happened, I thought you'd forgotten. Or you'd lost it. You didn't." She scooted over to hug him. "This is the happiest Christmas of my life."

"For me, too, sweetheart."

"Braxton, honey, there's something wonderful you need to know. We—"

Three bangs on the front door echoed through the house.

"Our guests are arriving." Brax kissed her nose. "We'll take up where we left off . . . later."

* * *

The table laden with food and drink, the parlor littered with the debris of gift exchanging, Skylla eyed the seated diners over the flickering of a candelabra. How heartwarming it had been to have gifts for everyone. Even Stalking Wolf had gotten into the spirit, had grinned like a boy upon unwrapping a Bowie knife.

Not simply diners, these were misfits come together to form a family.

Braxton sat opposite Skylla. Flanking them were ranch hands, plus Geoff and Pearl. Stalking Wolf wore buckskin, his ink-black hair braided. A bewildered mien on his broad face, he addressed the obstacle of a fork. Kathy Ann and her girls, both scrubbed and clucked over by their new mother, sat to his right.

Chatter and the clink of silverware vibrated in the air. A recently hired Mexican woman began to clear the dinner plates to ready the diners for mincemeat pie. The trail cook René Boulogne, a charming yet temperamental Norman of forty sporting a strawberry-blond mustache, appeared crestfallen as he contemplated the half-eaten turkey. "I am not very pleasing."

Confused stares shifted to him. Skylla bit her tongue to keep from chuckling. He had an endearing problem with verbs. Pleasing really meant pleased.

Lately, with Skylla's permission, René had taken over the cookhouse. When he robed himself in the vestments of touchy cook for the upcoming trail drive, she would miss this study in extremes, as well as his tales of faraway France.

He continued. "You did not like my turkey."

A chorus of "Not so!" greeted this charge. "With all this bounty," Skylla said, "we don't have room for turkey."

"I like turkey," a small voice put in. All eyes turned to the four-year-old Indian girl. She ducked her chin and cuddled her new baby doll, a gift from Skylla and Braxton.

"Would you like some more?" Kathy Ann asked sweetly.

"Yes, please." With a child's ability to grasp new things easily, she cut the slice with care and ate it, showing René Boulogne that his cooking was indeed well received.

The cook beamed.

Kathy Ann smiled proudly. "Pansy, you're a good, good girl. Mother is proud of you."

Pansy. Her stepmother had given Eyes Like a Leaf that name. Kathy Ann was giving her savage world a gentility that had been buried within her. *Claudine and I didn't fail after all. No! Braxton deserves the thanks for turning her around.*

Kathy Ann then wiped the chin of wee "Violet." The tot sat on pillows and grinned with four teeth at Kathy Ann, who now patted her stomach. "Wolf and I haven't decided on what to name the new one. I'm partial to Ambrose."

Ambrose. After her adoptive father. This made Skylla even prouder. Her glowing sister couldn't be more content, despite all, even the responsibility of a ready-made family. Braxton had been right to permit the marriage.

"Wolf," said Kathy Ann, "what about Ambrose?"

"Sun In Her Hair, cease!" Stalking Wolf quit eating the strange food and, setting aside his eating utensils, folded his arms over his chest. Though his look was stern, love shone in his eyes. "Medicine man will name the boy."

What will Braxton and I name our child? Skylla wondered if their babe would be a boy or a girl. Would it look like its mother or its father, or neither of them? None of that seemed as important as giving birth to a healthy child.

So far, she hadn't had a sick moment, which had thrown her off. Now that another monthly hadn't appeared, there could be no explanation save for pregnancy. As near as she could figure, Miss or Master Hale would arrive in July. A year after Braxton had answered that advertisement.

If only Claudine were here. And happy. Skylla would forever mourn the ending of their friendship, as well as her stepmother's untimely death. *You didn't allow John Hale to ruin this holiday, why are you allowing Claudine to do it?*

Skylla pulled herself together. Fingering the cameo fastened to the neckline of her dress, she smiled. Earlier, she'd thought, This isn't the same brooch. Of course it was the heirloom. She'd forgotten what it looked like, that was all.

"Let's see." Geoff took a sip of wine. "We're going to take five hundred head to Kansas next month. Do you suppose we'll try for a thousand in '67?"

"That's what the boss done said," replied Luckless.

Geoff got into a lively discussion with Luckless about the cattle drive. Snuffy just ate. So did Pearl, who had a good appetite for an expectant mother. Though as quiet by nature as the cowpoke, she smiled now and then.

Skylla sipped coffee and said a prayer of thanks for this brood. Who would ever have thought last Christmas, in the very worst of war's hell, that so much bounty would be hers— theirs!—this year? And next year . . . Next year a new face would grace this table. As would a high chair.

Correction. There would be three high chairs. Wow, what a roar would fill this dining room!

"Sounds like someone's at the door." Braxton placed his serviette on the table. "I'll see."

"Keep your seat, honey. Guadalupe is right behind you with a nice piece of that pie René worked so hard to bake."

The Frenchman puffed out his chest.

Skylla left the table, walking to the parlor and opening the door. To Webb Albright. A bittersweet smile on her lips, she said, "Please come in."

"No." His mouth grim, he lifted a small box. "This was in Claudine's saddlebag. I found it after, after . . . She wanted you to have it—your name's written on the box. I figured Christmas would be a good time to bring a remembrance."

Skylla could have cried at the poignancy of the moment. She touched his elbow. "Please come in and have an eggnog."

"No. I've got to be going." He shoved the box into her hand. "Merry Christmas, Mrs. Hale." He hurried to his steed, got in the saddle, and rode away.

"What was that all about?" Braxton strode up.

"The grief of a troubled man." She lifted the box. "He

brought this." Unwrapping it, she took the gift in hand. "Oh, my goodness. It's a cameo. She knew I'd wanted yours."

Skylla swallowed the lump in her throat. If only she could thank Claudine . . .

Braxton stepped to the side, and bright lamplight spilled over the brooch. Shock and confusion then struck Skylla, and her eyes went to her husband's ashen face. "This is . . . this is your mother's cameo. How can that be?"

"Skylla, we need to talk."

Chapter Twenty-six

When the last guest at the Christmas feast departed, Braxton repeated his words of thirty minutes earlier. "We need to talk."

Skylla had spent a troubled half-hour, imagining all sorts of reasons for her husband's lying about the cameo. How many other things had he distorted? What did she really know about this father of her child? "I'm waiting."

"I didn't give you my mother's cameo." His handsome face was contorted. "I sold it in Menard. To finance our wedding."

Once, she had thrown this option out to Claudine. It was certainly the most reasonable possibility, and now it had proven truthful. "Who would have money to buy a cameo? And why did you feel the need to lie about this?" She pointed to the one he'd given her.

"Because I sold it to a whore."

"What . . . what caused you to call on a whore?"

"These are hard times. Jane was the only person with money for frippery."

"Jane?" Skylla echoed, not caring for his familiarity with the woman. An argument from the past arose in her mind.

"Claudine mentioned the cameo, but I cut her short. She had it in her possession days before she died. No matter what Winslow Packard said, Claudine schemed against me." No longer would she grieve for the woman who was not a friend. "She knew you'd been to a whore. She figured tangible evidence would reinforce her charges against you. They were true, weren't they?" On his face was guilt. It hurt Skylla to press the issue, but she did. "How well do you know that whore?"

"As well as a man can know a woman," he replied in a hollow voice. "But, Skylla, I didn't—"

"No. Don't say a word." She wanted to pummel him, to make him hurt as she did, but fear of expressing her anger made her proceed with caution. "I need to be alone."

She wanted to tear something to shreds; better a pillow than a deceitful husband. But how did one deal with a deceased villainess? Raising her chin in wounded dignity, Skylla made for the darkened bedroom. Yet he wouldn't leave her be.

Not five minutes later, he stopped in the doorway, a dark figure against the light behind him. Gone was the frock coat. He strode toward her, lighting the lamp. His features pleaded for understanding. Seated on the bed, she fiddled with the clasp and handed the cameo to Braxton. "I'd rather not wear this."

He gave the brooch a tiny toss, as if it were hot in his hand, then caught it and set it on the nightstand. Taking a sidestep, he crowded her sight. She stared at her father's stickpin and closed her left hand, letting her nails dig into the palm. "Why did you go to a whore when we were engaged?"

Braxton hunkered down, getting eye to eye. "I didn't sleep with her."

It took Skylla's store of patience not to tear him limb from limb. "I should imagine you did little *sleeping.*" Her gaze went to the masculine part of him so evident against the material of his trousers. "Where has that thing of yours been?"

The crook of his finger raised her chin. "I swear I haven't

touched her since before the war." Her teeth ground together as he persisted. "I swear to God I haven't."

How could she believe a hot-blooded man hadn't taken care of his needs? She shoved the hand away that he tried to place on her cheek. "Don't make me say things I'll regret later. Leave me be. I want to be alone tonight."

"Where shall I go? Perhaps the pigsty, so I can be with the other swine?" He rose to stand. "I won't be turned out because I made your wedding special, while you hoarded a king's ransom."

"Hoarded a king's ransom? You weren't on the premises when Kathy Ann discovered the treasure," Skylla said, marshaling an even tone. "I find it very difficult to like you right now."

"Same goes for you, cupcake." He didn't bother with the door as he stomped away. The front door did close with a slam.

She went to the parlor and let her temper go, picking up item after item to toss at the doorway. "Damn you, Braxton Hale! Damn you for a liar and a whoremonger!"

Somehow she got undressed and into bed. Her bladder warned her about not taking care of necessities, but she told it to leave her alone. Some time later, arguments from the heart intruded on her anger. He'd said he wanted to make their wedding special. He'd sworn his hands hadn't lately touched that whore. But why did he have to go to such a woman to sell the cameo? Simple. Like he'd said, who else could afford a bauble?

"I'm not going to make excuses," Skylla muttered and got out of bed, unable to deny her screaming bladder.

The chamber pot stood ready, but some unknown something propelled her to the outhouse. On the trip there, as well as on the return, her eyes scoured the surroundings for her aggravating husband. He wasn't in the pigsty.

By the cookhouse a tepee had been erected, a couple of Indian ponies tethered next to it. Kathy Ann and family had stayed over. Skylla took comfort. She'd have her sister's presence in the morning. As for tonight . . .

Where was Braxton? She marched into the bedroom, then locked the door. She took up her brush and yanked the bristles through her tangles, taking solace in physical pain. When she turned to the bed, she saw Braxton. In the far corner, standing in the dim light, wearing nothing but his britches.

Neither spoke a single syllable.

Her blood began to heat, and it wasn't in anger.

He stepped into a ray of moonlight, and his tall body became limned in silver. "Forgive me. Forgive me, Skylla. 'Cause if you don't, I'm going to lose my mind."

She opened her arms.

Just before dawn, he still held her tightly, whispering tender words into her ear. Their love played sweet, gentle, for he'd cherished her with a reverence that took her breath away. Then he'd loved her with such passion that she believed an earthquake had shaken them to pieces.

She couldn't tell him about the baby now, not while rolling along the tremendous hills and valleys of making love. Baby news wasn't something to blurt out.

Way past first light, René tapped on the window. "Are you wanting breakfast?"

Braxton jumped from bed, jerking on clothes. "This may be Christmas Day, but ranching never takes a holiday."

No way would she demand he neglect the Nickel Dime for their splendid news. Instead, she got presentable, then moseyed out to the cookhouse. She might have abdicated the cookstove, but her fingers weren't yet weaned from lifting the lids on pots. Still, she grew impatient to call Braxton aside.

She said to René, "You take over."

"D'accord." His hand made a shooing motion. "You are not needing. Too many cooks spoil the soup."

She'd rather spoil her husband, which didn't necessitate ruining René's soup. The matter of the cameo was dead, as dead as Claudine, and that was that.

Already she'd garbed herself in the trousers and shirt she'd long ago decided were the only proper clothes for ranching. Intent on saddling the dappled mare dubbed Pretty Girl, she started toward the stable.

"Morning, Skylla." Kathy Ann walked toward her, worry on her moon-shaped features. "Are you all right?"

She flushed, realizing she hadn't thought about family since that trip to the outhouse. Kissing her sister's cheek, she said, "Did you sleep well? Did your family?"

Kathy Ann would have none of this banality. "What did Major Albright do to upset you?"

"Nothing that Braxton and I didn't work out."

"That's obvious enough. You look like you spent the night being tumbled."

"Guilty!"

"It pleases me to see you happy."

"That goes double for you." They embraced, and Skylla considered their new closeness. For years she'd given her friendship wholeheartedly to Claudine, yet Kathy Ann had become an enduring friend. She confided, "I'm on the way to break wonderful news to Braxton."

"That you're pregnant?"

"How did you know?"

"Wild guess." Kathy Ann winked. "Congratulations!"

Fingers smoothed blond braids. "I'm so happy about your baby. Just think, our children will be playmates."

"I'm looking forward to that." Kathy Ann spoke softly. "I know you're in a rush to find Sarge, but before you chase off, I have something to give you." She reached into a beaded pouch that hung from her shoulder. "We exchanged a lot of presents last night, but I held one back. Sergeant gave me this." She placed a gold coin in her sister's hand. "You know the night."

"I remember." A warmth swirled as Skylla slipped the coin into her breast pocket. "I'll forever cherish it. Maybe I'll even"—she winked conspiratorially—"save it for my firstborn to use in case of emergencies."

"Do that, Skylla. You do that."

The sisters parted, the elder one making for the stables and the gray, Pretty Girl. Soon, with the wind in her hair, Skylla was on her way to Safe Haven Canyon. Trouble met her as she topped the first rise. Winslow Packard rode toward her on a stout mount.

The county clerk brought his big horse to heel. Pomade glistened in the sunlight as he doffed his hat. "I bring bad news," he said without preamble. "After you paid your taxes a couple days ago, I tried to abstract the deed to this ranch."

Yes, she'd paid back taxes, but she couldn't fathom what he meant about the deed. "I beg your pardon?"

"I find no record that a title passed to Titus St. Clair."

"You must be mistaken. The Confederate county clerk said there was no problem with transferring the title to my name."

"Well, Mrs. Hale, that's a Reb for you."

She clenched her teeth. "Word has been running wild here lately, Mr. Packard. You Reconstructionists are doing your best to make life uncomfortable for Southerners." With a haughty glare, she added, "But there's something more here, isn't there? I believe you have some sort of ax to grind over Claudine. Why was she in your office that day?"

He pulled a cigar from his coat, bit the end, and spat it at the ground. Next, he lit a match, cupping his hand around the flame as he ignited the stogie. Blowing smoke toward Skylla, he replied, "She asked me to destroy the deed book. I didn't buy into her conniving ways. But she did give me pause to wonder about the legality of your claim."

Oh, Claudi, you didn't! But she had. "If the deed isn't legal, fine. My husband and I will buy the ranch."

"Do that, Mrs. Hale. Be at the courthouse steps on the morning of January fifteenth. That's when the sheriff will conduct the auction." He turned his mount around. "By the way, I've set the opening bid at fifty thousand dollars."

His crop struck his prancing mount and he galloped away.

* * *

Winslow Packard took delight in this altercation with Claudine's kin. That redheaded bitch had gazed upon his meager equipment with disgust, which reinforced the laughter that rang in his head. Many a whore had scorned him. But he would have the last laugh, for he had the power to break Claudine's family.

He eased his mount into a canter, then recalled the day Claudine had called to beg that he destroy public records. As he had told her, he wouldn't do such a thing, and he wouldn't have, no matter how many times she might have gone down on him.

"Zephyr, I shouldn't have been weak at the funeral," he said to the stallion. "I shouldn't have eased the family's mind about her change of heart, her intentions to make peace."

Zephyr, snorting, twisted his neck to listen to his master, and Packard elaborated, "There's no need for weakness now. There's no deed to the Nickel Dime. I will have the place for myself. I will have what that Rebel bitch connived to get."

Shaking, Skylla stared as Packard faded over a hillock. He hadn't been joking. Fifty thousand dollars! The San Antonio bank held forty thousand in the Hale account. Ten thousand short. An impossible amount. She must find the deed.

What had transpired to transfer the ranch to her name? Her uncle's will in hand, she'd called on the county clerk. Bernard Loez, his dark hair an unruly shock, had assured her the deed wasn't necessary. "We've got it on file," he'd said. Had he been lax?

She couldn't solve her problems in the pasture. She rode fast for the house and hurried inside, Kathy Ann and Pansy, along with Guadalupe, behind her. Speaking hurriedly, she explained the situation to her audience. "We've got to turn this place upside down," she then declared.

Kathy Ann ordered Pansy to look under every bed, every

table; they also searched the attic. Skylla conscripted Guadalupe. First off, they shoved the bed aside to lift the trap-door. Skylla peered downward. Nothing. Nothing but dark and a scurrying of varmints. Poking her head out the window, she called René as he ambled past with a bucket of slop: "Help!"

The muscular Frenchman moved every piece of furniture in the·house, save for the woodstove in the northern corner, in which Guadalupe had built a fire to hurry drying last night's freshly laundered table linen. No way could the papers be in that red-bellied stove!

Everyone came up empty-handed. What a way to spend Christmas Day. "Braxton," Skylla said. "He'll know what to do."

Brax wasn't particularly worried about Packard's threat, though he did hate to see his wife derailed. Gripping Pretty Girl's reins here at Safe Haven, she stood shaking. His new stallion sized up the mare; Brax hobbled Diablo, then tried to comfort his own pretty girl. "Titus didn't buy the Nickel Dime. The Republic of Texas gave it to him. For fighting at the Battle of San Jacinto, in 1836."

"But where is the deed?"

"Doesn't matter. The Land Office in Austin will have a re-cord of the land grant. The records of the decade when Texas was a nation unto itself are kept there."

"Yes, he was given a grant by the Republic," she replied. "Years later, when he left Mississippi and got to it, he decided the land wasn't for him. It was in East Texas, timber country. He wanted to ranch in wide-open spaces. He didn't have any trouble trading for this property, since it sat in Comanche territory. The original grantee wanted to be closer to civiliza-tion."

Brax shook his head. "That isn't what he told me."

"It's what he said in Biloxi, on his way to Virginia."

"How'd you find out about his will?"

"He left it with my father. Papa didn't mention it, not until the War Department notified him of Uncle's death."

"He didn't leave any other papers, did he?"

"None." Skylla leaned back against Pretty Girl. "Search your brain, honey. What *exactly* did he tell *you?*"

Brax stared at the longhorns grazing on buffalo grass. A hawk flew through the December sky, dipping a wing. The rush of Safe Haven's spring echoed in Brax's ears. It had been here at the canyon that Titus told a circle of cowboys gathered around a dying branding fire how he'd gotten the ranch. "He said the Republic gave him land, for the reason we both know. He said the Nickel Dime didn't sit in desirable country, but he wanted it anyway. Like you said, for wide-open spaces."

"Is that it?"

"I'm trying to think."

Brax ambled over to the fire built to heat branding irons. A quartet of the new cowhands were lassoing heifers, then bulldogging them to the ground for the ropers to hog-tie. Luckless and Snuffy, the branders, took over from there. The sizzle of smoking hide clogged the air. This wasn't much different from the day Titus had related his tale, except on that long-ago day it had been twilight, and colder.

What more had been said? Nothing came to mind. Brax returned to his wife. "Could be I drew my own conclusion."

Skylla twined her fingers into Pretty Girl's dark-gray mane. "Would the Land Office have a record of property transfers?"

"I doubt it. That's county business."

"What should we do?"

"Go to Austin. If we can't find Titus's papers. But they've got to be here. He wasn't the sort not to put important items away for safekeeping."

Skylla's pugnacious little nose lifted. "I told you. We've searched the house from stem to stern. Maybe he left the deed with his banker in Galveston."

"He didn't leave his fortune there, why would he leave the deed to his ranch? We'll search again. The boys can scour the outbuildings." He set the men on the mission.

Skylla climbed into the saddle. Brax did likewise. And husband and wife rode hard for the house. At the same time they tied their mounts to the hitching post, the dinner bell rang. And rang. Brax wasn't hungry, nor did Skylla want to take time out for a meal. She hurried into the house, taking the steps at an amazing clip, considering her leg.

Right behind her, Brax ground to a halt, seeing the mess in their home. "Y'all did tear stuff up."

Kathy Ann, followed by Stalking Wolf and their hazel-eyed girls, quit straightening the parlor. "How can we help?" she asked.

Brax took a moment to contemplate the incongruous sight of a Comanche chief doing housework, and to admire the likable young woman emerged from the hellion.

"You take the downstairs this time," Skylla said to her sister. "Braxton and I will search upstairs."

René Boulogne burst through the door leading to the dining room from outdoors. Everyone stood still as the apron-wearing Frenchman bellowed. His face red with pique, he charged, "You ignore the dinner bell. I am very upsetting."

Skylla sighed. "Upset, René. We are all upset. We've got to find my late uncle's papers."

"Forget dinner," Brax ordered. "Round up whoever's handy and tell them to spread out. Fast."

The French cook did as ordered.

No matter how diligent their combined efforts, nothing turned up. Night had fallen by the time the seekers quit, cowboys and cook trudging to the kitchen for their now-cold meal. The family dropped onto chairs in the front room and admitted defeat, but Brax hadn't given up.

"I'm gonna search the hidey-hole again."

Truth be known, he got the willies just considering crawling into that pit, but this ranch had become as important to him as it had always been to his wife. He marveled at how lucky he'd been, not getting caught in the web of his lies, except for the one about the cameo. His eyes traveled to Skylla, and his blood warmed as he recalled last night and the peace they had found in each other's arms. He intended to spend the rest of his life holding her and thanking the fates for luck.

For now, though, they had to find the deed. "Will you hold the lantern for me, sweetheart?"

"Braxton, we've looked twice."

Wide-eyed, Pansy and Violet clutched their mother's skirts and began to suck their thumbs. Pearl gripped Geoff's hand. "Pappy, mammy, and a dead dog called Sammy. Careful of snakes, Bubba. We don't need any more trouble."

"Hello? Anybody home?"

The feminine voice wafted in from outdoors. Company—just what they needed. Christmas visitors. Skylla went to the window. "It's a stranger. She's tying her horse to the hitching post."

It would be a lie if Brax told himself he wasn't relieved at the reprieve. Unfortunately, that reprieve was not what he'd figured. After this half-year of lying and scheming to get his hands on the Nickel Dime—after these few months of wedded bliss—Braxton Hippocrates Hale looked upon the face of his reckoning.

The tall middle-aged woman caught sight of him, elbowed her way indoors, and threw herself into his arms. "My baby!" She covered his face with kisses. "How's my baby? Where's Geoffie? Oh, there you am. Come here, honey chile. How you boys been? I been missing y'all and missing y'all!"

Brax allowed himself a moment to delight in her arrival. He gave her a big sloppy kiss, then stepped back to let his brother have a turn. "Welcome."

There wouldn't be any need to send to California. With enough ammunition to kill a marriage, Bella Hale had arrived.

Chapter Twenty-seven

Who was this straw-thin black lady? Bella? She had to be. Skylla gaped as Braxton picked the caller up, whirling her around and around; Geoff joined the happy reunion. Pearl sidled up to her sister-in-law. They locked hands to watch the threesome, each of them talking at once. But why, in his obvious elation, did Brax have such a peculiar look on his face?

From the corner of her eye, Skylla noted Kathy Ann standing by the staircase, holding her little girls by the hand. The serving woman hovered in the dining room. His arms over his chest, Stalking Wolf stood by the topaz-polishing wheel.

When the newcomer caught sight of him, she leaped off the floor, screeched, and jumped into Braxton's arms again. "What's that red Indian doin' in this house!"

"He's kin, Bella. He's married to Skylla's sister. The Hales are at peace with the Comanches."

"Phew. Bella thought she gonna have to get back on her horse and *ride!*"

Skylla had been right. This was Bella, the slave Elizabeth Hale had emancipated not long after her husband left. The freed woman who'd stayed with the jinxed Hales through thick and thin, mostly thin. The woman Geoff thought his mother.

"I hope you're here for good." Skylla wouldn't wish a return to Vicksburg on anyone who'd endured the Siege. She squeezed Pearl's hand reassuringly, leading her shy sister-in-law to the threesome. "Welcome to the Nickel Dime Ranch. Since our husbands are too excited for introductions, I'm Skylla. Braxton's wife. And this is Pearl. She's married to Geoff."

A satisfied smile spread over that blade-sharp ebony face. "Two pretty girls, even if one is a red Indian. Lordy, Bella's baby boys done good."

Bella's boys. It didn't surprise Skylla that the woman took a proprietorial stance. It wasn't unusual in the South—she had done so much to rear her "baby boys."

Kathy Ann took charge of hospitality. "Guadalupe, go to the cookhouse and have René fix a tray of turkey sandwiches and some hot tea."

Skylla offered Bella a seat. The woman dropped her bony self into Brax's favorite horn chair. "It sure good to be here. Lordy, it's good."

"Everyone. Sit down, please." Skylla made a circular motion with her hand. "This is indeed a special Christmas treat! May I present Bella Hale? She helped rear Braxton and Geoff." Recalling that Geoff didn't know about the circumstance of his birth, Skylla amended, "She is Geoff's mother."

When the introductions were finished, Kathy Ann led her husband and girls to the settee. Skylla and Pearl settled down, while Braxton and Geoff collected dining-room chairs. Skylla wondered . . . was there some reason why her husband chose not to sit close to her or to Bella?

She began chatter, Geoff joining in. Like Pearl, Braxton didn't say a word. Out of character for him. Guadalupe served the repast, and everyone partook of it. Everyone but Braxton and Skylla.

The new arrival placed her empty cup on a table. "Bella been praying and praying for the boys to find good ladies.

When Brax tell Bella about that mail-order husband business back in Vicksburg"—she clicked her tongue and rolled her eyes—"Bella try to talk him outta it. She say, 'um, um, no telling what you gonna be rollin' in.' Bella wrong on this one. And she sure glad it lastin'."

Skylla, casting an eye on her fidgeting husband, refilled the teacup. "I'm pleased by your approval."

"Bella, you must be tired." Braxton dug at his collar. "Why don't I show you to your room?"

"Now you just keep your seat, baby. Bella not tired a bit. Massa Petry give her enough money to eat and sleep proper, and to ride a good horse what don't rattle these ole bones."

Skylla said, "So, you've spoken with Virgil Petry recently. How is he?"

"Worried." Bella sat up straight. "Massa Petry been sick something bad, too sick to make the trip with me."

"Sick?" Braxton spoke hurriedly. "What's the matter?"

"Wastin' disease. But he more worried sick about sendin' my baby here. He say my baby married the wrong lady." She smiled. "Bella sees that ain't so. Her baby got hisself a plum."

While the older woman added her other "baby" and his Indian wife to the list, Skylla couldn't take much heart in the praise. Why would Virgil Petry be worried about Braxton? While he'd written to say she must do everything in her power to protect the Nickel Dime, he wouldn't have sent a shady character to marry Claudine. What in the world could he have against Braxton? Well, there had been that petty gossip about women in Vicksburg. Gracious, if that was all, Skylla had nothing to fret about.

"Massa Petry worried about this ranch. But Bella sees there ain't nothing amiss in this happy home." She sipped more tea. "She sure happy to find this place. Talk about worried. Bella been half worried to death, scared she gonna lose her boys in this big ole world. She scared all the way around."

"Braxton, didn't you tell Bella where to find you?" Skylla asked, finding it peculiar that he would confide in the woman about becoming a mail-order husband without mentioning specifics.

"No'm. He—"

"Must have slipped your mind," Braxton corrected, his face green.

Had he taken ill? Surely, he'd say something if his stomach wasn't agreeable.

"Skylla, do you think René has some dessert fixed?" He ran his hand down that green face, another sign of agitation. "Pansy and Violet look like they could use something for a sweet tooth. And I know Bella has a sweet tooth, don't you, Bella?"

She nodded.

"Guadalupe will see to dessert," Skylla said.

Kathy Ann, Violet on her lap, shot her sister a questioning look. What's wrong with him? Sizing up Brax's demeanor, Skylla saw something disturbing. He feared something Bella might say.

"Wolf, I'm tired." Kathy Ann stood up, sensing trouble. "You've filled me full of a baby that's flat wore me out. Let's hit the buffalo skins. Come with Mother, girls."

She half dragged Violet and Pansy to their feet, but handed them over to their father. "I need a good-night kiss, sis." When she placed her lips against Skylla's cheek, she whispered, "You know where to find me. The tepee. I love you. And Sarge loves you, too. He's crazy for you. Keep that in mind."

Skylla, whose heart had begun to race, looked up into Kathy Ann's concerned face and saw her champion. Did she need one? Surely not. There had to be a good explanation for the riddle of Bella and her baby boys.

Kathy Ann and her family took their leave amid a chorus of good-night wishes. Pearl, having stayed silent, looked as if she yearned to go with them. Geoff appeared to be a man wishing for the floor to open up beneath him—quite an unusual reaction for a man to have upon seeing his mother for the first time in months.

Meanwhile, Braxton abandoned his chair and crossed the

room to stand at Skylla's side. He hunkered down on his booted heels. Uneasiness marked his mouth with grim lines, and something quaked in Skylla. *I may need a champion. There's more than a riddle hidden here.*

"Did you have a pleasant trip?" she asked Bella. "Did you ride all the way from Mississippi?"

"Yes'm. Bella took a stagecoach far as it come, then bought that sweet mare Tina in San Antonio. It sure better this trip. Um, um. After Bella cryin' and wavin' goodbye to her babies, she been scared that ole *Jackie Jo* gonna sink goin' around that awful ole Horn. She been scared of ships ever since that ole slave trader caught her and shoved her in that awful ole slaver. That been over thirty years ago. Bella didn't forget, no she didn't. She done jumped ship in that ole Tampico down in Mexico. Weren't no way she gonna go all the way to California on that ole *Jackie Jo.* "

"My goodness. You do have a tale to tell." Skylla paused. "You mentioned California. Such an interesting place! I'm curious to know what was sending you to the blue Pacific."

Geoff patted his mouth. "It sure is getting late."

"Go to bed then, baby. Bella ain't through talkin'." Bella smiled at Skylla. "You wanted to know about California. Bella figured they was halfway—"

"What's the matter with us?" Braxton broke in. "You must be burning up in that coat. Some damned fool lit a fire when it must be seventy degrees outside."

He jumped to stand and rushed to help her with her wrap. Then Bella settled back on the settee. When he said to Skylla, "Let's me and you check on that dessert," she didn't argue.

"We'll be back shortly," she said but knew they wouldn't. Her intuition told her: Whatever was going afoul had to be worse than anything that had gone before. He had done something. And it was *bad.*

Surely not.

Surely it wasn't as horrible as she suspected.

* * *

Her husband caught her arm as Skylla stepped toward the cookhouse. Guadalupe, carrying a tray of pie, emerged from René's domain. Braxton said, "Tell the family Skylla and I have a problem. Horses. Yeah, a problem with the horses. Tell them we don't need any help, to make themselves at home. Or show Miss Bella upstairs to one of the bedrooms. Tell her I'll bed her horse down in the stable. Guadalupe, my wife and I don't want to be disturbed."

This sounded serious, which didn't come as a surprise.

It was serious.

After Braxton indeed penned Bella's pinto mare, he shuffled Skylla into the tack room adjoining the stables. They faced each other. His face pulled tight by this mysterious mess, he stood, arms limp. He fought for something to say; Skylla allowed him to fight this inner battle alone. But she refused to allow him to leave the tack room without revealing the full story, whatever it was.

The hush between husband and wife allowed normal sounds to intrude on her thoughts. A stabled horse neighed, knocking against a stall. A mouse raced between Braxton's legs. By rote, Skylla calculated how many people could stay alive from its meat in a soup. Old habits died hard. Her shudder didn't compare to the turmoil of not knowing what Braxton intended to say.

"Skylla, you'd best sit down."

She looked around, catching sight of a bale of hay. On the makeshift chair, she hugged her knees. "Am I going to need a shot of Uncle's whiskey to get through this?"

"I'll go get some."

"No! We need clear heads. What is it you fear Bella will tell me?"

He rubbed his hand down his face again, then bent to right a branding iron that had tipped over. His thumbs acting as anchors, he slipped his fingers behind his waistband. He began to pace the tack room with his eyes to the ground. After two turns up and down the straw-cluttered dirt floor, he dropped down to rest his back against the wall opposite to

Skylla. Drawing up one knee, he laid his wrist across it. "Skylla, I blackmailed Virgil Petry into handing over that ivory chess piece."

"That's a relief." She expelled breath. "I was afraid you were going to tell me you'd broken out of jail . . . or something."

He went white, she could tell even from this distance.

He said, "In a manner of speaking, I did break out of jail. I blackmailed Petry so he'd coerce the captain of guards into destroying my records and leaving my cell unlocked."

A terrible pain went through her heart. Her Braxton a jailbird? She couldn't imagine this as true. "What . . . what was the charge against you?"

"Disrupting martial law. And thievery. I cheated a guard in three-card monte. I was looking to spend years locked up—the Yankees didn't abide nonsense. So I did what I had to do to get out." His every expression and gesture bespoke a man climbing to the gallows. "Titus owed me money, and I wanted it. You didn't have any money. Which gave me no choice but to get my hands on the Nickel Dime, then sell it. I was hoping for a gullible carpetbagger, so I brought colored glass to seed Topaz Creek with. Geoff and I . . ." He looked away. "We had plans to meet Bella in San Francisco." His eyes slammed closed. "I intended to sell this ranch and take off with the proceeds."

Unable to accept the truth—praying she'd heard him wrong—she raised her hands to the sides of her face, as if the action would keep all her foolish illusions captured within her. Yet a clear picture of perfidy and conspiracy sprang to a mind even more reluctant to accept the truth than her aching heart.

Pain struck, this one not in her chest. She rubbed her left leg, her hand dipping into the indented scar. It hurt as much as when she took the Minié ball. *Why couldn't I have died right there and then? Why did I have to live? Why couldn't I have been spared this worst kind of suffering, the death of a heart?*

The urge to flee from this land—from her husband—burned within her. Yet she wouldn't. Not until she knew the whole ugly story—the truth Claudine had tried and tried to tell her. "What did you intend to do with the refuse from this plan? What did you intend to do with me?"

"Take you with me, of course."

She stared at the husband who'd become a stranger. "Not true. I can tell. I hear it in that hollowness of your voice. You were planning to desert me all along."

"Only in the beginning. I've changed from what I was before. Skylla, you mean more to me than life itself. If I could do anything to change the way this all started, I would."

Despite Kathy Ann's assurance that he loved Skylla, her fierce belief in him was gone, clearing the way for her to see through his facade. He was a liar and a crook. How could she ever put faith in anything he might say in the future?

Why hadn't she seen the signs, even after Claudine had warned her? Little lies, small untruths. His lack of interest in a beautiful and vivacious, though penniless, redhead more than eager to make him lucky number five. What about his tenacity in getting an heiress to the altar? What about his unyielding resolve in getting her into the marriage bed? Well, his grasp on the ranch wouldn't have been legal unless an annulment could be forestalled.

It hadn't been for love that Braxton said, "I do." It was for the ranch. Why else would any man want a scarecrow who lurched when she walked? Except when she could prop herself on a pot of gold and jewels.

Dropping her unfocused gaze, Skylla heard Braxton stand, heard him walk toward her. She felt his presence as he knelt at her feet. She rejected the hand that tried to take hers. "Keep your distance."

"If I do, I can't tell you I love you. That I changed my mind about California, probably the first moment I laid eyes on you in the magnolia grove."

"Love is only a word, Braxton. Only a glib four-letter word, useful for getting what one wants from a weaker person."

"Have you no more faith in me than that?"

Faith? Only from his father had she heard about his fam-

ily—which confirmed her suspicions about the liar and trick-
ster who was his brother. *What's Calibornion?*

How these co-conspirators must have roared with laughter
behind the back of a stupid, gullible cripple. What fun Braxton
and Geoff must have had at the ease with which she fell into
the trap. She could almost hear their hysterics.

She clutched her middle, protecting the child conceived
while its sire connived. How could she shield the babe from
the liars and thieves of the Nickel Dime?

"What can I do to make you forgive me?" He stood.

She feared what she needed most—him. And she hated herself for this weakness. *How can he love me, when I can't love
myself?* "Forgive you? You actually expect me to say, 'Oh,
please, honey, please do take St. Clair land—do send a card
to let me know you're having a wonderful time in California.
And help yourself to some riches while you're at it.' Surely
you don't think I'm such a dunce that I'll let you continue to
live the leisurely life, complete with a fat bank account."

Thunderous fury distorted his face. "You didn't mind my
cheating—as long as you had something to gain from it."

"Don't lower me to your level."

He clenched his teeth, his nostrils enlarging. "I have
schemed and cheated for your benefit. I have worked your
land. I have put food on your table. I have given you my very
soul, both in the light of day and in the privacy of your bedroom." The storm and strife in his expression eased. "If you
need me to do so, I will lie or cheat, scheme or steal, for your
benefit. I would lay down my life for you, Skylla Hale."

Rocked by how much he offered, she nonetheless forced
herself to remember his glibness. "What would my uncle
think, if he knew you'd deceived his family?"

Braxton's countenance filled with malice. "Titus St. Clair
was a jeering, no-good son of a bitch. If the Yankees hadn't
killed him, I would have."

The temper she had tried to control flared, and she did
nothing to control it. Grabbing for a currycomb, she hurled

it. He didn't so much as flinch, even when it glanced off his shoulder.

"You'll regret these things you're doing," he ground out. "You always regret your actions. Later."

"Not this time." She stood, determined to face the enemy eye to eye. "May you burn in hell, Braxton Hale."

"Knowing how my father damned the Hale family, you would curse me to hell?"

"I don't care what you feel. Collect your band of misfits, liars, and thieves. Get on those nags you rode in on. Get gone!"

He grasped her elbow cruelly. "I won't be turned off this land. I am here to stay. As your legal husband. You're in no position to order me to leave."

By law, if anyone left, it would be Skylla. Biloxi came hurtling into her thoughts. Her father swinging lifeless from a branch of the Spanish oak in front of Beau Rivage, vigilantes turning their hate on the St. Clair women. "Get out of Biloxi, or the three of you will be next!" they had shouted, advancing with nooses in their raised grips. Like scared rabbits, Skylla and Kathy Ann fled, dragging Claudine to safety with them. The vigilantes hadn't even allowed the St. Clairs enough time to bury Ambrose.

Skylla had lost one home. She wouldn't lose another. She owed her child more than that. But what could she do? Would the laws of Texas protect her? To the devil with the law! Yet the government could end up with the Nickel Dime and all its appurtenances.

Let Winslow Packard try to seize it.

Skylla would fight like a tiger for the ranch that Uncle had bequeathed her. Her child would grow up in the home that was its birthright. Whatever that took, she would do it. With no wool covering her eyes.

Bestowing a look of contempt on her husband, she spat out, "You are a whore, Braxton Hale. You sold your body to get this ranch. But then . . . blood will tell."

"What does that mean?"

"It means you are the image of your selfish father. Quite a pair of bookends, the two of you." She pulled her elbow free. "It's not over yet. I'll fight you—be it in the Courts or right on this spot—for all that you have lied and cheated to get."

When she started to pass him, he grabbed her arm, yanking her to him. "Dammit, be reasonable. Yes, I made mistakes. Bad mistakes. But I love you. And I need you."

She shoved her way out of his arms, rearing back and slapping him soundly. The reverberation of the blow ringing, she watched him rub the reddening outline of her hand. Some of the life died in his face.

Like a dying man surfacing for the third time, he took her into his arms again, asking, "What happened to my sweet and understanding wife? Remember how many of your loved ones died knowing your anger."

"Claudine blackmailed me into feeling guilty, but I'm smarter now. I won't take it from you."

"Sweetheart, you're being unreasonable."

With an "Oooh!" she brought her knee up hard against his groin, then took a backward step when he ground out, "Damn you, you hellcat!"

As he lunged for her once more, her hand grabbed a branding iron. "Stay back." He didn't. Arching an arm, she whacked him on the side of the head. He fell, stunned. Shaking his head from side to side, he tried to get up.

For a split second she wanted to comfort him, to beg his forgiveness.

No more the fool, though, she pressed the branding iron against his chest, giving it a shove that sent him to the straw again. "You have twenty minutes to collect your vile entourage. Then I want you off this place. If you don't leave, I will shoot you dead, Braxton Hale."

Chapter Twenty-eight

His every muscle ached from days of riding bareback, chasing through the Comancheria on a buffalo hunt in the middle of a January blue norther. Squatting Indian-fashion in front of a campfire in Stalking Wolf's village, Brax stared into the flames. It was Skylla he saw. She who couldn't forgive him.

"Do you want firewater?" the chief asked.

Brax elevated his line of sight to his brother-in-law, extending his hand for a gourd of whiskey. He took a more than ample quaff, enjoying the burn.

"A wise man does not surrender when his woman is angry." Stalking Wolf folded his arms over his chest. "Go to her."

Brax shrugged one of those aching shoulders. "I lost one wife. What's losing another one?"

Indifference, at least outward indifference, helped him pass the endless moments of each endless day.

Earlier, Pansy and Violet had curled up beside him and were now sleeping. He gave each girl a pat on the arm. "I'm bushed, Stalking Wolf. See you tomorrow."

"Rest, Yellow Hair. Tomorrow we hunt more buffalo."

Why not? Brax didn't have anything better to do. Calling up the remains of his strength, he creaked to his feet and trudged toward his borrowed tepee. Along the way he passed the abode Pearl's family had made available to their daughter and her quadroon husband. Stalking Wolf had provided separate sleeping accommodations for Bella, who didn't care much for the savage life. Good old Stalking Wolf, always providing.

The Comanche chief had left his beloved wife at the Nickel Dime to console her sister. This, Brax appreciated. He'd lost Skylla, but he wanted her watched over.

Oh, Skylla. Give me one more chance at the dance.

She wouldn't. The week between Christmas and New Year's Day, Brax had tried to make amends, had wanted to reason with her, had needed to show his love. She had refused to see him. He'd given up, withdrawing from her as well as from the Nickel Dime, when the sheriff showed up with a posse to run him off the place. His option? Return to the bosom of jail.

Brax neared his tepee. Home sweet home. What was a home without the best wife a man could ever hope for in it?

He walked over to give good-night pats to Molasses and Impossible, tied close by. Paying particular attention to Impossible, he rubbed the horse's long nose. "Do you reckon she ever thinks of us, old boy?"

Impossible neighed.

"Damn, boy. I wish I knew something I could do to show her I love her. But what? If I knew of anything, I'd do it. What can I do? There's the trouble over the deed to the Nickel Dime, but my hands are tied, since I can't get onto the property to search for papers."

Impossible sneezed on his hand.

"Shit. Shit, shit, shit."

Brax did an about-face, washed his hands, and headed for the tepee. He drew back the flap, and got an eyeful of Electra reposing on the buffalo skin. She yawned, then hissed. There wasn't a woman alive who wanted him, he decided.

"Move over, gal." He shoved her aside, then lay in the bed

of his making, and brought the cat's corpulent body to him. "This is a helluva bed I've made for myself, isn't it?"

She looked up, giving him an examination.

"Damn, it's cold. You may be fat, but you aren't fat enough to keep a man warm." He drew another buffalo skin around his shoulders. It was still cold. Damn, the cat's breath was sour. "No-good bastard that I am, I shouldn't even want anything better than a cold bed to look forward to."

Jesus, he'd been reduced to talking to dumb animals. Sympathetic now, Electra arched her chin against his. He fell into the sleep of a broken man.

"Sergeant. Sergeant, wake up."

He lunged from the buffalo hides. Rubbing his eyes, he saw Piglet bending from the waist to stick her head through the flap hole. "Skylla. Is she here?" he asked hopefully.

"No. She's gone to San Antonio—the old records for Mason County are filed there. It's her last hope. There's only a week left 'til the auction, and that sidewinder Packard has been surveying the property."

"Did she send you to fetch me?"

A sorrowful look on her face, Kathy Ann shook her head.

"You say she's in San Antonio? Is she all right?"

"Stupid question. Of course she's not all right. She's lost the love of her life."

"No two people ever loved half as much as we did." A stab of pain lanced Brax. "Does she . . . ever mention me?"

Kathy Ann entered the tepee, letting the flap fall behind her. She kicked away the hides, disturbing Brax's female friend. "Sarge, seems this would be a good time for a certain Reb to show a Blue Belly sidewinder not to mess with Texans. Then a certain Texas man ought to park his sweet behind in a certain woman's bed. He could be waiting for that certain woman with a romantic gift and a thousand 'I'm sorry's.' "

"That is exactly what a certain Texan has in mind." Where he'd get a romantic gift was another problem.

Kathy Ann offered her pudgy hand. "Come on, Sarge. I bought a jar of peaches off a peddler. And René and I made fudge."

"Piglet, you are a damned good woman."

By the morning cookfire in the Comanche camp, Brax gathered his band of misfits, miscreants, and true friends, with the exception of Bella, who'd expressed an interest in learning beadwork. "Let's turn that house upside down. One more time."

Stalking Wolf, Kathy Ann, Geoff, and Pearl got on their mounts. On a borrowed one, Brax led them to the Nickel Dime. They called for reinforcements, the original quintet fanning out in the house with Luckless, Snuffy, and René joining the entourage. Brax had to avoid getting sentimental, seeing his wife in every nook and cranny. He had a job to do. Three hours later, snake eyes. Crapped out.

He stood amid the upturned parlor. "Kathy Ann, where are the peaches and fudge? There's nothing for me to do but crawl into bed and hope for the best."

Crawl. Why not do some crawling around under the house? He'd looked into the trapdoor, had seen nothing, then had moved on. He had to give that damned trapdoor one more try. He addressed the task with no passion save for the desire to please a woman.

Brax lifted the creaking door and took a peek into the dank hole. A rat scurried past. He shivered. Gooseflesh raised the hair on his arms as he contemplated that yawning hole.

"Makes me sick to think about what's living and what's not in that hole," Kathy Ann commented, putting words to her brother-in-law's frame of mind.

"Ugh," Stalking Wolf grunted, summing it all up.

Pearl gripped Geoff's hand; he said, "Pappy, Mammy, and a dog once known as Sammy. Careful of snakes, Bubba."

"There's nothing down there." Pearl sounded hopeful.

Luckless spoke. "I ain't going down in that there hole."

"Me neither," added his buddy Snuffy.

"Nobody asked you to," Brax said.

René stepped forward, put his hands on Brax's shoulders, and in Continental fashion kissed his boss's right cheek. Brax nearly jumped out of his boots; the kisser nearly got a fist in the kisser, but Brax called to mind foreign customs. "Boulogne, you're in Texas. Texans don't kiss nobody. Except their sweethearts."

"It is better in Cherbourg. We kiss everyone in my town." René pouted, but offered a handshake, which was accepted. *"Bonne chance, monsieur.* Good luck. Like Monsieur Geoff said, the snakes, they could be down there."

"Hush," Kathy Ann ordered, her voice a croak.

Quit. Quit, Hale, and now. You don't want to poke your nose under the house, so don't.

Why should he search for the papers to a damned old piece of frontier hell? With forty thousand dollars banked, why not accept that the Nickel Dime was lost and be done with it. Hell, the Yankees were welcome to it. Except . . . Except that Skylla loved the place. And he did, too. It had been his salvation. Without his wife and her ranch, he might as well reconcile himself to life in a Comanche village. "Here goes."

Feet first, Brax lowered his cowardly self downward. About three feet of space separated the floor from the ground. His knees buckled as he crouched down and shouldered his way into the black hole. Winter frost iced the den, and the chill seeped into his bones. The pitch of his voice resembled a boy's as he called, "The lantern. Quick!"

And then there was light. On second thought, he'd be better off not to see this Hades. A nested rat reared on hind legs to hiss at him. He'd never seen bigger teeth. Something scampered behind him. He didn't want to know what.

He prayed for deliverance, and shoved his stomach to the damp stinking earth. Brax propped himself on an elbow. "Put the lantern in my hand." He looked up at Kathy Ann's worried face. A corona of concerned faces circled hers. Right then, Brax would have given five years of his life to be up there with them.

He grabbed hold of the light.

Something fell onto his hand, and it would have taken a better man than Brax Hale not to cry out. He screamed. Screeched was more like it.

"Sergeant, are you okay? Get out of there!"

"Bubba. Bubba! Answer her."

"You all right, Yellow Hair of Good Medicine?"

"The snakes. Regard the snakes," René cautioned.

"Bubba, you never did teach me to suck poison from a snake bite!"

"Hold your horses, all of you. I'm all right," Brax lied, wishing he had a big slug of Titus's best whiskey in him. Even rotgut would do.

One hand pressing into the earth—he'd rather be pushing it into a fresh cow patty!—he waved the lantern from side to side. He saw plenty of nothing. *I've gotta turn around.* Somehow he managed the feat.

Once more he waved the light. More nothing. Wait. Maybe not. He angled the lantern toward the north end of the house, steadying his hand. There was something over there. Something that looked like a box.

Hot damn!

Don't get your hopes up. It could be nothing. And knowing that devious Titus St.Clair, it probably is nothing.

There was but one way to find out. Two vent holes had been built into the house's foundation, but those lay east and west, rendering each useless as far as easier access went. Brax would have to crawl to the other side of the house. There was no other choice, outside of cutting a hole in the floor above the box. Hell, he wasn't that much of a sissy.

Calling up courage from somewhere, he got onto all fours, bumping his butt on the floor. It was slither like a snake. So he did, the lantern in hand. A dozen times he spat dirt from his mouth, and blew it from his nostrils.

At last, though, he reached his destination.

It was a box. A strongbox. Made of some sort of metal, probably lead, from the weight of it. How the hell was he going to get it and the lantern back to the trapdoor?

"Friends," he shouted, his voice muffled by the confines. "I've found something. It better be wonderful. Or I'm gonna go back to Virginia to dig up Titus St. Clair's bones—and break all two-hundred and six of them!"

"How will we know 'til you open it?" Kathy Ann asked.

"Get another lantern. Lower it down here. I'll leave this one here to use as a beacon."

"Just a minute."

It seemed like three lifetimes before the second lantern rested on the dirt. Box in hand, Brax extinguished the lantern he held and started slithering back. The return trip went faster than the initial one. About twenty feet from his destination, the mother rat, frantic to defend her squeaking infants, ran over his legs. By now he'd gotten somewhat inured to the environs.

"Sorry, Mama," he murmured.

He kept going. He reached the trapdoor. At last! "Stalking Wolf, grab this. You others, help him. It's heavy."

They reached down and hefted on the strongbox. Then a cheer went up.

Spent, Brax took a deep breath. "This had better not be for nothing," he muttered. "And that woman of mine sure better be appreciative. She will. I know she will. I can't be that wrong about her. I hope."

Like a prisoner given a reprieve, he levered himself up.

That was when it happened. Something—something like a needle—pierced the heel of his hand. Pain shot upward, even hurting his teeth. He yanked his fingers up. A creature small and fragile fell away. In the yellow glow from the lantern, he saw a scorpion, its venomous tail curled over its segmented body, skipping away, gleeful in its vengeance.

The poison raced through Brax's veins. And he envisioned his death. Better men than he had died of a scorpion bite.

He wouldn't even be able to tell Skylla goodbye.

Chapter Twenty-nine

The family Bible clutched in her hand, Kathy Ann prayed over him, for medical science and even the Comanche shaman had exhausted all avenues of treatment. Sergeant had been at death's door for two days.

A doctor stood over Brax's bed, bathing his fevered pallid face. Yesterday, John Larkin Hale, M.D., had arrived, repentant and hoping to reconcile with his surviving son. Yes, surviving. John Hale brought sad news. His young son Andrew had succumbed to pneumonia. Grief had wrenched the doctor into coming to grips with his first family and doing something about his muddled past, as he had told Kathy Ann.

John Hale existed as living proof that what goes around, comes around. He watched his last living son slipping away—and agonized over a dying child.

John Larkin Hale had begun to pay for the wrongs he'd done.

Brax spoke, his voice weak. "Was the . . . deed in the strongbox?"

How easy it would be to lie, but Kathy Ann couldn't fabricate

stories for the man who had turned her life around. Why mention that they'd found another trapdoor? The woodstove had
sat atop it. He could have reached down into that hole, yet
he'd have reached for nothing. The strongbox there brimmed
with Confederate bills. "I'm sorry, Sarge. The deed wasn't
there."

"I wanted to prove my love. Oh, God, I wanted to secure
this place for her." He tried to swallow. "Have the boys carry
me outside, lay me under a magnolia tree. I want to die in
the magnolia grove where I first saw Skylla."

"Eureka!"

Skylla, in the Bexar county clerk's office, sniffled over the
musty deed book and jabbed a finger against the page con-
veying the ranch's title to Titus St. Clair. "There it is, Mr.
Packard. Proof positive you can't take my ranch."

His jowls went gray; she would have bet the ranch he regretted accompanying her to San Antonio. "You're too new
to Texas to know how our public records have shifted
around," she said as Packard slammed his hat atop his head.
"I must remember to bake Herr Kreitz a nice vinegar pie for
sending me here."

"I hope he chokes on it."

The big Yankee stomped out of the vault, and Skylla knew
intuitively this was the last Texas would see of him.

Although victory was hers, it rang hollow. she had the land,
but she'd lost Braxton. As if she ever had him to begin with.

"Are you Mrs. Hale?"

Skylla swung to a pretty fair-haired, green-eyed girl of about
twelve. "Yes, I am. Skylla Hale."

"I . . . I may be your sister-in-law. My dad is John Hale. My
name is Abigail Hale. I'm called Abby."

So this was Braxton's half sister. Well, the family looks were
inherent in yet another of the Hales. "I know who you are.
Yes, we're sisters-in-law. How . . how did you find me?"

"Talk gets around in San Antonio. Someone told my grandmother a Hale was snooping around in the courthouse. Oh, fiddlesticks, I mean no offense by 'snooping.' " Abigail blushed. "Anyhow, my dad told me I had a married brother, so I couldn't help wondering if you were the same Mrs. Hale. Dad said you're pretty and dark haired."

John Hale had confessed to his second family? Perhaps he wasn't the rogue of first impression. "I'm married to Braxton Hale. Your brother. There's quite a resemblance between you."

"I'd like to meet him."

"You'd best concentrate on Andrew."

That pretty chin dropped. "Andrew is dead."

Wordlessly, Skylla opened her arms: The girl lunged into them, and her tears wet Skylla's bodice. "Abby, life probably doesn't seem too fair right now. You can't understand why you had to lose your brother. And you probably wish you'd been nicer to him."

"How did you know?"

"Oh, I know, sugar. I do know."

Grief made Skylla ache. Considering the tenuous grip one had on earthly anchors, she questioned her actions that night in the tack room. If there was even a chance that Braxton returned her love, should pride keep her from making the most of each and every moment in this earthly home?

Hadn't Braxton pledged his love and affection? Words were only words, but actions spoke true. He had given all of himself and his energies to her, and what had she done in a time of travail? Tossed her beloved aside.

After she'd threatened him, would he give her a second chance?

Abigail looked up with those magnetic green eyes. "Will you take me to meet my brother?"

Skylla knew where to find him, Stalking Wolf's village. "What would your mother say if I took you to Mason County? I should imagine she wouldn't be pleased."

"She's not feeling too well right now, being sad over Andrew.

We could ask Grandmother Rourke. She brought me here. She's in the hallway."

The Hale females locked hands and went to find Mrs. Rourke. Abigail's grandmother was formidable. At least six-feet tall, she stood erect, a stern glare in her steel-gray eyes.

"Are you Mrs. Braxton Hale?"

"Yes, ma'am."

"My granddaughter needs to meet her brother. Her mother and I are willing to let her. Unfortunately, that bounder son-in-law of mine has already taken off to do business with your husband, so Harriet and I can't count on him. And I won't leave my daughter. Are you willing to help Abby?"

John Hale wanted to find Braxton? That was good. Very good. The father wouldn't go after the son unless his intentions were sterling. "Yes, ma'am. Yes, ma'am, I am."

Skylla would return to the ranch, then have a ranch hand fetch her husband. She asked God for one more favor: *Please let him stay, once he gets there.* She would ask him to remain. If she got the chance . . .

Chills wracked him, despite his fever and the quilts Kathy Ann and Bella had tucked around him. He lay abed, slices of orange and blue cutting across the twilight sky. A magnolia leaf drifted to his chest. Magnolias. He'd vowed he'd never smell them without thinking of Skylla—his sole succor. While passing away with her scent in his nose.

Damn, he was going to miss his lady. What he wouldn't give to have a few more days, weeks, years with her. He couldn't count on an eternity together. She'd fly right to heaven. The last place Brax Hale's soul would end up.

The venom ate through his body, leaving him with patches of consciousness. Hallucinations, too. He thought he saw his father's face. His earthly father. The devil knew Brax Hale wouldn't be meeting God. And he'd leave without helping Skylla keep her ranch. *No!*

"Try this broth, son." That sounded like John Hale.

There was a hell on earth. Or Brax had died and just didn't know it.

His lids closed, like sandpaper over his coal-hot eyes. Someone pried open his mouth, then dribbled chicken broth onto his tongue. He swallowed. He took more of it. By the time he'd had several sips, he forced his eyes open. And saw John Hale.

"Am I dead?"

"Not yet."

"What are you doing here?"

"Trying to save my son."

"Have you seen Geoffie?"

"Yes. I didn't say anything about Geoffrey Bain. It's better that way. I'm through breaking hearts."

That would be a first. "How did you find me?"

The doctor wiped his son's chin. "Through Sheriff Klein in San Antonio. You gave him your name. And where to find you."

"Go away."

"I'm told you've forgiven me."

"That's not the same as—" Brax tried to rearrange his body on what felt like a bed of nails. Couldn't. Couldn't move. "I . . . understand what you . . . did. But I don't wanna see you."

"Don't go to your grave without forgiving me, son."

That entreaty settled in a cobwebbed brain. "Did you put poison in that broth?"

"Your wife cooked the broth."

Brax felt a surge of strength. "Where is she?"

"Sleeping. The first rest she's gotten since arriving two days ago."

Skylla was here. That was good. Unless she'd come to gloat over his funeral. No. She wouldn't do that. "I bet René was . . . upsetting about the broth."

"He was gracious." John chuckled at the allusion to the Gaul's verb usage. "I'm glad to see your humor's returned. That's an encouraging sign."

"Does it mean I don't have to forgive you?"

"Absolutely not."

The scrape of chair legs grated in Brax's ears as his father brought a seat over.

"Son, ever since you were in San Antonio, I've been thinking about Natchez. At last I see myself as I was. I'm sorry I hurt your mother. Despite everything I said about her, she was a good woman. Too good for the likes of John Hale of Natchez."

This, Brax identified with.

A tear made a runnel down John's face. "I'm sorry I hurt you kids. If there were anything I could do to make up for my sins, I'd do it."

"There's no changing the past."

"There's always the future."

Brax recognized the irony in his father's remark. Soon, he would have no such chance. Curiosity settling into his feeble heart, he prompted quietly, "Tell me about your family."

John launched into a complimentary account of his wife and daughter, ending with, "She's twelve, Abigail. A pretty little blonde. I've told her about you. She wants to meet her big brother." A moment went by. "She's here. Will you see her?"

Why not? He had nothing more to lose. Yet when he said, "I want to meet her. If I beat that scorpion, I'd like us to be a family," he'd made peace with his resentments.

"My prayers are answered."

For the second time in his life, Brax Hale felt the kiss of another man. This time he didn't have a fit. "You didn't say anything about the boy. Andrew."

His father looked away. The words came slowly, wrenched from the soul of a man who had made too many mistakes. "The angels took him. Christmas Eve. He's up there with the other Hales. I can't help but believe Elizabeth is seeing after him."

For fifteen years Brax had yearned to hear his father say something nice about his mother. Those words mellowed the effects of the venom. "Don't forget Diana and Susan. And Lilly. And Larkin and his wife. They were Hales, too."

John took his son's uninjured hand. "And Diana and Susan and Larkin. And Lilly and Larkin's wife."

Brax squeezed the fingers that clasped his. "I wish I could tell them you had a change of heart. 'Fraid I won't be seeing them. I'm bound for the devil."

"Only if you don't make up your mind to get well. You've got to. Not for me. For your wife. She's a noble woman."

"I know." He let the tears fall; they pooled in his ears. He cried for all that he would leave. Skylla and her ranch—and the children he'd never been able to give her.

"Braxton."

That wasn't a male voice. "Skylla?" A tender hand touched his jaw; a sweet scent enveloped him. A wondrous vision formed. "I love you, sweetheart."

"I know," she whispered. "I found the peaches and fudge. That was dear of you."

"All Piglet's doing. But she owed me."

"I know all about it."

He worked hard at focusing on the sweetest peach in the world. "I'm sorry about the ranch."

"Don't be. I found what I was looking for."

He wanted so much to hold her, yet he couldn't. "Will you do something for me? I don't want to die without your forgiveness."

"I've forgiven you. Will you forgive me?"

"There's nothing to forgive." He luxuriated in the sight of her. He tried to raise his stung hand to touch her cheek. Futile. Pain shot through him. The hand was a huge purple ball of pus. But he had to know . . . "Do you still love me?"

"You know I do." She placed her chilled cheek beside his feverish one. "Get well. We've got a baby to rear."

"Whose?"

"Ours."

A baby. A real live baby was growing. He hadn't fired blanks. Brax experienced a jubilation he'd never known before. This was a solemn trust The Man Above had rested upon his weakened shoulders. A child was the second best reason to get well. "Make it grow up to be a good person."

"You make it. Come July, I'm going to push your child into this world. And you'd better, by darn, be there to catch him."

"Too late for that."

"You're a gambling man. How about we engage in a game of chance?" She lifted her hand. Her fingers gripped a gold coin. "Let's flip to see how hard you fight that tiny scorpion. I choose tails."

Brax laughed softly. "I pick heads."

Epilogue

July 4, 1866
The Nickel Dime Ranch

Just as the roosters began to crow on Independence Day—
six months to the day after a sidewinder named Packard had
slithered out of Texas for good, and eight decades before the
people of Vicksburg would again celebrate the Fourth of
July—Brax yelled, "Push!"

Skylla Hale gave a mighty shove.

Two men of medicine attended the birth of yet another
Larkin Hale. The boy greeted the world with a loud and ex-
ceedingly healthy protest, the womb being a much more gen-
teel place than the frontier of Texas.

Lark Hale, fair-haired and dark of eye, learned to cope. He
had a host of misfits, liars, and thieves to help him along the
way. And he had a few angels, too. His mother nursed and
weaned him, and Aunt Abigail took him under her tender
wing.